True To Your Boots

A Novel

Lexie Sloane

Caffeinated Llama

Library of Congress Control Number: 2026907766

Trigger Warning: This book contains sexual intimacy and references to both traumatic death and death due to illness, grief, PTSD, vehicular collision, corporate bullying, and substance abuse.

ISBN (paperback) 979-8-9953316-0-5

ISBN (e-book) 979-8-9953316-1-2

For Dad
So some of your many contributions
may be immortalized in print.

Prologue

It was like that Imagine Dragons concert back in college. I stood, front row in the pit, my ribs bruising from the swell of people pushing me into the railing. The pulse of percussion rattled my brain, and the amplified bass stretched over my skin, infusing its rhythm over my own until we were in sync. Until my heart slammed against its cage to prove its worth.

Like that, only I wasn't at a concert. I was at work. No instruments, no throngs of people. Just me, Kip, and the squeak of her chair as she shifted.

I pushed a palm into my chest and moved away from the office window, regretting the eggs I had for breakfast. "I can't watch."

"They sure do like the rush," Kip agreed into the pages of the Hidden Meadows account book. Her birth certificate listed her as Nancy Stein, but she preferred Kipper, so that's what everyone called her.

From our single-wide trailer between the round pen and the horse barn, I had a perfect view of the boys at work. Today's activities deviated from their normal routine. Jason was jogging our newest addition, a wild mustang, in circles to shake off some of its angst.

Maybe that's what I needed, a few laps.

Jason wore his leathers and the white Stetson I'd bought him last Christmas. I'd teased him when he asked for it. *"White? Really? On a working ranch? Isn't that bad luck or something?"* And when he ripped off the Christmas Cow paper, I'd announced, *"I'm not buying you another one when this gets stained."*

He had pressed the stiff, pale felt to his chest and leaned forward to kiss me. *"It's perfect, baby. I have all I need. One and done."*

"Ditto."

He was it, and I'd lied. I would have bought him a hundred hats if he'd asked. That night, we'd promised to buy the ranch. And then I soaked his white hat in Scotchgard.

Motion outside ceased in an eerie calm as Jason brought the horse to a stop at the center of the pen, a tableau like one of our ranch postcards. Ranch hands hovered at the outer edges of the circle, and customers in wide-brimmed sun hats and chunky sunglasses watched from the shade of velvet mesquite trees.

He'd worn his white hat every day for the past six months, but today, it seemed ... out of place. Showy and overconfident.

I frowned.

Kip's chair squeaked as she shifted. "He'll be fine."

But an uneasy feeling shook my confidence, like heavy winds building around the nexus of a tornado. Silly, since Arizona rarely saw tornadoes. It must've been the humming breeze of the air conditioning working at full capacity.

Still. "He refuses to wear a helmet."

Kip scoffed. "As did his ancestors."

His people caught and trained horses in nothing but leather long before Phoenix became ... well, Phoenix. How could I protest? It was his male bravado that first attracted me. I spun my wedding band around my finger. Horse's blood practically ran in Jason's veins–Phoenix's local horse whisperer–the reason Terry agreed to sell us the ranch when he retired. Our very own heaven on Earth: rusty mountains under a forget-me-not sky.

I chewed the inside of my lip.

Kip peered over her readers at me. "Ava, go sit down! You're starting to make *me* nervous."

The ringing of the main office line cut off my rebuttal. I sighed, leaning a thigh into the edge of my worn wood desk, and reached for the receiver. "Hi! I'm so glad you called Hidden Meadows Horse Ranch. This is Ava."

My eyes drifted back to the window.

Jason was checking the saddle, running a hand over the horse's flinching withers. The animal flicked its head from side to side.

"Of course!" I told the caller. "Would you like to saddle–" A desperate puff of laughter escaped me. "I'm sorry. Would you like to *schedule* a tour?" *Focus, Ava.*

After flipping through the appointment book, I rattled off the open slots. "And what's the best number to reach you?" The ten digits barely fit on the tiny line. "Uh-huh. Seven-six-one-three?"

Whistles and cheers rose outside.

"Great, Carla! We look forward to seeing you and your daughter next Tuesday!"

"Another one?" Kip asked. Her chair croaked as she leaned back to settle her full attention on me–a rare occurrence. "You know, you're lucky that boy is so devoted to you."

"It's not for lessons. They're looking to board."

Rumors had spread that our lessons hit capacity because my very handsome husband ran them. I popped off the desk like I had ants in my cutoffs. Jason sat up in the saddle now.

"Boarding," Kip muttered. "That's something."

"Don't sound too excited," I teased.

"How about a little less sass, and a little more work?" She angled back to her books.

I stared at the white roots sneaking in under her auburn dye job, a rich, variegated white that spoke of wisdom and maturity, which she insisted on covering in an unnatural hue of red. I'd never hide my proof of having lived, learned, and loved. Of surviving the first few years of motherhood. If people asked me why I let my hair turn, I'd tell them I earned it.

Outside, the mustang reared, but Jason held fast, staying on with a squeeze of strong thighs. Ironically, it might be him who gives me my first gray hair. Nina was an easy baby.

I plodded around the side of my desk, flopped into the wheezy second-hand swivel chair, and gave it a reluctant spin. Cobwebs danced overhead with each pirouette of the ceiling fan. Work waited for me. Accounts to review, feed orders to submit, flyers to make for the Rodeo ... I needed to track down Terry to sign for the repairs on the horse barn.

I kicked my embroidered cowboy boots up on the desk and started chipping at my blue nail polish. Little midnight flecks fell onto my yellow top. Jason's hat swooped by the window like a ghost. "Hey, Kip, white hats aren't bad luck, are they?"

"What?"

"Never mind. You want some coffee?"

She snickered. "Why don't you go take a walk? Or check on Nina?"

"What if the phone rings?"

While she excelled at finding mistakes and missed payments, Kip lacked a certain grace with customers. After a few complaints, Terry unplugged her phone.

She sighed, flagging a page with a yellow Post-it. "Fine. I'll take some coffee."

I jumped up and crossed to the folding table in the corner that served as our kitchenette—coffee maker, hot plate, microwave, and a dented mini fridge shoved under the table.

A crowd had gathered around the pen outside. People held their phones over their heads, taking pictures. It looked more rodeo than our annual, organized one. My stomach churned.

I fitted the paper filter into the black tray and measured coarse coffee grounds from an extra-large tin can, but halfway through, I lost count of my scoops. Then I second-guessed if I even wanted coffee. "I think I'll check on Nina while this brews," I told Kip.

"Good idea."

"If the phone rings, let it go to voicemail."

I was halfway to the door when Kip stopped me. "You plan on putting water in that coffee?"

"Oh, right." *Focus, Ava!* I used my legs to lift the heavy water jug. I'd nixed the water cooler dispenser. *A penny saved is a penny–*

Urgent shouts erupted outside.

My eyes sliced to the window. People were staggering away from the arena with wide eyes, their hands flying to their mouths.

The jug fell with a sloshy *thud* on the corner of the table and cracked open, spewing water everywhere. My husband's white hat sailed over the scene.

But it wasn't on his head.

1

Ava

"Call Robert McClintock," Steven told his car.

The dash shifted to phone mode and started dialing Rubber Duck Car Wash.

"No. Damnit. End call!" He tried again, enunciating each syllable. Again, it pulled up the wrong name. "I don't have time for this. Ava, can you–"

"On it."

I dialed the contact manually, his ever-reliable office admin. My long black braid slid over my shoulder as I held his cell to his ear.

"Ranger Rob!" Steven greeted. Not a forest ranger–Rob marshaled at the golf course where Steven took his clients. "Unfortunately, we're about ten minutes out." His eyes cut to me with an accusation. "Drama at the daycare."

None of Rob's business, but okay.

"Yup. Getting on the freeway now. See you soon."

I ended the call for him and sank into my seat. The city's flat landscape gave way to a crop of jutting mountains as we headed south, and a low sun lit a cloudless blue sky.

"Let's get Chinese on the way home," Steven said, rolling but not stopping before turning right on a red.

I smothered a grimace. Taking a three-year-old to a Chinese restaurant–any restaurant–topped my cringe list. Right above artificial popcorn flavor, wet socks, and leather interiors ... What Arizonian in their right mind chose leather? But it was too hot to cook.

I shrugged. "If you want to."

Steven was smart, well-dressed, financially independent, and ambitious, just not kid savvy. He knew not the struggle of extracting an unwilling child from a mountain of preschool stuffed animals. Nor the effort required to wash white rice out of my three-year-old's long, thick hair. Of course, chocolate wasn't much better.

I twisted to assess the damage in the back seat. Melted chocolate everywhere. Face, hands, everything in reach, thanks to the protein bar I gave her despite my better judgment. *There goes another hundred bucks for detailing.*

Tuesdays were expensive.

Steven glanced into the rear-view mirror at Nina. "I wish you hadn't given her that."

"She was hungry. It's all I had."

"She couldn't wait thirty minutes?"

As I said, not kid savvy. But he'd never been around kids before me, so I gave him a pass.

Thirteen minutes later, he parked his shiny black Mercedes in front of an empty shopfront sandwiched between a Circle K and a Mexican carry-out, and pecked me on the cheek. "Be right back."

He grabbed his slim-fit navy sports coat from the backseat, checked it for melted chocolate, then slid the narrow cut over his crisp white button-down. Every dark brown hair in place, every pleat pressed. Always ready to sell.

"Robby!" he greeted, strutting up the sidewalk to meet his client.

My pencil skirts and patent heels matched his campaign. Yesterday, we were referred to as Phoenix's power couple. It made me laugh because everything, from dating to our living arrangement, resembled a business deal.

I'd agreed on a first date more out of loneliness than active interest. And cohabitation because of financial strain. In exchange, I fulfilled his overtime needs. The routine felt reliable. Nice. Quiet nights didn't torment me anymore. Nothing and no one could replace what I'd lost, but maybe I could settle for *nice*.

Despite the AC, the evening summer sun beat straight into my window, clinging to the leather interior like a bad Yelp review. Yes, leather. We all make sacrifices, right? At least my skin didn't burn like Steven's did. Thank you, Mom, for my Latina genes.

A family of four exited the Mexican restaurant with enough crinkly plastic bags to feed an apartment complex. My stomach grumbled. Nina pushed against her five-point harness, whining, kicking, and smearing more melted chocolate.

"How about," I said, producing a baby wipe from my purse, "we play I-Spy?" My words sang with the feigned enthusiasm of an elementary school teacher in December, but Nina only grunted. I twisted back to wrestle the chocolate off her hands.

Her limbs flailed. "Mama, I want wockets."

"Sorry, Crackerjack, I don't have your rocket magnets. I didn't know we'd be stopping."

She pressed her chest into her seatbelt. Sweaty black curls clung to her sticky, red face. "Out!"

I searched the car: listing postcards in the glove compartment, extra sunglasses in the center console, for-lease signs sticking through the half-folded down back seat. Nothing would interest a toddler. Inside the empty store, Steven and his client chatted with animated arms and eager smiles.

"I spy with my little eye–"

"No!" Nina shouted.

"Okay." I snagged a postcard to fan myself. "How about hide-and-seek?"

"Yes. Yes. Yes!"

As soon as I released her harness buckle, Nina scrambled toward the folded back seat. I closed my eyes and started counting. "One, two, three ..."

Little clops reverberated like distant thunder as she crawled over the lease signs and into the trunk. I kept counting, even when I suspected she'd reached her destination.

"... Eight, nine, ten! Ready or not!" In an overly loud voice, I wondered, "Hmm. Where is Nina?" Making a show of searching everywhere was her favorite part. I checked the seat pockets, behind the sun visor, the footwell of the driver's seat, everywhere, complete with narration, until only one place remained.

"Well," I sighed, "I guess I'll have to get out and check the trunk. But I don't know how she could've gotten in there."

Her little snickers from the back made me smile.

I opened my door and stood, ripping my legs free of the passenger seat. Inside the for-lease property, Steven and his client compared golf swings.

When I opened the trunk, Nina jumped up and shouted, "Boo!" knocking over a stack of blue client folders.

I threw a hand to my heart. "Whoa! You scared me! How did you get back here?"

"I cwalled twrough the seat!"

"You did?" I reached past her to drag the mess of real estate contracts closer, to re-stack them and to tuck escaped pages safely back inside.

"Mama?"

"Mhmm?" Creased side down, I tapped the edges until they were even, and re-alphabetized the labels.

"Dis time, you hide."

"I'm too big to hide in the car," I told her. "I would never fit in the cupholder."

She burst into giggles. "Dat's silly."

"Well, where do you think you get it from?" I flipped a folder, searching front and back for a label. Steven must've been in a rush. I opened the cover to find the account name listed on the cover page.

"Mama, peas!"

Some moments shift so swiftly, it feels like a rug yanked out from under you. One second, you're flying high, living with a sense of naïve invincibility, and then *poof!* Your magic carpet disintegrates. No warm-up. No warning. Just a total freefall into a turbulent sea below.

My eyes skated the property address, and suddenly, I was hitting violent waves. Sinking as newfound lead pulled my stomach into a liquid vacuum without sound.

Reason gasped for air. *It's a misunderstanding.* One year ago, grief threatened to consume me, but a single hope pushed me through. One goal. One place. And Steven *knew* that.

Something didn't fit. I flipped the page to scan the offer.

Nina tugged at my arm. "Mama, peeeeeas."

Details catapulted off the page, little flaming fireballs searing holes in my plan. I tried and failed to fabricate some explanation. Words blurred, and the world radiated a habanero haze.

"MAMA!" Nina jumped on a lease sign and cracked it straight down the middle. "You hiiide!"

Everything I'd done ... all those midnight hours, late child-care fees. Moving into his house so I could build my down payment!

The doors to the empty store swung open, and the men

exited with hearty pats on the back. I needed to think, to be strategic.

"You bet!" Steven called as he sauntered toward his Mercedes. "See you in a few!" He stopped at the trunk, unaware of the active five-foot-four volcano wearing stilettos in front of him. "Oh, come on, Ava. You know I hate it when she climbs on the signs. Look at this mess!"

Could a human combust?

Think, Ava.

But I couldn't. My anger slammed all the doors in my head like a petulant teenager.

"What's this?" Steven said. "Did she break it? Nina!" He hauled her out by her armpits, and she hid behind my legs, curling her fingers into my skirt.

Steven shook his head, running a finger along the cracked sign. "Damnit! This needs to go up tomorrow. When the hell am I going to have time to replace it?" He looked at me, his extended-hour lackey.

I pressed my lips together, fearful of what might come out.

"Fine." He scoffed. "I guess we're going back to the office after dinner. Get in the car. Rob's meeting us at the Chinese place. Jesus ... look at this mess." He tried to grab the folder from me, but my fingers held fast.

It took a second, but I knew exactly when it registered. When his cocky offense turned to a groveling, deflated defense.

2

———

Ava

A LONG STREAM of air rushed from Steven's mouth, like a moving tire that accidentally picked up a nail. "Shit."

"Language." In the year I'd known him, I'd never seen him speechless. I waited. He wouldn't get any roadside assistance from me.

He smoothed a pale palm along his dark, cropped hair, scanned the parking lot, and waved to his client as the older man pulled out of the lot. "I planned to talk to you about this."

"Really? Before or after you sold it?"

"Before. I mean, in general."

I threw my arms out wide, a replica of Christ the Redeemer. "I'm here."

"This offer came in yesterday," he insisted. "I didn't realize it was the same ranch until today when I printed it."

"Well, that would have been a good time to find me. At my desk. Where I live six days a week!"

"And say what?"

I stared at him, unblinking as molten acid rose in my chest. Was it a ploy? Date me, distract me, and screw me over? I couldn't decide what upset me more–that he'd violated my trust behind my back, or that I'd let him?

His mouth opened again. "Can we talk about this later? Rob is probably at the restaurant."

"Steven, I don't want Chinese right now!"

"Shit, Ava, this is bad timing!"

I cupped my hands over Nina's ears. "Language!" For a fleeting beat, I thought he intended to apologize.

"You're upset." I didn't like the shift in his tone. "Let's cool down. Have some dinner. I'll even treat you to dessert. Then we can talk about it."

"You can't buy my cooperation! We can talk about it later, or we can talk about it now. My response won't change. Tell your client that the property is not for sale."

Steven shrugged out of his sports coat and laid it across the signs in the back.

A black truck rumbled into a spot in front of the Circle K. A group of teens spilled out of the Mexican place, conversation at full volume, plastic bags swinging. Nina tried to climb back into the trunk, but her little legs wouldn't reach. All around me, the world carried on like I didn't hover on a cliff's edge.

"It's not that simple, Ava."

"Then you're overcomplicating it," I seethed, clutching the folder to my chest. The one that should have *my* name on it.

"This client is a game-changer. A major hotel chain? This could make my career! I can't call him and tell him *no deal* because my girlfriend wants it, and she saw it first."

I shook my head, insulted that he made it sound so child-ish. "How did you not know? I talk about it all the time. This place is everything to me!"

"Everything?" he challenged.

Hidden Meadows held the last traces of Jason. If I lost our ranch, I lost him forever. My fingers clenched the folder. "This is not new. This paperwork is weeks in the making."

"Come on, Ava. I'm between a rock and a hard place." His hands went out like a judicial scale. "Secure my career. Appease my girlfriend." One upturned palm hovered by his shoulder. The latter dropped past his hip.

The brutal honesty in that little gesture settled it. "Enjoy being single."

"Are you kidding me?"

"And good luck finding an admin half as competent as I am."

"For fuck's sake, you can't qui–"

"Language!"

The squeal of tires drowned our words, and in that halting moment, I realized Nina no longer stood beside me. I spun to see a man in a baseball cap sprinting into the lot, shouting, and grabbing my child from the path of a moving car.

"Oh, my God!"

The folder in my hands fell to the pavement, my heart surged up my throat, and the world melted into a blur. Every worst-case scenario battled for real estate in my head.

The stranger held Nina to his chest, slamming his free palm into the hood of the culprit's striped mustang. "Slow down! This is a parking lot!"

I rushed to the scene. The man supplied my outstretched arm with Nina. She latched onto me with all her limbs as the driver sped around us, yelling profanities until he was out of sight.

When the shock fled, Nina's tears started. I began a visual inspection of injuries. Head, arms, legs, feet ... "Nina, are you hurt?"

Her answer comprised intensified wails.

The man paced a circle, pressing a hand into his chest the way people will their heart to slow. My arms were full, or I'd have been doing the same.

"Is she okay?" he asked.

Her sobs grew louder.

"I-I think so." I blinked up at my all-American hero in his frayed baseball cap and worn jeans.

His chest heaved under a snug gray tee. "That idiot peeled outta here like this was the freaking Indy 500." He shook his head. "Unbelievable."

I hugged Nina, absorbing her cries. "Thank you. Thank you so much. I–She was right there. I was ..." Too busy arguing with Steven?

"Just glad I saw her," he said.

Following his eyes to the front of the convenience store, I noticed a dented case of beer sitting in a puddle of its own making.

"Ava!" Steven yelled, still beside his car. "Let's go!"

I was a horrible mother! What if this stranger hadn't ... if he hadn't ... I should've been watching her! My gaze bounced between the two men. One active, one passive. The stranger wore dusty jeans and had a faint, familiar earthy odor to him. Steven always reminded me of a department store cologne counter. Relief and adrenaline filled me up with no place to go. Perhaps that's why I crossed the few feet to the stranger and threw my free arm around him. The man was a rock. As in, solid. *Good.* I needed something stable.

"Thank you." I gushed again. "Words feel wildly insufficient."

His hand settled on my back like a friend. "You're welcome."

I wanted to stay there, under his arm, an umbrella from this emotional downpour. But this man didn't know me. Or I him. So I forced myself away. "Let me buy you a new case of beer?"

He looked over his shoulder at the mess, his baseball cap shading his face and making his expression difficult to read. "Nah. There's plenty of good ones left."

I yelped when Steven appeared at my elbow. His sharp, artificial sea breeze hit me before his words did. "Is Nina okay? Do we need to take her to the ER?"

I turned, narrowing my eyes at his 180.

The stranger ran a palm over his frayed cap. "I don't think the car actually hit her."

Steven reached his arm out to Nina's rescuer. "Thank you. We really appreciate what you did."

When they shook hands, Steven's looked frail by comparison.

"No problem. I was telling your wife I'm just glad I saw her."

"We're not married," I blurted, but as the words blew from my mouth, Steven's arm settled over my shoulder.

"Well, if everyone's fine ..." Steven murmured in my ear as if it were a sweet nothing, "We can still make it to dinner."

Is he serious?

I stepped out from under his hold, giving the stranger my back out of respect for Steven, although I couldn't say he deserved it. In a hushed voice, I said, "I meant what I said. If you intend to sell my ranch to anyone but me, there is no *we*."

For once, he had the good sense not to speak. He slid his hands in his pockets, eyes directed at his feet, perhaps thinking meek might change my mind.

I knew better. "Steven."

"Ava." Sympathy and understanding dripped from his voice in two-dimensional sincerity. "You haven't set foot on that property in a year."

"That's not the point."

"You kind of abandoned them."

"I didn't, I–"

"Have you even talked with Terry? What makes you think it's still yours?"

Low blow. And a gross oversimplification. He couldn't know my struggle. How each passing day added one more brick to my chest. How every time I picked up the phone, my throat closed until I couldn't breathe.

Steven cupped his hands on my shoulders. "Ava, I'm sorry. I know this isn't what you want to hear, but if it causes you so much pain, maybe you need to let it go." His eyes cut over my shoulder to the man behind me.

It was always a show with him.

"Steven, I think I made a mistake."

He rubbed my arm. "It's okay, Ava. I forgive you."

"No." I stepped back. "I don't think we're suited for each other. Work-wise, or–"

"Ava, you're just emotional because of the whole near-hit thing."

Behind me, the man scoffed. An echo of my well-capped sentiments.

Steven's eyes shot up over my shoulder again, this time like tiny little tin swords in a gladiator match. I used to appreciate how unassuming he was: a partner, not a dictator. But now I wondered if that's only how he wanted me to feel. What would happen if I didn't bend the way he intended?

"I'd like you to take us home," I told him.

"What about dinner?"

"I don't want to go."

A vein in Steven's temple started pulsing. I stared evenly at him. For the first time in a year, I didn't question my decision. Impatience, frustration, and hurt moved across his clean-shaven features. Then anger puffed up his skinny chest. I took an instinctive step back. Into a warm, solid wall of rein-forcement.

Steven stiffened, his amiable game dropping into hard, sour lines. With both hands, he smoothed back his already perfected hair. "You know something, Ava? You are your own worst enemy." Then he turned and marched to his car.

"Hey!" I started after him, but my stupid heels in this heat were my undoing. I couldn't match his pace. Not with Nina plastered to my chest. "Where are you going?"

"Mr. Bodyguard can take you home."

"Steven!" Never had I been more tempted to throw my shoe at someone. "Hey!"

In the space of my next heaving exhale, all that remained of my recently appointed ex were the black tire lines marking his abrupt departure.

Mentos in a soda bottle.

That was me. Except I'd capped it too well, so it piled up, building silent pressure. Then another Mentos dropped in.

"Oh."

A horrible realization.

"Oh, no."

The cap twisted counterclockwise.

The stranger moved in close. Too close. Worried eyes stared out from under the bill of his hat. "What? What's wrong?"

Deep breath, Ava.

It was coming. Everything I tried to keep down. On a forced inhale, I caught a whiff of my hero's earthy scent. It hit my brain, freezing the moment like dry ice.

Horses. He smelled like horses.

His arm shot out to steady me. "What's wrong? Are you okay?"

"I-I ..." My heart sped. But not out of anguish. More like when you're at the top of a roller coaster. I staggered back. "He has my purse."

The bill of his ball cap followed my gaze as I searched down McDowell.

Steven's car was out of sight.

3

Eli

A GUST SNAGGED her hair out of her braid. It whipped her face, making her look exotic, like she should be on a beach somewhere. A photo, 'cause she wasn't moving. Or breathing. When I tapped her shoulder, an angry, feral scream rushed outta her.

"FUNNEL CAKE!"

Most people liked funnel cake. Apparently not this woman.

"Ha! Classic." Behind us, the cashier from the Circle K loitered on the sidewalk, phone out, catching the whole thing.

"Excuse me a sec," I said, but I doubt she heard me. I walked in front of the cashier's camera and waited till his eyes flicked up to me.

"Oh, hey. You forget something?" he asked.

"Yeah." I tipped my head to the convenience store.

The tone twanged as he went in ahead of me. With his eyes glued to his screen, the teen walked right into the counter. Puberty had no mercy—he had zits all over his face and neck. But that didn't give him permission to blast the misery of others.

I grabbed a bag of mini Reese's cups from the rack next to the register and tossed it on the counter.

The kid snagged it, scanned it, said, "Three forty-nine," all while still on his phone.

I tapped my card on the reader. "Hey, you get that scene out there on video?"

"Only the end. Super lame. I missed the whole kid/car thing."

"Can I see?" I held out my hand.

He didn't even pause, just gave me his cracked Samsung.

Kids. "You know what's lame?" I asked, watching the first few seconds, then deleting the video. From the trash, too. "Posting people's private lives on social media." I handed it back.

Casey, according to his name tag, stared at his photo grid. "What the hell, man?"

I tore into my Reese's. "Have a good night."

"Hey! You can't–"

The tone twanged again as I shoved the glass door open and left.

Back outside, in the top-ten-reasons-never-to-live-here heat, I panicked at the empty lot. But then I saw the stranded pair on the sidewalk. The mom chewed up the concrete in long, swaying strides. She reminded me of a cheetah in heels.

My feet stopped by my leaking case of beer. Like the cars at the intersection, tonight's plan hovered in a kind of in-between, waiting for the green go-ahead. I toed the soggy box. Judging by the spill, only one or two casualties.

I could go back to my dad's, eat my Reese's, have a beer, and go to bed. Check off one more day in this hellhole. If anyone asked, I had 48 days left. Less if I could find Dad a ranch manager. What a job that was turning out to be.

That's all to say, I had nothing to offer a pretty woman stranded in a strip mall. Nothing but a ride and chocolate peanut butter cups. But the orange sky behind her had this glow-y effect that you get at the end of cheesy movies. I wondered what other swear words I could learn from her.

The candy bag crinkled in my grip. I cut a glance at my truck.

Oh, what the hell. Worth an ask, at least.

The light turned green, engines revved, and I left the beer on the sidewalk, headed straight to the rescue. Or trouble. Or both. "Hey, you good? Can I give you a ride somewhere?"

The woman spun and hit me with the most intense brown eyes I'd ever seen–quenching like Coca-Cola. An oasis right there on McDowell Road. *Damn.* If I were a moth, pretty sure I would've combusted, and not only because her stare tried to burn me alive.

"Absolutely not!" she said. "I don't need some hunk playing hero!"

I took a step back, hands up.

She stopped short. Her shoulders dropped a good inch. "I'm sorry. I didn't mean–I'm not mad at you. You've been very kind. Thank you. For the offer, but ..." She blew out a breath.

My lip twitched. Black skirt, shiny white shirt, fancy heels–she probably came straight from the office. What's that rule? The hotter they were, the crazier? A wiser man would've backed away. She watched me shift the bill of my hat lower.

Dad always said I was reckless.

I shot out my hand. "I'm Eli. Eli Anderson." Then, like an idiot, I tugged it back, determined not to be my old man. Plus, her arms were full. "I'm not trying to be a hero or anything." *Wow, smooth.* "Just offering you a ride."

She didn't have her purse. She didn't have anything. In comparison, my day didn't seem so bad. Maybe my misery wanted a drinking buddy.

Her eyebrows lifted. "You're joking?"

"About?"

"Eli Anderson? That sounds like something from an old western."

"You don't believe me?" I pulled out my wallet, ID up.

She shifted the kid to take it. "Elijah T. Anderson. Where's your mighty steed?"

I cracked a smile. "It's more of a turbocharged V8."

With a nod, she scanned the parking lot again. I got it–she had a kid. I might be a creep. But she was the one holding my ID and all my money. My eyes got stuck where her top teeth dug into her bottom lip.

She handed back my wallet.

"Thanks." I itched the back of my neck. God, this heat. Even with the sun going down. Why did people choose to live here? Her skin shone with sweat, too. And with a kid clinging to her like that? How could I help them?

I glanced at my Ford F-150, but it didn't have any answers. It felt wrong to leave them. Mom would've called it *divine intervention,* insisted I'd stopped at *that* Circle K for a reason. Looking at the woman, her kid, I kinda wanted there to be.

In a world full of shitty people, how could I convince her I wasn't one of them?

"If it were my sister stranded," I said, "I'd want someone to help her out. Someone who wasn't a creep." Though Hannah would just kick their ass if they tried anything funny. Hell, she'd kick *my* ass for trying to help her. The woman in front of me stood taller, eyes sharp as a hawk. Maybe an ass kicking wasn't off the table. I mean, those heels could do a lot of damage in the wrong places.

"I don't have any cash," I told her, "or I'd give you money for a ride share." Still nothing. I held out my candy bag. "How 'bout a Reese's Miss ...?" I drew out the end, hoping she'd feed me her name. The other guy had said it, but I'd been a little keyed up.

After a long pause, she finally gave in. "Ava."

"How about a Reese's, Ava? Peanut butter cups are perfect for crummy days."

The kid twisted her hungry eyes to the candy. No more tears. *What a relief.* I was afraid I'd been too slow. Or too rough scooping her up.

"Can she have one?" I asked.

Ava stared at the bag. "Fine. Why not? Just *one*, Nina."

My phone dinged in my pocket, but I ignored it. I watched Nina's little fingers pick a candy. "How about you?" I angled the bag at Ava.

She sighed–hopefully the giving-in kind, and not the annoyed kind. That's when I saw goosebumps covering her arm, even though it had to be a hundred degrees. Her eyes drifted down the road again.

"Forget that punk," I wanted to say. Instead came the words, "You wanna go find him?"

"No. I might do something I regret."

"Like what?" *Kiss and make up?* I'd seen too many women let their men walk all over them.

"Like punch him in the spot where his integrity is supposed to be."

I smoothed a hand over my mouth. She probably wouldn't appreciate me laughing.

"What the heck?" she finally muttered. "This day can't get any worse." The orange bag crinkled as she stuck her hand in and took a chocolate.

While she chewed, her smoky brown eyes dipped to my T-shirt and jeans. I probably smelled like a barn, all coated in dust and horsehair, but she wasn't that close, so maybe she wouldn't notice?

"Do you work with horses?"

I took a step back. "Yeah. For now."

Horses ... horsepower–I'd pick machines over livestock any day, but life didn't care what I wanted.

She nodded in slow motion. Then her eyes dropped to my pocket, where someone was blowing up my phone. "Don't let us keep you."

I blew out a breath.

Don't be Dad.

"Sorry, let me check ..." I found twelve messages from my buddy Ryan, the last one all in caps.

Ryan: SCREW YOUR OLD MAN! THIS IS BIG $$$

More gigs.

The guy always had jobs lined up. I read the latest bid and almost choked. *Tempting.* Too bad my ass had to stay in hotter-than-hell Phoenix. I shot off a reply.

Another text came as I shoved my phone back in my pocket. I didn't need to see what I was missing. Doing the right thing felt hard enough.

Ava's voice pulled me out of my brood. "Um, can I borrow your phone?"

"Yeah, of course." I practically threw the thing at her.

Real smooth, Eli.

"Thanks." She stared at the screen for half a second, then shoved it back at me. "Oh, um, maybe you-do you want to ..."

Ryan: Come on! Aren't you tired of jerking off?

"No." I handed it back, fighting the urge to assure her I didn't do that ... Not all the time.

"N-no?"

Frigging Ryan. "I mean, no, I'm not answering that. Make your call."

She readjusted the kid on her hip and got really interested in her feet as she put my phone to her ear. "What's it called?"

I didn't realize she was talking to me till her eyes tipped up. "What?"

"The ranch, where you work?"

I frowned. "It doesn't really have a name. It's a boarding ranch."

She shifted. Glanced around the lot again. "How many horses are there?"

"Four."

"Four? That's not a lot." She looked relieved as she ended the call and handed the phone back to me. "No one's answering."

"You got family nearby or something? Somewhere I can drop you?"

"I just called them, but ..." She groaned, running her hand over her hair and gripping her braid like a lifeline. "I don't know what to do."

"Mama?"

Ava petted the kid's head. "Yes, Crackerjack?"

"I wanna go home."

4

———

Eli

THE AIR CONDITIONING blasted from my vents. We drove north, up a rocky mountain, supposedly to some ranch. I had a soggy crate of beer in the back of my truck. My cab smelled like McDonald's, and in the passenger seat was a woman way outta my league. She sat ramrod straight, arms wrapped around her kid like a harness. Nina dug salty fries out of her red and yellow cardboard box.

I avoided fast food on the road, but the smell pulled the teenage addict out of me. "Can I have one of those?"

Nina licked her finger before handing me one.

"Thanks." Just as greasy as I remembered. "I'm going the right way?"

"Yes."

I glanced at Ava. She looked ready to eject. Was it something I said? "I knew I should've gotten you one, too."

She blinked over a smooth, tanned shoulder at me. "What?"

"A Happy Meal."

"They're for kids."

I cut her sideways smile, wondering at her age. Maybe a few

years more than me? Not that it mattered. "We're all kids at heart."

The road curved, so I had to go back to driving, but her focus stayed on me. Hopefully to admire my winning jaw line.

"I'll reimburse you once I get my purse. For the gas and the food."

Or was she noticing my frayed, old baseball cap? "No need."

"Really. I'm sure this is out of your way."

I shrugged.

After a lull, Ava said, "Can I ask you something?"

"Anything." I waited while her eyes roamed the dashboard, while she fiddled with the air vent, and adjusted Nina's position.

She sat back, heaved a sigh, and ran a slender hand along the center console. "You have a nice truck."

What's that supposed to mean?

"Thanks?" After a beat, I added, "You're not gonna steal it, are you?"

"What? No!"

Her shock convinced me. "Okay, good. 'Cause I just paid it off."

"No. It's ... It's a refreshing change from luxury sedans."

With those kinds of clothes, I had trouble seeing her in anything but a "luxury sedan." *With luxury guys.* Hell, here I was, a Ford Pinto.

"Surprisingly refreshing," she added. "I think I need a change." Her face steered back to me, studying me from top to bottom. Long enough, I figured she'd found something wrong.

"Elijah T. Andersen ..." she repeated, just like when she'd read it off my license. "What's the 'T' stand for?"

My lip twitched. "Guess."

"Seriously?"

"Man's gotta have some secrets."

She huffed, but there was humor to it. After a beat, she said, "Thomas?"

"Nope."

"Travis?"

"No."

"Tucker?"

"No, ma'am."

"*Ma'am*?" She laughed. It was like the sun poking holes in the clouds. "Are we in a western?"

"Do you like westerns?"

Her eyes climbed over me again. "You don't look like a cowboy." They stopped at my face.

I shoulda shaved this morning. "No?"

"No. It's those boots."

I glanced down at my steel-toed Cats. "What's wrong with them?"

"Nothing, they just aren't cowboy boots."

"Mama, help." Nina shoved the wrapped toy from her Happy Meal at her mom's chest.

Ava ripped it open. "Trenton?"

I shook my head, smiling.

"Toby?"

"Toby? What? No! Come on." I waited for her next guess, but it didn't come.

It's because her eyes were wide on the wrought iron sign mounted over the road. *Hidden Meadows*. It was the only thing not gray or rocky for miles. Ava frowned out her window as we drove under it and past a quarter-mile line of tree stumps.

The road dumped us on a wide dirt patch. "Where do I park?"

"Um ..." She'd gone pale. "In front of the arena." She pointed to the ring. Half of its posts teetered at odd angles. When I cut the engine, she unbuckled her seatbelt and slid out of the truck, kid and all.

I met her around her side, scanning the scene. No cars. No people. "Is this the right place?"

"Yes. But ..." She glanced back at the road we'd just traveled. "Are you okay?"

"There used to be trees." The way she hugged Nina to her chest reminded me of that kid in Charlie Brown with the blanket. I followed her into what looked like a ghost ranch. Lots of splinters and dust. A horse huffed, but I couldn't see it. I shoved my hands in my pockets and kept two steps behind her. She looked so outta place. Curiosity had me glancing left and right. The place seemed vaguely familiar. What were we doing here?

When we reached the barn, a hunched form in the shadows turned toward us. "Ava?" it called. It wore an unbuttoned brown flannel over a white t-shirt. Not a spirit– just a man one missed meal shy of a flagpole. But what had me staring was the massive white mustache dominating his face.

Ava's posture changed as he came out into the sun. Her back got straight, and her voice cracked. "H-hi, Terry."

Deep, leathery lines stretched around a grin. At least I think that's what hid under the hairy white horseshoe. "Well, I'll be damned." The man set a screwdriver on a post at the mouth of the barn, then dug his thick, gnarled fists into his sides. "What a surprise! Look at you! Both of you!"

I rocked back a few steps to let them have their reunion.

Ava widened her stance and adjusted her kid at her hip. "Nina, this very shaggy man is Terry."

Terry stared at Nina with hearts in his crinkling eyes. "I knew you when all you did was poop and drool." He tapped her on the nose. "You like my mustache?" he asked.

She shook her head.

Kids. Gotta love their brutal honesty.

"It's gotten a little long," he admitted, combing his fingers through it. "Probably time for a trim."

"I'm sorry to just show up like this," Ava started. "I tried calling but–"

"Oh, stop!" He swatted the air like her words annoyed him.

I wondered at her hesitance. The man was obviously pleased to see her–them.

His eyes wandered over to me. "Who's this?"

Hold up. Was this her dad? I stepped forward, but Ava cut me off.

"This is Eli. He gave me a ride. I actually came to pick up my truck."

Truck? My pulse spiked. I studied her profile. She just kept getting more interesting.

"Mmhmm." Terry nodded, still eying me. "Eli, good to meet you." He held out a calloused hand, which I took.

"And you, Sir."

He laughed. "Sir? Ava, you pick 'em good."

We spoke at the same time.

"Actually ..."

"Oh, no–"

But Terry was already walking off, saying, "It's a little different from when you left."

Ava skipped after him in her heels. Her footing wobbled over the uneven ground. "That's an understatement," she told him. "Your hair alone has me reeling."

I took up the rear.

His laugh reminded me of an old wagon wheel rolling over clumps of dirt. "Kipper threatened to leave if I cut it."

"Oh, really?" Her tone sounded teasing.

Ava's stride grew longer and more confident as we walked toward a sun-beaten single-wide past the barn, across from another cockeyed ring. It might've been brown once, but now it matched the rest of the gray landscape.

Nina watched me over Ava's shoulder. Those little eyes were curious. Or maybe calculating. I covered my face with my hands, then took them away and mouthed "peek-a-boo." That earned me a smile. *Definitely curious.* I hid my face behind my hands again and peeked through my fingers. That made her giggle.

"What happened to all the trees?" Ava asked, glancing back at me.

I dropped my hands and shrugged. Nina giggled harder.

"Some kind of disease," Terry was saying. "Spread to the lot of 'em. Cost a fortune to cut down. But cheaper than a lawsuit."

Ava's feet slowed, then stopped. "Hey, um, where's the trailer?"

When Terry turned, his caterpillar of a mustache drooped, like the thing got dehydrated. I felt a little dry myself. My shirt stuck to me, and the sun seared the back of my neck.

The older man sighed and ran knobby fingers through his wild hair. "We had to haul it out. The whole inside was covered in mold."

"Oh."

Who knew a single syllable could sound like heartbreak? My eyes dropped past her shapely legs to her classy heels, now dull and covered in dust, looking for clues. *Truck. Trailer?*

"I would've saved it if I could," Terry told her.

"No. I understand."

He studied her under a dark, bushy brow, arms now crossed. I couldn't see her face, but the way her shoulders sank, like twin battleships, gave me a weird indigestion. Something happened here, something that kept her away. We had more in common than I thought. If I'd known I'd be bringing her into the thick of it, I would've forced the Happy Meal on her. Or at least an ice cream sundae.

"You gone in to see ol' Kipper, yet?" Terry asked her.

She shook her head. "Don't let her hear you call her old."

"What? Eh." He waved a dismissive hand, but his weathered

face turned red. "I'll go in with ya." He climbed the steps of the single-wide and held the door open for us.

Ava's eyes lingered on the prickly weeds growing in the splitting planter boxes under the windows as she entered.

Terry put a hand on my chest as I reached the door. In a low voice, he asked, "How's she been?"

"I, uh ... she's having a rough day."

"Has she been eating? She looks too skinny."

"I heard that," Ava muttered from just inside a small, dusty office. "And you're one to talk!"

The moment to correct him passed again. He waved me inside and let the door slap shut behind him. Ava stood in the center of the room between two desks. Terry moved in next to her. I felt like the fourth wheel of a tricycle, but it beat facing Dad back at the ranch. I could do no right with that man.

"Well, well. Look who the cat dragged in," said an attractive older woman from behind her desk. She dropped a highlighter on an open notebook and tapped her glasses down her nose to stare at us. Her stern face reminded me of a high school math teacher. "I heard you were selling houses now. What brings you in here, fancy pants?"

Ava glanced at me, but when I met her eye, she blinked away. "We just came by to say hi. And get my truck."

This Kip woman didn't go gooey like Terry. In fact, the room felt a little crowded. I faded back, pretending to be interested in other things. A dented desk on another wall hid under a bunch of cardboard boxes. A ceiling fan covered in spider webs groaned as it spun. Nina hung on her mom's side like a baby monkey playing with a dangling earring.

"Ouch, baby." Ava grabbed the kid's chubby fingers. "No, thank you."

Where was the kid's dad?

The woman behind the desk pushed her glasses back up

her nose. "Well, while you're here, tell this old goat to call it a day, before he breaks something."

Terry's laugh brought to mind sandpaper. "Kipper, I've been fixing barns for forty years. I know what I'm doing."

"I wasn't talking about the barn." She shot him a scolding glare.

Ava elbowed Terry. "She has a point."

"Not you, too?" he grumbled. "Shoulda known you women would gang up on me."

"Maybe it's because we care," she shot back.

"Alright. Alright." Terry slapped my shoulder. "How about you and I take a look at that truck? It might need some coaxing."

I snuck a peek at Ava, feeling bad for leaving her.

"Come on, Loverboy." Terry steered me to the door.

"No, I–" I nearly tripped down the stairs, not watching where I was going. "I'm not–We're not together." Finally, out in the open, and the man strode way ahead of me. If he heard, he didn't respond.

I jogged to catch up. What did a city girl qualify as a truck? My bets were on one of those new Mavericks, or a Santa Cruz. *You have a nice truck ... a refreshing change from luxury sedans.*

Oh God, so help me if it's an Escalade!

I followed Terry around the back of the single-wide where he hauled up the door of a standalone garage. Inside was a friggin' dual-tone Chevy. A C10. Early 70s, judging by the trim. Interest revved up to a full-on crush.

Who was this woman?

"I think the battery's a goner," Terry commented. "But she never came by to get it fixed after she had it hauled."

"Is it open?"

"Yup."

I ducked into the cab, released the hood, then came around

the front and slid my fingers under the hot metal for the release. The hinge groaned as I lifted it overhead.

Sweet mother of automobiles, the thing was beautiful.

"You know much about cars?" Terry asked. Something odd struck me about his voice. Humor?

"I know a thing or two."

"Guess that adds up." He leaned over the engine with me. "What do ya reckon?"

"I can bring my truck around and give her a jump. See if we can get her started. Then go from there."

"Good plan." He patted my back, then strode off, saying, "I'll leave you to it. Gotta finish something before I lose the light."

I spun my key on my finger, feeling optimistic for once. Finally, a chance to do something I was actually good at.

5

—

Ava

KIP LEANED back in her chair and removed her Dollar Tree readers to study Nina and me. "She's big. She's three now?"

I nodded.

"Geez, she looks just like him."

Every response caught in my throat.

She straightened, folded her hands, and rested them on the desktop. "So ... You still hell-bent on buying this place?"

"Of course. I've been working overtime to build up my down payment."

"Hmm." Her deep-set toffee eyes held mine in challenge. "We weren't sure you'd come back."

I swallowed my rising guilt. The reel from that horrible day didn't cycle through my head like I had feared it would. Then again, the brittle, treeless landscape, the odd angles of the round pen, the splintered fences, they looked nothing like the ranch I remembered. My heart ached at the signs of a slow struggle. Piles of broken helmets, forgotten tools fading in the sun, barn doors hanging by a single screw. Unlike Jason's swift death, Hidden Meadows screamed the end stages of a long, drawn-out illness. All preventable if I'd found the strength to stay.

I watched Kip watching me, wishing for something other than indifference in her smooth expression–even anger or disappointment. I'd deserve it. I'd let them down, and I owed it to everyone to revive this dying friend.

"Let me ask you something," Kip said. "Why would you dump all your hard-earned money into this place?"

"B-because ..." *I made a promise? This was home? I wanted my old life back.* I doubted those sappy answers would penetrate her pragmatic shell. "It can't be that bad. You're still here."

"Yeah, well, someone needs to keep an eye on that stubborn geriatric coot."

"It has nothing to do with your love for the job? Or this ranch?"

Kip shrugged. I hadn't considered that once my name transferred onto the deed, everyone would leave. Including her. An ominous cloud swelled over my head. "You'd rather the other buyer tear it down?"

"What other buyer?"

"The corporate offer." I tilted my head, eyes narrowing. *Terry didn't tell her?*

Kip leaned forward, placing her elbows on the desk, a dip in her lip, and a single wrinkle forming between her eyes. "Corporate, huh? How much are they offering?"

"More than I can match." A number so high it didn't need a verbal confirmation.

She sighed, steepling her fingers. "Didn't realize he'd put the place on the market."

"He didn't." I'd checked.

One win. I just needed one win. I'd been confident the prospect of leveling the ranch would push her into my court, but she sat there, pressing her fingertips into a pensive frown.

"You're a good kid," she said. "Smart. Hard-working. Stubborn as hell, just like Terry, but I figure that serves you pretty well." She paused, looking at me for confirmation, but none of what she said felt complimentary.

I waited for the "but."

"You have a good heart," she went on. "And he'd do anything for you."

That's when I realized this conversation had backfired. "Kip–"

"Now, I know you've got your reasons. But think about what you're trying to achieve and ask yourself if buying this ranch is the only way to do that."

My voice took a defensive turn. "I just want my family back."

"You don't need a ranch for that. We've been here all along. Where were you?" Finally, I saw her eyebrows come together in anger.

"I, I couldn't stay–"

"No. No, no." She waved her hands in front of her face, then dug a fine-boned finger into her desk. "I don't mean *here*. I mean, where were you? You didn't even call."

I locked my jaw, holding back a rush of things that had no name. Emotions all marbled together, impossible to separate. A lump threatened to choke out my words. "I-I didn't know what else to do."

She shook her head, her gaze dropping to her desk. "It was hard enough losing him. But you too? And Nina?"

Back then, I couldn't see the arena without reliving the replay. Or bear hearing Kip's deflated sigh at every canceled lesson. Or Terry's weary gait when he came into the office for cheap, bitter coffee. There were times I'd wondered, how can emptiness feel so heavy? Moments when the air vanished from the entire world. The need to fill that void consumed me. I had to get back to where we'd been.

"I'm sorry, Kip." It came out as a whisper. "I messed up. But

I want to make it right. I-I thought if I could stop seeing him everywhere, if I–" I couldn't stop it. Guilt rose past the road-block in my throat and leaked all over my face. "If I could get through one d-day–"

"Oh, stop that." Kip's chair squeaked as she stood.

I swiped a hand across my wet cheeks, then froze as she wrapped her arms around Nina and me. Traces of rosewater lifted off her skin. Not once in the five years I'd been there had she ever hugged me. Not even when I told her I was pregnant.

My heart shattered into a million fragments, each reflecting wasted time and missed opportunities.

"You have every r-right to be mad at me," I stuttered into her shoulder.

"No," she scoffed. "Never mad. Worried maybe. And a little disappointed."

"I'm sorry."

"We just wanted to know you and Nina were okay." She squeezed me tighter.

"Kip, stop. You're making me cry."

"Nonsense. You were already doing that."

"Well, you're making it worse," I blubbered.

She stepped back, holding me at arm's length, waiting while I composed myself. Nina stared at her, unblinking.

"You good?" Kip asked.

I took a deep breath, blew it out, nodded, wiped my eyes.

"Good." She let go of my arms. Then, in true Kip fashion, she added, "You tell Terry I did that, and we're not friends anymore. Got it?"

I nodded again.

Nina put a hand on the top of my head. "Mama, why are you crying?"

"Miss Nina," Kip declared, saving me from a watery reply. "You remind your mama not to take everything on by herself." A tall order for a three-year-old. A strange expression crossed

Kip's gaze. She dipped her head and cleared her throat. "Now, go make sure Terry's not doing something stupid, will ya? I've got work to do." Halfway out the door, just as the sun hit my face, Kip called out. "Ava?"

My feet paused on the top step. "Yeah?"

"It's good to see you. Both of you."

I'd fled this place so I could finally breathe–short, dissatisfying breaths, but breaths all the same. Steven's office kept me busy. Paperwork, showings, deadlines ... very few quiet moments for my mind to wander, for the grief to overwhelm me. I'd refused to burden everyone with my broken heart, but in my numbness, I'd missed that theirs were breaking, too.

The sky yawned dusty pink with orange highlights. Maybe that meant new beginnings? I set Nina on her feet, searching for Terry, Eli, and my truck.

"We used to live here," I told her. She wouldn't remember early mornings in the stable, and pony rides on the sweep. "Every morning, we'd greet the horses." I sighed. One day, we'd get back there.

"Mama, where's da horsies?"

I glanced at the barn. "Good question." Getting the ranch was only the first step.

The reliable growl of an engine caught my attention, but it didn't sound like mine. I led Nina toward the sound, rounding the corner of the single-wide as a sputtering, high-pitched groan hit my ear.

"Roxy!" A smile shone through my emotional exhaustion. "You fixed her!"

Eli's truck idled nose to nose with mine. An automotive kiss of life. He slid out from behind the wheel of my Chevy, exuding confidence in his slow stride, and something borderline painful pinched in my chest.

"Far from fixed," he said. "But she'll run for now." After a brief pause, he added, "Someone should look at her. Sooner rather than later."

When was I going to have time for that? I had to find an apartment, a job, and convince Terry to ignore the dollar signs raining down from a soulless industry. "How soon?"

"You hear that whining?" Eli asked.

I listened. It sounded like it always did. "Not really."

He walked over to the open driver's door and put his foot on the accelerator. "Hear it now?"

"Sort of?" I really tried to listen for it, but something happened in my brain. Everything went in one ear then just sort of faded around his hands, now smudged with grease from touching my parts–my truck's parts.

"The timing's off," he said. "Could be a few things. But if you ignore it, you could burn out your engine."

I heard the words, but what registered were things like how his mouth curved down at the edges, and the way his Adam's apple settled low as he waited for my response. That some family heritage made his eyes almond-shaped. That the little wrinkle in his forehead just under the bill of his hat painted him compassionate instead of cocky.

"I'm happy to take a look," he was saying, "back at my dad's place. Get it running smoothly."

So, help me. "Y-you're a mechanic?"

"Yeah."

My chest spasmed as my eyes traced down his arms to the black smudges that marred his hands. Very nice hands. Strong hands that knew their way around an engine. The stress of the day had finally induced a heart attack.

Nina pulled at my grip. "Stay close," I told her, letting her go.

Eli removed the jump-start cables. "So, you're a realtor?"

I narrowed my gaze at his tone. "Why do you say it like that?"

"Like what?"

"Dripping with disappointment."

"I didn't ... It's nothing." He tossed the coiled cables into the back of his truck.

"It doesn't sound like nothing."

He scrunched his face, like his next words were bitter. "Relators are always talking up school districts, equity, thirty-year loans ... That's just not my thing."

"What is your thing?"

"Easy. Open roads and new places."

My eyes kept dipping to where his shirt stretched across his chest. "So, you're kind of a nomad?"

"I guess you could say that."

Nina came running up with a handful of rocks. "Mama! Hold deeze."

"All of them?"

She dumped them into my open palms. I waited until she'd run off before discarding one that looked suspiciously like poop. Eli watched with a warm half-smile.

"Kids," I explained. "And just to clear the air, I am not a realtor. I'm an office admin. *Was* an office admin. I just quit."

"Yeah? 'Cause of Mr. Mercedes?"

I sighed, the anger rising all over again. "Yeah. 'Cause of him."

A lazy stillness stretched between us as we watched Nina collect more treasures under a warm watercolor sky. One thing I loved about Hidden Meadows? You couldn't hear the city traffic or the music from the car next to you at the stoplight. The world was quiet. I think I missed that the most. Being swallowed up in nature.

Eli's boot pivoted on the rocky soil. "You got somewhere to stay tonight?"

"I was going to stay here, but my old trailer's gone." A sinking ship hit the bottom of unfathomable depths.

Our home. Gone.

I kept my eyes on Nina.

After another elongated silence, Eli said, "If you wanna stay in a trailer, my old man has one on his ranch. You're welcome to it."

I grimaced at even considering it.

"Is that weird?" he added. "Since we just met?"

Before I could respond, Terry snuck up behind us.

"Listen to that!" He wiped his hands on his jeans before giving Eli a pat on the back. "Good work, son."

Maybe it was the hue of the setting sun, but Eli's ears looked a little pink.

"You know," Terry said, combing his fingers through his mustache, "you look so darn familiar. Do you work down at the feed store?"

"No, sir. I don't live around here. I'm just helping my dad for the summer."

"Who's your dad?"

"William Anderson. He's an–"

"Bill! Bill's your dad? Well, shoot!" Terry turned to me. "Remember, we had a guy come out to design the event arena?"

I shook my head.

"Ah, maybe that was before your time. Anyway, they boarded here, way back." He turned to Eli, a new light shining in his eye. "How's your mom? If I recall, she was the rider in the family."

A muscle jumped in Eli's jaw. "She died. About 15 years ago."

"Oh no. I'm sorry. What happened?"

"Cancer."

Terry *tsked*, shaking his head in regret. "That's terrible."

"Yeah." Eli repositioned his cap on his head exactly like he'd had it before.

Nina returned with another load of rocks. And a bone.

"Hey, Crackerjack, let's leave this one here." I handed back the lower mandible of some long-dead rodent.

"No! I want it!" She shoved it back at me, and a tooth broke off.

Terry laughed. "That's Jason's kid, alright."

In my peripheral, I caught Eli curl his hands over the bill of his hat. Maybe it was his visible discomfort that motivated me. Maybe I needed to release the pressure that had been building since I found that unlabeled blue folder in the back of the Mercedes. Steven's words regurgitated like a Taco Bell Gordita. *Have you even talked to Terry?* So, I said it without preamble.

"Hey Terry, you still plan on selling me the ranch, right?"

6

Ava

"You prepared *to work your hiney off?*" Not exactly the response I had hoped for.

Under a darkening sky, I followed Eli's Ford to the opposite edge of town.

We turned into a dirt driveway, slowing to a stop at a metal cattle guard. No property indicator, no sign. Nothing. Eli hopped out and forced the gate open, metal wheezing and scraping the ground. *Who doesn't name their ranch?* But Terry vouched for his family, and I lacked a better option. Eli waved me through, closed up, and took the lead again.

Here's hoping I don't regret this tomorrow.

Gravel popped under my tires, and Nina's rock collection rattled in the glove compartment. My yellow headlights danced over grooves that wove through the road like dried-out rivers. Eli seemed like an upstanding person. I mean, he saved my daughter from a moving vehicle! I glanced to my right, where Nina enjoyed her freedom, lying across the bench with the seatbelt strap behind her because Steven had her car seat. *Mr. Mercedes* ... The nickname fit. Steady anger simmered on my back burner. What an idiot I'd been!

The day had unraveled faster than a snag in a handmade scarf, but Eli was right. Chocolate helped. And now I had Roxy. I found myself craving another peanut butter cup. Until a horrifying reality hit.

Oh. My. God.

I had just accepted candy AND a ride from a stranger! And he didn't even need the chocolate. The minute he turned mechanic, I had regressed into a billboard victim! Steven was right. I was my own worst enemy.

Up ahead, ominous glowing orbs morphed into friendly porch sconces. We approached a well-lit, Craftsman-style home sandwiched between an open-air stable and a three-car garage. When Eli's truck stopped abruptly, I had to slam on my brakes. My arm shot out to hold Nina as a broad gray horse ambled past Eli's front bumper, unfazed.

"Mama, look!" Nina rose to her knees and pressed her face against the passenger window. The animal outside stopped to rub its flank against a parked white truck, much like a bear scratching its back on a tree.

I cranked my window down, intending to ask Eli where to park, but a man with white hair stormed out of the house.

"Eli!" Light glinted off his glasses as he labored down the front steps, fists swinging. Given the exasperated tone, I assumed this was Dad. "What did I tell you about Chuck?"

Eli slid out of his truck and blocked the man from view. "Sorry. I forgot."

"You *forgot*? People don't pay us to lose their animals, son. Put him back where he belongs."

Chuck swung his attention to the men with lips curled into a smile, then bobbed his head.

Nina giggled. "Mama, he's laughing!"

I smiled despite myself, thinking I should suck it up and get my purse from Steven. I didn't need to insert myself into someone else's family drama. But did I have the energy for another fight?

"So, you let him wander around while I'm gone?" Eli was saying.

"You'll never learn if I do it for you."

Eli ran a hand over the top of his hat. "Fine. I'll do it in a minute. I need the RV keys."

"Oh?" The older man's tone shifted. "You found me some help?"

"Not exactly."

Reflective eyewear peered around his wide shoulders. "For crying out loud, Eli!"

Great. I was the stray dog that every kid tried to convince their parents to keep.

Eli threw his palms up. "It's not–"

"I don't want to hear it. Just put Chuck away! I'm going to bed." The older man lumbered up the porch steps, slamming the front door behind him.

Maybe I could ask Terry to camp on his couch? Or borrow money for a hotel? I grimaced. *And give him a reason to doubt my hiney?* I needed to prove I could take things over, not advertise how messy my life had become. I shifted behind the wheel. The old wool blanket draped across the bench seat scratched the backs of my legs. My hiney was tired of sitting.

Eli stood, chin to his chest, hands on his hips. He'd seen me vulnerable; now this window into his life ignited a sort of camaraderie.

He turned and strode with purpose to my open window. "I gotta put Chuck away. If you want, you can head over." He twisted and pointed into the darkness past the stables. "It's down by the barn."

"I'll wait for you. If that's okay."

He glanced at the house. "Sure. Be back in a few."

Ten minutes later, we left the friendly porch lights for darkness and uncertainty. *"If you wanna stay in a trailer ..."* Want had little to do with it. But my nightmare remained dormant, so I had hope.

Nina stretched forward to open the glove compartment, and *all* her rocks tumbled out. "Mama, help!"

"Leave them, Crackerjack. We'll pick them up when we stop."

We drove past the stables, and the dim silhouette of a trailer materialized like a ghost, hiding beneath the shadow of a massive tree. I blinked away a memory that tried to superimpose itself onto reality as I put the truck in park behind Eli's. Everything was for Nina. I could, and would, do hard things– whatever it took. For her.

"Now, Mama?"

"What?"

"Can I get my rocks?"

"Sure."

She crawled out of her seatbelt and slunk into the footwell.

The red glow of Eli's taillights made an eerie scene as he thudded up the wooden steps to the trailer door. It creaked open, and he disappeared inside. A silent beat later, the interior lit, then the front exterior. The unit boasted slide-outs and a deck large enough for a chair. Nina searched for her treasures in the dark. It was well past bedtime. She moaned when some of her bounty dropped back into the footwell.

"Can we look for them tomorrow?" I asked.

"No!"

Too tired to fight it, I opened my door to give her light.

Earthy odors wafted in like outstretched arms bearing unwanted gifts. Familiar hues of horsehair, manure, and dirt. At first, like weak tea.

I'm okay.

But the arms wrapped around me and their scents bloomed into a heady bouquet. My fingers flexed around the steering wheel.

I'm fine.

We weren't at Hidden Meadows.

Nina started counting her rocks, oblivious. "One, two, four, seven ..."

I could feel it coming, like the warning vibrations of a stampede. On this unremarkable Tuesday. I tried taking a deep breath, but the musky tang of the ranch surrounded me. Consumed me.

The reel began–no pause button, nowhere to run. *The white trash bag floating against a cerulean blue sky. His white hat crushed into the red dirt.* White wasn't hope or purity. It was sorrow. Death. Panic. Desperation.

I can't do this.

"Mama?"

In place of my heart swung a wrecking ball, determined to break me open. I held my breath.

Not my ranch.

I squeezed my eyes shut, and Jason's lifeless ones gazed skyward.

Not my ranch.

My pulse thumped like techno bass.

Jason's head weighed heavily in my lap. People gasped. My fingers fumble over the nine and the one on my phone. Why isn't it working? Help. We need help!

"Ava?"

The soft touch on my arm jolted me out of my skin. My eyes flew open to find Elijah Anderson at my side.

He was frowning. "What's wrong?"

My heart hammered, and my breath shook. "Nothing." *Everything.*

This was the reason Nina didn't know horses. The reason I'd packed my boots in storage.

He studied me, gaze narrowed with doubt. "You wanna come up?"

If I couldn't do this, how would I take over Hidden Meadows? A lot had changed since Jason's death, but I kept my promises.

Eli pulled the door wide. My pencil skirt had hiked up on the drive over. To pull it down now would only draw attention to it, so I squeezed my thighs together and wiggled off the bench, wobbling as one of my stupid heels found a gopher hole.

Eli threw a hand to my aid. "You good?"

"Mhmm." My sensible pencil skirt had just become a micro skirt. *Great*. Now I *had* to fix it.

His eyes dipped as I adjusted the material. "Probably shouldn't tell you this, but I'm a leg man."

"Yeah ... Let's not make this awkward, or anything."

He placed his hand on the top of his head and exhaled a self-deprecating laugh. "Sorry. I don't suppose you can forget I said that?"

"Not a chance."

"What if I told you it's because I was a leg doctor?"

I fought the urge to mess with my skirt further. "*Do* you work in orthopedics?"

"No, but I can give you the name of one that promises a perfect smile." He flashed me his own endearing example.

"Right ..." I couldn't tell if he was trying to flirt or if he was just ironically funny.

Nina scuttled across the bench behind me, rocks and all. I scooped her up and held her to my chest like armor. This kid. She fueled my motivation when I wanted to quit. She gave me strength. And in that moment, she was giving me one of her rocks ... which missed its mark and slid down my shirt.

Her little voice echoed my thoughts. "Uh oh."

A tired curse danced on my tongue, but I managed an "I will get that later." I caught her searching hand before it dipped down into my shirt. Hopefully Eli wasn't also a breast man.

We walked single file, me on the balls of my feet, Eli trailing behind, up the wooden steps to the open RV. I adjusted Nina as we entered, and her rock slid past my waistband and hit the ground.

To my horror, Eli stooped to pick it up. "What do you think?" To his credit, he did not look at my legs.

"I think I'd like to crawl into a hole."

He handed the smooth, white striped stone to Nina. "Now you know how I feel. But I meant the trailer."

"Oh."

It looked like every RV I'd ever seen, down to faded tan upholstery, peeling vinyl wallpaper, and stale air. Not so dissimilar from Jason's and my first home. *Only home.* I focused on the differences: three stairs to a bathroom and a bedroom slide-out on our right. *More privacy.* A wide living area with a movable couch and a flat screen TV. *Space to stretch out.* A dinette set tucked in the slide-out on my left, and past that, the concise kitchen. *With a full-sized refrigerator.* Still, a pesky knowing clung to the cubbies and cabinets tucked in every corner, the way the unit popped and shifted when we moved inside.

"It's fine." My reservations had nothing to do with the state of the trailer.

"It's hot," Nina whined.

Eli checked the control panel opposite the door. "I just turned on the air. It should cool down. Water's hooked up, so you can use the sink."

I nodded with eyes fixed on the tiny kitchen. I used to thrive cooking on two coiled burners and a half-sized oven.

Eli crossed in front of me and frowned. "You say it's fine, but your forehead's all wrinkled." His finger drew squiggly lines in front of my face as he said this.

I covered the top of my head with my hand. "It's not!"

He chuckled. This close, I noticed a slightly crooked canine in his otherwise even smile.

He peeled my hand away, tracing his index finger horizontally across my forehead. "Right there."

For a fleeting moment, I forgot what we were talking about. "I was–I was thinking of my old trailer."

Nina jerked back, almost head-butting Eli in the chin.

"Sorry." I set her down, and she immediately started exploring.

Eli shoved his hands in his pockets. "I threw a clean blanket on the bed. There's sheets up at the house if–"

"This is fine." Clean sheets wouldn't fix my problems. "Thank you, Eli. For the ride and the trailer." I had to remind myself I wasn't a stray. I was a wife. And a mom. And I had an entire life I was working to build.

"No problem." He smiled at his feet. "Guess I'd better get out of your hair." Those feet took him to the deck out front. "Good night, Ava."

"Good night, Eli."

The door clapped shut behind him.

Silence. Stillness.

I kicked my shoes off with a sigh, but my relief was short-lived. There were no files to go through before morning, or schedules to verify with Steven. Without the distraction, dark thoughts crept around the edges of my brain like a vignette.

"Mama!" Nina called from the bedroom. "I hear horsies!"

Enter Nina's second wind.

"The horses are sleeping right now," I said. *Except for Chuck.*

"But I hear them!"

"And speaking of sleep–"

The door to the trailer creaked open. Fight mode coiled my

muscles as I spun to face a familiar gray tee and hat combo. "Eli! You scared me!"

"Sorry." Without my shoes, he stood half a head taller than me. "Sorry. I should've knocked." He held up a can of beer. "I thought you could use one. Or two." His other hand revealed another.

When I didn't respond, he set them on the dinette table. Instead of leaving, he scratched behind his ear. "You should come up to the house for breakfast tomorrow."

Thoughts zeroed immediately to his dad. "Thank you for the offer, but–"

"It's not good to start the day on an empty stomach. Oh." He frowned. "But Marley's cooking."

"Who?"

"Thing is, I wanted to look at your truck before you go."

My eyes involuntarily dropped to his hands. "I appreciate your help. I really do. That's why I can't ask for more."

"Up to you." He shrugged and meandered back to the deck. "Good night. For real."

"Good night, Eli."

I stood, staring at the closed door for a good minute, expecting him to storm back in. But his truck rumbled, and through the window, his taillights bounced down the road until they were nothing but fading red dots.

That's when loneliness flooded in. Like a car careened off a bridge. Or a monsoon.

"Mama! Mama, look!"

The distinct, repetitive creak of a mattress crept down from the bedroom. "Nina, I hope you're not jumping on the bed!"

"It's fun!"

I didn't even have time to remind her of the five little monkeys before the *thud*. Wails followed.

I grabbed a warm beer on my way to the bedroom.

"Mama! No pants!"

I'd just closed my eyes, and here we were, awake again. "No pants," I murmured, curling my bare legs into my chest.

Nina flopped across me, all elbows and chins.

"*Oof!* Ouch, baby!" I guess we were doing this. I squeezed Nina in a morning hug. She squealed–a defibrillator setting my heart back to its normal rhythm. I held tighter, digging my nose into her hair as sunshine reached through the windows, bounced off the mirrored closet doors, and bathed the little bedroom in an optimistic glow. But it didn't reach me. Because one by one, my promises and my failures filtered to awareness. What I had to do, what I could lose, but most of all, the familiar undertones that surrounded me.

I pushed myself up on the tan velour blanket that covered a naked mattress, and Nina went rolling.

She giggled as she climbed back on top of me. "Again!"

My insides felt dry and brittle as a beached sea sponge. "No more, Crackerjack. We have to go to Steven's house."

As I stood, something caught my eye, and my fragile heart shuddered. I could've focused on the dark wood finishes and rubbed bronze hardware in the unit. Or Nina star-fishing across the bed.

Look away.

My throat clamped, but my heart yearned to see him. Behind Nina, Jason sat propped against the upholstered headboard, reading a worn paperback.

It wasn't real.

Of course, it wasn't. But I didn't blink it away, even as my eyes blurred. He turned a page, and I begged the image to look up at me. His calm energy used to fill the space–any space–seeping into everything and everyone. It washed over anger and stress, a warm embrace, a strong-armed, sun-soaked cocoon. When Jason was near, you knew everything would be okay.

This filmy facsimile of him held none of that.

"Mama, I'm firsty."

I forced my attention to Nina. "Okay. We'll work on that."

"Mama? Why is your eyes like that?"

"Like what, baby?"

She stared at me, an old soul stuck in a child's body.

I rubbed my face, wiped at my eyes, and when I looked back at the bed, he was gone. "I'm just tired."

Nina gasped. "Mama! Mama! Horsies, me-member?" She launched herself up and teetered to the edge of the mattress to stare out the window.

A weak smile lifted my lips. "I guess we'd better get dressed, so we can meet them?"

"Yes! Yes!" She bounced to the floor, this time landing on her feet, and got dressed in record time.

My eyes kept drifting to the empty headboard as I shook out my wrinkled office wear. If Jason were alive, he'd be laughing. "*What the heck are you wearing, boo?*" he'd say, before taking an appreciative gander at my butt.

I missed that.

I bent to wedge my foot into cursed heel number one before helping Nina put on yesterday's dirty shirt. Once in the kitchen, my eyes fell on the only food-safe container available–the empty beer can in the sink. Would it be wrong to offer her water in that?

"I wanna banana," she whined, hanging on my leg.

"You said you were thirsty." I rinsed the can and refilled it from the tap. A sniff and a cringe later, I dumped it and tried again. The sharp sting of sulfur remained. *She won't drink this.* I didn't even want to drink it.

Nina heaved her weight onto me. "Banaaanaaa!"

The flashing clock on the microwave lied—it couldn't be 2:43. I glanced out the RV window. The picturesque white Craftsman with black shutters stood like a mission on El Camino Real. It struck an odd juxtaposition beside utilitarian stables made of galvanized steel and corrugated aluminum.

"Tell you what, Crackerjack?" I led Nina to the door. "Let's see the horses, then Mama will get her purse and buy you a big bunch of bananas. Deal?"

"Yay!"

Despite her initial enthusiasm, I had to drag Nina behind me as we approached the animals. "It's okay. They can't hurt you, see? They're fenced in."

In the nearest corner stall, a beautiful gray Andalusian with a mercury-threaded mane nosed at an empty feed bucket. She was an animal that emerged from the mist, regal and mysterious, a creature of legends and myth.

Well, she would've been ... Mud caked halfway up her leg. The heavy scent of manure hung in the air.

They need to clean the stalls.

We inch-wormed into the stable; me stepping forward, Nina pulling back until we stood under the aluminum roof in the aisle between the two rows of enclosures, four on each side. Half were empty. Plywood walled off the first stall on our left. From my tiptoes, I spotted tack and tools hanging inside. Next on the left lived a large black Tennessee Walker, but he moved away as we came near. An empty stall separated him from a brown-white Painted at the end, who tossed her head and paced the narrow space.

"See that?" I pointed to the agitated equine. "When they act like that, you keep away."

Nina tried to crawl into my skirt.

"Are you scared?"

She nodded.

I picked her up and took her to the stalls on the right, toward someone I recognized. In the daytime, his spotted pattern gave him an ombre effect, transitioning from a smooth light gray at his thick center to dark charcoal ears, muzzle, and hooves. My fingers brushed against the padlock that hung from the latch of his gate–the only gate that had one. Chuck lifted his head and sniffed the air before meandering over to greet us. The languid movement reminded me of Eli.

"Good morning." I offered him the back of my hand, explaining to Nina how we greet unfamiliar horses. "Be calm. Let them smell you." He nudged his nose against my skin, lighting a unique thrill I'd somehow forgotten. "Aren't you handsome?"

As I ran my palm down his muscular neck, time slowed, and my pulse with it. The world fell away. It was only Nina, Chuck, and me. The shift of hooves, the flinch of muscle, his warm breath billowing on my chest. A wave of acceptance washed over me. There were no expectations here, no deadlines, no judgements.

I twisted, bringing Nina closer so she could pet him, but she reared back as Chuck slid his head through the bars to nip at my blouse. Nina whined, kicking at his long nose and square teeth.

I grabbed her leg as Chuck jerked his head back into the enclosure. "Careful! He's just saying hi." Nina locked her arms around my neck in a choke-hold and unleashed a high-pitched wail of distress.

I retreated to the center of the aisle. "I guess they're a lot bigger up close, huh?"

When she nodded into my neck, another seed of guilt burrowed. If I'd been stronger, she would have never known a life *without* horses. I shouldered us and all my regrets out of the stable.

One thing at a time.

First, I had to deal with Steven. And convince Terry I could handle Hidden Meadows.

7

Eli

*"Hey! I'm parked here!" The weird mechanical beeping got louder
as the semi backed closer to my truck.*

"What are you doing? Stop!"

He wasn't gonna stop.

Right before impact, I realized why it sounded off. Not a truck. It
was my alarm. *Shit!* I bolted up and checked the clock. *Double
shit!*

Shoving into a pair of jeans, I hopped my way to the door.
Don't be too late. I thundered barefoot down the stairs of my
garage studio, through the garage, and stopped short in the
mudroom.

Marley's voice echoed from the front door. "Can I *help* you?"
Must be an unspoken rule that teenage girls had to act like
DMV employees before their lunch break.

"... truck won't start."

Ava!

I grabbed a t-shirt from the dryer and shook out the wrinkles as I passed through the kitchen.

"Oh, that's convenient," Marley was saying. "It got you here, but suddenly it won't start?" Seventeen. Acting like hot shit. She looked older, especially with all that make-up on her eyes, but as soon as she opened her mouth ...

"It needed a jump yesterday, too. We ... Is Eli here?"

"Let 'em in, Mar!" I skidded to the door, still pulling my shirt over my head.

"Ugh." You could hear Marley's eye roll. "And you complain about my shorts! Whatever. You asked for it."

She stalked past, and I *didn't* mention the crescents the entire world could see under the hemline of her so-called "shorts." Hell, half her shirt was missing, too. I can't believe my aunt let her pierce her belly button.

I turned to Ava. "Hey! You're here." The color on her cheeks reminded me of strawberry lemonade. "Ignore Marley," I said. "She's not a morning person."

"I can hear you!" Marley shouted from the kitchen.

Nina clung to Ava's upper half, peeking at me through messy black hair.

I pushed the door wide open. "Are you hungry? Come in."

"Actually, if we could just get another jump start ..." Ava's eyes searched over my shoulder, and I realized she must've been worried about Dad.

That made two of us.

The crazy part? He'd probably love someone like her, dressed all business-y. Even with the wrinkles–another thing we now had in common. The sun seemed extra bright for once, and I didn't want her to go.

She must've caught me staring because she looked down at her clothes and smoothed a hand over her skirt. "Too formal for breakfast?" That full bottom lip tipped into a tight smile.

I wanted more.

"I probably look wrinkled and ridiculous," she said.

"No, you look ..." Gorgeous? *Come on, Eli. Play it cool.* This wasn't a date. "You look ready for breakfast."

"I just need a jump."

I went to fix my hat, but my hand hit hair, and I realized I'd left it upstairs. "If the battery isn't holding a charge," I said, "you'll just get stuck at your next stop." And I'd be back to long, thankless days in the sun and nighttime standoffs with Dad. "Where are you headed?"

"To get my purse."

"From Mr. Mercedes?"

She nodded, shifting Nina to the other hip.

I wondered if her arms ever got tired. "You should get a new battery before you stop again." I leaned back, glancing through the wide opening into the kitchen, at the clock on the wall. "Shops aren't open yet." And some sales guy would try to upsell her some fancy-ass hunk of lead. "Why don't you grab something to eat first? A cup of coffee? I'll look up a battery for you."

Marley clanked in the kitchen, reminding me that breakfast was more of a punishment than a promise.

Ava hesitated.

I stepped back. "You coming in, or what?"

She grimaced. "Or what."

"At least get some coffee."

Her eyes skated toward the kitchen. "Fine."

I closed the door before she changed her mind and caught her gawking straight back at the living room.

"Wow."

As far as views went, I guess "wow" said it best. Dad had this giant-ass window instead of a wall so he could stare at the big red mountain behind the house. It was the one good thing about the room. Better than the stiff brown leather couch and fancy flat stone fireplace. It felt stuffy. More like a hotel lobby than the house I grew up in.

Ava walked through the entryway, past the top landing of the stairs that took you to the den, straight back to the floor-to-ceiling windows. "Rusty mountains and a forget-me-not sky." At least, I think that's what she said. "No wonder you picked this spot."

"Dad picked it."

"Well, he did good. He should send in for a spread in Better Homes and Gardens."

I had no idea what that meant. "Kitchen's this way." I ticked my head to the side, then led them into the smell of … burning?

Marley stood at the stove, sour-faced, beating the inside of a pot with a wooden spoon. All she needed was a pointy black hat.

I came up next to her. "What. Is that?"

"Oatmeal!"

I shook my head, smiling. *This kid*. She made me crazy, but I wouldn't trade her. "Only you."

Ava's eyes grew two sizes as she scanned the kitchen. She'd put Nina down, and the kid was grabbing at her skirt. I tried to see what Ava saw, but it was just a bunch of black and white to me. The only thing with any personality was the old scratched-up kitchen table. Though why Dad got a twelve-footer for one man made no sense.

"Oh my gosh!" she said. "The light! These countertops! Those cabinets! It's like walking into a centerfold!"

"A what now?"

"A–" Red bled into her cheeks. "I mean–it's gorgeous. The kitchen." She tugged at her skirt, which, thanks to Nina's fussing, had crept up to mid-thigh. "Nina, stop that."

Who knew kitchens could be sexy? I patted Marley's stiff shoulder and moved to the large center island. Just for kicks, I dragged my finger along the black marble. Ava's eyes followed the trail. *Interesting*. Maybe it was kinda sexy. For a kitchen counter. My fingers curled into a fist, derailing that train.

I squatted in front of Nina. "Morning, kiddo! You hungry?"

She watched me through narrow slits.

"We have cereal, apples–"

"And *oatmeal*," Marley interjected.

"I want a banana," Nina blurted.

Ava squeezed the kid's hand. "I told you I'd get one later."

"Banana, huh?" I stood. "I think I can find one of those. Ava, how do you take your coffee?"

She gave me the same suspicious once over, but my patience paid off. "Splash of milk."

The white swirl in her cup evened out by the time I exited the pantry with the bananas. I held out her drink. "One coffee for the not-real-estate-agent."

She carefully looped her fingers into the handle. "Thanks."

I pulled a banana free from the bunch. "And one monkey snack for Short Stop, here."

Nina wrapped her little fingers around it, and it killed me–she reminded me of those baby gorillas on the Discovery Channel.

Ava nudged her. "What do you say?"

"Peas!"

"Other one, baby."

"Fank you!"

Can this kid get any cuter?

I pulled another banana from the knot and held it out to Ava. "Want one?"

"No, thank you."

I shrugged, peeled it, and took a huge bite.

Her eyes zeroed in on my mouth.

"You sure?"

"N-no. I mean, yes. I'm sure."

"Am I making this oatmeal for nothing?" Marley slammed the wooden spoon on the counter, but it bounced and rained oats before landing on the floor.

Silence followed.

Then Ava surprised me. "I'll have some."

Bold. Brave. "Your call," I muttered, despite my utter respect.

'Course, she'd never had Marley's cooking. I took another bite of banana, and she definitely watched me swallow it.

Light from outside made the room glow-y. The sun was definitely brighter. But that's when I noticed a lack of Toyota Corollas out front.

Shit.

"Mar, have you seen Nick?"

She shrugged.

"Sorry," I told Ava. "I'll be right back."

I left through the front door and jogged to the empty barn. Empty except for a bunch of hungry horses and mountains of manure. *Of all the days.* Phone to my ear, I marched back to the house, but he didn't pick up. "Nick, man. Where are you? Bright and early, remember? This was your last chance. Hope you're on your way."

I stopped for a second on the porch, dragged my hands down my face, already hearing Dad's, *"I told you so."* Maybe I could take care of this before he made an appearance.

Back in the kitchen, Nina and Ava sat at the table, and Marley stood at her cauldron. "Mar, I need you on mucking."

"What? No!" Tan globs went flying when she spun to attack me with her death stare. "You said if I cook, I don't have to muck." She stabbed the gooey spoon at me. "*You* said I suck at mucking!"

"What? No, I didn't."

Marley dropped her voice into a dopey drawl. "You realize the point of mucking is to take the poop out of the horse pen."

"Is that supposed to be me?"

She jammed her spoon at a bubble rising in the pot. "Since you're so picky, you do it."

Why did everything have to be so dramatic with her? "I can't. I gotta fix the gate before boarders come."

"What boarders?" Marley snarked.

Good point.

Ava was watching me. I shoved my fingers through my hair. It needed a cut. "Fine. Okay." I could figure this out.

Then Dad walked in, and all the air in the room went out.

He had on his brown cowboy boots, Levi's, and same-as-ever golf polo. "Eli, a word?"

Great, I was hoping to hit rock bottom by breakfast. For a man who didn't want to muck, he sure dressed the part. I followed him around the corner to the souless living room. "Dad, before you say–"

"Eli ..." He stretched out my name, looking to the heavens like he hoped Mom might jump in.

"She needs help with her truck. And she's got a kid," I said, even though he didn't ask. "I told her to come in for breakfast."

"This isn't a B&B for humans, it's a B&B for horses."

"I know."

"And that fifth wheel is for our ranch manager."

"Which we don't have yet," I reminded him.

"The way you're going, we aren't going to have one."

"I'm happy to leave, anytime."

He crossed his arms. The floor creaked under his weight. "Look, I don't care what you do in your personal time. I'm not asking you to be celibate–"

"Will you stop it!" I cut a glance at the wall separating us from the kitchen. "That's not what this is."

"All I'm saying is, keep it separate. You're here to work."

As if I needed reminding. I held his stare. "They needed help. It's what Mom woulda done."

"Yeah, well, she'd be doing a lot of other things around here, too." His eyebrows lifted. A challenge.

This was why I stayed away.

Dad started toward the kitchen. I threw my hand out to stop him. "Uh, since you got your boots on." He was already ticked at me, what could it hurt? "Can you muck?"

His eyes went skyward again. "Lord, help me, Eli." For a non-religious man, he seemed to pray a lot. "Luke?" he asked.

"No, Nick."

"I told you. I told you when you brought them on–"

"Yeah, yeah. I've already dealt with it. I get it."

But *he* didn't. These kids needed something to stay outta trouble, and I knew the ranch could give it to them. Well, maybe not Nick, not anymore.

Dad was shaking his head.

"You want to do the gate instead?" I asked.

His lips got thin, and he turned his head to the side, as if looking at me offended him. "Just fix it. The darn thing's near impossible to open."

Good. Done. Fine. I turned before he loaded on another lecture. He followed me silently into the kitchen, not bothering to hide the once-over he gave Ava and Nina. To her credit, Ava didn't even flinch. I considered introducing them, but Dad didn't seem interested in knowing more.

He went to the coffee pot. "Get me an egg, will ya?"

I opened the fridge and came out with leftover bacon and two hard-boiled eggs. Marley scraped the sides of the pot and glared at me. For a second, I almost gave in, but then I remembered the last time I buckled. My stomach hurt for days.

I spun Dad's egg on the counter next to him. He missed the hellfire in Marley's eyes while he was busy peeling it.

"Who the hell am I making this oatmeal for? Seriously?"

"Hey," I said. "Watch your language. There's a kid in the room."

"Oh, I'm sorry. Where's the rainbow-pooping unicorn I'm making this oatmeal for?"

Props for creativity. "Sorry, Mar, I gotta get that gate fixed. Ava, can you hang for a few?"

She shrugged.

Yeah, it was a cheap move. Where could she go with a dead battery?

"Uncle Bill?" Marley asked, sounding like she lost her dog. "Oatmeal?"

Dad shoved half his egg in his mouth. "Sorry, kid. Stalls won't muck 'emselves."

For once, we agreed on something.

8

———

Ava

THEIR ABRUPT EXIT left me gaping.

It's just oatmeal. I thought men would eat anything.

Marley turned back to the pot, head down. Her dark, delicate features and willowy curves reminded me of a pixie. And despite the brutal stare-down I'd received at the front door, perhaps she was just as delicate inside? What a contrast to Eli. His angular, broad planes spoke gladiator. Or bull rider.

I stood from the table. "Is it ready?"

When I sidled up beside her, I understood. She was using the wooden utensil to mash her disappointment into the now lumpy oats.

"I think it's done," I whispered, reaching between her and the stovetop to turn off the burner. "Where do the bowls live?"

It took several flings to get the hot, sticky cereal to separate from the spoon. Dark flecks seasoned the mush that held its shape like Play-Doh.

"Only a little for Nina," I said.

She slung a huge glob in the second bowl, bigger than the first. And another into the last bowl. My breakfast jiggled like Jello, and smelled like cardboard, but I intended to eat it because it mattered to this girl that someone did. I carried all three servings to the table, and Marley tossed a Tupperware of brown sugar and a bag of raisins on the table, choosing the seat opposite us. Even with extra sugar and a silent prayer, Nina tested the tip of her tongue on the spoon and promptly labeled it "yuck."

Marley glared.

"She's three," I said apologetically. "Don't take it personally."

But she did. She shoved off the bench, dumped her half-eaten bowl into the sink, and stormed out of the kitchen. I ate what I could, tossed the rest, then washed the bowls and soaked the pot in soapy water. As the bubbles dissipated, I considered Steven. I didn't feel sad about ending it, which didn't surprise me. My heart was closed for business. And I'd never pretended otherwise. But ending it meant I had to move all our stuff *and* hunt for a new job. My stomach sank.

I found a rag and scrubbed at the sides of the oatmeal pot. The water turned murky, and the burnt bits floated to the top. That's how I felt. Old emotions and new hopes drifted around inside, making everything cloudy. When I finished scrubbing the pot, it would be clean and ready to cook with again. The dirty water and all the gunk would disappear down the drain. I wondered what would wash away with my dirty water?

"Mama," Nina tugged on my wrinkled blouse. "I wanna go see the horsies."

Kids–the only safe assumption was that they'd change their mind. "Okay. But we have to stay out of the way."

Ocotillo popped up around the property like twisted clusters of spiky green birthday candles, their fiery persimmon flowers reaching skyward. I loved that color.

We kept to the perimeter of the stalls. Nina observed the horses from the safety of my arms and outside of nose reach. I kept my eye on Eli's dad as he mucked Chuck's stall, waiting for our cue to vacate.

His movements were jerky, and every few minutes he'd stop to flex his hand. *Arthritis?* He fixed his hold on the rake, but with such a loose grip, a twenty-minute task could take him all day. When he winced, I conveniently forgot my creed and led us to the edge of Chuck's enclosure.

"I can muck if you need a break."

Chuck shoved his head over the bars at us, so I ran a palm down his roan muzzle. Nina squirmed on my hip.

Bill glowered. "This is a business, not a petting zoo."

"I know." I set Nina on her feet, initiating an instant tantrum.

"Nooo! Mama, uppy!" She grabbed at my skirt.

"Nina, not right now."

Bill grumbled something to himself, wiped his palm on his jeans, then readjusted his hands around the wooden rake handle.

"There's a phrase I like," I said over Nina's fit. "Work smarter, not harder. You've got a perfectly capable volunteer right here. One that owes you for a bowl of oatmeal, a banana, and a night's stay."

He looked over the top of his glasses at me. "You ate Marley's oatmeal?"

"I did."

He tilted his head, studying me from a different angle. Nina continued to wail and tried to climb me.

"You ever mucked before?"

"A few times." No need to brag.

"In those clothes?"

I laughed–a quick, tense burst. "No. I, um ..." I hadn't thought of that. I glanced down at my shoes. *Not impossible*, but it wouldn't be pretty.

"There's a pair of spare boots in the end stall." He came to the rails, his eyes slicing to Nina, who continued to howl. "Hey. Knock that off. You're hurting the horse's ears."

The sound stopped, but her mouth hung open as she stared at him with teary eyes.

"What're you going to do with her?" he asked.

"She can watch." What other choice did I have?

"And when she wanders into one of the other stalls?" His head tilted toward the prickly painted horse on the end.

I stared at him, curious how he missed her whole afraid-of-horses fit. "She won't."

He eased between the horizontal bars to stand next to us. "Guess I'll have to stay here." The resigned deflation in his tone made for a begrudging offer.

"It's okay. You don't have to watch her." I squatted to Nina. "Mama's going to help clean the stalls. The horses can't touch you if you stay outside the bars. Okay?"

"No." Nina smooshed herself into me. It almost sent me to my butt.

"What's your name, kid?" Eli's dad towered over us with his hands on his hips.

I couldn't blame Nina for her cautious, over-the-shoulder stare. In fact, relief flowed through me. Even after my horrible example, her stranger danger remained intact.

"Welp," the older man said, turning to the stall. "This here is Chuck." Then he pointed to the one next door. "The gray one is Misty. She's a gentle thing. 'Cross the way there, with the diamond on her forehead, that's Royal." In the far-right corner, the Paint huffed as if incensed at being left out. "The feisty one there is Sugar. But she ain't all that sweet."

Nina remained unmoved, her arms locked around my neck.

"And I'm William," he told her. "Scratch that. Call me Bill."

She didn't call him anything, just scooted into me until I had to throw a hand to the bars to catch myself.

"What's the matter?" he said. "You don't like horses?"

"Nina doesn't really know horses," I explained.

With an audible inhale, Bill bent, pressing his hands into his thighs. "Nina? That's your name? Well, Nina, which horse is your favorite?" His curt tone didn't inspire a reply. "You like Misty?"

Nina's dark eyes drifted to where the gray horse sunned.

"Yeah, a charmer, that one." Bill's expression turned thoughtful. "Some folks say she's a unicorn."

Nina's arms unlocked from her chokehold so she could study the mystical creature.

I stood, brushing the dirt off my skirt.

Bill rose with me. "What about you? You got a name?"

"Hi. I'm Ava." I held out my hand.

He stared at it before accepting the greeting. Maybe trying to evaluate my ability to do manual labor? A dry palm encased mine. Not calloused, like I'd expected from a ranch owner. "Well, Ava, you'd better get those boots on if you plan to finish today."

I held back a laugh. I liked him. "You got it, boss."

It could have been my imagination, but when he cleared his throat, I thought I saw the corner of his mouth turn up.

9

———

Eli

Where is everyone?

The house was empty. I checked my phone, not that I expected Dad to suddenly learn how to text. But I did have a message from Ryan.

Ryan: Dude, you're killing me!

Eli: I told you I gotta hire a manager first.

Ryan: Why can't your dad do it?

Good question. I knew squat about ranches. Did avoiding another argument count as a reason? We had an interview scheduled later. Maybe I'd get lucky. I left the house, weeds crunching under my boots as I worked my way to the barn.

Eli: I hear there's a great opportunity outside of Phoenix. Long-term. Private housing. Flex hours. The ladies have names like Sugar and Misty.

Ryan: Screw you.

*Ryan: The sun's messing with you. Do I need to come
rescue your ass?*

Dad and Ryan: that combination had high school chemistry class written all over it. I started to shoot a response when movement caught my eye. Ava, jumping around out front of the tack room, trying to yank off a rubber boot. Her back was to me.

"Seriously?" she groaned. "You're worse than my heels!" When the boot finally slid off, she threw it, and it knocked over the mucking rake. "If you give me a foot fungus ..." The tone of her threat made me feel sorry for the footwear.

"You tell that boot who's boss."

She spun and met me with hot pink cheeks, hair spilling out of her ponytail. "Eli! How long have you been there?"

I stepped forward to right the rake. "You shopping for new shoes?"

"No. Just borrowing them so I could muck." She stood flamingo-style to work off the second boot.

"You were mucking?" My eyes fell on her hiked-up skirt. "In that?"

"Ha, Ha. I know. But Bill's arthritis was bothering him."

Bill? As in my dad?

I watched her brush the dirt off her feet and shove them into those fancy heels of hers. Man, she was pretty. Even with the dark shadows under her eyes.

"What?" she asked.

"Hm?" The seconds stretched like the countdown of a game show, and I had no answers. I readjusted my cap, blaming the barn. "Where's Nina?"

"With your dad."

I laughed, but she didn't even crack a smile. "Wait, seriously?"

"About this tall, wears glasses?" She held her hand up over her head.

Did I walk into a different dimension? I studied her, looking for little differences. A tattoo, a scar ... "My dad is watching Nina, and you're mucking stalls?"

She nodded. "Yes. Well, I'm done now. They just went up to the house."

This, I had to see. "Perfect. I'll go with you." Ava led the way. "I'm done with the gate, by the way," I told her. "And I found a battery for your truck."

"Oh. Thank you. Can you send me the info?"

My sister Hannah accused me of having a "pathological need to help." Her words. But as I appreciated Ava's confident stride up the porch steps, I had to wonder who was helping who here? I'd been awake for two hours and hadn't hated a single minute. "What if I go with you today? We can take my truck." Before she shot me down, I added, "We'll get your purse, grab a battery, then come back here so I can install it for you."

"Okay."

"Okay? Really? You don't wanna argue first?"

She laughed. Addictive like that first hit of nicotine. "No, I'm not really in a place to turn down help at the moment."

I lurched forward to get the door for her, fisting my free hand to keep it off the small of her back.

We found Dad and Nina in the living room, sitting on the stiff leather couch with a big book opened across their laps. My crabby old man, watching a kid?

On purpose?

The man grouched at anyone under twenty-five. He didn't do kids. I'm convinced he didn't even like me when I was one. The silver lining? I never had to suffer the when-are-you-gonna-start-a-family talk.

He looked up at me over his glasses. "You finish the gate?"

"Yeah. You, uh, having fun?"

He ignored my question and glanced at Ava. "What about you, Missy? You leave me any stalls?"

"I did not, but you can save your tears for after we're gone." Ava flashed him a bright smile.

Damn. How could I get one of those?

"Thanks for watching Nina." She moved into the living room to collect the kid, sticking her on her usual hip-perch.

Dad pushed on his legs to stand. "Eh, it was nothing."

Ava turned to me. "Is it okay to use the bathroom before we go?"

"Yeah, 'course." I threw a thumb behind me. "By the front door." I guess I stared too long, because when they disappeared into the bathroom, Dad snuck up on me.

"Cute kid."

I cut a narrowed side glance his way. "Yeah. She is."

His jaw rolled over, chewing on some thought, and when he returned my stare, a question flashed on his face. "Ava seems nice."

I dug my hands in my pockets, feeling a little like I was driving on a spare tire, waiting for it to pop. "Yeah, I guess."

Dad gruffed, then landed a hearty slap on my back. "Welp, guess you've got the rest under control." He moseyed into the kitchen.

Under control? As I looked at the closed bathroom door, I couldn't help feeling under-*something*. Under-settled? Under-qualified? Definitely not under-standing.

We ended up with more than her purse. Two hours later, everything Ava owned was strapped into the bed of my truck, including a toddler bed and dresser.

"I cannot believe the eggs on that man!" Ava reached over the seat to pass Nina a tube of "HappyBaby Puffs," whatever those were. Apparently, something good, 'cause Nina squealed from her little fighter-pilot seat in the back. "*Don't.* Drop them," Ava said. "Mama has to deal with something."

I clocked Mr. Mercedes lurking by the door to his house, about as intimidating as a chihuahua with the shakes. Still, it was his turf. "You want backup?"

"No. But I wouldn't object to shaving his head in his sleep. To take him down a notch."

Damn. "Remind me never to get on your bad side."

"I can assure you, he had it coming." She slammed the door and strutted up the walk.

I almost went after her. In my experience, weak men played dirty. But also, no good ever came from telling a woman she couldn't do something. So, I waited with Nina, AC running, glad as hell it wasn't me in her crosshairs. Steven tried to touch her, and she slapped him.

"Oh, shit," I laughed. Then my eyes met Nina's in the rearview mirror.

She blinked at me.

Oops. "Hey, kiddo. Don't repeat that, okay?" I held a finger to my lips, and she copied me. "How you doing back there? Still eating your kid crack?"

I twisted to face her. She made a yum-num-num sound. Half the cereal stuck to her lap, hands, arm, and even the side of her face. The other half was on the floor.

"You like those, huh?"

Straight out of a cartoon, she repeated, "Yumnumnum."

"Tell you what?" I leaned over the front seat to scoop the pieces off the floor mat and dumped them on her lap. "I won't tell Mom about the spill if you don't tell her I said a bad word."

She shoved a fistful of puffs in her mouth as the passenger door swung open.

Ava threw herself inside. "Let's go."

"Yes, ma'am."

I pulled away from the curb before her ex could catch up. Nina may have missed it, but I saw the long, slender finger Ava used to say goodbye. We cleared the forest of cookie-cutter houses to nothing but the hum of the engine. Ava's knee started bouncing as we waited for a light to turn.

"Hey. You did the right thing." I grabbed for her hand, and tiny electric zaps shot up my arm.

She blinked down where I held her, teeth digging into her bottom lip. I pulled my hand away before all the blood left my brain. Flexed my fingers on the steering wheel.

Open roads never warmed my veins like that.

Ava tucked a soft-looking strand of black hair behind her ear. "I hate to admit this, but I don't know what I would've done without you."

Her words gave me something I didn't know I needed. "You would've figured out something."

"Maybe." She sighed. "Where am I going to put all this stuff?"

"Let's deal with one thing at a time. First, you need a truck battery." I pulled into the auto parts lot.

Ten minutes later, we were driving home with a new battery and a load of bags stashed behind Ava's seat.

"How long do you think it will take to install?" she asked.

I hesitated to give her a number on account of the bags. I'd lied, saying I needed stuff for another project. No one would take care of her truck the way I could. Getting my hands on her Chevy was the first thing I could remember looking forward to since rolling into Phoenix. And I had a suspicion she'd say no if I asked.

"You don't have another place to stay lined up yet, right?"

She gave me a funny look.

I fixed my hat. "What I mean is, do you want the trailer another night?"

"I'd better not."

"Why?"

"Your Dad, for one."

My dad. Last night, I had the same concern. But today? "You know, I think he might like you better than me."

"I highly doubt that! Besides, isn't the RV for your ranch manager?"

"Lucky for you, we don't have one yet."

She stared silently out the windshield. Nina grunted behind us, her fingers toying with the harness clip.

"If you stayed," I said, "I could work on your truck. I won't charge you."

"I can't ask that of you."

"You're not. I'm offering." Would it look bad to beg? "Where would you go instead, a hotel? That would cost you what, hundreds of dollars for a week? Save that for when you find an apartment. Somewhere with a pool. Kids love pools."

"Pool!" Nina cheered. "I wanna go to da pool!"

"Not today, Crackerjack." Ava tilted her head back to rest it on the seat. Then she turned sharp, narrow eyes on me. "Why are you doing all this?"

I took a second to answer. "Mom always told us it's our job to take care of each other."

"I think she probably meant your family."

"She meant everyone."

"I can't, Eli. It's too much."

"Would it sway you if I said we're down a ranch hand and could use the help?"

Nina shifted and started groaning from the back.

Ava chewed on the inside of her lip. I couldn't explain why this mattered so much. We'd just met, but around her, everything felt better.

She smoothed her hands over her lap, and suddenly, my palms felt sweaty. "Your dad said it wasn't a bed-and-breakfast."

I frowned. "You heard that?"

She nodded.

"That's on me. I should've given him a heads up." Nina cried out again in one of those high–pitched kid squeals that reminded me of a bomb about to detonate. "Tell you what? I'll call him right now." I pulled out my phone and had the line ringing before she could argue.

"Eli ..." Ava sighed.

I loved the way my name hung on her lips, even to scold me.

My old man picked up on the second ring. "What do you need?"

"Hey. I'm here with Ava and all her stuff. They need a place to stay while she looks for an apartment."

"And?"

I shifted, second-guessing my read on him from this morning. "I don't think they should stay at a hotel. It's a waste of money, and something could get stolen. And Nina needs space to play." My heart kicked up a few beats. If he said no, I'd look like such an ass. "I want to offer her the RV for a few more days."

"You're asking my permission this time?"

I rolled my eyes. "Yes." Cars wove around us on the freeway. "She mucked for you," I reminded him.

"Is she there with you?"

"Yes."

"Let me talk to her."

"What?"

"Just put her on, Eli."

I handed the phone to Ava. "He wants to talk to you."

Her eyes got wide as she took it. "H-hi Bill."

I merged into the exit lane. Why did he want to talk to her?

"A few days," she said to my dad. "A week at most." A pause.

"No. Yes, but only after a long day. I'm trying to acquire a ranch ... Hidden Meadows?"

Oh, come on! Was he interrogating her?

In the next pause, her eyes slid to me. "Yes, he did. He's been very helpful. Okay. Thank you."

She handed back the phone after ending the call. "I guess I passed the five-point inspection."

I parked alongside the RV, behind Ava's truck. She hopped out first, and when she opened the rear door, only a few baby puffs flew out. "Wow, Crackerjack, you did good!"

I held a finger to my mouth, and Nina giggled.

We unloaded my truck together.

"I can stick the furniture in the garage until you need it," I offered, trailing her up the steps with an armload of bags. One foot into the trailer, I could tell something was different. "Did you clean?"

Nina wove between our legs into the unit.

Ava shrugged. "It was mostly dust."

I followed her back outside. "You didn't have to do that."

"I was up anyway." After a pause, she surveyed the landscape. "I love the ocotillo along the fence. It reminds me of spikey seaweed. That's silly, huh? Seaweed in a desert?"

I studied her ocotillo, wondering what she wasn't saying. Why, after a long day, would she scrub the inside of someone else's trailer? Her eyes slid back to me. It made me antsy, but not in the way staying in one place did. More like I had something important I needed to do.

I grabbed another bag from my truck bed. "Got a guy coming for an interview in a few. I'll get that battery installed after. And bring you some towels and sheets."

Ava followed me up the steps. "Thank you."

"Yeah. No problem." I put her bag inside. "Feel free to use

the main house for whatever. Food. Internet. Air conditioning."
Now I was just stalling.

She tilted her head to the side. "You're very accommodating today."

I grinned. "Only for women who think I'm a *hunky hero*."

Her mouth fell open. "Please never refer to that again."

"Why? You don't think I'm hunky anymore?"

She smacked my arm. It tingled, but in a pleasant way. Then two perfectly pronounced little words filled the silent room and secured my end.

"Oh, shit!"

We both turned to Nina. This was bad. I had the wrong shaped head to go bald.

Ava gaped. "What did you say?"

Nina put her finger to her mouth and shushed her mom.

Shit, shit, shit! I started a retreat to the deck. Gravel crunched under large tires in the distance as a dusty white truck drove up to the house. *Perfect timing!* "Whaddaya know? That's probably my guy." But my traitorous feet stalled right in the middle of their escape, the second she said my name.

"Hey, Eli?"

"Yeah?"

"I'd appreciate it if you didn't cuss in front of Nina."

I nodded, then jogged off to meet this potential hire before Ava found out I fed her kid food off the floor.

A hired-on ranch manager meant I'd done my job. Meant Dad was happy, and I didn't have to stick around and take his criticisms, Marley's cooking, or this heat. Meant going back to making decent money and having no responsibilities. Every morning, starting fresh, not worrying about much of anything.

But against all reason, I hoped this new yahoo didn't make the cut.

10

Ava

I SHED my pencil skirt for worn-in cutoffs, and I couldn't help wondering what Eli-the-leg-man would think of them. Then, with Nina engrossed in a nature show on TV, I took my phone to the deck. The AC and the shade from the tree kept the interior of the trailer from simmering. A small win as I leaned against the railing, victim to the full flame of the afternoon sun and Steven's haunting comment.

What makes you think it's still yours?

To stay there would've torn me in two. But Hidden Meadows contained the last traces of my husband. He was mixed in the soil, waiting for me to follow through on my promises. To reclaim our home and live our dream. And I was running out of time.

By the stables, Eli led a man with an obnoxious swagger to the horses. Sugar reared at their approach, and the stranger slapped Eli on the back, laughing.

Ugh. No thanks.

Eli noticed me out on the deck and stared in my direction so long I had to point out that his interviewee had wandered off without him. He ducked under the brim of his hat before jogging to catch up.

As I watched him go, something light and carefree tickled under my skin. Before I could chicken out, I dialed Terry.

We started with small talk. He thought Eli was my boyfriend and laughed when I tried to correct him. I dropped the topic, more eager to resolve our other little dispute.

"It's not that I don't want to sell to you," he said.

"Then what is it?"

"Well ... you saw what it's like here."

"So, you're selling it to a corporation instead?"

After a pause, he said, "You know about that?"

"Is it a done deal?"

"No! No, it isn't anything." A chair squeaked under new weight on his end. "I wasn't looking to sell. A man came by in his fancy blue suit and handed me an envelope, told me the place was worth millions."

"You know they'll level it before the ink's dry?"

"Not much left to level ..."

"Terry! You're acting like the place is already past hope!"

He met my accusation with silence.

Would the corporation have known about Hidden Meadows if not for Steven? Our relationship sailed onto full screen, replaying every red flag I ignored out of loneliness and desperation. How had I justified the office flirtation? Why did I concede to that first date? Or carry on after our underwhelming first kiss? Traded vibrance for monochrome, and paraded around in shoes as impractical as agreeing I didn't need my truck? I'd let him bulldoze right over me, just like the intended future of Hidden Meadows.

Frustrated tears burned my eyes, but crying wouldn't stick my life back together, only make my view muddier and this valley harder to climb out of. I'd promised Jason. If our dream died, he'd be gone forever. One day, our ranch wouldn't be a torrent. It would be an anchor.

Dirt and sweat didn't scare me. "I still want Hidden Meadows. I know the market has shot up, so if you want to negotiate a different price–"

"You know it ain't about the money."

"What's it about, then?" Did no one honor promises anymore? Did they have expiration dates? If so, I missed the memo.

Air hissed between his teeth, and I could almost see him twisting his bushy handlebar mustache. "You know, horses do better in herds." My brow furrowed in confusion. But before I could ask what he meant, he said, "I need to see to a few things. Can we talk later?"

"Sure." After the call ended, I leaned over the railing, afraid I might be sick. "I'm not a lone horse."

My whole plan was falling apart. I could either give up, accept my fate, and pretend to be happy, or hold on to hope. Power through with faith that I'd reach the end and it would all be worth it. I stared out at the ocotillo. Somehow, they found the strength to make beautiful flowers with almost no water.

Hidden Meadows aside, I needed a job and a place to live.

I climbed the wooden stairs to the front door of the main house with Nina on my hip and two computers under my other arm. The colorful lineup of painted Adirondack chairs made for a welcoming greeting. I could see myself kicking back in one of them, beer in hand.

"What are you two trouble-makers doing?"

I spun to find Bill at the bottom of the porch steps. "Oh! Hi,

Bill. I didn't see you come up." I set Nina on her feet. She went straight for the bright red chair and started climbing.

His eyes fell to my computer. "You working?"

"I need to send out an email." More specifically, a letter of resignation. "And look for an apartment. Eli said we could use the Wi-Fi?" Bill's frown made me wonder if I should have left Eli out of it. "But I don't want to be underfoot. I can do it from out here."

He watched Nina play on the chair, his serious expression adapting an air of mischief. "I'll tell ya what? If you eat Marley's muffins, you can come in where it's cool and hop on the Wi-Fi."

I laughed. *Is he serious?*

"That'll get me off the hook," he confided. His mouth remained a straight line, but little smile lines appeared next to his eyes.

"How many muffins are we talking about?"

"Eh, let's say two."

Two? That's it? I called Nina. "Come on, Crackerjack. We're going inside." To lure her into cooperation, I handed over her LeapFrog tablet, my digital babysitter for only very necessary occasions.

Bill led us to the kitchen. A bowl of fruit sat in the middle of the granite island, and next to it, a colorful plate piled high with dark brown hockey pucks. He leaned his palms on the counter. "Take your pick."

I selected the smallest, least burnt muffin. "You have a beautiful house."

"Thank you." He watched my cautious taste and grimaced on my behalf.

I forced the salty, bitter bite down. "Is it just you and Marley living here?"

"Marley's just here for some summer reflection." At my raised brow, he added, "She's my niece." He grabbed a glass from the cabinet, filled it with water, and held it out like a peace offering.

"Thank you." I drained it, then forced the rest of the muffin down. "So, it's just you?"

His expression sagged a little. But in the next breath, he straightened and said, "Genius loci."

"What?"

"The Wi-Fi password." He spelled it out with a mix of letters, numbers, and symbols that made my head spin.

I whipped open my laptop. "Hold on. One more time." It took three tries.

The afternoon passed with Nina and me sitting side-by-side, our heads buried in our screens. I planned to write a saccharine resignation letter to Steven. Did a part of me hope he'd realize his mistake and apologize? Yes. But after the confrontation at his house, I knew miracles like that were saved for Hallmark movies at Christmastime. I couldn't believe he thought I was shacking up to make him jealous!

Bill set a plate next to me with another muffin. "Thanks for taking one for the team."

"I believe that's two, actually." With a fortifying breath, I picked it up. It stared back. Literally. Extra-burnt spots straddled the center like two dark, bread-y eyes.

Bill's smile looked as natural as the scowl I'd met him in. "I'll leave you to it, then." He patted my shoulder and wandered out of the kitchen.

As I chewed, and chewed, *and chewed*, I wondered, *did I just make a new friend?*

The repetitious music from Nina's counting game became the underscore to my clacking of keys. I scrolled through apartment listings, some with pools. After scheduling a few tours, I pushed on to the next task.

If Terry sold me the ranch ... No, scratch that. *When* Terry sold me Hidden Meadows, I would need a steady paycheck. Not only to secure a loan, but to have income for renovations. I wondered if I could squeak in a preapproval using my newly resigned job? How would they know?

Hours later, my stomach rumbled. I drummed my fingers on the pitted wooden tabletop. What next? The clock read almost five. *Shoot!*

I rubbed Nina's back. "Hey, Crackerjack. Time to turn it off. We need to go shopping." Groceries were cheaper than eating out, and until I secured an income, we were officially on a budget. She whined, melting into the table like a popsicle in the sun. "You can pick something out. You want Fruit Loops?"

"Did someone say Fruit Loops?"

I spun to find Eli in the archway, wiping his hands on his dusty jeans.

Sweat highlighted his skin, and streaks of motor grime marred his clothes. "I haven't had those since I was a kid."

Was he always that tall? "Oh. Hey."

White teeth flashed in an unabashed smile. His were more pronounced than his dad's, but he had the same crinkle lines in his eyes. "Oh, hey, back atcha."

I tripped on the bench as I stood. "A-are you done with the battery?"

"Not yet. Just here to grab some water." He moved to the sink and filled a cup at the tap.

I thought he said it would be quick? His throat flexed, his Adam's apple bobbed with each gulp, and thirst seized me like a lasso, tightening when a satisfied sigh left his chest.

I forced myself to swallow. "Let me guess. You were one of those beer-chuggers when you were a kid."

His eyes lost their crinkles. "I was a lotta things when I was a kid."

"Well ..." *Way to kill the mood.* "I was all work and no play. Not much better."

Awkward silence fell between us. He scratched behind his head, apparently unaware of my cut-offs.

Maybe that was a good thing.

"I need to go to the store," I said.

Nina moaned, sliding off the bench and flowing into a puddle under the table–not unlike what I wanted to do. We stared at her. Kids got away with everything.

"But ..." I added, "I need my Chevy."

"Oh." He ran a hand over his hat. "Take my truck." He disappeared into the hall and came back with a set of keys.

Nina continued moaning, a long, theatrical death scene.

He nodded in her direction. "You want to leave her here?"

I wouldn't sic a tired three-year-old on my worst enemy. Also, how could he finish the battery if he had to entertain her? And why did my imagination keep drifting to images of Eli's hands working under my hood? "It's okay." I curled my fingers around his keys, noticing a round keychain with a mountain range that read, *Get Lost.* "We won't be long. So ... Fruit Loops. Anything else?"

"Nope. I'm good."

I nodded, grabbing our computers before my greedy hormones convinced me his stare was anything more than polite attentiveness.

"Hey, Ava?"

I paused. "Yes?"

"I really like your shorts."

Nina nodded off on the way home, and I enjoyed twenty blessed minutes of silence, bedtime be damned. But as I pulled up to the house and stared at Roxy's back end sticking out of the garage bay, my calm dissipated. No more playing dumb.

A battery doesn't take this long.

When we'd left the auto shop, I had suspected all those extra bags meant Eli planned to fix her, and I said nothing. Look where denial landed me. I forced a swallow, trying not to overthink it. Realistically, this meant one less task on my list.

Nina didn't even flinch when I lifted her out of her car seat and draped her across my chest. I had two choices: hide and pretend Eli's hands weren't all over my engine. Or face him, return his keys, and chew him out for thinking he could put his hands wherever he wanted without asking. The clink of metal on metal drifted out from the third bay and sent little thrills along my spine.

Was there a third option?

I grabbed Eli's keys and the box of cereal with my free hand, all signs pointing towards a cliff edge.

This didn't have to be a big deal. I'd seen many mechanics in my life, and I'd only fallen in love with one of them. Logically, I needed my truck running, and Eli could do that. Simple. Nothing more. I just. Wouldn't. Look at him.

I Zen-walked toward the open garage, telling myself it was to keep Nina sleeping. The tinkering sounds grew louder. Classic rock music danced in the stagnant air, mixing with the burnt odors of lubricant and gasoline. A colony of butterflies readied for flight under my rib cage—the fluttering when you're nearing the front of the line, Sharpie and new album in hand, and you can actually see the lead singer and his perfect white teeth.

I could pretend it was Ray down at the smog check on 7th– definitely not my type.

But Ray never wore dark blue coveralls and camel-colored work boots, like the ones sticking out from under my truck. My steps fell amidst a minefield of blackened parts and pieces.

Jason was a mechanic before discovering his calling with horses. I'd met him under similar circumstances, which gave me reason enough to abort.

Under the cover of an Eagles guitar solo, I laid Eli's keys silently on the workbench next to his box of Fruit Loops, right where he'd see them.

Now, to creep out undetected.

"Ava, is that you?"

I Zen-froze.

"Hey, can you grab me a towel?" His muffled voice drew my eyes to his long, sturdy legs, now bent, boots planted on the ground. "Hello?"

"Yes, sorry."

Why am I apologizing?

I backpedaled, scanning the workbench, then the piles of tools and parts on the floor. *Towels, towels…* "Shop towel?"

"That'll do."

With a wad of blue paper towels, I squatted next to the Chevy and stretched my arm underneath. Sweat pasted my camisole to my back, and Nina's limp form moved with me, her steady breathing blowing hot air onto my neck.

Eli's fingers fumbled over mine before finding the towels. I yanked my arm back, half-expecting singe marks where our skin met. Instead, I found a black grease streak across my palm.

I stood too fast, and the world tilted. "Your keys are on the workbench. Thanks again." Time to go.

"You okay?"

"Yup."

But before I could leave, he shifted himself out from under the front end of my truck, and the image impregnated my brain. Long, solid limbs and casual confidence hit me like an arrow.

The discarded parts on the floor slowed my escape. I

grabbed a shop towel on my way out and tried single-handedly to rub at the blackish stain on my palm.

"Ava, wait!" Eli hopped over the mess and cut me off, stopping in front of me in all his sweat, grease, and coverall glory.

Well, funnel cake ...

He wasn't hard to look at before, but now? His head tilted to study me, then nodded to Nina's sleeping form. "Tired kid."

Why is it so hot in here?

His mechanic's suit sleeves were pushed up to his elbows, revealing a dusting of hair that ran over smooth, lean muscle.

Ray on 7th. Ray on 7th ...

My left arm burned from holding Nina. Part of me wanted her to wake up and give me an excuse to leave. The other, less responsible part wished I had somewhere to put her down. I hadn't seen this latter part of myself in a while, and I wasn't sure what to do with her.

My eyes drifted to the open hood of my Chevy. "I thought you were just replacing the battery?"

"Yeah ... well," amusement tinted his deep, warm tone. "If you let me finish, I promise I'll make your engine purr."

My back muscles undulated from the bottom up. Were we talking about my truck? "I'm not criticizing your skill. It's just, you didn't even ask."

He shrugged. "I was already under there and had most of the parts."

"Because you bought them yesterday?"

He grinned from ear to ear, denying nothing. Then he laughed, glanced to the side, and rested his hands on his hips. He could've been Mr. July in one of my old calendars. "I couldn't help myself."

"Oh, no?"

"Ava, I think you underestimate how sexy your truck is."

"Please don't say that word."

"What, sexy?"

I inhaled sharply, hating how his deep vibrations settled over me in an intoxicating plume. I dropped my eyes to the floor, but even his darn boots called to me. The whole place smelled sharp, like a shop. His hair stuck out at every angle, and he even had a swipe of dirt across his face.

Was he *trying* to be a stereotype?

"How much is this going to cost?" I needed something to get angry about because the alternative scared me.

He crossed his arms, which was arguably worse. "Don't worry about it," he said.

"I'm not *worried*. I trust you'll give me a fair price–"

"Ava, I'm not gonna charge you."

"Well, you should. You did the work." Our eyes locked–his radiating confidence. I wouldn't win this stare-down. *Fine.* "What did you fix?" I'd look up fair prices later.

"What? You want a list?"

"Yes."

His eyes narrowed. "Why?"

Because you're too hot to be giving me gifts like this. "So, the next time I take it in for a service, they don't sell me something I don't need."

He blew out a stream of air and ticked off fingers as he said, "Plugs, fluids, oil filter, hoses ..."

That didn't sound too bad.

"... belts, radiator fan, alternator ..."

Alternator?

"Rotor, condenser cap." One side of his mouth curved up. "And I de-greased the engine."

"No." I shook my head, grinding the coarse paper towel into my hand on a second attempt to remove the grease stain. Or maybe to clear the layer of intrigue that coated me like sweat. Quite the feat while holding Nina. "There's no way you could've done all that in one day."

He studied me for several seconds, then his eyes lowered to my hand. "I've got something that will get that off. Come here."

He dropped his towels on the floor and moved deeper into the garage. Cardboard slid across concrete, flaps scraping open as Eli dug through boxes, one after another.

Upon noticing I hadn't moved, he pointed to the rear corner. "Hey, you. Sink."

My traitorous feet obeyed. I picked my way past mounds of tiles, tires, and scrap wood. I told myself it was the only polite response given his efforts. Dried blobs of black and white paint coated the sides of the large metal paint sink. I twisted the hot-water handle and stuck my hand under the stream. None of this seemed to bother Nina, who slept on.

I wasn't ready when Eli leaned in behind me, one solid, muscular arm reaching past mine to shut off the water. Heat rolled off him like a seductive bonfire on a cold, starry night.

Maybe he was a terrible kisser.

Guilt instantly flooded my senses. "*I have all I need. One and done,*" Jason always said. He'd been talking about me.

Eli twisted off the lid of a round white tub the diameter of a corn tortilla. "Scrub first, then water," he murmured. The vibrations slithered past my guilt and coiled happily in my stomach.

I watched in a grating mix of horror and thrill as he swiped his finger into the tub, then took my grease-smeared hand in his. Breathing ceased as he massaged the gritty paste into my palm. Each little circular scrub shipped me further out of reality. Like an all-inclusive cruise with a drinks package. *Vacations are good, Ava.* You were supposed to take them. Maybe I was overthinking this.

Nina stirred, her low, sleepy moan sling-shotting me back to shore. I yanked my hand free and fumbled with the tap, but my slippery grip accomplished nothing. Eli leaned in to assist, and his body closed in on mine.

I stuck my hand under the tap, practically crawling into the sink to make space between us because every skin cell he met was doing backflips.

"Mama?" Nina mumbled, popping her head up and looking around. "Where's my Fruit Loops?"

I shook out my wet hand as Eli turned off the water, and I practically rammed him over on my escape. I was a mom. Moms didn't get vacations. "I'll b-be back. Later. For my truck."

I had no doubt he could restart any neglected engine. Even mine. And I had no business doing that.

11

———

Ava

ELI MUST'VE KNOWN what he was doing, because now I couldn't get my engine to shut off. I gave up trying to sleep and tiptoed to the couch with my phone to search parts and labor costs for old trucks. *Oil filter, hoses, belts ... a fan?* Sweat trickled down my back, even with the AC pumping. *Condenser? Plugs?* I squirmed as I tapped out "de-grease engine" in my notes.

That was normal, right? Everyone's engine needed that?

The internet searches took forever to load. Still, I knew it would be more than I could afford.

I'm not gonna charge you.

Why? Why do all that for free? No one was *that* nice.

I rubbed my clean palm on my thigh, trying to erase the ghost of Eli's touch. Terry's hug had lingered, too. Maybe I was just deprived of physical touch for too long. Steven was hardly the affectionate type.

Yup, that must be it.

Sleep found me eventually, because I woke gasping for breath in a mold-infested trailer. Until the clean scent of lemon Windex hit my nose, and the streams of sunshine pulled me from my nightmare. Terry's words lingered like an echo.

"The whole inside was covered in mold."

I jumped up to check on Nina. She slept on clean sheets, occupying the mattress in perpendicular conquest, trailer walls all bright and spore-free. Sounds and smells of Bill's stable drifted in. Just a day like any other. But the bad dream felt like an omen. What happened to all the belongings I had stowed in the fifth-wheel Terry had to haul away?

I fished in my suitcase for a tank top and cutoffs, but the mundane task did little to calm a biting urgency.

"Mama?" Nina appeared over my shoulder in her red Elmo nightgown.

"Morning, Crackerjack. Are you hungry?"

"No."

"Do you have to go potty?"

"No."

One of these days, I'd stop making that a question. "Well, I think I'll have some cereal." *And organize my thoughts.*

I lured her to the dinette table with Fruit Loops. As I chewed my own, the crunch canceled all other sounds, and my brain fixated on the sad truth.

My old clothes, my boots, they were probably trashed, too. I shouldn't have let Steven bully me into leaving so many boxes in there. Practically everything from my old life: stories scratched into leather and sewn in denim patches. *Stupid, Ava.* What had I been thinking?

I cleared my bowl to the sink. "Hey Crackerjack, when you're done, let's see who's awake."

We strode to the stable, but instead of Eli, we discovered a lanky kid in dark skinny jeans, a black hoodie, and orange Chucks, sporting lots of facial piercings. *Lots.* Rings on eyebrows, studs on lips, a barbell at the bridge of his nose, gauges in his ears, and I'd hazard a guess there were more we couldn't see. With a jerk of his head, he sent long dark bangs flopping out of his eyes.

I couldn't stop myself. "Did those hurt?"

Nina stared. "Mama, why he has that on his face?" His glare sent her hiding behind my leg.

Diffuse, Ava. "Cool kicks. I love the orange."

More glaring.

I tucked a strand of loose hair behind my ear. "Um, have you seen Eli?"

Instead of answering, he walked away.

Wow. Visions of me trying to single-parent a high-schooler danced around my head like drunk birds. I clasped Nina's little hand. "Don't ever grow up, okay?"

Eli answered the front door in another snug tee, jeans, and his worn brown baseball cap. Suddenly, I didn't know where to put my hands.

Would it kill him to get a larger shirt? "Is my Chevy ready?"

"Well, good morning to you, too." He flashed a bright smile.

"Right. Sorry. Good morning."

"We sawed a robot!" Nina blurted.

He glanced at her, then at me. "A robot? Here?"

"I think she's referring to the kid at the stables," I said.

"Oh." He laughed. "That's Luke. You were at the barn? Did you wanna go for a ride?" His eagerness wooed me, and for a moment, I forgot why we were there. Jaws that chiseled should be illegal.

"N-no." But as I said it, I remembered him mentioning he was shorthanded. And Ava Garcia was not a freeloader. "We were looking for you."

His wattage went up, and he gripped the doorframe overhead, displaying a set of equally perfect triceps. "Oh, yeah?"

Guilt squeezed through me. Was Jason up there, watching me ogling another man's arms? I forced my eyes to the row of colorful chairs lining the deck. "I, um, I didn't forget our deal. I still plan to help with the horses. But I have somewhere I need to go this morning."

"It's all good. Luke wanted the hours, so you're off the hook."

"Oh."

Eli's eyes narrowed as he studied me. "You're disappointed?"

Was I? "How else will I earn our keep? For the trailer, the food, and everything." I waved a hand around to embody *everything.*

"Hmm." As if in answer to a silent prayer, his arms came down and fell to his sides like a normal person. "I guess more is better, right?"

Unless it's Marley's muffins.

"How about you start tomorrow?" he said. "I'll tell Luke you're coming."

I nodded. Great. Done. Moving on. "So, my truck?"

His smile turned mischievous. "Actually, this is perfect. I need to run out for a part, so I'll take you."

Which meant it wasn't ready.

"No. That's not necessary. I'll just wait." I didn't want an audience for this errand. It might involve begging and crying over lost boxes. I'd put it off this long. What did a few more hours matter?

"Nonsense." Eli grabbed his keys off the hook in the entryway, his long, sturdy legs strutting to his truck like a Levi's ad. The kind that dropped panties worldwide.

How was this man single?

When he opened his driver's door, he turned to catch me staring. "You getting in, or what?"

Fix your face, Ava!

Nina wrenched free from my grip to run after him. Thanks to the early heat, sweat slid down my back. Terry would have finished feeding and mucking, probably retreating to the air-conditioned office. Would he peruse Steven's enticing offer as he sipped his second cup of coffee?

"Fine," I said. "But only because this is time sensitive. And I need to stop at the bank on the way back." Pressure built in my chest as I climbed into Eli's passenger seat. I hated depending on others. In the end, people did what was best for them. Or they died.

I couldn't decide what bothered me more–my stray thoughts, Terry's reluctance to honor our deal, or the prospect of losing all my stuff. It was like I'd drew the Cinderella card in Candyland and got sent back to the beginning. I didn't have the time or money to start again from scratch.

Eli pulled into the parking void and shut off his truck. Heat instantly chased out the cool air from the AC. Beyond the lot, Terry was resetting an arena post.

"Do your thing," Eli said. "Nina and I will go explore. Right, Shorty?" He twisted to smile at my very agreeable toddler.

"O-okay, thanks." My breath shook. I slid from the truck to approach the man who would either make or break my heart. I had no plan, just a rash impulse and the hopes the old go-getter me might show up.

Terry's mustache curved up at the sides. "Two visits in one week! Maybe I should buy a lotto ticket."

"You'll see a lot more of me when you sell me the ranch."

Instead of affirmation, he nodded to Eli's truck. Nina giggled from atop Eli's shoulders as they traipsed toward the barn.

"Thought that friend of yours got your truck running?" Terry said.

"Yeah. Well, apparently, my engine needed de-greasing."

Terry's head fell back, and he laughed so hard Jason probably heard it. After wiping a stray tear, he said, "He seems like a nice kid."

"He is." Maybe *too* nice. I couldn't help wondering what he had to gain?

Silence descended. Terry's hands settled on his hips as he regarded me, thick eyebrows pinching together. No banter this time. "Nothing but bones here, Hon."

It did look a little ... skeletal. "I like challenges. Remember that first family rodeo?" Everything went wrong.

He nodded with a wisp of a smile. "It's a lot of work. All day, every day."

"Good thing I don't plan on doing it by myself." I mimicked his stance.

A whistle sang from Terry's teeth as he surveyed the faded expanse of broken gates, weedy walkways, and dried-out shrubs. But these were *our* dried-out shrubs. Each leaf was a part of mine and Jason's story. Our dream. "I'm not afraid of a little sweat."

"Tell ya what?" he said finally, and I was already nodding. "You give me something to look at. A plan of how you're gonna make this all work."

My eager agreement wobbled like a bobblehead. "I can do that."

"By the end of the week?"

"Yes, absolutely." I needed a business plan for the loan anyway.

"Okay, then."

"Okay, then," I repeated, relieved. That almost felt too easy. Now, for the other thing. My pulse thrummed faster. "Hey, while I'm here," and faster. Why was this the harder question? "I had some boxes. In the trailer ..." I knew the second my words were out. When his mustache drooped.

"I'm sorry, Hon."

A fissure split through my chest. "It-it's okay. It's not your fault."

"We had to toss all but one box."

"There's still one? Where is it?"

"Under your desk." Terry must've seen the hope on my face. "Go."

I raced to the office, startling Kip as I burst through the door.

"Is there a fire?" she asked.

"Hi, Kip. Sorry. I just–" I forced the rusty office chair back, and there, under the desk, just like Terry said, was one lonely cardboard box, its surface darkened but not overcome with mold.

Please, please, please.

Of everything I'd left behind, there was one item–an external extension of myself. Breath bated, I fell to my knees and pried back the brittle flaps. Somehow, this felt like the epicenter of my future. Would the old me be there? Could the past still be revived?

Euphoric tears pricked the backs of my eyes. Inside the box, vivid coral embroidery wove across leather like a treasure map. I pulled out my scuffed-up cowboy boots and hugged them to my chest.

"Oh, yeah." Kip towered behind me. "Figured you'd want those back."

My boots. My time machine to my favorite era. To my favorite me. They were way too expensive, and naïve Ava knew not the wrath they would wreak on a wannabe-cowgirl's feet. A rite of passage. A lesson that we all start at the beginning.

I heeled out of my sneakers and pulled them on. A custom fit, a fingerprint within the scarred leather. Scars that proved I'd survived. Grown stronger. Found my calling.

It was a sign.

No more artificial light, frigid summer climate control, and teetering towers of paperwork! This Mama would get her vitamin D the old-fashioned way.

12

Eli

Luke barged through the double glass doors into the den. He flipped his hair to the side, crossed his arms over the band logo on his black shirt, and stared at me from the other side of the coffee table.

Perfect timing.

Dad insisted I take a stab at the ranch paperwork, but hell if I knew where to start. This stuff should go to H&R Block. Or at least someone with a desk. Upstairs, I heard Dad grumbling at the coffeepot. Not even eight in the morning, and the forecast predicted grouchy, with a 100% chance of complaining.

I dropped a stack of papers on the table. "What's up, Luke?"

"That yuppie horse lady has her kid with her."

I stood, regarding him. His thumbs poked out of holes in his long-sleeve shirt. "Ava?"

"Yeah. Whatever. She's being, like, super bossy and asking stupid questions."

"She's supposed to. You're training her."

"No! Like weird ones. Like what I drink and stuff!"

I grabbed my hat off the blue couch and shoved it on my

head. That did seem like a weird question. "Did you get through the checklist?"

Luke threw his skinny arms out. "No! 'Cause she's stopping me every time I do anything and–"

"Okay. Okay." I raised a hand to stop him. "I'll talk to her."

Luke had a big heart and a hair trigger. I'd hired him, hoping to boost his confidence so he'd make better choices. I figured teaching Ava the ropes would inflate the kid's ego. Apparently not.

Marley strutted out of her room all made-up, looking too old for her own good. A sweet-smelling cloud followed her. *Great, just what I need.* Luke flipped his hair again, clicking his tongue piercing against his teeth. These two were gonna give me gray hair.

Marley gave Luke a head tilt and a "hey." Then, in almost non-existent shorts, she jogged up the stairs.

"Hey, Mar," I called. "You gonna put some clothes on?"

She gave me the finger, then strutted out of sight.

I didn't know what to do with her. Luke's focus stayed on the steps long after she'd gone. I'd already warned the kid that Marley was trouble. Too late, I realized that was half the draw.

I ran a hand over my chin, staring at the lust-struck teen. He did better solo. Which meant I needed something else for Ava to do. My eyes dropped to the stacks of papers on the coffee table. A mess like that needed a professional. Someone organized and smart. Someone who used to work in an office.

I lifted my hat and reseated it. "Hang here," I said. "I'll be back." It was perfect. Luke would get his barn back, and the paperwork might actually get done.

I jogged down to the barn, stopping in the empty aisle between the pens. "Ava?"

A *clink* in the tack stall snagged my attention. I walked to the end of the row, ready to defend Luke and deliver new instructions.

Only, the second I saw her, my mind turned blanker than Dad's staff roster. The boots. That's what did me in. Suddenly, she looked like she was made to wear dust and horse hair. Born to squeeze those jean-clad thighs around a horse. Not afraid to end the day–or night–coated in grit or sweat. *Maybe even my sweat.*

I shook my head to clear those thoughts.

Ava was tying Nina's shoe, so she didn't notice me standing there, gaping like an idiot. Her hair hung in a long ponytail over one shoulder as she bent and recited a rhyme. "Bunny ears, bunny ears, playing by the tree–" She looked up. "Oh. Hey."

"You ... changed."

She straightened, tightening her ponytail. "Yes. I do it every morning."

In that moment, I had to agree with every stereotype I'd heard about barns. I was a horny teenager again. And I couldn't stop staring.

She glanced down at herself. "Do I have something on my–"

"No. Sorry. Uh ..." I flexed the bill of my hat. "Nice boots."

"Thanks! They're–" She did a double take of her kid's hair. "No! Nina! That's for horses!"

Her toddler tugged at the handle of a horse brush, but her hair wrapped around it like Cthulhu had its prized ship.

Sighing, Ava dropped to her knees and started extracting one dark tentacle at a time. "I'm guessing you're here to talk about Luke?"

"Yeah." I shoved my hands into my pockets. "I'm sure you didn't mean anything by it, but–"

Nina screeched and lunged away, wrapping her fingers over the brush and hair.

Ava reached for her. "Nina, let go!"

"No!"

"It's stuck in your hair."

"No!"

"You can argue till you're blue, but that doesn't make it true." She wrapped an arm around the kid like a seatbelt and freed tangles with her other hand, grunting as an elbow landed in her stomach. "Next time I'm braiding your hair." She yanked the brush free and stood before Nina could get it from her.

A full-on tantrum exploded.

Ava inhaled and turned to me, holding the brush over her head. "I'm sorry. What were you saying?"

My eyes jumped between the two, then stuck on the hysterical kid rolling around in the dirt. "I, uh–I wanted to talk about Luke."

"Is this about the oats?" she asked.

"Oats?"

"Luke was feeding the horses way too many oats."

I opened my mouth, but didn't know what to say. "Too many oats?"

Nina's volume escalated. I stepped aside to avoid a kick in the shin.

"All I said," Ava half shouted, "was it's like drinking a Red Bull, then being told to sit still all day. Sugar is already twitchy. And she hasn't left her stall since we've been here."

Stubble *chafed* under my nails as I scratched my cheek.

Good point.

"Thing is, Luke's a little sensitive. And him being here is keeping him from being somewhere he shouldn't."

She nodded, and I figured, being a mom, she understood. "I'm sorry. I'm not trying to make things difficult for you." Her eyes cut to her screaming, sweaty kid. "Nina, enough!"

The heat always made me crabby. Maybe bringing them indoors would help? "Listen, I think Luke needs space." I moved closer so I wouldn't have to yell, and Ava's fruity shampoo had me losing track of the conversation.

She blinked at me. "Space?"

"Yeah." Right. *Focus, Eli.* "I have a different job for you. One that's not in the barn."

"Stable."

"What?"

"It's not a barn," she said. "Barns have walls.

"Really?"

"Whatever." Ava put the horse brush on a shelf above Nina's reach. "Just tell me what you want me to do." She didn't sound so thrilled, and she clearly had her hands full.

I hesitated. "I've got paperwork that needs going through."

It was like watching a birthday balloon sink to the floor after the party. "Paperwork? Fine. Great."

No. Not great. She hated it.

I took off my hat, repositioned it, shoved it back down. "It's up at the house."

Her eyes cut to Nina. "Can you just give me a few minutes?"

"Sure. Take as much time as you need." She didn't look at me again.

I trekked back to the house, feeling like the villain. Like everyone was pissed at me. The pressure of this domestic trap closed in, and my fingers itched for the steering wheel. I pushed my way through the glass doors into the den, tracking dust on the carpet. How the hell was I supposed to know what to do? I wasn't a rancher. With all the papers back in the cardboard box Dad had given me, I stomped upstairs.

My frown sank into a scowl when I found Luke and Marley shoulder-to-shoulder at the kitchen table. The cord to a pair of earbuds hung between their heads.

I thumped the box onto the tabletop. "Break's over."

Luke stood slowly, returning Marley's earbud with a chin-lift and a "Later." The flirty fingers Marley waved back iced my irritation cake.

I waited until Luke left before leaning my hands onto the

beat-up wood surface. "Mar, you gotta stop. Crap like that leads him on."

"What am I doing?"

"Playing music for him? Those shorts? That look?"

"What look?"

"Don't play dumb."

"So, now I'm dumb?" She pushed off the bench. "Whatever! Look who's talking!" She stormed back downstairs and slammed her door.

My hands tightened into fists. I should've been driving through canyons, windows open, The Eagles blasting, headed to my next short-term gig. But no. I was stuck here, pretending I knew what to do about everyone else's problems.

Dad wandered into the kitchen and peeked into the box. "Ah, finally getting around to those. Remember: categorize, calendarize, prioritize." He gave me a hearty pat on the back. "And good luck."

"Thanks, but, not gonna need it. Ava's got it covered."

"Got what covered?"

"This." I jerked my chin at the box.

"Eli—"

"What? She insisted on helping! It's a perfect job for her." *Liar, and you know it.*

Dad frowned. "I don't want strangers privy to our finances."

"First, you tell me to delegate! Now you're saying only delegate the shit that doesn't matter?"

"Everything matters, Eli. I just asked you to sort the invoices."

"Oh, that's it, huh? Have you looked in here, in oh, I dunno, the last decade?"

Dad's expression hardened. This was turning into another Reese's kind of day. "It's not about easy or hard. I'm trying to give you tools."

"I already have a set, thanks."

Dad threw his hands up. "For crying out loud, you know that's not what I meant."

Why was I there? What did he want from me? "I'm fine. I don't need your tools. I'm not begging for money, or blowing college funds on drugs and hookers."

"Well, that's a relief." His sarcastic tone didn't help my mood. "I just want you to stop running."

"I'm not running." The way he lifted his eyebrow pissed me off. "See my feet standing here? Do they look like they're running?"

"Your mom's death affected all of us."

"God, Dad, just drop it! It's hard enough being here in this hellhole."

He got silent. Finally.

Ava should've been up by now. I crossed to the huge kitchen window, worrying she and Luke had another run-in. But I only saw one skinny, black-clad kid at the barn. *Stable. Whatever.* Where was she?

"Can I ask you something, son?"

"You can ask ..."

"What are you going to do when your body can't keep up? It doesn't last forever, you know?"

Ava's words messed with me. "*... having a rough time with his arthritis.*" My old man had hunched over drafting tables most of his life, ate donuts for breakfast, pulled all-nighters with a wooden pencil and a ruler. We were not the same. "I'll be fine."

Dad was shaking his head. "It doesn't work by sheer will. Eventually, things wear out. You're gonna want a home base. Someone to help take care of you. Of things. I'm telling you."

"I'm not alone on the road."

He scoffed. "You think *Ryan* will be any help?"

"There it is," I mumbled.

"That kid is one bad choice after another. I don't want him bringing you down."

He didn't care where I was, just who I was with. Dad always hated my best friend. We weren't kids anymore. If I had problems, I had problems, but at least I didn't drag him into them.

I caught movement out the window. Ava and Nina came out of the trailer and picked their way around the weeds to the house.

I glanced at Dad. "We done?"

He didn't reply. But he also didn't vacate the kitchen.

I met the girls at the front door. Nina appeared first, looking like a victim of a peanut butter and jelly sandwich attack. She had sticky globs all over her face, hands, and shirt.

"Don't drop that," Ava uttered, following her in. "Please go sit at the table."

Peanut butter smeared the bench as Nina climbed up one-handed. Her legs dangled, and she hummed as she poked between the pieces of bread, then licked her finger. The same kid who'd been screaming over a horse brush.

"Okay," Ava said, filling her lungs. "Where's your paperwork?"

Eight-thirty, and Dad was putting another pod in the coffeepot. I ignored him and dragged the cardboard box down the table, out of Nina's reach. "In here."

Ava's chin went down, and her eyebrows went up, and if I didn't know better, I'd have thought she just swallowed a bee. Meanwhile, Nina swung her feet happily under the table.

I stared at the inside of the box. "It, uh, it needs to be sorted so we can balance the accounts." Dad's directive. Did it sound like I knew what I was talking about?

In gut-twisting slow motion, she drifted to my side and lifted a page from the top of the stack with long, delicate fingers. Her silence was killing me.

She pulled out another invoice and studied it. "Has this been paid?"

I didn't have the ball bearings to look her in the eye.

Glancing back at Dad was a worse mistake. If he cared so much, he should've done it. "Uh ... I dunno," I told her.

"It's just one box, right?"

"Yeah."

Ava ran a hand through her ponytail. It swayed, then settled on her back. If I'd ever had a chance with this woman, I was murdering it one stupid sheet of paper at a time.

"I'll do my best," she said. "But this is ..." She stared at it like she wished she'd never met me, like looking at me made her wanna hurl.

At the other end of the table, Nina smooshed her bread together and licked the jelly that oozed out of the sides. I should've said something. Apologized, maybe.

My old man leaned against the counter, sipping his coffee, no help at all. One by one, Ava laid pages on the table. Making stacks, I realized. Invoices for supplies. Invoices for boarding.

I scrubbed a hand over my jaw. *Categorizing.* At this rate, she'd be there all day, taking her punishment in silence. Only, I'd never meant it like that.

She probably hated me.

13

Ava

IT LOOKED like a year's worth of paperwork. In a *box!*

Did I anger the universe? Sure, owning a ranch meant accounts and books. But, books! Not *a box*. Why? How? But it didn't matter. I owed them. If this is what they needed, then that's what I'd do. "Will you need this table for eating?"

"What?" Eli asked.

"This might take days." Days in which I had hoped to be in an apartment, a new job.

Eli drummed his fingertips on the wooden tabletop. To his credit, he appeared remorseful. "What if we worked on it together?"

"That would help."

Bill cleared his throat and set his coffee cup in the sink. "I'll watch Nina."

After explaining my system, Eli and I stood side by side, working in silence for several minutes.

"I'm sorry," he said suddenly, pulling out another thick stack of documents. "I know you'd rather be at the stable."

I shrugged. "What good is my help if it's not what you need?"

"What I need," he repeated, more to himself. He pulled out his phone. "How about some music?"

"If you'd like."

"What do *you* like?"

My eyes climbed to his hopeful expression. I couldn't remember the last time someone had asked me that. "I-I don't know."

He studied me, then dipped his head to his phone. After a minute, a solid beat paired with an instantly likeable twang of country guitar bounced around the spacious kitchen. "How's this?"

I resisted the urge to tap my toes. "This is good." Sorting turned into a line dance of rustling papers, and I didn't hate it.

"Can you read this?" Eli held a page in my face.

"Not that close, I can't." I pushed his arm back, firm, warm muscle teasing my fingertips. Instead of reading the faded print with me, he watched the side of my face. "D-Dodd's Feed?" I said. "Budd's Feed? Put it with feed orders for now."

"As you wish." He leaned in, twisting to face me as he set his page down, almost as if he planned to scoop me up in a slow dance.

Why is he so close?

Then came an unwanted rebuttal: *You didn't mind when he was covered in motor oil.* I read the work order in my hand three times, but all that registered was the brush of Eli's shoulder every time he placed a page on a pile.

I elbowed his side, though I couldn't erase all of my smile. "Do you mind? I'm trying to work here."

"Yeah, me too." His head bobbed to the song as he inched closer.

Just ignore it. "How did the interview go?"

"The interview?" He paused, receipt in hand. "Oh. Yeah. Well, he showed up on time."

"That's rare," I observed, only half joking.

"Right?"

"But?" I asked.

He sighed, leaning his palms against the table's edge. "He seemed like an a-hole." With a *huff*, he added, "Dad's expecting way too much for this position."

"It might be easier to find someone trainable."

"Won't do us much good."

I took a turn studying his profile. "Why not?"

He pulled a face. "We're not cowboys. Dad's a retired architect. I don't even know why he has a ranch. Only thing I can figure, Mom loved horses, so he did it for her."

My eyes fell on Eli's industrial work boots. Functional, but steel toes were overkill for ranch wear. "Do you ride?"

"Used to." He put his page on a pile. "You?"

"Same."

"Why'd you stop?" he asked.

The bottom of the box materialized. I pulled out the last item, a piece of mail with red letters that spelled out *final notice*. "What's this?"

"Dunno." Eli took the offered correspondence, opened it, read it, then shoved it back into the envelope and tucked it in his pocket. "I'll give that to Dad later. Now what?"

I selected a pile. "Now we order each stack by date."

"Calendarize," he muttered.

"Hmm?"

"Nothing."

He picked up a neat-ish stack of invoices and curled up the bottom corners to read the printed dates. We plowed through the task much faster than expected, his interference in my personal space notwithstanding. When my stomach grumbled, I glanced at the clock. Nina would be due for her nap soon.

I smoothed the edges of the last ordered pile and resisted the urge to fix Eli's stack. "We should put these in binders so they stay organized."

"Good idea. I'll ask Dad if he has some."

"I'll come. It's near Nina's naptime, anyway."

I followed him down the set of stairs at the entryway, into a large den with wide exterior French doors that boasted the same majestic mountain view as upstairs. Surrounding the den were interior doors, presumably leading to more rooms.

"There's a whole other house down here!"

Bill glanced up from his spot on the floor. "You guys done already?"

He and Nina were hunched over a square coffee table, drawing. Behind them sat a plush blue couch opposite a large mounted TV. Creamy wall-to-wall carpeting grounded it all in cozy appeal—such a contrast to the clean, modern upstairs.

My real estate training kicked in. "How many bedrooms does this place have?"

"I gave it five," Bill said. "The master suite, three down here, and Eli's got the studio over the garage."

I took a turn, imagining how the rooms behind closed doors might look. "I love the layout." Then his words sank in. "Wait, you designed this house?"

His eyes drifted to Eli, but his son was busy scowling at his phone.

"What's with the face?" I asked Eli. "You don't like your studio?"

He glanced up, tucking his cell away. "Huh? Oh, no, it's nice. Maybe not as sexy as the kitchen," he teased.

My face flamed. Did he remember everything I said? I stepped in to study Bill's and Nina's drawings. "Wow, Bill. You're quite the artist." The house he had sketched rivaled listings for future build-sites. Nina's picture looked like a torn pizza box with a smiley face.

"Years of designs," he told me. "I started before all this computer rendering software."

"Hey, Dad," Eli interjected, "we got any binders?"

Bill carefully detailed a panel on the front door. "We do not. But if you're running out, I could use a ream of paper."

Eli sighed, then looked at me. "Just a binder? What kind?"

I chewed on the inside of my lip as I thought it over. "Three-inches? Actually, make that two of them. And some dividers? Or colorful sticky tabs. Anything to flag sections?"

"Do you just wanna come?" he asked.

My eyes dropped to the happy pizza box. I'd already strayed off course enough for one day. "I should get Nina down for a nap."

"Okay. Just call me if you think of anything else."

"I can't."

He crossed his arms. "Why is that?"

"I don't have your number." I meant nothing by it. Logically, I couldn't call him if I didn't have it.

"Give me your phone."

I regretted it the instant I handed it to him, fretted over the grin that stretched across his face as he tapped away at my screen.

"There. No excuses now." He passed it back. The heading of my newly saved contact read, "Hunky Hero."

Oh my God. Of course he remembered! Heat returned to my cheeks. I needed to stop saying things like that. Or just stop speaking in general. "Thank you."

"You're very welcome."

Once Eli left, Nina negotiated fifteen extra minutes to finish her drawing, which turned into two new drawings. I joined them, sketching a horse that shared a striking resemblance to a potato on stilts.

Bill looked at Nina's latest scribble thoughtfully. "It needs some color."

"But not right now," I interjected, "because we've put off naptime long enough." Then I realized something. "Shoot! Do you have a three-hole punch?"

He shook his head. "Left all that stuff at the office when I retired." He stood with a groan. "When you call Eli, tell him to get me colored pencils. Prismacolor. Not that off-brand crap." He started for the stairs. "I'll be around if you need anything."

"Thanks, Bill." I stacked our drawings into a neat pile. "Okay, Crackerjack. Time for a nap."

Nina popped to her feet and bolted out the glass doors. I followed, but instead of heading to our trailer, she zipped straight to the stable.

"Excuse me, missy! Where do you think you're going?" But my heart wasn't in it. I had to call Eli, anyway. When I caught up to her, she had two feet on the bottom rung of Chuck's fence. "Please don't climb those."

"I not." She climbed to the next rung.

I pulled out my phone. "You are. I see you are."

I lifted her off and set her on the ground, staring a little too long at the contact screen. What would Eli save *my* number as? Summer Stray? Drama Mama? Sexy Truck Lady? I shook my head and tapped the call button. Who's to say he'd save it at all? When he answered, my stupid heart hiccupped.

"Hello, Eli?"

"Who's this?"

Did I sound that different on the phone? Did he get a lot of calls from women?

He laughed. "I'm kidding, Ava. Whatcha need?"

"Are you still at the store?" I lifted Nina off the rails again.

"Yeah, I'm on a shopping spree. I found a love letter in my truck stashed full of cash."

"What? No! It's not a love letter, it's a thank you note for working on Roxy." Did it sound like a love letter? I tried to remember what I'd scrawled in my haste. "If it's not enough, let me know."

"An 'XOXO' at the bottom might be nice."

"I meant the money."

He hummed a thoughtful note. "If I leave my window open, will I get more love letters?"

"It's not a–Nina, no thank you!" This time, when I pried her off the fence, I stuck her at my hip, where she kicked and squirmed. "I have something to add to the list," I told Eli. "We need a three-hole punch and some colored pencils."

"Okay."

"Prismacolor," I clarified. "Not the off-brand crap." A long pause stretched on the other end. "Bill's words," I defended.

"Anything else?" Something in his tone changed.

"No, that's it." I couldn't stop myself. "Are you okay?"

"Huh? Yeah, it's just weird. Dad hasn't drawn in years."

"Maybe he's feeling inspired?"

"Maybe." Why did Eli sound so disturbed by that? After a lull, he said, "Is that all?"

"Yeah."

"Great. See you soon." I hung up before I gave him anything else to quote me on.

While Nina napped, I scheduled an apartment tour. Not my first choice, but the pool outweighed the dated interior and exterior stairs to the second floor. After naptime, I offered Nina a snack, then returned to the main house with my computer tucked under my arm again.

Bill was sitting on the porch in a blue Adirondack chair with an iced tea. His stare stretched a thousand miles past the nearest ocotillo. Lonely shadows lurked in the creases of his face. They were the same lines I saw when I looked in the mirror.

When he noticed us, he offered a weary smile. "Uh oh, here comes trouble."

Nina pulled free of my hand and climbed into the chair next to him, leaning back to copy him, but the sun hit her face straight on. Bill stretched to his left to shade a hand over her eyes.

"Better?" he asked.

She nodded with a toothy grin. He was such a natural.

"Do you have grandkids?" I asked him.

"N-ope." Disappointment. Regret.

His single word weighed heavier than its Merriam-Webster meaning, and it compelled me to feed him. A silly notion, considering I had so much to do. Sillier still, because cooking in the RV in this heat defied all common sense. But when people grieved, you brought them casseroles. When your friend sobbed over a breakup, you arrived with ice cream and a bottle of tequila. This man needed tamales.

"I was thinking ..." Would he resist if I asked him outright? Bill waited for me to finish, his sweating iced tea halfway to his mouth. Melting ice shifted with little clinks. "I'd like to make you dinner."

His stubby eyebrows shot up. "Well, I've gotta say, it's been a long time since a woman told me that." Sorrow faded, and the crow's feet returned to his eyes. "I should treat you to dinner. Figure I owe you for whipping Eli into shape over that darn box." He squinted up at me. "What are you offering?"

"Tamales. Unless you want something else?"

He took a sip of his iced tea. "I'm easy. I'll eat anything."

"Except for Marley's apple muffins," I pointed out.

"Except for that."

Poor Marley. She'd tried.

"Or kale," he added in a gruff voice. "And that fake meat stuff. If it ain't chicken, don't call it chicken."

I threw a dramatic hand to my chest. "I would never."

"Good."

I missed this—lazy afternoon banter. Easy company. I missed sharing home-cooked meals and corn husks coated in tamale sauce, piled high in the center of the table like poker chips. I wanted cold beers and laughter under a sky full of stars. I bet the stars looked huge this far outside the city. When my phone buzzed, I whipped it out.

"Is Eli on his way back?" Bill asked.

I frowned. "What? Oh, I don't know." Steven. *Again.* I tucked it away and glanced at the long, empty driveway. Mr. Hunky Hero had been gone for almost two hours. Not that I was counting. I had *hoped* to finish the binders and move on to other things.

"You reckon he got lost?" Bill asked.

"In an office store? Maybe."

An hour later, still no Eli. I sent off a few more resumes, then gave up on him, and loaded Nina into the Chevy for our apartment tour. The unit was ready for lease, so we headed straight to the office to complete paperwork. That meant pre-made pork tamales from the *Carneceria.* A wiser choice given the circumstances, though not as good as homemade.

Eli still hadn't returned when we pulled into Bill's ranch. *Whatever.* Packing took priority over binders. Inside the RV, swollen rice kernels boiled with bouillon and tomato paste in my cheap Teflon pot. I wiped the sweat off the side of my face as I haphazardly checked the liquid level. Then I bounced to shoving things back in boxes. Mainly Nina's toys, which she pulled out every time I resumed my spot at the stove.

"Nina, leave them there!"

"Mama, I have to go potty."

Oh. *This is a first.* "Okay." I wiped my hands and walked her across a sea of stuffed animals to the bathroom. It still had a sour twinge, but nothing like that first day. Nina climbed onto the seat and sat there, legs swinging as she talked non-stop about everything from horses to the hair inside my nose.

"Are you done?" I asked.

"No."

"Are you sure you have to go?"

"Yes."

Burnt rice wafted through the small space. *Shoot!* "Nina, I'll be right back."

"No!" She grabbed my arm.

"Dinner is burning." I fought to pull free without yanking her off the toilet seat. "Nina, let go. I'll be right back." With gentle force I escaped, only to trip over a box of clothes on my way to the kitchen. The handle was hot when I moved the food off the burner, and not only did I kill the rice, but I also scorched my new pot.

"Mama!" Nina wailed.

The trailer was too hot, too messy. How did I think I'd be ready to move in the morning? With so many tasks? Make dinner, pack, clean, wow Terry with a business proposal.

"Mama! Come back!"

All I really wanted was a nap. Better yet, a shower. But I wouldn't get either. It was too much! I blew through the front door and onto the deck. Why did everything have to be so hard? I was trying to stitch our lives back together, and seams just kept splitting everywhere. I couldn't keep up. And somehow, I had to figure this out. On my own.

A throat cleared.

I whipped around to see Eli standing on the bottom step with two white shopping bags. "You want me to come back later?" He preemptively twisted away.

My hands curled into bionic fists. "Where have you been?"

He shot me an incredulous look. "Where have I …? Ava, do you have any idea how many kinds of colored sticky tabs the office store sells?"

"You spent four hours picking out Post-its?"

"Of course not. Why are you yelling at me?"

"I'm not yelling!"

Eli slanted a look at me.

I closed my eyes and forced my fists open. Took a deep breath. "I'm sorry. It's not you. I'm just …" freaking out about doing all this on my own. "Are those the binders?"

He chewed on a piece of gum as he studied me, mouth turned down. Then he climbed the stairs, one boot-fall at a time, bags swinging. When he held his arms out, I thought he meant to offer the office supplies, but suddenly they were going around me and pulling me into his chest.

Panic surged. "W-what are you doing?"

"Giving you a hug."

My first instinct was to push away, but the firmness of his body against mine made me lightheaded, the soft, sun-soaked fabric of his shirt wooing. I could still pick up hints of soap or deodorant, even after a full day of heat. I didn't hate it. His strong, confident embrace hung on a beat longer than normal and spoke without words. I'm not sure what it said, but I gave in just before he let go.

"Better?" he asked.

I squinted, trying to navigate through my brain fog. "I guess. Yeah."

He grinned. "Good. Wanna see what I got?"

His smile could've won awards. The way his eyes formed perfect crescents, and his full bottom lip took center stage. How the divot in his chin became extra prominent.

I blinked down at the open bag. At the rainbow of office

supplies inside: binders, colorful tabs, post-its, highlighters, and ... *gel pens*? "Wow. You really did go on a spree."

He looked so pleased with himself, and that golden retriever energy sucked the anger right out of me. "I'm sorry I snapped at you."

He shrugged. "You can make it up to me."

I refused to open that can of butterflies, no matter how much they fluttered to the surface. "Was it the office chairs?"

"What?"

"Did you have to try them all out, give each one a spin? Nina always bee-lines it to the chairs when we go."

His chuckle drew my eyes to his mouth. "No. I had other errands." He really needed to stop smiling. Though now it was more of a smirk, making my insides do weird acrobatics.

I forced an inhale. "Since you're here, can you take something to the house?"

"Sure." He followed me inside the trailer, not yet noticing my toddler, standing smack in the center of the living room, amid piles of once-packed toys, bare from the waist down. "Holy hell, it's hot in here."

The urge to weep punched me all over again. "Nina! We are packing, not playing! And where are your shorts?"

She ignored me and ran straight to Eli's legs. "Eli, play with me!"

Bless his heart, he wasn't even fazed. "Hey, monkey. I have something for you." He rifled through his bag and handed her a package of sparkly stickers.

I grabbed her discarded clothes from the bathroom and wrestled her legs back into her bottoms.

When I rose, Eli gave me a strange look. "Did you say *packing*?"

"I did. We signed a lease for an apartment today."

His shoulders sank.

"It has a pool," I added, like he needed assurance. Or maybe it was for my benefit. I tucked a loose hair behind my ear. "Don't worry, I'll finish the binders before we go."

He said nothing.

I dug out a Dollar General Tupperware and started spooning rice, working to avoid the burnt bits and Eli's disappointed expression. His sudden silence felt more oppressive than the heat.

When he finally spoke, it came from right behind me. "You made us dinner?" I could smell the spearmint on his breath. And the intimate way he said "us" resonated more like a candlelit dinner than takeout. Or maybe the extra heat emanating from his body messed with my brain.

"Who said there's enough for you?" There was. "It's for your dad. I'm thanking him for his hospitality."

"Our hospitality."

If I stepped back, I'd fold into his chest. That's how close he stood. I topped the rice with hot tamales and tucked a dish towel under the container so it wouldn't burn his hands. Sweat dripped down my temple as I pivoted to hand it to Eli. "I don't have a vegetable."

To have someone stare so intensely at you must turn every hopeless romantic's heart to mush.

He took the container. "It smells good."

Did that make me a hopeless romantic? "I-I didn't make them. The tamales, I mean. I bought them."

A crease in the letter "A" formed between his eyes as he glanced at the four tamales still in the steamer behind me. 'A' for alluring. For assuring. There he stood, a boy who rescued strays. "You aren't eating with us?"

'A' for adultery.

"No." I wasn't a stray. I had a life. A promise to keep. A husband to honor. "Enjoy the food, Eli."

He dropped his eyes to the home-ish cooked meal. "I'm sure we will."

His departure left an emptiness in my bones. I slumped into a chair at the dinette table, where I discovered an envelope that hadn't been there earlier. The one I'd slipped through Eli's open truck window the day before. Upon further inspection, I found all the cash. And a note.

Save it for when you take me out to dinner.
XOXO Eli

I snorted. "That's one expensive dinner."

Then my eye caught the sparkle of shiny stickers all over the TV. *Nina!*

I dropped the envelope back on the table as I stood. What was I thinking? Who had time for dinner dates?

14

———

Eli

I MET Ava and Nina at the door with my biggest smile, even if it was ninety percent fake. *Heaven help me,* she wore those cut-offs again.

"Morning, ladies." This couldn't be it. Their last day. The last time I'd see them.

Ava's eyes traveled from my mouth to the cup I offered her. Coffee with a splash of milk, the way she liked it. "Is this for me?"

"Mhmm." I wasn't above bribery. Our fingers brushed when she took the cup, and I should've been ashamed at how my blood raced.

She stared at her coffee with odd intensity, still no smile. Nina, on the other hand, had a full-on scowl. "Rough morning?" I asked.

"She's mad," Ava explained, "because I made her walk."

"I know what she needs." I waved them into the kitchen with me and grabbed a banana off the counter, but Nina stomped straight past and climbed under the table. "Or not." Maybe she didn't like the stickers?

"Don't read too much into it." Ava inhaled the steam from

her coffee like a Folgers commercial, then tipped her cup in a slow, glamorous sip. "Mmm. I needed this."

I reclaimed my mug from the counter and took a plain ol' boring sip. "Did you get your stuff packed?"

"I did." She fought a yawn. "I even had time to throw together a business plan."

"Wow. When did you sleep?"

Her shoulders lifted, then dropped.

"*Did* you sleep?" I wondered if my fake smile looked as bad as the one she shot me.

"Terry wants something *today* that shows I can take on the ranch without going bankrupt." She cupped both her hands around her mug. "It's almost there. I just need to research a few costs."

"Ava!"

"What?"

I tried not to notice how bloodshot her eyes looked. Women didn't like it when you pointed out that stuff. "If I'd known you had things to do, I wouldn't have made you work on our crap."

"You didn't *make* me do anything."

I ran a hand over my hat. This was all wrong. "And today you're gonna move all your stuff?" The grouchy gremlin under the kitchen table would make her day extra hard. "I wish you'd said something. How can you think that late at night, anyway?"

"I have a degree in agricultural management," she said, taking another commercial-worthy sip. "So, throwing together a proposal is basically muscle memory."

Well, shit.

I finally brought Dad a manager, and we couldn't keep her.

She knocked back the rest of her coffee and put her empty cup on the counter. "Should we finish the binders?"

"No, I'll do it. Go get the costs for your plan. Or take a nap, or something."

She frowned. "It will go faster if we do it together."

I didn't want fast, I wanted to savor her. Soon she'd be gone, and then what would I look forward to when I woke up in this dry, dusty hell? "The hard part's done. I think I can handle punching a few holes."

"Okay, fine." She tucked her bottom lip between her teeth, and it came out shining. "Lucky for you, we're almost out of your hair."

What if I wanted her in my hair? Her fingers, her face. I cleared my throat. "Did you see my note?"

Instead of an answer, she pulled her buzzing phone out of her shorts pocket and glanced at the screen. "Oh. Sorry, I–I need to take this." Then she moved to the window, giving me her back. "Hello, this is Ava Garcia."

I studied Nina, still under the table, and wondered if there was room for two under there.

"Yes, absolutely! I'm still interested," Ava said into the phone. "Tomorrow?" She turned to me and mouthed a silent question. I nodded even though I had no idea what she was asking.

"Yes, nine is great! Thank you. I'll see you tomorrow." After ending the call, I got to see an Ava-exclusive victory dance. A kind of raise-the-roof, hips-don't-lie number. "I have an interview!"

Energy radiated off her like a bug zapper, and I leaned in. "Yeah? Where at?"

"Rock 'N Roll Landscaping."

"Well, you're gonna cause a lot of trouble forking dirt in those shorts."

She straightened, dropping her arms. "It's for an office position." I must've made a face, 'cause then she said, "What's that look for?"

"Nothing. It's just ... You were ready to stab me over paperwork yesterday."

Ava landed her hands on her perfectly proportioned hips.

"First of all, that box was a nightmare! I mean, why would you keep your paperwork that way?"

Dang it, she would've made a perfect manager. And not because of her killer legs. "I dunno. I think Dad wants me to suffer. What's the second thing?"

She raised a dark eyebrow at me.

"You said, *first of all* ..." I made my voice high and stuck my hands on my hips.

She chuckled, and I finally earned one of those bright, heart-stopping smiles. "'A' for effort," she said, then sighed. "It's a job. With benefits *and* flexibility. I need both to get Hidden Meadows up and running again."

Benefits? Maybe that's why we weren't getting any hits on the job listing? Were we supposed to offer that kind of stuff? "Then, congratulations."

"I don't have the job yet."

"You will."

"I hope so." She tucked loose hair behind her ears. "Thank you for agreeing to watch Nina. I don't think I'll ever be able to pay you back for all your help. Truly."

"You could take me to dinner."

She opened her mouth, but hesitated. "I'll be busy for a while."

"So? Make it a quickie." Her face fell before I realized my mistake. "N-no. I meant, like, takeout."

"Is that what you want?"

Shit. Why did I have to get so tongue-tied around her? I fixed my hat, fingering through the hair under it. "I'd rather have a full sit-down dinner. With dessert."

She studied me, chewing that darn lip again. "Maybe we can take a rain check?"

"Sure. Name the time. I'm all yours."

Then, the craziest thing happened. Her eyes dipped to my mouth.

What *did* I want? I was leaving soon anyway. Was it worth starting something, just to pass the time? Would Ava go for that? She seemed more like a serious-inquiries-only kind of woman. Except, she was studying my lips like the dessert menu. Then, in the next breath, she bolted into motion, hauling a whining Nina out from the table and vacating the kitchen.

I trailed behind. "I'll help you get your stuff to the new place."

"Okay."

"Okay? No argument?"

"Why bother? You'll just do it anyway."

I smiled at her back as she rushed down the porch steps, leaving behind the sweet, fruity smell of her shampoo.

Yes. I definitely wanted to start something.

With a pep in my step, I went to find Dad. He was down in the den, sitting cross-legged on the floor with a stack of foam squares, piecing interlocking edges into a triangular tunnel.

I frowned. "Whatcha doing?"

"Making a fort for the kid."

"With my gym mats?"

"They were just sitting in the mudroom. You got a problem with it?"

"No, it's cool." I wasn't using them anyway. "But the, uh–the girls are moving into an apartment today."

"Oh." He paused, staring at the half-attached foam.

I should've been used to seeing his disappointment by now. "Ava has a job interview tomorrow. She asked if I could watch Nina."

"Oh, yeah?" Dad sized me up over his glasses. Did he think I couldn't do it? "I'll finish this, then," he said, returning to his masterpiece. A body snatcher. It had to be. He looked the same, sounded the same, but his behavior?

My phone buzzed in my pocket. I ignored it. "Hey, do you need me for anything?"

"Nope."

"Fine. I'm gonna finish the paperwork stuff, then help Ava move into her new place."

"Okay."

"Luke's down at the stable."

"Great." Was this a test? Him just waiting to catch my mistake. Screw something up?

Whatever. I rocked on my heels and made for the stairs, but then I remembered something. "Oh. There was a late-notice letter at the bottom of the paperwork box."

"Stick it on my bed," he said. No explanation.

I crossed my arms. "Why aren't you paying your business taxes?"

"We aren't making that much. I doubt they'll notice."

"They sent you a letter. That means they noticed. Can't they shut you down, or take the house, or something?"

"They won't."

"Dad."

Finally, my old man graced me with his attention. "Why are you so worried? Do you want this place?"

"No. But I don't want you losing your house. Do you need money?"

"No."

"I can help you out. I'm not a total deadbeat." My phone buzzed again.

"I don't think you're a deadbeat, son. And I don't need your money. It was an oversight. Put the letter on my bed. I'll take care of it." The letter was a *third notice*, which meant he'd gotten two others. *Before* he filled that damn box. How many more came in after that?

He grabbed another mat square and started attaching it. "Oh. Henry called this morning."

"Henry?"

"Misty's owner."

Right. One of the boarders that, as Ava pointed out, never came by.

"They want to end the contract and move her somewhere else."

"What? Why?"

Dad leaned back to admire his work. "Said it was out of their way, no good place to exercise her."

I threw my arm at the glass doors, to the huge horse ring I could see from where I was standing. "No place to train her? What the hell is that?"

"I'm disappointed, too. But it's no good arguing if we don't have what they want."

"What *do* they want? A grassy meadow? Good luck finding that in Arizona!" *No place to train, my ass.* A weird pressure pushed at me from the inside out. Something unfamiliar and uncomfortable. "So, what does that mean?"

"Welp," Dad pushed himself up off the floor. "We should find another boarder."

"Shit." I ran a hand down my face. "Hey, how many boarders would it take to cover health insurance for a ranch manager?" Dad stared at me thoughtfully. It made my skin itch. "Don't read into it. I just wanna hire someone before I fry to a crisp."

"You know, all the paperwork you sorted would help you figure that out."

My phone went off again. I pulled it out and saw I'd missed six calls from Ryan. "Fine," I told Dad. "I'll look later. I gotta take this." Sweat dripped down my back the second I exited through the glass doors and stepped into the summer heat. A daily reminder of where I'd landed.

With a swipe, I answered Ryan's call. "Hey man, what's up?"

"My disco stick."

"I don't need you to blow up my phone to tell me that."

"Dude. Who spit in your beer?"

I stared out at the ring. It was a perfectly fine place to exercise a horse. Hot. But I couldn't control the weather. "It's too early for beer."

"Maybe that's your problem," he drawled. I heard a woman in the background. "You need a vacation. You should take a week. In Texas."

"I told you. I promised my dad–"

"Stop with the excuses. It's not until the end of August. Five figures, man. For five fuckin' days! This is *the* gig!"

Yeah, probably crossing a picket line and walking straight into a shitshow.

A feminine giggle filled the silence on his end, which irritated me. Magnified my lack of a social life. "You sound a little busy. Call me later."

"I can multitask. Right, Baby?" Several affirmative sounds came from Ryan's company.

"Why are you calling me?"

"I need my right-hand man."

"Sounds like you have enough hands at the moment."

"But these hands. Won't. Be. In Texas." With every pause came a grunt or groan telling me he was enjoying himself.

"Ryan, no amount of money would make me want to touch your junk."

He laughed. "You haven't heard the offer yet."

"No."

"Maybe you need someone to touch your junk?" At my silence, he went on. "Five days. Plus a few days driving. That's all I'm asking."

"Ryan."

"Fuck, man, what can your dad do? You're a grown-ass adult!"

"It's not–" I exhaled, tired of this fight. "I'm trying to do the right thing."

Ryan's side went quiet for so long, I thought the call had dropped. Then he said, "Dude, you're not housebroken, are you?"

"Bye, Ryan."

"It's a cage!"

"Yeah, I'm done." I hung up, but his comment hit below the belt. Ryan and I, we'd been freedom seekers since we were kids. I scrubbed my hands down my face, aware of the pressure from all the things that kept piling on. Damnit, maybe Ryan was right. Maybe I needed to let off some steam.

The fresh, white paint failed to make Ava's new apartment feel less like a cinderblock cell, what with its whopping novelty window by the front door and a dinky excuse for one in the bedroom. The cheap furniture ate up all the space, and the concrete stairs to the second floor were definitely not kid-friendly.

What's she paying for this?

I put a stack of boxes on the flimsy coffee table in the living room/dining room/kitchen. At least the air conditioning worked. "Where do you want to set up Nina's bed?" I asked.

Ava came out of the single bedroom with Nina hot on her heels. She pursed her lips and looked around. "I don't know. Lean the pieces against the wall for now."

"Mama! I wanna go swimming!"

"Later, Crackerjack. We have to finish bringing our stuff in."

The place made my head hurt. "Maybe I should take the bed home and store it for you."

Ava ran her fingers through her ponytail, sweeping her eyes through the space again. She blew out all her air, and her shoulder sank like an inner tube at the end of summer. Ready for the off-season. "No. It's fine. I'll figure it out."

Instead of arguing, I went out for another load. The place felt more crammed than the trailer. What was the point in moving? When I walked in with the last few boxes, Ava was leaning her elbows onto the breakfast counter, butt jutting into the alley kitchen behind her, tapping on her phone.

"I can't thank you enough for your help," she said. "I'm not sure how I would've done the dresser with those stairs."

The handle jiggled when I closed the front door behind me. "No problem." Frowning, I dug out my keys and used the multi-tool on my keychain to tighten the screws, but they spun in place. *Stripped. Figures.*

"What are you doing?"

"The handle is loose," I answered. "I'm trying to fix it."

"I can ask the super to do that."

Based on the state of the complex, that wouldn't accomplish much. "So, uh, the people at the ranch you're gonna buy, are they your in-laws?" I don't know what made me ask. Maybe I was wondering why she didn't stay with them?

"No. Not technically. Jason was like the son Terry never had. So, that would make them my adopted family-in-law? Except, they're not together, Kip and Terry." I could hear the clicks of each letter as she wrote something on her phone. "Jason never knew his parents. That's why he wanted a family so bad."

She had a kid, so of course she had a man in her past. Served me right for asking. I gave up on the handle. "Where are your folks?"

She straightened and started going through the kitchen cabinets. "My dad died in a tractor mishap when I was in high school. My mom left of a broken heart shortly after that." She said it like you'd give directions to the nearest gas station.

"Left?" I asked.

"Died."

"Wow. That's a lot."

She shrugged, tapping more into her phone.

So, she knew what it felt like, too. I studied her as she moved, a woman on a mission through her new kitchen. Not sure what I was looking for. A stray tear? A shudder? Could someone actually die of a broken heart?

I wandered across the living room to stand opposite the bar from her. "Well, you met my dad, the uptight retired architect."

She shook her head. "I can't believe he designed his house! Five out of five stars."

My mouth curved with a wave of pride for that centerfold kitchen. It beat the hell out of the bite-sized cubby Ava stood in now. White laminate counters weren't nearly as sexy as black stone. *Shit.* That sounded *housebroken.*

Ava's phone blared on the counter between us. She glanced at the screen, frowned, then answered it. "Hello?" Half a breath later, "Oh, my God! Stop calling me!" Another pause. "Not unless you're retracting your client's offer?"

This ass-wipe again?

"I'm blocking this number." She swiped out of the end-call screen and to the recent call log.

"Mr. Mercedes is still bothering you?"

"Not for long. There. Blocked."

"He'll probably call from a different number," I told her.

"Then I'll block that one, too."

This reeked of bad news. I didn't like it. If I'd known, I would've fought harder to keep Ava at my dad's place. "You could change your number."

She replied with a half-assed laugh. "That seems a little excessive."

"The guy's been harassing you. What's he gonna do when he can't get through?"

She crossed her arms and narrowed her eyes at me. "You sound like you speak from experience?"

"I don't need experience. It's common sense. The man has no boundaries."

"He's a wimp, Eli. He's not going to do anything."

"It's the wimps that fight dirty."

She held my stare, and a long challenge filled the silence. But neither of us won because Nina appeared in the living room in a ruffled swimsuit, goggles, and bright red flip-flops. Nothing like a cute kid to break a moment. But something about her get-up looked off.

"Mama, I'm ready!"

Ava set down her phone and sighed. "Not like that, you're not."

"Pool! I wanna go to the pool!"

"Your suit is on backwards."

"No, it's not!"

"Let me fix it." She ushered Nina down the hall, leaving me in the living room/dining room, staring at her deserted phone.

What was his aim? He wanted her ranch? And her relationship with Terry was keeping him from getting it? Out on the road, I'd seen people go homicidal over less. I pushed off the counter and back to the front door to test the deadbolt. It took effort to slide into place, but it worked. The window had a lock, the screen appeared intact, but a scrap of wood in the track wouldn't hurt. Maybe I had something in the back of my truck?

I was just about to run down and check when Nina came bolting out of the bedroom with a mischievous giggle, and hid behind my legs.

"Nina!" Ava called from down the micro-hall. "Ponytail!"

I twisted to get a look at the kid. Her swimsuit faced the right direction, but her hair looked like one of those before-pictures in a hair ad. "The sooner she gets your hair fixed," I said, "the sooner we can go swimming. I might even teach you the cannonball."

Her eyes lit up.

Ava wandered into the living room holding a bright pink hairbrush, but she headed straight to a stack of boxes. "Where did I put the towels?"

She pried the top one open, then strained as she shifted it to access the one below it. Nina followed like my little shadow as I moved in to help search the stack.

"Thanks." She paused, shook her head, glanced at me, then trailed her eyes down to the little face that peeked out from behind my knee. "What am I thinking? Nina, we can't swim yet. I have to go to the store. We have nothing for dinner."

The kid whined behind me. Ava seemed so ... all over the place. I'd assumed she was like the binders we'd made, neat and organized. But in that moment, she looked more like the box.

"You know," I leaned in close until my mouth was right at her ear, and whispered, "this is exactly what pizza delivery was made for."

The kid must've heard because she jumped up and down, making her little flip-flops squeak. "Pizza! Pizza! I want pizza!"

Ava's expression borderlined desperate when she turned to look over her shoulder at me, putting her lips that much closer to mine. "I suppose I already owe you dinner."

I grinned, inches from her face. "You *did* see my note." Her eyes flicked to my mouth, and my blood went south for the winter. "I'll take a meat-lovers with stuffed crust."

From that close, I could see her pulse thrumming in her neck. "A-Anything else?"

Recognizing a nice kitchen didn't make me housebroken. I was just picking up on the things Ava liked. And in that moment, I think she liked me being that close. "And maybe a salad, for good measure."

15

Ava

EVERYTHING WAS fine until Eli showed up in that darn swimsuit! Curses to the pizza delivery driver who called in sick!

Why couldn't I just enjoy the simple pleasantries of sharing a meal? Being around Eli felt natural, and he was great with Nina, all the makings of a solid friendship. Except my thoughts circled like a vulture around a certain somebody's bare chest as he dove into the pool in his Walmart swim trunks, the ones he purchased while picking up our pizza yesterday. No one should look that appetizing in clearance board shorts. His playfulness, that subtle "V" made by a shameful amount of abdominal definition! I was the worst widow, fantasizing about Eli shirtless when I still owed my husband a ranch!

"What are you doing?"

The question caught me off guard, and I spun on my pile of horse manure to find Eli approaching the corral with a strange look. Instinct took over. "What's wrong? Does Nina need me?"

He stopped at the edge of Royal's stall and rested his elbows on the horizontal bars. The dark Tennessee Walker, whose home I was cleaning, kept to his opposite corner, his tail swishing to starve off flies. "No, she's fine. Dad's teaching her poker. Are you mucking?"

"Yeah, why?"

Seriously! How could a human look so delicious leaning against a fence? It didn't seem to matter that this time he was fully clothed. I was probably just deficient in something. Even a gas station hot dog looked good if you were hungry enough.

Not that Eli was a hot dog.

He adjusted his hat. "I figured you'd be getting ready for your interview."

"Last night, didn't you say Luke was sick?"

Fess up, Ava. He *was* hot. Hot when moving boxes. Hot when eating pizza. Downright blazing, dripping in pool water under a setting sun. *Hot and off-limits.*

My phone buzzed in my pocket. Probably Steven from yet another number. I sighed, fixing my grip on the rake, and returned to my self-ordained task. In a month, Eli'd be gone anyway, and I'd be elbow deep in ranch renovations. *Hopefully.*

"Yeah, but it's almost eight," he pointed out.

"And?"

"Isn't your interview at nine?"

"No. They pushed it to ten."

"Well, don't you need to prep, or primp, or whatever?"

My eyes slid back to his. "Primp?"

"O-or whatever?" Pink tinted his ears. It was enough to make a sentimental girl ovulate.

Maybe I was. Ovulating. "What, you don't think I should roll in all sweaty and covered in horsehair?" Color bled into his cheeks and neck.

In reality, I should've been at the apartment unpacking or following up with Terry. Instead, I was ... what was I doing? My phone went off again. I forced my eyes back to the mud and scraped the soiled stall with extra fervor.

"Someone's calling you," Eli said unnecessarily. "Is it him? Mr. Mercedes?"

"Probably."

"You gonna block him?"

Steven's persistence used to be an endearing trait. Now I just found it annoying. "When I'm done."

Eli pursed his lips, then ducked through the bars and strode right at me, his broody aura giving him an appeal that must've made old western film stars popular. *Giddy-up cowboy.*

His t-shirt grazed my arm as he stopped only inches away, heat radiating through the thin cotton, his pulse vibrating the air around us. I was trying to do the right thing, swear to God. Could he feel how hard my heart thumped? Would he believe me if I blamed the mucking?

"Give me your phone." He had his own in-hand, thumbing up the voice memo app.

"Why?"

"Because I think you should report Mr. Mercedes for harassment, and I'm gonna help you get proof."

Ah. He planned to record Steven's voice. Which I would've figured out all on my own if I wasn't so ... distracted. "It's fine. He's just being a pest. I can deal with pests."

"Yeah? And when the whole swarm follows?"

"We're talking about a human. He's one man. Not a colony of wasps."

"I think you're underestimating him."

I sighed at Eli's serious expression, then reluctantly handed over my phone. He frowned at the missed-call screen, but I assured him Steven would call again.

Who knew an exhale could sound angry? "Next time, could you try not arguing with me?"

My hackles rose. "Hey! I didn't ask for help. Not that it's your business, but I refuse to let Steven dictate my schedule by dropping everything to field his calls."

"I'm not saying you do that, I'm just saying, let's be smart and–"

"Let's?" When did this become a "we" thing? "No. This isn't your fight, Eli. And I'd appreciate it if you stayed out of it." I snagged my cell from his grip, shoved it back in my pocket, and turned on my heels to bob through the horizontal railings. Was he right? Maybe. But hell if I wanted him to swoop in and fix things! I needed to prove I could do this on my own. Otherwise, how the heck would I run an entire ranch by myself?

When I returned with a wheelbarrow, Eli held the stall gate open, forcing me to pass him. The zest of his deodorant tickled my nose, not unpleasantly. I held my breath, but he trailed me right into my pile of manure. Back to inches apart. *Seriously?*

What's a girl gotta do? "I can finish this on my own, thanks."

My phone buzzed in my pocket again. This time, he didn't comment. Only stared at our feet, letting the seconds tick by. Judging by the twitch in his jaw, it was a struggle.

"Thank you."

He accepted my truce with a bashful, one-sided lip lift that very nearly resembled a smolder. "You're welcome."

Lord help me.

"Hey, I was thinking," he said, performing his signature move–running his fingers through his hair and re-adjusting his hat. He hesitated so long I'd have checked my watch if I had one. I didn't primp, but neither did my plan include going to my interview smelling like a three-day-old shirt. A smell that apparently offered no discouragement on his part.

Finally, I gave him a little push. "You were thinking?"

"I know Luke can be ... challenging," he said. At my drawn brow, he rushed on, "And I'm sure he'll get over his whole 'Yuppy Horse Lady' thing."

"Y-Yuppy Horse Lady?"

"His words," Eli defended, casting me a glance. "He's a quick learner, and he's reliable. He just gets defensive."

I was feeling a little defensive myself. "Eli, where are you going with this?"

He planted his hands on his hips and blew a lungful of air at our feet. "He needs some training. And I'm not a rancher. Dad doesn't have the patience, so I was kinda hoping ..." he met my gaze again, letting his meaning hang, unspoken.

"You were hoping he'd listen to Yuppy Horse Lady?"

My eyes fell on the hollow of his cheek as he chewed on his next words. "The kid needs a thing."

"A *thing*?"

"You know, something he's good at, that he can do even on the crappy days. To lift him up when he's feeling low–so he doesn't make bad choices."

I nodded in understanding. "A thing."

Concerned creased Eli's forehead under the bill of his cap; a layer I'd not seen before, and it made me wonder, *what's Eli's thing?* "I want to help," I said, hefting a healthy scoop of manure into the wheelbarrow. "But Luke doesn't like me. I think he'll respond better to you."

"Yeah, but I didn't know about the oats."

"And now you do. Imagine what else you'll learn by summer's end." I gave him a playful wink to soften my rejection, realizing too late how flirty it came off. Luckily, Eli's cell started ringing before he could respond.

He checked the screen, then brought it to his ear. "Dad? Did you mean to call me?" A pause. "No. We're at the stable. Just come out. What?" His eyes narrowed and sought mine. Something passed through them. Anger? Defiance?

I tilted my head in question, and he turned away.

"No. Just–" he spun, surveying the grounds. "I'll be right there." To me, he said, "Ava, do me a favor? Go into the tack room to check the horse blankets for rips?"

"What?"

"Wait there till I get back." He didn't elaborate, just turned and strode purposefully toward the house.

Horse blankets? What just happened?

I complied, but only because it couldn't have been about Nina, or Bill would have called me. This was their ranch, after all. I was only a guest.

Nearly thirty minutes later, Eli stormed into the makeshift storeroom, a large ring of keys jingling from his hand and an expression made of steel and fury. I'd sifted through the stack of wool, all solid and tear-free, then organized the leads and bridles, putting the nicest ones in the front. I got the distinct impression he noticed none of that.

"We've been leaving the gate open," he said without preamble. "That's going to change." He pulled a key off the ring and held it out, halting a full two feet from where I stood.

Alarm crawled up my spine. "Why? What's going on?"

He studied me, his lips locked.

"Eli?"

"Doesn't matter. You gonna take this?"

I edged my hand out, and he pressed the laser-cut metal into my open palm. They didn't have a ranch sign to graffiti or a water tower to shoot at. No clues stood out in his appearance. "What happened? Is your dad okay?"

"He's fine. Don't lose that."

I curled my fingers around the key and sank it into my pocket. He may as well have said, "Not your business." And how could I complain? I'd argued the same point. "Okay. Thank you. Am I allowed to go now? I do have an interview to *primp* for."

The hardened edges of Eli's face faded as a smile snuck in. "Thought you said you didn't do that."

"Well, I need a shower at least. I'm sure I stink."

He stepped forward, closing the distance between us, and tilted his nose to my hair. "Nah. You smell good."

My words strayed off somewhere in the interlinking channels of my brain. He offered no tension-breaking chuckle. Just those intense burnt-caramel eyes on me. It would never work. We were opposites. I hustled, he played. I wanted roots; he'd never stay.

"You and Bill are good with Nina?"

"Yup, they're having breakfast."

"Another one?" Nina must be gearing up for a growth spurt. Or maybe I wasn't feeding her enough?

Eli grasped my shoulders, spun me, and marched me out of the tack stall. "Go. Do your *not-primping* thing." The weight of his hands sank deep into my skin, warming the lonely little corners of my soul. "And good luck on the interview."

"Thanks."

I wanted a hot dog. But if I kept my distance, the temptation would pass. And I wouldn't wind up with a bellyache later.

Still got it!

Roxy's engine purred, just like Eli promised, and I got the job, just like he'd said I would. Part of me couldn't wait to share the news with him. The other hastily threw up roadblocks to keep me on track–something to pick apart another day. I turned up the radio, tapping the steering wheel to the beat of a country song as I cruised down the lone paved road toward Bill's ranch.

All but officially employed, I had some unknowns to solve: long-term daycare for Nina, a loan approval, a revised business plan per Terry's questions. But the momentum of my accomplishments pulled me forward, and the fight felt a little less taxing for once. *Progress.*

Bill sat alone on the porch in a blue Adirondack when I pulled up to the house. I parked next to Eli's truck, then snagged my purse and the white bakery bag next to me before hopping out.

"How'd it go?" he asked.

"Really well. It's not official yet, but they want to hire me!"

"Well, look at you!" His genuine pride filled me like a birthday balloon.

I hiked the steps and joined him on the porch. "How was Nina?"

"She did great. We did a little of everything today. Brushed the horses, made pancakes, played cards."

"Poker, was it?"

"Go-fish. And she kicked my behind. Twice."

I laughed. "You shouldn't have let her win!"

"I didn't." Based on the smile lines behind his glasses, he didn't seem too sore about it. He rose from his chair. "Anyway, I just put her down for a nap about twenty minutes ago." His back elongated. "She's in the den. Fell right to sleep."

I gaped at him, wondering how I'd gotten so lucky to end up here while simultaneously fretting how to avoid Eli while I waited for her to wake up. "You're amazing. Especially since Eli agreed to watch her."

Bill shrugged. "He was a little busy."

Busy doing what? "Well, thank you." I opened the white paper bag and offered Bill first pick.

"What's this?"

"Some of the best baked goods in Phoenix."

"I do love a good pastry." He pulled out an apple fritter, holding it up to admire its assortment of glazed bumps and dark crevices. "Oh, yeah. That's a good one." His first bite ended in an appreciative moan. The same reaction I'd had upon discovering the hole in the wall bakery five years ago. I beamed.

"Holy hell, this is good," he said around a mouthful. "Do me a favor?"

"Of course."

"Don't tell Eli."

I furrowed my brow. "About what?"

"About the pastries. 'Cause I'm not sharing." At my smirk, he added, "He'll thank me. He's always complaining about extra sugar and being fit or some such nonsense."

"Really? When we first met, he was buying peanut butter cups and beer."

Bill brushed the glaze off the side of his mouth with his fingertips, the jovial creases fading from his eyes. "He does that sometimes. When he's had a bad day."

The day he got saddled with me and all my drama. He bought Nina dinner and took a scolding from his dad, all so a stranger didn't have to crawl back to her newly appointed ex. Without complaining once. And then he fixed my truck! Who did that? Who was that selfless?

That's when I remembered the envelope of cash in my purse.

"Can you hold this for me?" I handed Bill the pastry bag, then skipped to Eli's truck and tried the driver's side door. *Unlocked, perfect.* This time, I tucked the payment inside the center console so that he'd find it after we parted ways. The thought stirred a strange weight in my chest.

Bill lifted an eyebrow when I met him back on the porch. "What's that about?"

"I'm trying to pay Eli for the work he did on my Chevy."

"I don't think he plans to take your money."

I dropped my voice to a whisper. "That's why I'm hiding it."

The older man chuckled and handed me the pastries. "I'm not getting in the middle of *that*."

Yes, *that* had taken on a life of its own, and I wasn't sure what to do with it. "Do you want the macadamia nut?"

"All yours."

I fished out a cookie and took a huge bite. Soft dough and firm nuts paired in a delicious partnership. I'd always thought macadamia nut cookies were more dynamic than gooey chocolate chip. My eyes slid back to Eli's truck.

"We don't always see eye to eye," Bill said, pulling me from dangerous musings. "Eli doesn't understand why I built the ranch. I don't understand how he hops around from place to place."

"It sounds exhausting, always being on the move."

"He's a skilled mechanic," Bill continued. "Good with people. Kids especially." He paused, and when I turned to him, he was studying me. "Sure would be nice if he stuck around."

"Have you told him that?"

"Don't know if you've noticed, but he likes to do the opposite of what I ask."

I thought back to that first night. "Opposite" didn't seem like the right word. "There's more than one way to tie a lasso. Maybe he just does things differently."

A sly smile crept up Bill's face. "Maybe." He tilted his head to the pastry bag. "Why don't you go offer him one of those?"

"What? You'd share the best pastries in all of Phoenix?"

He shrugged. "I'm not afraid to pull cheap shots."

"You think he'll stay for cookies?"

"Perhaps."

Hmm. I regarded him with suspicion.

Bill tilted his head toward the house. "He's in the kitchen."

"The kitchen?" I glanced at the front windows and then his Ford. Dang it! He probably saw my whole charade!

I found Eli at the long table with the binder we'd made, scribbling something on a pad of paper, much like a kid finishing his homework before the bus came. My eyes skated over his broad shoulders.

Yeah, maybe the high school linebacker. Fit, indeed.

"Whatcha working on?" I tried to keep my voice light, non-committal.

"What?" He straightened, flipped the top sheets back into line, and stood before I could look over his shoulder. "Oh, nothing. How'd your interview go?"

"Good. Great, actually. I pretty much have the job."

A sunny smile lit his face. "I knew you would." His eyes drifted to the bag in my hands. "What's that?"

"It's, um, doughnuts and cookies."

"Aw, honey, you shouldn't have."

Suddenly, he was moving into my bubble. *Again.*

"They're full of sugar and fat." I gulped. This wasn't high school football, and I wasn't the quarterback, so there was no need to be so close.

After a peek inside the bag, he cut me a devious look that all but melted my good sense. "These are my favorite."

I watched speechless as he extracted a peanut butter cookie. Unlike Bill's reaction, Eli's groan of pleasure hit low in my belly and left me breathless. Maybe it was the intense eye contact? Heat surged simultaneously up and down my body as he chewed. Sharp angles, flexing muscles, paired with soft lips tempting enough to bite. *Dynamic.*

He inched closer, his Adam's apple bobbing as he swallowed. *Heaven, help me.* If I didn't draw a line, the curve of his lips would take us in the wrong direction, roadblocks be damned.

When his gaze dropped to my mouth, my stupid drummer missed a beat. Feral instinct pulled me in, drew my eyes down his face. To the manly growth of stubble. He made me feel young, vibrant. Maybe it was his carefree take on life? Like the world still held endless possibilities. Maybe kissing him would send me back to a time before responsibilities. Before all the sacrifices. Before grief. What would it be like to live without those, even for just a few minutes?

One and done.

Jason's promise blew in out of nowhere, pelting me with guilt and shame, jolting my senses back into rhythm. *What am I thinking?* Kissing wasn't a time machine. It wouldn't erase anything, only add complication.

Libido and guilt had been throwing me around the ring all day. I needed to regain charge of this stupid match, needed to stop staring at his mouth as if it might save me.

In fact, his one-sided tease of a smile might just kill me.

I snagged the bag back from him. "One is enough for you."

My hasty exit took me to the den where I spent the rest of Nina's nap lying on the floor next to her, staring at the ceiling. When had I become so desperate? I needed to stop relying on others, to stop prioritizing goodness over reality. Ultimately, Eli would follow his own interests. He had a life. And so did we. And they were hundreds of miles apart.

I made a promise to my husband well before I set foot on Bill's ranch. Until I secured Hidden Meadows, I had no business with side hustles.

I needed to discourage Eli. To shut down the flirting for good.

16

Eli

I STARED out the kitchen window, drinking my coffee. Dirt, rocks, and more dirt. Without Ava, the whole ranch felt bland. The nice thing about being on the road? If a place got boring, you just moved on.

Dad shuffled into the kitchen in his polo and jeans, straight to the coffee. Someone had to tell him ranchers didn't wear golf shirts, but it wasn't gonna be me.

"Got any plans today?" he asked.

I pulled out my phone. "Working on one." *6:19. Too early to text her?* "No Luke again today. Kid's got a bad case of food poisoning."

"Bummer. Welp, I'm sure you'll figure it out. Just don't ask me to muck."

"Wouldn't dream of it." A minute passed on my screen, but all I saw were Ava's cola eyes turning drunk when she watched me eat that cookie. She was definitely interested. And there was something I'd been dying to do. Been up all night thinking about it.

Dad opened the fridge. "Good idea. Call her."

"You think it's too early? I mean, who? Call who?"

"Tell her I'll watch the kid." As fast as he showed up, he disappeared around the corner with his insulated travel cup.

He's in a good mood.

Another minute turned over on my screen. *Just do it.* Better to text early, before it got too hot.

I was stuck on a call when Ava showed up to leave Nina with my dad. By the time I met her at the stables, she'd already started raking. This time she wore a loose shirt and jeans. Still sexy as hell. I leaned against the railing. She seemed to like that yesterday.

"It's rude to stare," she snapped.

I grinned. "Nina's building a fort with Dad. Well, it's mostly built. She's overseeing."

"Great. Thanks for the play-by-play."

"Just saying, they're good for a while."

She didn't even look up. "I'm sorry. Am I going too slow for you?"

"Whoa. What's with the hostility?"

She stuck the fork in the manure and shot me a kick-to-the-nuts kind of look. Good thing there was a fence between us. "What do you want, Eli?"

Did I miss something? "Are you okay?"

"I'm fine." She went back to cleaning poop and ignoring me.

Push it, or back off? "I'm just saying, we have all morning."

"I don't know where you're going with this, but I will throw this rake at you."

My laugh made her scowl. I ducked through the bars and crossed to her. She had the same feisty energy as Sugar. Muttering about bubbles, she wrenched her pronged weapon back, and it rained manure.

Even more reason to go for it. What did I have to lose? I looked her dead on so there'd be no confusion. Stood close enough, she'd have to stop and face me. "We should go for a ride."

"Eli, personal space!"

I took a half-step back and repeated myself. She pressed her palm into my chest, and I let her shove me a few more inches, if only because I liked her touching me. "Better?" I asked. Something was off. She was like a bridge troll. A sexy one. I just had to figure out the riddle. "Ava, let's go for a ride."

"Like on a horse?"

"Of course!" I laughed. "What'd you think I meant?" I couldn't tell if the pink in her cheeks was new. "We should go now. Before it gets any hotter."

She frowned and narrowed a glare at me. "Why?"

"Why?" *Wow.* Another hit to the nuts. "Uh, because it's a sunny day and ..." I took off my hat. Fixed the mess underneath. "And because I want to?"

She turned her back to me.

"It will probably make you feel better," I added.

"I said I'm fine." If that rake had a pulse, her white knuckles would've choked it out.

"You know how to ride a horse, right?"

Annoyed eyes cut to me. I could almost see her hackles rise. "Of course, I do! Do *you*?"

"I'm a little rusty. Maybe you can show me a thing or two." She didn't take the bait. "Tell you what," I coaxed. "I'll saddle the horses. You want Sugar or Chuck?"

"Eli, you can't just ride other people's horses without permission."

"Then I guess it's good I just got off the phone with the owner."

She huffed, just like Sugar, and threw the rake out in a wide sweep, scraping metal teeth over my boots.

I stared at the little lines scored into the leather toe. "Well, now you owe me."

"I don't owe you anything. You shouldn't be so close. In fact, if you had time to go for a ride, why did you call me to muck?"

I frowned. That didn't seem like her at all. "I guess I'll take Sugar out on my own."

The rake stopped an inch from my foot, and Ava shot me a doubting stare.

"What?" I teased. "You don't think I can do it?" I took a step closer, toe-to-toe, face-to-face. Was it me, or was she holding her breath? "Are you worried about me?"

"No!" came her too-fast response. Her focus dropped to our feet. "Will you back up, please?"

"You're worried about me." I didn't bother hiding my smile.

She tucked an errant wisp of hair behind her ear. "I'm worried about the horse."

"Fine, for Sugar's sake, then. She needs some exercise."

Ava stabbed the prongs of the rake into her poop pile. "God, Eli. You can be so aggravating."

Aggravating? She wanted to talk about aggravating? Aggravating was this need to touch her. Urges twitched under my fingers, taking way too much brain power to hold back. That flash of skin at her waist, where her shirt hiked up, it taunted me. The way the sun slid across her tanned arm, I wanted to slide my hand across it, too. This woman had no idea what it took to hold back.

I curled my fingers into fists. "Go for a ride with me? Please?"

She chewed on her bottom lip as she cut a glance to Sugar, then back to me. *That bottom lip ...* It kept me up at night. I waited for the snap–the refusal. I had no more cards. If she said no, I'd have to walk away. Did I read it wrong? Had I imagined that lusty look in Dad's kitchen?

With a breathy exhale, her shoulders sank, and she finally sheathed her daggers. "*I'll* ride Sugar. But I'm saddling her." She took a step back. "Give her some time in the ring first."

When I didn't move, Ava deadpanned. "And wipe that stupid, slap-happy grin off your face. You're like a kid on Christmas morning."

I grinned wider. "All that's missing is the bow."

"Eli."

"Ava?"

She tilted her head to one side and stared at me. Wisps of hair escaped and flew around her face. I couldn't stop myself. I reached out and tucked one behind her ear.

Her body stilled, and my favorite word rolled off her tongue. "Eli?" If only I could record it as my ringtone.

"Yes, Ava?"

Did she know she wet her lips as she stared back? Heat traveled down my body like adrenaline, only better. Way more addictive. My heart thudded, my eyes dipped to her mouth, and the world narrowed to the curve of her jaw and her honey skin.

Plump, very kissable lips parted. "You're standing in my manure pile."

The words buzzed in front of me, edging around my head, looking for an opening or a back door, finally seeping through my thick skull. I glanced down at my boots, now covered in muddy horse poop. "I'd stand in worse to be near you."

Ava fisted her hand, looking like she wished it were around my neck. Then she opened it and shoved it into my pec. "Go. Put Sugar in the arena while I finish up."

"Yes, ma'am."

Her voice as my ringtone, her handprint tattooed on my chest—hell, I could almost die a happy man.

With a scrapper in one hand and Sugar's hoof in the other, Ava watched me saddle Chuck. "Check your strap. It looks loose."

"This must be how Luke felt," I mumbled.

"What?"

"Nothing."

I tugged the leather to the next notch. If it was too tight, Chuck didn't complain. He seemed more interested in nosing Ava's back. Can't say I blamed him.

She returned to scraping mud off Sugar's hoof, stiff as a ship boarded up for a storm.

I tested the saddle. It didn't budge. "How's this?"

No response. Maybe she had trouble seeing from under the brim of that sexy straw cowgirl hat she'd grabbed from her truck? Sauntering over, I hunkered down to her level, while she tried her best to ignore me.

"Hey." I tapped a finger under the brim so it lifted from her eyes. "Relax. This is supposed to be fun."

She pushed it back down and moved to the next hoof. I followed and tapped it up again, smiling. Now that I'd seen that lusty stare, it got harder not to just kiss her. I imagined it everywhere. Pushed up against the tack room wall. Dragging her across the bench in my truck at a stoplight. Lifting her onto the edge of the kitchen sink when her hands were all soapy, and her legs could wrap around me.

This time, when she shoved her hat back down, she said, "What, are you five? Knock it off!" Then she pushed past me to the tack room.

I ran a hand down my face. Took off my hat and slapped it against my leg. *What did I do wrong?*

We finished saddling in silence, and I started wondering if this was a bad idea. But as soon as Ava threw a leg over Sugar's back, her shoulders dropped. She lifted her face to the sun, and I could practically see the walls coming down. I scanned the ranch from Chuck's saddle. Yeah, the world felt lighter from higher ground. Perfect timing. I needed a lift.

Hooves on the rocky terrain tapped out a beat as we took

the trail behind the house and climbed the mountainside. Ava handled Sugar like a pro, finding the best footing, totally in control. It had been years since I'd taken a trail ride, but Chuck and I found our groove, too. Except for when he kept stopping to eat the vegetation.

The farther in we rode, the more the world slowed, the less important stuff seemed. Life was simple. Just me and a pretty girl on horseback. Nothing else mattered. Not gigs, not bills, not the stupid shit I did in high school, or the hell I'd put Dad through. The ride cleared my head better than any day under a greasy engine.

We stopped at the peak. Phoenix looked like one of Dad's models. Little boxes with tiny reflective surfaces. Fluffs of green polka-dotting the side of the freeway. A sharp wind whipped over the cliff and dried the sweat on my neck. Ava cried out and threw a hand to her head, but too late. The gust caught her hat and blew it clear off. I tossed her my reins and dismounted to run after it. Not gonna lie, it felt a little heroic when I brushed off the dirt and handed it back.

"Thank you." Her lips curved up—a little ray of sunshine.

"There it is," I said.

"What?"

"That smile I've been waiting for."

She forced the corners of her mouth down and shoved the hat back on. "You know, for a mechanic, you ride well."

My turn to force down a grin. *Play it cool.* "That's because I'm not a mechanic."

"You're not a mechanic?"

I stuck a foot in the stirrup, but Chuck thought it would be funny to wander forward and make me hop after him. "Come on, man." *Definitely not cool.* The only silver lining, it got a snicker out of Ava. "No." I hoisted myself up and settled back in the saddle. "Mechanics is just something I can do."

"Oh." Did she seem disappointed? "What would you call yourself, then?"

Adventurous? Carefree? I glanced back. She was studying me. Pretty sure those things wouldn't impress her.

I shrugged. "Not sure yet."

"Hmm." Her eyes slid to the open sky.

"What about you? You're not a real estate agent?" I teased.

"Office administrator, thank you very much."

Was her ice finally melting? "Right. That. You're not an office admin. So, what are *you*?"

Instead of spouting some ready answer, she stared at the city below. I urged Chuck backwards to stand beside Sugar. Sweat, horsehair, and dust itched my nose, and the heat made my muscles lazy. I'd peg her as a cowgirl, but if she didn't want to admit it, that was fine. Who cared about titles, anyway?

"Be a good boy," Mom said as she was dying.

"Good Boy" was a title. One that came with a bunch of expectations. A set-up for letting everyone down. I gave Chuck a neck scratch. Sometimes, titles only made things worse.

Just when I figured she'd forgotten the question, she looked at me and said, "I think ... I think I'm just lost." She may have been talking about herself, but it was like she'd seen straight through to my soul.

Lost.

The word burrowed in my brain. Into places no one saw. Thoughts and feelings I'd never shared started burning my tongue like hot sauce. Dad once told me, "Pain either fuels a man to meet his potential, or leaves him for dead." We were fighting about the drugs he found under my bed. At the time, I thought he was talking about the pain in his ass I was causing him.

Ava let out a heavy breath, then blinked away. "Sorry. That's probably not what you meant."

"It's a good answer." Her sad smile made it difficult to swallow, and a new title came to mind.

Yours.

I shoved it away. She didn't want a romp or a fling. She wanted plans and picket fences. A full five-course dinner, and I was just a fast-food hamburger. No amount of condiments would make me look like a steak.

She made a clicking sound and turned Sugar toward the trail. "We should probably head back. The horses need water."

"Sure."

As I followed silently, I hoped the new, sharp sensation in my chest wouldn't leave me for dead.

17

Ava

It didn't tear me apart.

My first ride since the accident, I'd anticipated panic or overwhelming sadness. But, once in that saddle, things just felt right. Whole. The sun blazed above, and we were drowning in sweat by the time we returned to the stables, yet eager energy coursed through me.

I ran the brush over Sugar's withers, catching Eli's sidelong glances as he gave Chuck the same treatment. He flicked his eyes back to his task, but every so often they'd return to me. We played that game for several minutes until I stopped and waited to catch him. It didn't take long.

I'd expected him to ride with the same authenticity as his boots, which were clearly not made for ranch work, so the confidence he displayed on Chuck threw me. I didn't know what to think. "Is there something you want to say?"

He cleared his throat. "You're buying a ranch. What are you gonna do about a ranch manager?"

Ah. Business was better than personal, right? "I had one lined up," I told him. "Augustino. He used to work at Hidden Meadows. He's amazing with horses and can fix just about anything." *If he's still around.* I chewed my bottom lip. New priority: call August.

"Why did he leave Hidden Meadows?"

"The ranch was hit with pretty negative media attention. Almost everyone left."

"Guess you're all set, then."

Hopefully. Maybe Eli would have better luck with a trainable ranch hand? Except, who would train them? I had too much on my plate to take on another role. "You know, if you could just get someone good with horses, my guy might be willing to train them for you. He might even know someone who's looking for work. I could ask. I have to call him anyway."

"Sure, I guess."

Eli resumed brushing. This time, his eyes stayed on the roan. Once we'd watered the horses, I followed him back to the house.

He stopped at the front door. "You want some lunch. I can make sandwiches."

"Actually, I should call August."

The little hollow at the hinge of his jaw flexed. I should've been relieved. The flirty smiles and playful banter had finally stopped. Eli lingered in the doorway as I pulled out my cell.

"Want me to stay and talk to him?" he asked.

Our ride was nice. Really nice. I didn't want to tarnish it. "No, we have catching up to do."

His shoulders held an edgy tension as he closed the door behind him, leaving me alone on the porch. I pressed a hand into my chest. No matter what I did, guilt surfaced. Why did everything have to be so complicated? This call was complicated, too. I'd ghosted August for almost a year. He may not even want to talk to me. My heart hammered as I put the phone to my ear. Each ring forced the muscle higher up my throat until, when he answered, I could barely speak.

"*¿Bueno?*" *Yes?* He sounded just the same as I remembered him.

"H-hi, August." I waited out an elongated pause. Why didn't he reply? Maybe he'd deleted my contact? Maybe I was just some random woman calling him?

Finally, he said, "I am looking at my phone, and I cannot believe it."

The familiar meandering lilt of his accent, the playful fall of his words, was like hearing my favorite song on the radio. "I know. I'm sorry. It's been a while."

"I started to wonder if maybe you changed your phone?"

"No. Same number. Same ol' Ava. I'm sorry I didn't call you. I have no good excuse."

"No. Not the same. But still, I am happy to hear your voice."

I twisted an errant strand of hair around my finger. "You're not mad?"

"*Mi Amor*, I can never be mad at you."

He'd always called me that, even in front of Jason. Something about it now coaxed my heart back into my chest.

"I am thinking maybe *you* are mad at me?" he said. "That is why you don't call?"

"Of course not! Why would I be mad?"

He didn't respond right away, and in that time, I tried to imagine his point of view. Losing his best friend, then the severed contact with his best friend's wife?

"I thought ... Maybe he was gonna be okay, no?" he said. "This is why I pulled you away."

I'd lost my mind in front of all those people. He'd been the one to take me aside while the paramedics arrived.

"Yeah. Me too." I let out a watery breath. "I'm sorry. I was never mad at you. If anything, I blamed myself."

"*Mijo*, that is crazy."

August's words poked air holes in my heavy conscience. "I should've asked him to wait a few more days. Or been outside, managing the crowd. Or picked up that stupid trash bag." Its sudden flurry into the air had spooked the horse. So simple, so preventable.

"All the time, you are thinking this?" When I didn't answer, he let out a low whistle. "So, you are calling me? Does this mean you finally say yes and marry me?"

An unfiltered laugh burst out of me. Another thing he'd say in front of Jason. "And disappoint that long string of devoted fangirls?"

For as much as he joked, he knew my heart lived in Jason's tender embrace. I hadn't realized how much I'd yearned for a connection to him. Someone who knew him as I did. My trepidation suddenly seemed so foolish. "Actually, I'm calling to see if you knew anyone looking for work? I have a friend who needs a ranch manager."

"You are that friend?"

I laughed again. "No, but I'm still planning to buy Hidden Meadows. And I still want you on my team, if you aren't already spoken for."

"You even have to ask? What's it called? The one for your friend?"

"It doesn't have a name. It's a boarding ranch thirty minutes south of Phoenix."

"What they are offering?"

Shoot, I should've asked. "I'm not sure. But they're having trouble finding someone, so I suggested a trainable ranch hand. The problem is, there's no one here to train them."

"You are there?"

"I am, but I'm swamped trying to get Terry to sell me Hidden Meadows."

Confusion tinted his tone when he said, "He not wanna sell to you?"

"It's kind of complicated." *Just ask, Ava!* "I was actually wondering if you could help train someone?"

August's end went silent. It occurred to me then that he might be out of state. Happy in a current job. That maybe I'd put too much hope in this plan.

"I'm so rude, I didn't even ask where you are these days. Or *how* you are! Are you still in Arizona?"

He laughed. "No, but tell me where and I will come by. We will talk more then."

I hesitated. Maybe this was too big an ask. "You don't have to. I don't want you to uproot your life. I don't even know if anything will pan out."

"But you asked for my help."

"I did."

"So, I say yes."

I sighed. Who could argue with that? "Okay. I'll text you the address."

A genuine smile traced my lips on the drive back to our apartment. I couldn't wait to see August! Finally, our past felt in reach. A slow revival, but each connection brought us closer.

The bland browns and tans of our two-story complex came into view. I glanced at Nina. She folded and unfolded a drawing Bill had made for her. The kind where when you creased the paper, it changed into something else. "You ready for some lunch, Crackerjack?"

If she answered, I missed it because when I pulled into the parking lot, my eyes fell on a familiar black Mercedes. "You have got to be kidding me!" Steven approached my truck in full-suited swagger before I'd even finished pulling into a spot. "F-ried funnel cakes! Nina, I'll be just a second." I slid out of the truck with the engine still running and closed the door behind me.

"Ava! I've been trying to call you." His friendly tone only raised my guard.

"And I've been trying to avoid you. What are you doing here?"

He tucked his hands in his pockets, but his feigned bashfulness didn't come close to genuine. Though his hair looked a little disheveled. Odd for him.

"I wanted to see you," he said.

"And you knew I'd be here ... how?"

He shrugged. "I didn't. It's just a coincidence."

Like I was buying that.

"I'm here to see Mark," he said. "We're friends."

Mark? Who's Mark? I glanced over my shoulder at the complex as a disheartening realization hit me. *My landlord.* And he was probably one of Steven's clients! *Double-fried funnel cakes!* Fine. So, he knew where I lived? That didn't have to be an issue. We were both adults.

"You look good," Steven said, pulling my attention back to him. No matter the weather, he never sweated in his crisp business get-up.

Does he bathe in antiperspirant? "What do you want?"

"Grab dinner with me."

"No."

"Why not?"

Seriously? "Because you are trying to steal my ranch out from under me."

"I wasn't trying to steal it. I had assumed you moved on. Got over it."

I blinked at him. "Got over what? My husband's death?"

"Yes. No. The whole ranch life."

"Why would you think that?"

"Come on, Ava. You're a rock star in the office. You could make a killing in real estate. Wouldn't that be better? For Nina?"

"I think we have different definitions of success. Garcias don't thrive under artificial light and cedar-scented diffusers."

"Fine, you can have a window office."

"You're missing the point. I want my ranch. The second I said it, you should have validated that and backed off."

"Ava." He ran a hand through his hair, moving the slicked spikes more out of place. "There are tons of ranches for sale. Cheaper. In better shape. Closer to town. I have three properties sitting on my desk that you'd probably love."

"Wow. Are you trying to sweet-talk me out of my dream? Real classy, Steven."

"No. I'm not telling you to give up your dream. Just be practical. Running a ranch is nothing like running an office."

"I see. Have you run a ranch before?"

This was dumb. Arguing with him would only kill brain cells. His focus would always be on the next sale. On pleasing the client. "Listen up, because I won't repeat myself. Terry and I have a deal, and I'm going to the bank tomorrow to get a preapproval. So, show those better, cheaper properties to your client. And don't call me. Unless it's to congratulate me on my new ranch."

I swung my car door open and slid into the seat before he could respond. Dramatic as it sounded, I left him there, gaping in the parking lot. If he knew Mark, he could find out what unit we occupied, but I didn't want to lead him right to our door.

Two hours later, I pulled back into the apartment lot sans Mercedes, the bed of my truck loaded with $200 worth of stuff I didn't need, a cranky toddler who'd missed her nap, and a creeping suspicion that this wasn't over.

The next morning, my phone pinged with a text.

August: I am at the gate.

Ava: Great! I'm almost there. See you in two minutes.

He had the same faded red Ford Ranger, scratched and rusted from decades of use and sun. I jumped out of my idling Chevy with a squeal and ran straight into the biggest, most satisfying hug I'd had all year.

"August! You're here."

Everything about him felt familiar and welcoming, his cinnamon chewing gum, the softness of his worn Diamondbacks t-shirt–the sense of home and belonging. This is what I fought so hard for.

He leaned back and laughed. "You missed me, no?"

"No. Not at all."

"Little liar." His thick accent made the accusation poetic. Dark, humored eyes squinted past me to my truck. "Is she there? Baby Nina?"

"She's not a baby anymore. She's changed a lot."

August's smile faltered slightly, and he looked back at me. "Well, you are not changed at all. Es-cept, you're looking a little eh … *flaca*." *Skinny.*

"I'll have you know I put on five pounds my first week in an office job."

"Yeah?" He made a show of looking around me. "Where did it go?"

I grinned. "Shall we?" I spun the key ring around a finger before unlocking the main gate.

August waited while I locked back up and took the lead. As we drove down the gravel road to the house, a strange chord of déjà vu vibrated through me. Relief mingled with trepidation. I stopped my truck at the stables and shot off a quick text to Eli. August parked next to me and followed me to the passenger door, grinning wide as a proud uncle when I unstrapped Nina's harness and fitted her to my hip.

"Little Nina, you grow so much!" He ruffled her hair, and she reared back.

Time for a proper introduction. "Nina, this is your daddy's best friend, August."

Her expression could only be described as skeptical. She wouldn't remember all the times he'd rocked her to sleep while Jason and I took sunset rides after work.

"You were very little to remember," August said. "It's good you're not trusting strangers. Soon I am not gonna be a stranger, okay?" Settled, he stuck his hands on his hips and surveyed the stables. "It's not what I expected."

"If you think this needs work, wait until you see Hidden Meadows."

He wrapped an arm around my shoulders. "You always have big dreams."

This was going to work. Under August's supervision and tutelage, Bill would get a solid, trained manager. Maybe even a little facelift for the ranch. August and I could reconnect and brainstorm for Hidden Meadows. And Terry would see that I wasn't doing it alone.

Then the lower-level side door to the house creaked open, and Eli walked out. In his coveralls, no less, sleeves rolled, forearms on display. *Why?* Was I being punished? August's arm suddenly weighed heavily across my shoulders. I tried to ignore it. I wasn't doing anything wrong, but my knowing friend let out a low hum, his eyes sliding toward me. Okay, so I had a type! In my defense, I didn't know Eli's profession before coming here. And who said I couldn't be friends with a mechanic? A sexy mechanic who approached us with a growing scowl.

I stepped aside so August could have his arm back. Eli halted a few feet in front of us.

"Eli!" I greeted a little too enthusiastically. "This is August. The friend I was telling you about." Good grief, what was wrong with my voice? *Take it down an octave.* "August, this is Eli, the one looking for a ranch manager."

Neither spoke for a good thirty seconds, and the optimistic dream from moments earlier unraveled like a thrift store sweater.

August's attention crawled over Eli's mechanic's uniform. "Ava says you need me to train somebody?"

Eli sized up August in return. "Maybe. Gotta find somebody first."

"I know a few guys might be looking for work. You want I can call them?"

"No. I'm good."

I had to grasp this loose thread before the whole plan came undone. "What he means is that they already have a listing posted." Eli cut a cool glance my way.

August scratched his chin, inhaled loud enough to hear, and scanned the stable again. "You're a mechanic?"

"Why? You need someone to work on your truck?"

He flashed his playful smile. "No."

The air around us solidified like Jello.

"You sure? I worked on Roxy." Eli ticked his chin to my Chevy.

"Roxy," August repeated, his eyes moving to my profile.

Surely there had to be a sinkhole somewhere on this massive lot to fall into. Eli crossed his arms over his chest. A trail of sweat dripped from his temple to his jaw. August lifted his chin defiantly. I'd never seen a Western, but I could hear the quintessential whistle of a standoff.

Great. They hate each other!

Voices drew my eye to the visible edge of the front deck of the main house. Luke leaned over the railing while Marley tugged on the back of his shirt.

"Hey Eli," Luke called. "Marley wants to know who the hot Latino Popstar is?" I guess he was feeling better.

"Shut up! I did not say that!" She punched his shoulder.

For the first time since I'd met him, Luke grinned. "Hot. Latino. Popstar," he repeated.

"I will kill you!" Marley screamed, locking him in a choke-hold and dragging him out of sight. He laughed through their entire, abrupt exit.

Nina tugged on my earring. "Mama, what's a tino pa-star?"

Eli frowned. August laughed. I still sought that sinkhole.

"I cannot sing," August admitted.

"It's true," I rushed to agree. "He's like a yowling cat."

Eli didn't look impressed. "I gotta get back to work. I'll bring Luke down tomorrow morning. Seven a.m. See how you do." Then he stormed off without a backward glance.

This was going to be harder than I thought.

August leaned in. "You don't need to frown for him. You want somebody, you can have me."

"What?" Was I frowning? "No, I'm just disappointed that he wasn't more friendly. He isn't usually like that."

August shook his head.

"What?"

"*Amor* ..." he exhaled as if I exhausted him. "You used to be so smart. Maybe I cannot marry you no more."

I shoved an elbow into his side. "It's just been a long year." I still didn't feel out of the brambles, but in the past few days, at least I could manage them.

Nina wiggled in my hold. I set her down, and she ran off to greet Chuck. We watched her tease the old gelding with a weed.

"Do you have somewhere to stay?" I asked.

"If I say no, you will offer me something?" He flashed a devilish grin, displaying straight, bright teeth. The two front ones were just a little too big, giving him a certain boyish charm that matched the beauty mark on his cheekbone.

"I have nowhere for you to sleep. But I'll cover your hotel while you're here."

"Helping you? Or helping your friend?"

"A friend."

He raised an eyebrow. "Your friend who works with cars?"

"Yup." *Don't look guilty. Don't look guilty.*

"Well, I stay with a friend, also. And she cooks better than you." He shrugged like facts were facts, and I could do nothing about it. "And she says I am always her favorite."

"Augustino Alejo. Are you trying to make me jealous?"

His playful smile got to me every time. Not romantically, but in a caretaking I-want-to-find-the-perfect-woman-for-you way. "Why? Are you jealous?"

"It's your sister, isn't it?"

"Shh. Don't tell nobody. I have to keep my image."

"What image?"

"A hot Latino popstar, *¿qué no?*"

I laughed. God, I missed him. It was so easy being around August. The more I climbed out of my shell, the more I regretted fortifying it to begin with.

"Okay, Mr. Popstar. Let me introduce you to the horses."

18

Eli

AVA MIGHT TRUST HIM, but I wasn't convinced. The guy looked like a young Enrique Iglesias, for crying out loud! With all of us there–me, Luke, August, and Ava practically attached to his hip–the stable felt crowded.

Luke threw an armful of hay in Sugar's feed bucket, and August immediately pulled some out and walked it to Chuck's stall, saying, "Only two flakes for each horse."

The kid shot him a look, then stormed off with the wheel-barrow, muttering, "What the hell's a flake?"

I jogged after him, sharing the same thought. Neither one of us was charmed by that accent. "Wouldn't it really throw 'em," I said, catching up to Luke, "if you came back with exactly what he asked for?"

Luke yanked an open bale apart with his hands, breaking the layers and making a mess. Maybe those were flakes? The layers?

"If they're working here," he grunted, "why do you even need me?"

"This guy isn't your boss," I told him. "He's just here to train someone. Maybe. This is like his interview."

At first, Ava's plan sounded good, but this August character was not what I expected. I'd figured he'd be older, like Terry. And who knew they'd be so buddy-buddy? Why didn't she call *him* when she got stranded at the strip mall?

"What about your girlfriend?" Luke said.

"She's not ..." I ran a hand down my face. "She's also temporary."

"Harsh. So what? She's like your booty call?"

"I meant she's temporarily helping with the horses, smartass." Did it look like we were–like she was ... I grabbed a handful of hay from the ground and put it on Luke's stack. "Ava likes horses, like you. And August is supposed to be an expert." If Ava planned to hire him for her ranch, he had to be good, right? And that's what we needed. Someone with horse skills. I didn't have to like him.

"Think of August like a math tutor."

"I got an 'A' in math."

"Okay. English, then." The kid went silent. I backtracked. "Listen, I hired *you*. I want *you* here. Let August share what he knows before he moves on. Maybe we'll learn something."

"Whatever." Luke spun the wheelbarrow on the front wheel and hightailed it back to the stable, leaving me in his dust.

Before following, I looked up "flake" on my phone.

Ha! I was right!

The rest of the morning didn't go much better. Every time August tried to show Luke how to tie a knot or scrape out a hoof, the kid shut down and stared off into space.

When the morning tasks were done, and Luke trekked to the house, August jogged up to me. "He's on, eh, service?"

I crossed my arms. "What do you mean?"

Latino Popstar crossed his arms back. "He looks like he don't wanna be here. Like maybe he's in trouble?"

"Community service?"

"*Sí.* Yes, community service."

"No. He's here by choice." I widened my stance. "He's a good kid. Just not a fan of new people."

"Actually," Ava interjected, "Eli runs a youth program for troubled kids. To boost their self-confidence."

"It's not a program," I said. "It's just Luke."

"And Marley," she added.

I waved her off. "That's different."

August stared at me, then dropped his arms and smiled. Always smiling. What the hell? This wasn't a photoshoot. "I'm gonna go for now. Maybe I come back tonight, when it's cooler, to help exercise the horses?"

I didn't need his help. So far, I hadn't seen anything impressive about this guy. But Ava stood behind him, holding her hands together in prayer, and pressing them into her pouty lips. "Fine."

They walked together to his truck, and I stalked into the tack stall, looking for something to do. I couldn't deal with Luke and Marley right now. Wasn't up for confronting Dad about his business numbers. I ran a hand over my hat. Just how good a friend was August?

"You know ..." Ava said. I turned to find her leaning on the opening of the stall. "If you bumped everything up an hour, you'd finish before it got this miserable." Sweat highlighted her face, her arms.

I glanced down at the darker areas of my shirt. "Luke's a teen. I'm lucky I can get him here before noon."

"Fair point." She puffed out a laugh. "I don't know what I'm going to do when Nina becomes a teenager."

Guess we were gonna pretend nothing changed. "I'm sure you'll be fine."

"Hopefully." Her smile faded. "It's just, losing her dad so young? And I keep disrupting our lives. That's a lot of trauma." She ran a hand through ridiculously shiny hair that she wore down. For him? "I don't know what I was thinking."

"Meaning?"

"The whole thing with Steven."

For a second, I'd thought she meant hitching a ride with me.

"I was so focused on saving money," she said. "On hiding my sadness so it wouldn't affect her. Trying to keep things *normal*. I mean, he is terrible with kids!" Her hands flew up. "How did I miss *that* red flag?"

I shrugged. "I heard somewhere that five percent of people are colorblind." She laughed, and it stole the anger outta me. "It's better she's young. My mom died when I was eleven. It sucked being aware of all the things I was missing."

Ava's sympathetic look was just as pretty as all the other ones. "That must've been so hard."

"The worst," I said. "Cancer stole my mom, but it also took away Dad. It broke him. Then I made it worse by being an impossible hellion."

"I'm sure you weren't that bad. You were dealing with losing your mom, too."

Ava's phone pinged a bunch of times in a row, breaking the moment. A moment I was kind of enjoying. She pulled it out of her pocket, and her face twisted in confusion.

"What's wrong?" I resisted the urge to demand her phone. "Is it Steven?"

Her eyes flicked up to mine, then back to her screen. "Huh? I–I don't know." As she scrolled, her face fell until she looked like she was gonna cry. "This can't be happening!"

"What? What is it? What happened?" I crossed to stand next to her and read the screen as she opened an email.

"Someone just opened a bunch of credit cards under my name!"

"What, like right now?"

"Yes!" She opened another email that looked the same as the first.

"Can't you call the fraudulent department or something?"

"That's not the point! Someone has my info." She tilted her head back and groaned. "I'm so stupid. I told Steven I was getting my loan preapproval today." Her eyes slid to mine, glassy and full of fury. "This will freeze my credit!"

"Why would you tell him that?"

"I don't know," she moaned. "He caught me off guard when he came by my complex yesterday–"

"Wait, he knows where you live?"

"Yes. Apparently, he's friends with my landlord."

My fingers curled into fists. First, he shows up at our ranch when Ava's got an interview, now he's going to her place! Was he tracking her?

Her phone started ringing, and her voice shook when she answered it. "Hello? Yes, this is she." But then her tone shifted. "Oh, hi!" I studied her profile in the pause. "Of course." She offered me a small, hopeful smile, mouthing "job." "For paperwork? Sure. How about tomorrow?"

How did she do it? Switch gears like that? She ended the call, took a deep breath, then stared at me with wide, searching eyes. My boots itched to move closer. But they didn't know the difference between casual flirting and booty calls, and apparently neither did I. The thing is, I'd thought about her like that. More than once. Knowing full well it wouldn't be anything long-term. Leave it to a kid to serve up the harsh truth.

"I should go," she said. "I have to, um ... I have a lot of things."

"Yeah." It wasn't right. She shouldn't have to deal with all that bullcrap. "Is there anything I can do?"

She pulled a face that looked almost painful. "I don't suppose you can watch Nina tomorrow? I can ask you dad–"

"Yeah. Of course. Whatever you need." God, I was such a sap. *She's parading around with her new, old best friend, and I'm begging for scraps.*

"Thanks." She scooped up her hair and tied it back with the hair band from around her wrist. "Hey, do you want me to swing by later? When August comes back?"

A better question–did *she* want to swing by to see August?

"It just seemed like ..." she paused, chewing on that lower lip, put on this earth to taunt me. "It's just, I was really hoping you two would get along."

I ran a hand over my hat. "No. Get your stuff done. I promise I won't start a fight." At least, I'd try. She hesitated, like she didn't believe me. "Scout's honor." I held up three fingers. Something I hadn't done in decades.

She nodded and walked out of the tack stall, and all I could think was, *Is this day over yet?*

I stared at my dad in disbelief. "You've been pulling from your retirement fund?"

Dad leaned against the kitchen counter and took a swing of his beer. "I'm in my retirement."

"Yeah, but this is a business. It should make money! It shouldn't be using what you'll need when you're not business-ing anymore." Even without a degree, I knew that! I glanced out the kitchen window, wondering when August planned to show up. "Dad, what happens when you run out of retirement?" This cowboy fantasy could drain his savings, and he didn't even care! "Do you need all of it? What if you just kept the house?"

"I don't *need* the ranch," he said after a long pause. The way he said it sounded like there was a "but" coming.

I'd done the math. Even with a full stable, he'd barely break even. Didn't help that he had the lowest boarding fee in Arizona.

"I'm trying to help you," I said, "so you're set up when I leave."

Dad put his empty bottle in the sink. "I gotta pee."

I watched him leave the kitchen. What wasn't he saying? Why skip out on his taxes? That wasn't like him.

My phone rattled on the table next to me, and I had to blink at the screen, sure I was seeing things. My sister never called. Not me, anyway. "Hey Hans. Did you butt-dial me?"

"You're at Pop's, right? Is he around? He's not answering his phone."

Wow, not even a "Hi, Eli, how are you?" My eyes cut to the wall that separated the kitchen from the bathroom in the entryway. "He's busy. Why?"

Her words spewed out, all messy and rushed over a poor connection.

"Slow down," I said. "You're where?"

"Getting off the freeway now."

"In Phoenix?"

"Yes, Eli! The horse is freaking out–"

"What horse?" A distressed moan came over the line, and the *clunk* of metal or hooves, or something in the background.

Shit.

"Are you safe right now? Maybe you should pull over."

"And do what? The horse is tilting the fucking trailer! I'm sure as hell not taking him out for a walk!"

"Okay. Okay, just focus on driving. I'll meet you at the gate."

I shoved my phone in my pocket as I passed Dad coming out of the bathroom. "Hannah's coming. Something about a horse."

"Hannah's here?" Dad's pleasure rattled me, but worry for my sister won out.

"I'm gonna let her in."

When I got to the gate, August was pulling up. *Figures.*

"You knew I was coming?" he asked through his open window. With a smile, of course.

"Nope. Flat out forgot." Then I remembered my promise to Ava. "Guess it worked out." I shoved the gate open. "I'll be over in a minute." He drove on as I waited for my sister.

I heard the horse's scream before I saw her truck. "Shit."

Hannah slowed to a crawl as she turned onto the gravel drive, her gaze jumping between the road and her rearview mirror. As soon as she pulled to a stop, I jogged up to the driver's side door. She rolled down her window.

"Want me to take over?" I asked.

"Yes, please." The single-horse trailer shifted and thumped as she hopped out.

I didn't bother locking up the gate. Better if Mr. Mercedes came here than harass Ava at her apartment, anyway. We drove to the stable. Hannah parked my truck next to August's. I pulled up along the line of pens, wondering how the hell I was going to move a bucking horse without losing a limb. August knocked on the passenger window of Hannah's truck. I rolled it down.

"I think it's better we put the horse in the ring," he said. "Bigger space for him to move, and wider gate, no?"

That sounded like a great idea.

I nodded and rounded the stable. August ran off to swing the arena gate wide open. He spotted me as I backed into it, like parking between two goal posts. Hannah nagged and fretted from the sidelines. Once positioned, I threw the truck in park.

August appeared at my open window. "You have a rope?"

"In the tack room."

He jogged to the stable and returned with a lead. I climbed out of the truck and watched him tie it to the handle of the trailer door.

Hannah inched over and poked my arm. "The key's in the

center console." She flicked her eyes to the Latino Popstar. "And by the way, I'd like an introduction later."

"You have a girlfriend."

"It's more of an open relationship."

"Yeah, well, get in line," I grumbled.

She raised an eyebrow.

"Not me! Never mind."

I didn't have the energy or the desire to explain it to her. Metal screamed against metal as the trailer shifted against the arena rails.

August tested the rope. "Okay. Ready?"

Adrenaline rushed through me. "Yeah."

He let out slack on the rope as he ducked through the fence and positioned himself by the hinges of the trailer door, outside of the arena area. I grabbed the key and tried reaching the trailer lock from around the side, avoiding the kick zone, but couldn't see what I was doing. The trailer shifted again as the horse thrashed inside. I'd never get the key into a moving target I couldn't see. *Screw it.* I slid in the gap between the arena rails and the back corner of the trailer opposite August, with my back pressed against the gatepost.

"Careful!" Hannah moaned.

The trailer shifted yet again, pinching the gap where I stood and pinning me in place. All the air rushed outta me.

"Eli! Are you okay?" Hannah.

It took two tries to shove the key in the lock. As soon as I jammed down on the handle, August pulled the rope, swinging the trailer door wide. It slammed into the arena's fence, sending shockwaves through the entire structure and rattling my skull. I tried to squeeze myself out, but couldn't. Pain lanced up my side.

Shit. I was stuck!

Two hooves shot out the opening, but the horse wouldn't come out of the trailer.

"He'll break an ankle!" Hannah cried, now worrying over the horse.

I couldn't have responded if I'd wanted to. Holy hell, I couldn't even breathe. When I started seeing stars, Hannah's truck inched forward, giving me just enough relief to slide free. No more than a second later, the trailer jammed into the post I'd been pinned to. The horse's screams gave me chills. I rubbed at my chest, tried and failed to take a deep breath.

August hopped out of Hannah's truck and ran up to me. "Are you okay, my friend?" He put a hand on my shoulder, looked right into my face with obvious concern. How could I hate this man? He may have just saved my life.

I nodded.

He patted my arm, then climbed the outside of the trailer to reach the window, and started talking to the horse. Making clicking noises. At first, nothing happened, but after a minute or two, the horse took a step backward, then another, until he found the edge of his enclosure, and finally, his way into the arena. As soon as all four hooves found dirt, he took off, racing, bucking, and huffing.

"You did it!" Hannah clapped, then reached out and hugged me.

I winced. Fire climbed hip to head.

"*Chica*," August said to my sister. "Move your truck so I can shut the gate."

She let go, but mouthed a silent "introduction" before strutting to the open driver's side door.

The world tilted a little. Thank God we were done.

August slammed the gate shut. "You maybe should sit, no?"

I shook my head. I didn't think I could. "Hey, August?"

"Yes?"

"Got a guy. Coming tomorrow." It took effort to fill my lungs. "For a job. Think you can size him up for me?"

The Latino popstar flashed a paparazzi smile. "You got it, boss."

No question. I owed the man a top-shelf beer.

19

Ava

BILL OPENED the door the next morning, and Nina ran right in. I greeted him with a "Good morning!" while scanning the room for Eli.

"Did you see who came in last night?" Bill asked, a secret glint behind his glasses. "If you have a few minutes, you should go look."

"Where am I looking?"

"The arena."

I discovered August out there, observing a new horse: a beautiful, deep bay with a midnight mane. It loped anxious patterns in the dirt, switching directions often. Sweat collected on his flank.

I slung my arms over the metal fence. "Poor thing."

"*Sí*. He is not happy," August agreed. "But he responds to commands. I will try to work with him later."

"Who does he belong to?"

My friend cut me a devilish grin.

"He's available?"

"A rescue. I don't know the details. Eli—his sister brought him last night."

"Eli has a sister?" As I said it, I vaguely recalled him mentioning her at the strip mall.

"*Sí*. She left already. I think she is a little ... *salvaje*."

"Really? I got the impression Eli was the wild one." I watched the Arabian change directions again, taut muscles strong and agile. Dust lifted in a haze under his hooves.

"He will make a good mount, no?" August observed.

Definitely. "What about as a stud?"

"Maybe."

One way to populate a barn was to build a herd. But I knew nothing about animal husbandry.

Luke dragged a half-filled plastic water bucket across the expanse of dirt to the ring and shimmied it under the lowest bar.

"Thank you, my friend," August called to him.

The black-clad teen stalked away without a reply.

"Yeesh, he must be baking." I drew my eyes back to the newcomer. "How long are they keeping him?"

August shrugged.

I held up a hand to shield the sun from my face. "He can't stay here. It'll get too hot. And what if one of these mystery boarders comes to use the arena?"

"Yes," August agreed again.

I had a sneaking suspicion several ideas already bounced around in that clever head of his. The Arabian stopped at the water bucket, huffing, then finally dipped his head to drink.

"So, how'd it go between you two?" Did Eli keep his promise?

"Eh. He's no good."

"What?" The word hit a worry-doused high note. "What's wrong with him?"

August's eyes slanted to mine. "I am talking about the guy who comes for work."

Oh.

"*Amor*. You kill me."

"Sorry, I thought you meant–That's right, Eli had someone coming out today. What's wrong with him? He's not trainable?"

"He wanna put the stallion next to the mares." August *tsked* and shook his head. "You gotta have some sense, no?"

"Good point."

"It's gonna cost money, but maybe we build a space? Big enough so you can put another horse? The gray one is calm. He will settle the stallion."

"Chuck?" I glanced at the stable to catch the mischief-maker chewing at the gate latch again. "That's not a bad idea."

A larger space would benefit all the horses. My eyes drifted over the blank canvas in front of me, and things started popping up everywhere. "What about a few other easy upgrades? A sign at the entrance. A trail marker there?" I pointed toward where Eli and I had ridden. "It could draw boarders to this location, highlighting access up the mountain. And some shade structures wouldn't be too hard– What?"

"Nothing." August forced the sides of his mouth down when they clearly wanted to go up.

"No, not nothing. What's with that look?"

"I am smiling. I can smile, no?"

"Mhmm. I'm just saying, this place has potential." Though maybe I needed to tone it down. This wasn't my ranch, after all. "I have to go fill out employment forms. Have you seen Eli?"

"He is inside, I think."

I found Eli sitting on the couch in the den, head back. Sleeping? When the French doors clicked closed behind me, he cracked an eye open and rasped, "You headed out?"

"I was planning on it."

In a fantastic portrayal of Frankenstein's monster, he leaned forward and used his hands to push himself up slowly from the cushions.

I frowned. "Are you okay?"

"Yup. Probably sitting too long." He seemed pale, though it could've been a trick of the light.

"Nina's with Bill," I said, "but I can take her with me." Something seemed off about him.

"It's all good. Go."

"I'm not sure how long I'll be."

"All good," he repeated. "We'll be here."

A prickle inched up my spine, but I took my leave.

As I drove away from the house, the prickle became a shiver, then a chill. I used to have such a strong intuition. Was it warning me now? Maybe Eli just had a late night visiting with his sister? Kicked back a few too many beers at the reunion?

To ease my nerves, I ran through my recent accomplishments. I'd frozen all my accounts and changed all my passwords. Terry had my plan revisions and a vague explanation for my missing preapproval. And I'd unpacked two boxes last night!

But waiting for my credit to settle would mean I'd need to provide a more recent paycheck for the loan. An undoubtedly smaller one. Which would affect my loan limit. *Ugh!* I groaned into the ceiling of my truck while I waited for the light to turn green.

Would Terry entertain a smaller offer? *No, Ava, you can't do that.* He'd already have to sacrifice upgrading his trailer: a rickety 1980's Terry Taurus fifth-wheel that no one's even heard of anymore. Duct tape and sheer determination were all holding the thing together. Would it survive a cross-country tour like Terry dreamed of taking in his retirement? I frowned as I pulled into the lot at Rock 'N Roll. If he accepted the corporate offer, he could easily afford a top-of-the-line unit, maybe even one of those Sprinter vans. I slid out of my Chevy and locked the door. Something to worry about later. First, I needed to make this job official.

Three hours later, I hopped back into my smoldering truck. Next week, my training began. No more procrastinating–I needed permanent childcare. By the time I parked next to Eli's truck, I'd accomplished a full-on sweat. I loved Roxy, but the old girl had no frills. No AC, no power windows. Just a knobby radio and ancient power steering.

The cool house beckoned me as I let myself in and removed my shoes, following familiar voices to the den. Eli and Nina sat on the floor at opposite sides of the coffee table, half a deck of cards between them. Most of the other half fanned out in Eli's hand. The color seemed to have returned to his cheeks.

"You look better," I told him.

He sifted through his cards. "What do you mean?"

"You seemed off this morning."

"Oh. My sister came last night. She's a hurricane. Quick in, quick out. Lots of drama." He looked across the table at Nina. "Do you have any threes?"

"What's that?" she asked.

With a smile, he flipped his card to show her.

Nina dutifully shuffled through her hand, which she held in a single stack, taking one card off at a time and setting each on the table for everyone to see. When she finished, she looked up and grinned. "Go fish!"

The scene warmed my insides, like that first toothless baby-smile, or handing over the keys to a proud new homeowner. Like the trail ride Eli had taken me on days earlier. I was seriously questioning the whole keep-my-distance approach.

He took a card from the pond.

"Did she nap?" I asked, conversationally.

"Yup." No details, no upward glance.

I tried again. "What did you guys do today?"

"Little of everything," he clipped. "Nina," he prompted, "your turn."

Okay then.

"Since you're occupied, I think I'll make a few calls." I trudged back up to the kitchen, trying not to take his lack of response personally.

The timing sucked. Every worthwhile preschool in our area had a waitlist longer than the Gila River. Or asked for tuition well above my price range. I expanded my radius, but heard the same spiel: "We'll call you if a space opens up."

"I'm happy to watch her," Bill offered as the Keurig hissed and gurgled. At some point, he'd wandered into the kitchen to make coffee. He tossed the used pod in the garbage and claimed his cup.

I needed long-term, but in the interim? "Thank you. Maybe just this week? I'm only doing half-days to start." I chewed on the back of my pen, pulling up another daycare from the map on my phone.

"The hours don't matter to me. Nina's a hoot." He disappeared into the pantry and returned with a pack of Famous Amos cookies. "Want one?"

"Sure."

As I nibbled on a chocolate chip cookie, I debated. *Should I seek something closer to Hidden Meadows?* Once I took over the ranch, trekking to the city would eat up half the morning. But with no clear timeline and so many unknowns, how could I make the right choice? Did I rely on Bill until we closed escrow? *No.* I couldn't do that. It was one thing to ask a doting grandfather to watch his grandchild, but a new friend? Perhaps he'd let me pay him? My thoughts wandered to the envelope of cash, probably still hidden in Eli's center console, and I suspected, "like father, like son."

Needing a break from childcare searches, I joined Marley to

make banana nut muffins. I played dumb, asking her to read me the recipe aloud. It forced her to follow it, step by step. She may have rolled her eyes at the process, but when she shoved the fresh-out-of-the-oven muffin in her mouth, it was worth it.

Her eyes lit. "Oh, my God! These are really good."

I reached over and took one from the cooling rack. They were still hot, and half the bottom stuck to the cupcake liner. Fluffy, sweet, and utterly delightful.

"You're right!" I grabbed two more. "We should go find Bill. I bet he'll want one."

Marley tucked her head down, but I saw it. A stunning smile. For the first time since I'd met her, she looked her age.

Thursday, we tried zucchini bread. And Friday, when I returned from Rock 'N Roll, a plate of homemade chocolate chip cookies greeted me.

On Saturday, I followed up with the credit companies, but they were still investigating my claim. Sunday, I took a lazy day at the apartment pool with Nina. It felt good to do nothing, but Sunday night, my laziness caught up with me. None of the six school waitlists amounted to any miracles. Come Monday morning, Nina would either pal to work with me, or I'd have to ask Bill for a full day. I didn't think my boss would appreciate a three-year-old underfoot, and because I didn't have Bill's phone number, I called Eli.

"Hey." He sounded winded.

"Hi. Sorry to bother you–"

"No problem. What do you need?"

I bristled at his tone. It wasn't rude, just efficient. "I was hoping to hear back from a preschool by now. I'm on several waitlists, but ..."

"Hold on." A cacophony of rustles and thumps filled the line, and his next words were muffled. "Hey, Dad? We're gonna watch Nina tomorrow, right?"

"It's a full day," I interjected.

To me, Eli said, "Yeah. No problem. She can hang with us."

"Okay, thanks."

"Yup. See you tomorrow."

"Oh! Wait. Can you give me your dad's number? Just in case?" I could've gotten it in the morning, but for some inexplicable reason, I didn't want to end the call.

"Yeah. I'll text it."

"Thanks."

"You bet." Then he hung up.

I stared at my phone for a good five minutes, my heart fighting an odd undertow.

A proud expression painted Bill's face the next morning as he stopped us in front of the closet under the den stairs. I'd dressed in business casual for my first official, non-training day. Back to synthetic blouses. I didn't go so far as a pencil skirt or heels, though. Nina chose her own outfit, making it her mission to wear every color and pattern she could find.

"I picked up some things this weekend," Bill said, pulling bag after Walmart bag from the closet.

"Some?" I peered into one such bag to find a watercolor palette, paintbrushes, and a thick pad of craft paper.

He shrugged. "I figured we needed some new activities."

The next one held a little doll with accessories. Another contained more Play-Doh than a Kindercare. Nina tugged at the bag to see inside. "Ooo! I want that!"

I could cry! But I didn't, because I'd put on make-up. "Bill, this is so thoughtful. What do I owe you for all this stuff?"

"Mama! Mama, look!" Nina held up a Play-Doh breakfast kit.

Bill waved me off. "Nothing. It was cheap."

Don't cry. Don't cry. "Wow. This is, just ..." It had been so long since I'd had someone in my corner. "Thank you. I wish I could repay you for all this."

He shook his head. "You already have."

My chest panged as I watched Nina dig through the new toys. Why did leaving suddenly feel so hard? I used to drop her off every day to head into a full-time job, and think nothing of it. "I made her lunch, and I packed extra clothes. She ate before we came, so she shouldn't be hungry." *What else?*

Bill put a hand on my arm. "We're going to have a great day. And so will you."

I swallowed the thick lump in my throat. It was no exaggeration that I wouldn't have been able to do this without him. "Okay. I'll see you around six-thirty or so?"

By the time I pulled into Rock 'N Roll, I'd collected my sappy emotions and shoved them in a drawer to savor later. My whirlwind day culminated with brain fog, a stiff neck, and a smile that stretched cheek to cheek. Time to see my favorite faces! I grabbed my purse and headed to my truck, shooting off a quick text to August.

Ava: Hey, are you at the ranch?

August: Yes. We are trying something with Denver.

Eli had named the new horse. I had to applaud his choice. It fit the Arabian's spirit.

Ava: Great! I'll be there soon.

August: ...

Not waiting for the bouncing dots to turn into his next response, I tossed my phone on the bench and drove the twenty-five minutes to Bill's place. A yawn snuck out as I pulled the Chevy through the open front gate. At some point, Eli had stopped locking it. I still didn't know what all the fuss had been about.

I reached for my phone to see if August had replied.

August: Eli is gonna take him on the trail

Him? As in, Denver? "What!"

I floored my truck over the gravel, manifesting a storm in my wake, my heart climbing up my throat. The trail? Denver wasn't ready for that! He'd been there less than a week!

The stable came into view, then the arena, with everyone crowded around it. Eli and Denver stood at the center.

It was too familiar.

Eager crowd. New horse.

I didn't even remember turning off the engine, just stumbling from the driver's door. "Wait!" I shouted. A rock concert bass thudded inside my ribcage. This couldn't be happening. "Eli, wait!" When I reached the edge of the arena, I was gasping for breath. I gripped the rails. Bill, August, and Nina stared at me with wide eyes. Eli gave me a brief glance, but continued saddling the Arabian.

"Please don't get on that horse," I pleaded.

"Why?" Right before my eyes, he fit the leather saddle over the curve in Denver's back. The horse shifted under the added weight, his nostrils flaring.

Oh God! This can't be happening. My silence had cost me everything. "It's not safe. You don't know this horse."

August came up beside me and put an arm around my shoulder. "Ava, it's okay. The horse is good, no? Eli, he has been working with him."

White hat. Blue sky. Red dirt.

Time couldn't dull that day. The details swam around me. I

was there. Jason's cowboy hat floating above the scene, stuck in time against a cloudless sky. My eyes fell on Eli's ball cap. If it went soaring, I'd never forgive myself. "Wh-what if he spooks?"

"He's not gonna spook," Eli said.

"You can't know that."

"Ava, chill. You're less likely to die riding a horse than driving a car."

Bile burned my throat as Eli affixed the bridle. My eyes stung with frustration and fear. This was just like before. And no one would listen! The edges of the scene splintered around me, memories sifting between the cracks. A breeze lifted the hair at the sides of my face, carrying a tang on its wings.

I wrenched out of August's arm and shot between the parallel bars into the arena.

"¡*Ay, chica!*" August called.

Denver flinched and sidestepped at my approach.

"I'm going to take Nina inside," I heard Bill say. "I'll be right back."

Eli caught my shoulders at arm's length. "Ava, stop yelling. What are you doing?"

"Get out of the ring!"

He huffed a humorless laugh and let me go. "What's this? Huh? I know how to ride. You *saw* me ride."

Jason was an excellent rider, and it took less than five minutes. *Five minutes* and he was gone.

I fitted myself between Eli and the horse. Despite the day's lingering heat, I could feel the breeze of the office fan spinning overhead, see the cobwebs swirling in the airy current.

"You're not getting on this horse," I told him. "I won't let you."

"You won't *let* me?" His eyes jumped to where August stood, then back to me.

I crowded him, shoved my hands at his chest to force him away from Denver.

He winced and staggered backwards. "Jeez, Ava. Knock it off. You're acting like a punk."

I wouldn't. He could call me whatever he wanted.

The squeak in my chair. Flecks of blue nail polish. August was saying something, but his words just gurgled like the water sloshing from the five-gallon jug. *Shouting. gasps.* People with their cameras held high. The two worlds collided in my head. *Somebody call 9-1-1!* I closed my eyes, but I could still hear it. All of it. What could I have said? What would've kept him here with me?

"Stop! Your stupid bravado is going to ruin everything!"

"Ava, what the hell? Get out of the ring!" Eli shouted back.

No! I spun to Denver and whipped the buckle out of the girth strap, yanking the saddle down in one fell swoop.

Denver reared.

"Son of a–"

Without warning, I was flying, skidding across the dirt. Not from a horse. By human hands. I rolled onto my back, stunned and breathless.

Eli fell to his knees, gripping his side. "Jesus, Ava! You could've been kicked in the head!"

"I-I–" He was in pain.

"Get out of the ring before you do something stupid!"

I wanted to slap his words back at him. But I couldn't speak. Couldn't think.

Lifeless eyes staring skyward. Helplessness.

August grabbed Denver's lead. "Ava, it's okay. He's okay."

It wasn't okay. Jason was dead!

"You didn't have to go it alone," Kip had said.

My eyes jumped between the blurry forms of the men around me. No one understood. They kept saying things like, "It's fine," "It's okay." But it wasn't.

Past, present, hope, grief. My chest was clawing out of my skin. I ran. Past the arena. Past the French doors. Past Marley and Nina. Into solitude. I don't even know where. Somewhere I could lock myself up and hide as a chasm ripped me in two. It didn't matter how many people I surrounded myself with, how busy I stayed. It followed me.

And in the end, I was always alone.

20

Eli

WHAT THE FUCK?

I stared at the saddle in the dirt. My heart raced. Fire ate up my whole damn torso. But all I could think about was how close that hoof had been to her head.

"Eli?"

"What!"

My dad didn't bother answering.

August pulled Denver to the side and tied his reins to the rails.

I tried to stand, but got as far as hunched, leaning on bent knees like an old man. Dust started settling. The heat hadn't bothered me before, but now it was damn near suffocating.

Bravado? Did she think I was trying to show off? Why was it that the harder I worked, the more pissed everyone got? Maybe I'd just take Denver and ride into the freaking sunset by myself. Except first, I think I needed to lie down.

August ran up and offered me a hand. "Are you good, my friend?"

"No."

"The horse, did it kick you?"

"No."

He stared at me for a few seconds. "Maybe we should take you–"

"No! Damnit, August. Just give me a second!"

Dad's boots came into view. "Perhaps this isn't a good day to take a ride."

"Ya think?"

"Don't be smart with me."

"No. That's Hannah's job."

Dad scoffed. "Hannah has nothing to do with this."

"Well, this is her damn horse, and we're taking care of it! Tell me how it's not about her?"

It went quiet for a blessed minute.

Then August made a sound like a deflating tire and said, "I thought maybe this would help her to get better. To see everything goes okay."

I forced myself upright. "What do you mean? Get better from what?"

He scratched the back of his head, making me wait. "This is a little like when Jason died."

"What? Jason, as in, her husband?"

"He tried to ride a new horse with a lot of spirit. A rescue." August's eyes cut to Denver. "The horse threw him. I think maybe that is what she is seeing."

"Seeing?"

Was she having a PTSD attack? *Your stupid bravado is going to ruin everything!* Was she talking to me? Or her husband? My eyes narrowed on August. And he knew?

"What the hell, man! Why didn't you say something?"

For once, the Latino popstar didn't smile. I glanced up at the house. Anger, worry, pain. It was too much to deal with all at once. I had to pick one.

"Do something with Denver," I told him.

I didn't wait for an answer. Just started jogging. Adrenaline masked my pain. I had no idea what I'd find. I thought she'd lost her mind, or maybe gotten all territorial about the horse. Or August.

Inside the den, Marley and Nina were sitting eerily silent next to all of Nina's doll stuff. They stared at me as Ava's sobs bled through the wall.

It came out a little breathless when I said, "Hey, Mar, take Nina upstairs?"

She stood without arguing. "Come on, Nina. Let's make cookies for your mom. It'll make her feel better."

Nina hesitated, but took Marley's hand and followed her up to the kitchen.

I moved to the bedroom door that separated me from the woman who flipped my whole world upside down. "Ava?" No response. Just more gut-wrenching sobs. I leaned my forehead against the wood and closed my eyes. This was my fault.

"Ava, honey, let me in."

I twisted the handle, but the door didn't budge. Even if her tears were for another man, I had to fix it. I shoved a shoulder into the wood until the burning in my side made me dizzy. Then I tried again, forcing it open enough to squeeze through. Enough to see her hunched on the floor with her back against the door. She immediately popped up and bombarded me with angry fists.

"Go away!" Each blow landed on a different sore spot.

Son of a bottle-opener. "Ava–"

"I said get out!"

I had no intention of running away. Tears cut trails down her face, and they ripped a hole in me. I wasn't her husband– probably nothing like the guy. I might never make her feel better, but I knew a thing or two about feeling alone. About how easy it was to let darkness eat you alive.

"I'm not gonna leave, but it would be really great if you could stop hitting me."

She landed a solid punch into my shoulder. I caught her next swing in one hand, but she brought the other fist into my ribs, and I saw stars. Still, the tears in her eyes hurt more.

"How could you?" she cried. "What are you trying to prove?"

"Nothing."

"Do we mean nothing to you?"

"No."

"Then why? Why would you do that? People need you, you know!"

Was she talking to me? Or Jason?

She pushed off my chest and spun, pacing to the other side of the empty room. Her body shook and started to sway. "I can't. I ..."

I moved in, catching her right before she crumbled, holding her to me, wrapping my arms around her like a seat belt.

Shudders ran up her spine, and her small voice cracked when she said, "It's my fault. I should have said something."

I brought us gently to the floor. "You did. That's why I'm here."

She shook her head as another sob broke outta her chest. I wrapped my arms tighter, like the saddle tie she ragged on me for. I knew her pain wasn't for me. I held her, anyway.

"Ava, I didn't know about your husband. I'm sorry I yelled. You just–you scared me to death back there."

She grew still, so still, except for the rapid heartbeat that smashed into my chest, threatening to swallow me whole.

"Ava, you gotta breathe."

She shook her head.

"No? You're not gonna breathe? Why not?"

"Because it might all come out."

It didn't already? I held her closer, broken ribs be damned. "Fine, let it."

"I can't."

"Yes, you can."

"I-I can't," she whispered.

"Hey." I rested my cheek on her head. She smelled fruity. Feminine. The kind of paradise you wanted to wake up to every morning. "You're not alone, okay? I got you."

She curled into me, like a cat on my lap.

Like I was safety.

Even though I never really felt all that stable. Even though I couldn't commit to a place, let alone a person.

21

Ava

SOME HUGS ARE GENTLE, like being folded into dove wings. Eli's arms circled me firmly–a living, breathing roller coaster harness. Solid. With intention. So different from the ghosts following me for the past year. I could've fallen asleep curled in his lap. But that ever-nagging sense of responsibility called. Nina would need an explanation and assurance that I was okay. When I straightened, Eli smothered a grunt, and the flash of pain from the arena rushed back at me.

I flew off his lap in alarm. "Oh, my God! Did you get kicked?"

His chest dropped in a slow-motion exhale, but he shook his head.

"But I saw you. You were hurting. You *are* hurting." I crouched in front of him and grabbed the hem of his shirt.

"Ava, it's fine." He tried to pull my grip away. "Don't worry about it.

I lifted the fabric a few inches, void of gratuitous intent. "Oh, my God! Eli!" And higher, until his shirt practically smothered his face.

"Ava, it's nothing." His hands circled my wrists and tried to pull them down, but they lacked the strength.

"Nothing?" A horrible, dark purplish-black bruise ran from his collarbone to his navel. "Wh-what happened? *When* did this happen?"

He collected my hands in one of his, using the other to fix his clothing and hide the offense from view. "Don't worry about it. You have enough on your plate."

I shook my head. "Eli, you look like you broke a rib! Or ribs. Have you been to see a doctor?"

"What can a doctor do? It'll heal. This stuff happens all the time."

"No, it doesn't."

"It does for me."

I realized I knew so little about him. "Well, then you should consider a career change, because this ..." My hands slid out of his grip and back to his shirt. He didn't fight me this time when I shifted it up, studied the patterns, dusted my fingertips over the discolored skin. "Did you ice it? Does it hurt when you breathe?" Anger snuck back in. "You were going to get on a horse like this?"

His chest shook, and when I glanced at his face, it portrayed pained humor. He was laughing.

Laughing! "Excuse me?"

"I'm just enjoying you finally fawning over me."

I dropped my hands. "You're ridiculous."

"You don't have to stop."

"Forget it. Clearly, you're fine." I rose, fully intending to storm out, but he was on the floor because of me. With a sigh, I held my hand out to him. He did a poor job of hiding his discomfort as I hauled him to his feet. "Let me take you to the doctor." Before he could form a "no," I added, "It would make me feel better."

"Ava ..."

"We'll take your truck. It has a smoother ride."

"No. You gotta get Nina home. You have work in the morning."

"Yeah, I do. So, stop wasting time arguing about it."

His eyes met mine in challenge, studying me, hopefully noting that I wouldn't relent. He ran a tired hand down his face.

"Okay. Just don't tell my dad."

"Why?"

"Because I don't want him worrying about me."

I considered him for a moment. "Fine. We can tell him we're getting ice cream. I just need to check in with Nina before we go."

Day two at Rock 'N Roll flew by much like the first: chaotically. I fought off a wave of exhaustion as I parked next to Bill's truck that evening. Eli's and August's were down by the stables. *So much for doctor's orders.* I knew he wouldn't refrain from heavy lifting or vigorous activity.

I grabbed my purse and the white pastry bag before making my way to the house. Nina's face popped up in the kitchen window, then disappeared to greet me at the door with a huge smile.

"Mama! Guess what?"

"What?" I stooped to scoop her up.

"We sawed a fwog eat his skin!"

"What?" Did we have frogs in Phoenix?

"On the TV. Abi showed me."

I peeked into the living room and saw several encyclopedias spread open on the coffee table. Bill's glasses rested on top of one. "Well, that sounds gross." I wrapped her in a tight hug.

"Mama, you're squishing me!"

"It *was* gross," Bill called from the kitchen.

I waddled in as Nina slid down my leg. "Abi?" I asked him.

"Oh. Something August said, and it stuck, I guess."

Huh. Abi, short for *abuelo*? I liked it, but the lines were beginning to blur. "Thanks for watching her."

"My pleasure. How was your second day?"

In truth, not exciting at all–typical office work that stole hours I'd never get back. But I didn't want to appear ungrateful. "It was good." I set the pastry bag on the counter in front of him.

"Ooo, for me?" Paper crinkled as Bill dug out his apple fritter.

I chewed on the inside of my cheek. God, this was embarrassing. "I, um, I want to apologize for yesterday. My husband was thrown from a horse, and he died, and I guess I'm still a little ... tender about it."

"Understandable." He didn't sound surprised at all. "There's only one in here?"

My smile returned. "Yes. I'm saving you from yourself."

"In that case," he said, taking a large bite, "go find Eli and tell him to get his clothes out of the laundry. I'm not his maid."

"That sounds more like I'm saving Eli."

Bill shrugged, then sauntered out of the kitchen with his pastry and a bottle of iced tea.

I considered doing the task for Eli. Was that too domestic? Too intimate?

"You're not alone. I got you."

Not any more intimate than cradling me in an empty room, mascara smeared down my face in creepy clown fashion. He'd seen me at my worst. Sadness, anger, and loneliness were suffocating me, squeezing all the air from my lungs, convincing me I'd never be able to refill them. Then there he was, reminding me to breathe. With two broken ribs, no less!

"I was thinking," I said to Nina. "We should help Eli, since he's been so nice."

"Yeah!" Her enthusiasm locked my decision.

"Come on, let's find the washing machine."

The long mudroom jutted off the kitchen and stretched its way to the garage. A washer, dryer, counter, and sink lined the left wall. Windows over a bench lined the other. An ideal layout with tons of light to make the task downright pleasant.

I grabbed a basket from the counter and started unloading the dryer, shaking out each item so it didn't wrinkle. "What should we have for dinner tonight, Crackerjack?"

"Pizza!"

"Pizza? Didn't we just have that?"

"We eated it for lunch!"

"Well, then we're definitely not going to have it again for dinner." I tried not to blush when I removed a pair of boxer briefs. Maybe this was a bad idea.

"I wuv pizza!"

"I can tell, but let's pick something different. How about salad?"

Nina reached into the dryer to help, but ended up dragging several items to the floor. "E-why doesn't like salad."

The way she said his name made my heart stutter. I picked up a shirt by her feet. "He doesn't? How do you know that?"

"He tolded me."

"Well, then I guess it's good we're not making him dinner tonight." I tucked the basket of clean laundry into my hip and eyed the door that led to the garage. I figured it would take us to his studio. What did Eli's room look like? Was he the kind of man who made his bed or left dirty dishes everywhere?

Nina followed hot on my heels as we entered the concreted double-bay. To my left, I found a staircase that folded around itself to a second level. We climbed, and as I reached for the door handle at the top, I wondered if this infringed on his privacy. Then I remembered all the times he'd inserted himself into my bubble, and I threw the door open.

The garage studio boasted more square footage than our entire apartment. Eli's bed dominated the rear wall, and the crevices in the mussed sheets fueled my already tingling imagination. So, not a bed maker. But otherwise, tidy.

Left of the door stretched a modern kitchenette with trimmed wood cabinets. No dirty dishes. Just a little pile of coins and receipts. An open door in the back, left corner revealed a full bathroom. But I veered right, to the wooden desk under a large window, and admired the view. You could see from the line of trucks in front of the garage, all the way to the front gate.

On his desk, papers mingled, overlapped. Numbers littered the margins–equations–but one value stuck out with its dark, double underline. Lifting the top page, I studied the surrounding notes and surmised it must be related to Bill's ranch and that *final notice* envelope.

"Mama, what's dis book?"

I turned to find Nina holding a magazine with a very attractive, very bare woman on the cover.

"Nina!" I dropped the laundry basket on Eli's bed and snatched the publication. "This is not for kids! Where did you find this?"

Her eyes grew glassy. "I don't know."

"What do you mean, you don't know? You *just* picked it up."

Her mouth pinched.

I fixed my tone. "I'm not mad. I just want to make sure it goes back *exactly* how you found it."

Nina remained silent. With a sigh, I scanned the bedside area, looking for clues, but in the end, I guessed and left it on the single wooden nightstand.

"Come on, Crackerjack. Let's see what the boys are doing." Before we found anything else.

Beyond the stables, a series of metal poles sprang out of the ground at regular intervals, forming an elongated oval. August walked the perimeter, shaking each post in turn, checking its sturdiness. I smiled. Eli must've agreed to a paddock.

"Mama, watch!" Nina ran ahead, approaching the nearest post, and swung herself in a sweeping circle. Like a pole dancer.

I grimaced, hoping the cement had finished setting. "Wow!"

As if he heard my inner thoughts, August walked by and gave her post a good shake. He bent down to tell her something, and soon she shadowed him, laughing as she gave each pole the same treatment. Eli wandered out of the tack room behind me, headed for a pile of tools near the edge of the work zone.

"Hey, you." His warm greeting had me falling in step with him.

Could I pretend I hadn't just been holding his porn?

"Hi. I just came to tell you I put your clean laundry on your bed."

His head tilted, and his brow crinkled in a silent query.

Context, Ava. My hands leapt into an interpretive ballet as I explained, "Your dad wanted me to pass on a message to get your laundry. I was already in the house, and you've probably been working out here all day, so I just ... did it for you." I shoved those dancers into my pockets. They did not know what they were doing. "Aaand, that sounds ridiculous when I say it out loud."

He stooped to pick up a toolbox and several extension cords. "Does, uh," a smile lifted the corners of his mouth. "Does that mean your hands were on my underwear?"

Oh God, just wait till he sees his magazine!

Upon further reflection, I was almost positive it hadn't been on the nightstand when we walked in. "Let me carry those. You're supposed to be resting."

He handed me the extension cords, but kept the heavier toolbox out of reach. "I like that you care."

His tone held no sarcasm, no teasing finish. Only unadulterated sincerity. So why did my mind flash to the outline of his body in his bedsheets? It would appear the intimacy shared in grief opened a door I couldn't seem to close. Or maybe now that our bodies had connected, albeit clothed, the seal had been broken? Who knew hugging was a gateway drug? I hid my burning complexion by pulling ahead as we walked back to the stable, but he matched my gait easily.

"Did you do your deep breathing exercises?" I asked.

"Not yet."

"Eli ..."

"We've been busy."

"The doctor said five deep breaths, three times a day."

"Yes, dear."

I ignored the domesticity in his tone. "You won't get anything done if your lung collapses, or if you end up with pneumonia!"

I pushed ahead, into the tack stall and slung the cables on a hook. When I turned, he was right there, in my bubble again. Only this time, it sent thrills up my spine. Without a word, he caught my hand and placed it on his chest. The heavy thud of his heart ignited my fingertips. *Dangerous territory.* When I tried to pull away, his grip tightened. Beneath my palm, his chest inflated as he took a long breath in, then it sank on a slow exhale. His eyes remained fixed on mine as he did it four more times.

"Happy?"

I swallowed. "Yes."

Six weeks. According to Dr. Kaplin, that's how long ribs took to heal. So, I needed to get my head out of the crevices of his sheets.

His lips curved up. "Ava?"

And that lopsided smile. Seriously! It was like navigating a minefield! "Yes?"

"If you're gonna hold me to doctor's orders, please stop looking at me like that."

"Like what?"

"Like you wanna devour me."

Not devour. For then there'd be nothing left for later. His focus flicked to my mouth, and his hand tightened around mine. Did kissing count as vigorous activity?

"Look, I know I'm not your husband, but ..." He traced the edge of my ear, maybe tucking hair back in place, maybe just touching me. Either way was fine. Ever since knowing the safety of his arms, it's all I could think about.

"But?" I prompted.

A knock rattled the tack stall entrance, stealing both our attentions. August stood there, his face unreadable, but I'm sure he knew what he had just interrupted. "Sorry, but Nina says she has to go."

"Go?" I asked.

"Go. To the *baño*."

"Oh." I extracted my hand from Eli's chest. "Yeah. Sure. Actually, we should head out. It's getting late." Dinner, bath time, and all those other responsible things. I was still a mom with a laundry list that never ended. "See you tomorrow?" I asked Eli.

He ran both palms over his hat, and with a pained expression, linked them behind his head. "Yeah. See ya."

My phone buzzed as I pulled into our apartment complex. Finally, a number I recognized! "Hi Terry, I was wondering when you'd call."

"Hey, hon." I could hear the smile in his voice. "You throw together a pretty impressive pitch."

"Think of what I could do with a few more weeks of fine-tuning." I tucked my cell between my shoulder and ear, hopped out of the truck, and opened the passenger door for Nina.

"I always knew you had a good head on you."

This all sounded positive. "So?"

"I rejected the other offer."

Ha! Steven could eat his stupid, ostentatious heart out! I inhaled sharply to hold in the squeal.

Finally! Finally, the pieces were falling right!

"There are a few things, though ..." I heard the kiss of paper as he sifted through pages on his end. "This plan for the entrance? Gotta tell you, those trees were a beast to keep up with."

"But that's what transformed the landscape into something so magical. You drive from a bland, arid desert into a hidden oasis."

I loved those trees.

"You don't have to make it exactly the same, you know. It won't hurt my feelings."

"I know." Nina and I climbed the stairs to our unit.

"What about some of these costs?" he asked. "How are you going to recover that without any business?"

"That's what the marketing plan on page six is for." But it was a risk.

"And how long you gonna have before everything comes due?"

I grimaced. He'd hit on the one flaw in my plan. I unlocked the door and let Nina in first. "That's why I'm working at the landscape place. The income will help cover daily operational costs. You'll see that I intend to take out extra on the loan for renovations."

Despite my confident rebuttal, he didn't miss the facts. "You're going to run a ranch *and* work a full-time job?"

I sighed, flipping on the living room light. His concern held validation, but what choice did I have?

"Pretty busy these days," he drawled.

I stared at the twenty-year-old carpet. At the faded patches and stains from various furniture arrangements and families in transition like us. He only knew the half of it.

"But we work hard for the things we want, right, Terry?"

"I suppose so."

"How about I come by tomorrow after work," I suggested, "and answer any more questions you have about the business plan?" Face-to-face always held more gravity. People had a harder time saying "no" when you were staring right at them.

"Well, you know I always love a visit."

"Then I'll see you tomorrow?"

"Sure. See you tomorrow, hon."

I ended the call and dropped the phone on the Formica counter to evaluate the contents of my fridge.

It didn't take long.

"Hey, Crackerjack!" I called. "You're in luck. We're having pizza tonight."

22

Eli

I DIDN'T SLEEP. Not a wink.

Every time I closed my eyes, I saw Ava's drunk stare, felt her hands on me. My brain started asking, *what if*? What if I kissed her? What if she wanted me, too? She had to, right? Why else would she go through my stuff? I hope she knew how much hotter she was than any of the women in my magazine.

Her truck crunched up to the house, and I met her on the porch.

Nina ran straight to me, holding a rock bigger than her hand. "E-why, look!"

"Whoa! Cool rock, monkey."

"I'm not a monkey!"

"No?" I crouched to her level. "But you like bananas."

She stomped her foot. "I'm not a monkey. I'm a girl!"

"Okay. Okay! But, I like bananas." I pretended to think. "Maybe *I'm* the monkey."

"No!" she giggled. "You're sexy!"

I swear, the whole world went silent.

My eyes cut to Ava, who stood still as a statue. Her face matched Nina's ladybug backpack.

"I'm what?"

"Sexy!" Loud and clear.

I had no control over the smile that hijacked my face. "Where'd you hear that?"

Ava suddenly reanimated, rushing over with Nina's stuff. "Can you bring this in? I have to run. We're a little behind this morning."

"Yeah, no problem."

Her skin brushed against mine as she unloaded all of Nina's bags into my arms. It made my hair stand on end. The woman was magnetic. She was halfway back to her truck as she called, "Bye, Crackerjack!"

I dumped the stuff in a chair and chased after her. "Hey, uh, Dad's got a doctor's appointment. So, I'm gonna watch Nina solo today."

Her face fell. "Is everything okay?"

"Yeah. Just some routine thing." She was close enough I coulda tucked her hair behind her ear again.

"Okay. Um, make sure Nina eats three food groups for lunch? It's all in there." She pointed to the lunch bag.

"Three food groups, got it."

"And she takes a nap at one-thirty."

"Yup."

Her eyes veered to my smile. "Don't let her sweet-talk you out of it, or she'll be a nightmare later. Oh, and I need to make a stop after work." She grimaced. "It might be an hour?" Then, she glanced around the property, everywhere but me. "Is August coming today?"

"No. Hey, Ava?" I waited till her gaze hit mine. "You look nice."

"T-thanks."

I shifted my weight, leaning closer. She froze as I pressed a kiss to her cheek. "Have a good day."

I knew *I* would. She thought I was sexy.

Shit.

Shit! Ava's gonna kill me. Dad went outside to meet her in the driveway. The day couldn't get any worse.

I sat with Nina on the leather couch in the living room, bouncing my knee, but the kid started moaning, so I made it stop. The couch was too stiff and too brown. It needed one of Mom's bright pillows. 'Course, we didn't have them anymore. My muscles itched to move, but Nina was leaning on me, cradling one skinny arm. Her eyes looked just like her mom's when she cried. The front door opened, and feet fell in rapid succession across the tile. Here it came–my slow, brutal death. I wasn't ready.

"Nina?" Ava ran in, dropping her purse on the floor. "Nina, baby, are you okay?" She landed on her knees in front of the couch and inspected the kid, oblivious to how her body rubbed against my leg. Oblivious that I was there at all. "Does your arm hurt?"

New tears leaked as Nina reached her good limb out to her mom. Ava pulled her into her lap.

"We iced her arm," Dad said. "But she moans every time we touch it."

Ava nodded, rubbing Nina's leg, her head, her good shoulder. "Okay."

The arm was broken. I knew it was. And I hated being helpless. When I popped off the couch, Dad eyed me with a warning. Still, I said, "Want me to pick up some baby aspirin, or something?"

"No, thank you." Ava combed Nina's hair with her fingers. "Hey, Crackerjack, we need to go to the doctor, so they can x-ray your arm."

Nina wailed, adding another layer of tears and snot to her face.

I squatted next to them. "Hey Kiddo, listen to your mom. She knows what to do."

Ava's sharp, angry eyes sliced to me. "Back off."

"Come on! It's not like I dropped her off the roof. It was an accident."

"Jesus, Eli." Dad tipped his head back as if the savior might drop through the ceiling and fix this.

Ava stood with Nina, fitted in her usual hip spot.

I followed. "Ava, I'm sorry."

"I can't believe you let her climb the rails!"

"She's a kid. Kids climb. I was watching her the whole time."

"Until you weren't? What were you thinking?" Ava squeezed her eyes shut and pinched the bridge of her nose.

Great, now she was gonna cry. Two for two. One of Mom's cushions would've been handy right about then. To smother myself with. I already felt shitty about the whole thing. "I get you're upset. Let me help."

"I don't want your help."

"Because of this?" This being the broken arm.

Ava inhaled, and I braced for it. "Did she eat lunch?"

I didn't answer.

"Did she nap?"

"Her arm was hurting."

"*That's* why, Eli." She shook her head. "I should've just brought her to work with me."

I wasn't a total screw-up! We had a great day until she fell. "You had her car seat! I couldn't leave her here to pick up pain meds. What should I have done, huh?"

"Eli," Dad warned, again.

No. I wouldn't stand there and not defend myself. "Kids climb. It's what they do, Ava."

Her expression turned so dark that the last few weeks of my life flashed before my eyes. "Fine. Let her climb one rung. Maybe two. But to the top of the fence? I mean, come on, Eli! She's three! Have some common sense!"

I'd been accused of a lot, but lacking common sense? Never. "You can't protect her from everything. Kids get hurt. That's life!"

"No. This accident was totally preventable! *You* made a bad call."

I raised my voice to be heard over Nina's crying. "Lots of people make bad calls. Even the parents, sometimes! Casts come in colors for a reason. She can pick a pink one! Unless you feel the need to choose one for her!"

"Elijah Tremain Anderson!" Dad hollered. "Take a lap and cool your engine."

But Ava wasn't done. "She shouldn't have to pick a color! Or spend the day in a hospital being poked and prodded!"

"Ava, you're being–"

"What? What am I being? A mother?" Ava's glare was lethal, on the verge of drawing blood. "Well, I was a mother long before I met you. So, don't tell me how to raise my child!"

"That's enough!" Dad's authority boomed through the room. "Ava, take Nina to the hospital. Eli, take a minute somewhere else."

I clamped my jaw shut long enough for them to leave the house. Let her be mad. Life happened. It didn't wait for permission. She should know better than anyone.

Dad closed the front door, and the room filled with silence. This was high school all over again, me staring at my boots, waiting for a scolding. After the customary pause meant to light the flame of self-reflection, all he said was, "That could've gone better." Then he crossed the tile floor and disappeared into the master suite. He didn't call me reckless or rag on me for being hot-headed.

He didn't have to.

For the first time since Ava showed up, I felt the pull of the open road–no expectations, no responsibilities. No one to disappoint. Did it make me happy? Maybe not, but it beat the cocktail sloshing around in my stomach.

"Damnit."

I stormed through the mudroom, up the garage stairs to my studio. Opened all the cabinets and drawers and stared at their contents. How long would it take to pack it all up? *Less time than it takes to cast a kid's arm, I bet.*

Even with the big windows, the room was suffocating, the walls closing in. What the hell was I doing there? I hadn't managed a single task Dad asked me to do. The place was losing money. Even if I found him a manager, how would he pay them? What was his deal with this house? This ranch? I took off my hat, flexed the faded bill, stared at the frayed seams. The hat my mom gave me on my first day of seventh grade. Her last gift.

Dang it. I couldn't leave. Dad loved this place, and long before this asinine summer commitment, I'd made a promise to Mom. I paused at the window, frowned at the tire tracks Ava's truck left behind.

If I'd learned anything about emergency room visits, it'd be late when they got home. Would she grab something to eat on the way back? Or skip dinner to get Nina into bed? I ran a hand through my hair, then returned my hat to where it lived nearly every waking hour.

What would Mom do?

The container of spaghetti sat in an insulated chest on the seat next to me. Ava's truck wasn't at her apartment yet.

I shut off my engine and waited. Shadows stretched as the sun went down, but the heat refused to follow. My mind chewed on the ranch, Luke, mornings that smelled like frying bacon instead of cheap hotel soap. I couldn't take my weights on the road. Having laundry so close was a huge plus. But those were comforts, not necessities. People were always saying, "Less is more." And I'd always been fine with less.

A familiar set of yellowed headlights bounced into the parking lot. My chest squeezed. Should I jump out to help her? Or wait until she put her stuff down? She slid out of her Chevy, threw a bunch of bags over her shoulder, then trekked to the passenger side, reappearing with a sleeping Nina draped across her chest. Spaghetti soured in my stomach. A bright red cast ran all the way up the kid's arm.

As Ava hoofed up the stairs to her apartment, I grabbed the cooler, hand on the door handle, but I hesitated. *Here, Ava, have some mediocre spaghetti.* This plan felt stupid now. Especially seeing how late they rolled in. And sitting in that sterile hospital room probably killed her appetite. I was just about to abort this stupid mission when movement caught my eye on the lower level.

"Oh, hell no." I left the spaghetti in the truck.

A familiar suit started up the outside steps. Steven made quick work, crowding Ava on her own stoop.

"What do you want?" she growled.

I jogged up, keeping my footfalls silent.

"I came by to check on you," he said.

"Bull. This is you, isn't it?" She ripped a piece of paper off her door and shoved it into his chest. Then she clocked me behind him. "Ugh," she groaned. "I don't have the energy for this."

When Steven turned, I was in his face. "Oh, look, it's the bodyguard." He crossed his skinny arms over a wrinkled shirt, and the notice from her door floated to the ground.

Eviction Notice.

My stomach pitted straight through the concrete.

"Seriously, everyone, just go away," she begged.

I mirrored Steven's stance. "Thought I made myself clear last time I saw you. You give her problems, you can deal with me."

"Oh, yeah? Well, we're not on your turf anymore."

"I can punch you anywhere." To his credit, he didn't flinch. Maybe he thought I was joking?

"I'll press charges," he said.

"It'd be worth it."

Ava covered a hand over Nina's ear as the kid slept on. "If anyone's doing the punching, it'll be me. Steven, if you're the reason I have to move again–"

"Were you aware that lying on your application breaches a contract?" Steven said.

Ava's jaw flexed.

He shrugged. "You signed a legal document claiming income two days after sending me your registration letter. An eviction is well within legal rights."

Her nostrils flared, and her lips got thin. "What is it you think this will accomplish?"

He slid his hands into his pants pockets. Even his back looked sleazy, full of petty threats because it had no spine. "My client is sending in a new bid. They'll be very disappointed if the second one gets rejected."

"Then talk to the seller," Ava shot back.

"How about *you* tell Terry you changed your mind, and I'll ask the landlord to let you stay?"

She laughed. "Seriously? That's your bargaining chip? Give up my dreams to stay in this crummy apartment?"

I narrowed my focus to Steven's skinny neck, playing out a few scenarios. Pretty sure my name sat at the top of Ava's shit list, so not much to lose there. But I wouldn't be much use to her if I had to call Dad for bail.

Steven kept talking. "You can't win this. You don't have the buying power."

"Terry values morals over money."

"Everyone has a price, Ava."

She tilted her head in challenge.

"Is it worth it?" he asked. "All this for a dried-out patch of dirt?"

"Absolutely."

"Your husband's dead. This won't bring him back."

Ava's expression turned stony.

Steven rocked on his heels, probably thinking he'd won. "Have fun finding a new place to live." He turned to leave so someone else could do his dirty work. Only now he had to get through me.

He probably thought days of stubble made him suave, but he just looked like a hobo. Shoving his fingers through his greasy hair, he said. "You got a nice place, by the way. Call me if you ever think of selling."

One night in jail. Two if I broke his nose.

"Eli, don't," Ava begged. "I can't deal with more drama tonight."

I forced open my fist and let him pass. For Ava. We watched Steven reach the landing, then strut to my truck and stick a business card on my windshield.

"That cocky son of a bi–"

"Language," Ava cut in, but it lacked conviction.

I picked up the eviction notice. "Tomorrow by noon?"

She released a frustrated groan, crouched to her purse, and started digging. I grabbed the bags at her feet and waited while she unlocked the door. No arguments when I followed her in. She disappeared into the bedroom with Nina.

Poor kid.

Papers covered the dining table, so I put the bags on the counter. Dirty dishes waited for her in the sink and on the stove. I hunted for the thermostat. It had to be ninety degrees inside.

"*... a mom long before I met you.*"

A mom without a partner.

Looking around, I could see it. She never got a break. I stationed myself at the sink and soaped a sponge. How many hours of sleep did she lose cleaning up at night? And now, she had to pack all her shit again? Where would she go?

Ava yawned as she came into the kitchen. "What are you doing?"

"Washing dishes."

"Yeah, I can see that." She reached past me to shut off the water. "I meant, what are you doing *here*?"

I wiped my soapy hands on my Carhartts. "I brought you dinner. It's still in the truck. But now I'm gonna stay and help you pack."

She pressed her fingers into her temples. "Eli, I'm tired. And I have a headache."

"Then go lie down. I got this."

"Eli ..."

All my life, I hated my name. Mom wanted biblical, Dad didn't. So, in true marriage fashion, as Dad told it, they "compromised." Now, those three little letters, my three letters, hit like a prayer when it came from her lips. Hell, she could have it all. Middle name, too. Say it any way she wanted. If Ryan thought that made me housebroken, so be it.

"If you're not gonna lie down, then put some ice on it." But her freezer had no ice. The best I could find was a bag of frozen corn.

Ava crossed her arms, stubborn eyes tracking me.

I closed the distance, icy kernels grinding against each other in my grip. "Where does it hurt?"

"Everywhere."

I pressed the bag to her forehead. "Here?"

Her mouth flattened into an annoyed line.

"I didn't punch your ex. Give me this? Please?"

Her shoulders dropped. She took the bag from my fingers and held it to the back of her head. "That day when you stormed into the stable all pissed off? When you gave me the gate key, that was because of Steven?"

"Yeah." The entitled prick took his yuppy Mercedes right up to the house. "Not sure how he knew you were there."

"Location app," she sighed. "Which I have since removed." She blinked at my chest. "I wish you'd told me."

"You had an interview. I didn't want him messing with your headspace."

"Well, thank you. I guess."

The anger was gone. Now she just sounded tired. There couldn't be more than six inches between us, but that half-foot tortured me. "Can you promise not to get mad if I say something?"

She pulled back. "The fact you have to ask makes me want to say no."

"Ava, that guy's been harassing you for weeks. Living here by yourself, you're totally exposed."

"Exposed?" She shifted the frozen vegetables to the other side. "Well, it's a non-issue since I'll be moving. Again."

"You said this landlord was his friend? What if the next one is, too?"

Based on the way her face fell, she hadn't thought about that. She dropped the corn on the counter and scrubbed her face with her hands. "I don't know," she groaned. "I was more worried about the fact that I don't have pay stubs from Rock 'N Roll yet. Eli, how am I going to get an apartment by tomorrow?"

"Move into the house."

"What?"

"Dad's got the empty room downstairs. The one where you, you know ..." flashes of her crumpling to the floor flooded my brain. "It even has an attached bathroom."

"No."

"Look, I know you're mad at me, but it's safer. Someone's always around."

"Steven wouldn't actually hurt me. He doesn't have the horseshoes for that."

"Uh, eviction notice? How is that not hurting you?"

She sighed, but didn't argue.

"I've got more reasons if you wanna hear 'em?"

Then, with eyes closed, she folded into the counter, pressing her forehead to the fake tile.

"You'd have help," I said. "Dishes, babysitting."

Her mass of hair shook from side to side.

"You wouldn't have to rush to drop Nina off. Or come home to rubbery grits. There'd be coffee ready when you woke up."

She peeled herself off the counter and pressed her fingertips to my mouth, and I swear to God, my heart stopped. Ten heartbeats passed like that. But on beat seven, her eyes fell to her fingers. Beat eight, she ran her thumb across my lower lip. Nine to ten, that drunk, devouring look surfaced, like before.

She pulled her hand away. "Thank you for the offer."

This argument mattered. For her safety. For Nina's. But all I could think was, *do it again.*

"I know you're just trying to help ..." she was saying.

I might die, but do it anyway.

"... so generous. I don't want to be underfoot ..."

Underfoot, underneath, underwear, undressed. It unraveled too fast to stop it. This woman, who'd been on my mind every night for the past two weeks.

"... need space."

Space–the last thing I needed. In fact, I compressed the six inches between us into three.

"You already have a full house." It sounded more like she was trying to convince herself.

"Got any more lame excuses?"

"They aren't lame!"

"They are. And you know it. How many deposits are you willing to lose just to make a point?"

"I-I have other excellent reasons."

"Such as?"

Her eyes dropped to my mouth again.

Say it.

"The thing is," she licked her lips, flicked her eyes back to me. "I want Nina to see her mom as strong and independent, so she'll grow up strong and independent."

"Those are two things I admire most about you."

"A-and I don't want her to think she needs a man to come in and rescue her, to fight her battles for her."

"What if I want to fight for you?"

Ava opened her mouth, but nothing came out on her first try. "Fight my battles, you mean?"

Those three inches between us begged to be crossed. This strong, independent woman in front of me stripped the world away, quieted all those pesky distractions. Made me feel grounded. And I wanted to give her the same thing. "Have you eaten?"

"What?"

"I have spaghetti for you in the car."

"I'm not hungry."

"Eat something," I said. "Get some rest. I'll be here at first light with boxing tape."

23

Ava

"*WHAT IF I want to fight for you?*"

I rubbed my hands down my face, but that didn't make his words go away. What did he mean? Why say that, act so sweet, then *not* kiss me? He had leaned in so close his breath grazed my face, turned my chest into a cage of butterflies, and then he just ... didn't.

Was he teasing me? Testing me?

No, this was better. I was supposed to be in charge, hold boundaries, because no amount of "sorry" could undo the damage or reverse the hours spent in the hospital.

Nina slept in my bed with me, and I had the bruises to prove it. At three AM, our day started, and crankiness saturated every faded, dated, and stained fiber of our soon-to-be ex-apartment. A pre-dawn breakfast and a dose of pain medicine later, I stared at the messy living room. Even with Eli's help, this would take more than half a day. And because I'd lied on my application, I had no recourse. Eli was right. Parents made bad calls, too. How hard would another move be on Nina?

I plopped onto the overly firm couch beside her as she flipped through her Daniel Tiger book. This day would be an uphill, off-road ride in a Prius. The weather forecast predicted triple digits by ten. And poor Nina, stuck in a cast that spanned knuckle to armpit? The air conditioning in Bill's house sang like a siren's call.

No. No more free handouts. No more temporary.

Nina needed stability. I could solve this. Problem one: I wouldn't be getting my deposit back. Assuming I found a place outside of Steven's influence, I'd have to pull from my down payment fund, which was already at the bare minimum. Problem two: My credit was still under investigation. A temporary easement for a background check wouldn't erase all the new cards opened in my name. What would a landlord make of that? And with no current pay stub?

Fury funneled through me. Who knew Steven could stoop so low? I had missed all the warning signs! And they were everywhere! His refusal to park my broken-down truck in front of his house. The late daycare fees *I* had to pay due to overtime at *his* request. He had quoted HOA rules and accused me of taking long lunches. But really, his selfish acts only proved he cared more about status than substance. I'd thought being with someone would feel less lonely, but the busy days only masked how alone I truly was.

Nina closed her book. "Mama? I go to Abi's house?"

I smoothed a hand down her hair. "I don't know. But I'm staying home today to make sure you're feeling better." I'd chewed my lip raw, fretting the call-out in my first week at a new job. When I pulled out my phone, knowing I couldn't put it off any longer, I saw a text from Bill.

Bill: Bring your stuff over. We'll set you up in the spare room. Talk about details later. Bill.

Eli must've said something. The boy who rescued strays. If I weren't so tired, I might've resented what that made me. This choice felt like two steps back.

But what other options were there?

At seven, Eli showed up in jeans, a faded green t-shirt, and, of course, his signature baseball cap. How could everyday clothes seduce their way under my skin so easily? The casual sway of his gait held no regret or reservation about what *didn't* happen last night, so as soon as he started taking things to his truck, I hid in the bedroom. Me, Nina, and a mountain of wrinkled clothes to fold.

How did he do it? Live out of a suitcase? I bet he had a system. Probably only enough clothing to get by. A single duffle to throw over his shoulder and disappear. Exactly why we weren't a good fit!

My pile taunted me.

Screw it.

I shoved unfolded shirts and shorts into a suitcase with extra force. "Nina, can you sit on this?" She found my request hilarious and sprawled over the suitcase in a fit of giggles while I forced the zipper closed.

I didn't finish by noon, but nobody sent for law enforcement.

We staged my belongings in Bill's den so I could assemble Nina's bed first. No sooner had I laid all the pieces on the carpet than she wandered in with a request.

"Mama, can we see the horsies?"

I'd vowed to be at her beck and call for the day, so I put down my screwdriver and walked her to the stable. She marched straight to Misty with her broken arm held high. "Look at my cast!" The painkillers appeared to be working. She spun a 180 and waved it at Royal with the same gleeful pride. "It's red!" Her little legs carried her down the line to Chuck. "It's broken." She slowed as she reached Sugar's stall, closer than she'd ever been to the painted before. "But I'm very bwave."

An unfamiliar truck bumped its way to the stable. Bill, too, on foot. The truck stopped at the end stall, and a stranger hopped out to greet Misty. Bill caught up, carrying a folder, and the two chatted before the stranger took an offered pen and signed a paper form Bill presented to him.

Nina tugged on my shirt. "Who's dat?"

"I'm guessing Misty's owner."

We watched the stranger fix Misty with a lead, swing the trailer open, and guide her inside.

"Mama, why's he taking her?"

"I don't know." They drove off, and a somber energy encompassed the stable.

"Where is she go-ed?"

"Probably to a different stable."

Bill wandered over, forcing a smile atop his worry lines. He leaned against the rails of the empty stall. Now he had four vacancies. "Got all your stuff moved?"

"Yes. It's in the den right now, but I'll work on getting it put away."

He glanced down at Nina's cast, and the corners of his mouth made a slow, steady descent like an elevator to the basement level. "What did the doctor say?"

"It's a fracture and a break. They had to reset the radius." It was horrible, and I hated every second. I'd have given anything to trade places with her. "They cast the whole thing so she doesn't stress it."

"Poor kid."

"She's a trooper, though. The nurses all loved her. We have *lots* of Disney stickers. Lots. Don't be surprised if she gives you one. Or ten."

Nina reached her good arm through Chuck's fence to pet him. He thrusted his head between the rails and rubbed against her in cat-like fashion, but one overly eager nudge sent Nina to her butt.

"Oops!" I jogged over, lifting her back to her feet. "I think he likes you *too* much."

"Bad horsie!"

"That's how they show affection. He's hugging you."

"No hugs! I has an owie." She pointed to her cast. "See?"

But Chuck ignored her, already busy biting down on the gate latch in an escape attempt.

Bill walked over and shoved the horse's head aside. "Stop that. It's bad for your teeth." He waited while I dusted Nina's bottom, then asked, "Did you get your dinner last night?"

"I did, thank you. It hit the spot. I knew Marley had it in her."

Bill ran a hand down the roan's neck and smiled. "Marley didn't make it. Eli did."

"Eli?" My obstinate heart fluttered. "Really?"

The new information only seemed to muddy the picture. Like painting a new color before the underlayer had dried. Why did every detail only draw me in more? I was supposed to be mad at him!

Bill studied me. "I wasn't gonna butt in, 'cause it's not my business. But he's trying. More than I've seen him do in a while. Maybe ever."

"*What if I want to fight for you?*" His words kept echoing in my head, and each replay left me feeling more foolish. "Well, next time he can try with someone else's kid."

Bill pushed Chuck's head away from the gate latch again. "Hey, I think peanut over there is ready for a nap."

I glanced past my shoulder in time to catch Nina stagger into the tack room. "I think you're right. I'd better finish her bed."

From inside the boarded-up stall came a *thump*, followed by a high-pitched whine. *This is going to be a long day.*

"There's one of those folding pads in the closet under the stairs," Bill offered.

If anyone deserved a kiss, it was him. "Thank you."

Bill didn't say he also had a fuzzy Minnie Mouse blanket and a dog-shaped pillow. This man needed grandchildren.

I rubbed Nina's head while she drifted off. She looked so fragile, sprawled on her back, the red cast jutting like a whack-a-mole club. But she'd handled the emergency room visit better than I had. I was no stranger to the happenings of life, as Eli insinuated. Those happenings fueled the fire of my caution. He didn't have anyone who relied on him, so how could he understand?

I pried myself off the floor before I too fell asleep, and crept upstairs. Bill sat at the kitchen table with a can of beer.

Beer? This early?

"Is she asleep?" he asked.

"Almost before her head hit the pillow." I sat across from him, stifling a yawn.

"You should take a nap, too."

"No. I have too much to do."

"Then how 'bout some coffee?" Before I could answer, he rose and crossed to the coffeemaker. "You take milk or sugar?"

"Milk, please." It felt wrong to be waited on. Wrong to take, take, take. I'd decided I would only stay long enough to collect paystubs and secure a new apartment. This constant moving grated against my nature. No wonder my nerves were in shreds.

Bill's phone pinged as he added milk to my cup. "*Dag nammit,* I'm getting old. Ava, I don't suppose you could do me a favor?"

"Of course."

He crossed the kitchen and set my coffee in front of me. "I forgot I have a guy coming out. Met him at Walmart. He works at a few ranches in the area. Seems to know a lot about the business side. If Eli's not back, would you give him a once-over for me? Maybe walk him around the ranch?"

"Sure." I picked up my cup and inhaled the steam before testing the temperature. "What time is he coming?"

"In about thirty minutes. He doesn't have to be a perfect fit. I just need someone who will do for now."

"For now?"

His gaze went far away. I'd seen that million-mile stare before.

No! The doctor's appointment. The late notices.

My mug landed with a *thunk* on the tabletop. Coffee sloshed over the edge. "Bill, are you sick?"

His glasses shot up with his eyebrows. "What? No! No, no, nothing like that."

I pressed a hand to my racing heart. "Jeez, you scared me."

"No. Not sick. Though I'm glad to know someone cares." He retrieved a paper towel and handed it to me before resuming his seat.

"Thanks." I'm sure Eli cared, but I said nothing. I mopped up my mess, then lifted his beer to wipe the ring from the condensation.

Bill's eyes went soft as he watched me. "You're a coaster person, aren't you?"

"Not usually, but this is a great table. It would be a shame to ruin it."

Contented crinkles deepened behind his glasses. He slid an aged palm across the wooden surface with a sigh of appreciation. "It *is* a great table."

A companionable silence wrapped us both in an afternoon lull. I sipped my coffee, grateful for the mini-break.

"It's for Eli," Bill said.

"The table?"

"The ranch. I built it for him. If he wants it."

"What?"

Dawning washed over me in a slow wave. Facts connected. Oddities suddenly made sense. Bare walls held space for art, neutrals waited for coordinating area rugs, throw pillows, and decorative plants. "Oh." The clutterless house wasn't a showy centerfold. It was a blank slate, waiting for someone to make it a home.

I frowned. Eli's "thing" was open roads and new places. He told me so on the first day we met. I chose my next words carefully. "Does he know that?"

Bill shook his head, curling his fingers around his beer can. "He needs to want it. If I have to tell him, it's not much of a choice."

"What do you mean?"

"He always does what he thinks is best for others." Bill took a heavy sip from his beer. "This was her dream house."

"Whose?" But I already knew.

"Leah's." He cleared his throat. "Eli's mom." After a long pause, he added, "Leah died of cancer."

"I heard. I'm so sorry." More sorry than three little words could express. I knew the pain of losing both a spouse and a parent.

The corner of his eye twitched–a fleeting moment of emotional surrender he fortified with another gulp of his beer. "It was hard. Hard for me. Hard for Hannah." His mouth formed a perfect St. Louis Arch. "But it was *really* hard for Eli." After a beat, he said, "It wasn't long or painful. Quite the opposite, really. So quick, none of us had any time to process it."

A house full of empty spaces, a kitchen furnished with an overly large kitchen table. It perfectly explained the hopes and dreams of the man sitting across from me. I studied his face and knew then I'd never get over Jason or the life we'd planned together. The family we'd hoped for. But I also knew I'd never be happy sitting at an empty table in a big empty house, missing a ghost. And it was safe to assume, neither would Bill.

My fingers played with the handle of my mug. "You designed a beautiful house. Eli would be lucky to have it."

"Thank you." He inhaled, and his shoulders lifted toward a new topic. "So ... You know Terry Evanston?"

"I do! Hidden Meadows is the ranch I'm trying to buy."

"We used to board there, you know."

"I do. That was actually what made me trust Eli enough to wind up at your ranch."

Some of the spark returned to Bill's eyes. "Leah always said no life was worth living without horses. She would've put them right in the backyard if she could've. But we lived in the city."

"Did you ever ride?"

"No." He laughed, but it sounded bittersweet. "I was always working."

"But you kept her dream alive."

He stared into his beer can. "Welp, I promised I would when I took her hand."

My own vow burned a hole in my chest. Promises. So easy to make. Not as easy to keep. But I was trying.

"I, uh," he scratched his chin. "I worry about Eli. Hannah's a whirlwind, but if she's in a bind, she'll ask for help. Eli? He's a suffer-in-silence kind. It's hard, never knowing where he stops for the night, wondering if he's eating well, if he's lonely."

It took every ounce of self-control not to tell Bill about the broken ribs.

I'd always thought babyhood had to be the hardest part of parenting because out came a tiny human and *boom*, you took her home with no training, no manual, and no factory reset, functioning on minimal hygiene and even less sleep. But one day, Nina would be an adult. Getting left behind sounded so much harder.

"You should tell Eli," I said.

"That I worry about him?"

"No, that you built him his mom's house."

Bill shook his head. "I won't guilt him into staying. It has to be his choice. Not what he thinks I want."

"So, you asked him to help you hire a ranch manager, hoping he'd like it here and decide to stick around?"

The older man chuckled. "Guess I'm not as sneaky as I thought."

I bit my lip, hesitating. "Speaking of sneaky, what's going on with the ranch? I saw the final notice."

"Oh." He settled his elbows on the table. "It needs some reorganization. But I'm waiting to see if Eli wants it before I put in the effort."

Sympathy flooded my bloodstream. What if it all worked out? For Eli to be close to his mom again through her love of horses. For Bill to have his son back. To fill this darn kitchen table with hungry stomachs and loud conversation. I wanted that for Bill as much as I wanted my own happy ending.

He drained his beer in one final gulp, then slapped his hand on the wooden tabletop. "Welp, now you know why an old poke like me is playing with horses." The bench scuffed backwards as he stood.

"What will you do if he doesn't want it?"

A devastating weight fell with his silence. Bill's eyes skated over the countertops, out the window, then back to me. "What does an old guy like me need all this house for?"

"But you put your heart into this place!"

"Sometimes there's only so much you can do."

My head pivoted right to left, defiantly. "You should just ask him. From what I've seen, you two make a good team."

"*That* is a recent development." His phone chirped, effectively ending our afternoon break. "That must be our Walmart guy."

I forced myself up, collecting the empty beverage containers. "I'll give him a tour and see what he says."

The faint roar of an engine drew my attention to the front window. One familiar Ford, and a Silverado I didn't recognize, pulled to a stop in front of the house. A wrapped mattress stuck up in the bed of the Ford.

My gut sank. I hoped that wasn't for me.

Eli's voice entered the house ahead of him. "Hey, Dad, there's a guy out front who says he's here to see the ranch?" He appeared in the kitchen holding a gray plastic bag, his shirt matted to his chest with sweat.

"I forgot to tell you," Bill said. "I ran into this guy at the Walmart. He manages some ranches in the area. I asked him to come by."

Eli dumped the shopping bag on the table. When he glanced at me, I looked away. "You want me to take him around?" he asked.

"Ava said she'd do it. Wasn't sure when you'd be back. Maybe you can both go?"

We responded at the same time.

"What?"

"Why?"

Bill winked and said, "Because I asked you to."

24

Eli

"Well, that was painful." I crossed the kitchen and dropped onto the bench across from Dad. Took my hat off, flexed the bill. "He could've just said 'not interested.'"

Ava hung by the island, all quiet. She'd *been* quiet. Even when the guy went off about how much our ranch sucked.

Dad pushed aside his newspaper Sudoku puzzle. "Oh?"

"Yeah, as soon as we get to the stable, he's saying things like, 'If you want to make this a *real business*, you have work to do.'"

"What kind of work?" Dad didn't sound offended at all.

"I don't know. Sand? Shades? Does he have any idea how much that stuff costs?"

Dad glanced back at Ava. Her lips were pressing together like words were just dying to get out. *Good.* She'd been giving me the silent treatment all day. I figured it was 'cause she wanted space, but it was killing me. She had to know I felt terrible about Nina.

I shoved my hat on. "Tell me I'm wrong."

Her eyes jumped between Dad and me. "Actually, he made some good observations."

What?

"Sand keeps the stalls cleaner." Her eyes cut to my arms as I crossed them. "A-and a shade over the arena would protect the horses and humans from overheating. I'd actually go further and suggest a misting hose around the top. It's cheap, easy, and a luxury that might draw fresh interest."

I stared at her.

Finally, she speaks, and it's a stab in the back. "Anything else you wanna add there, boss? Throw down some fancy grass? Build a cafe?" The second I said it, I regretted it.

"I'm going to check on Nina."

And back to silent treatment.

Dad returned to his puzzle. "So, he's a no-go?" He penciled in numbers, erased one, wrote another. "Guess we'll have to keep looking."

I dug my fingers under my hat. What was that manifestation thing people did? You visualize what you want? I closed my eyes and tried to imagine myself not saying stupid shit.

"What's in the bag?" Dad asked.

I opened my eyes. "What?"

He nodded at the shopping bag on the table.

Linking fingers at the base of my skull, I stared at the ceiling. "It's a floor puzzle. For Nina. Kinda hoped if I kept her on the ground, Ava would give me another chance."

"Smart."

"Yeah, well, she won't even look at me today."

"I'm sure she'll come around."

I thought she had last night. Turned out, she was just too tired to fight with me. God, I'd wanted to kiss her, but Luke's comment messed with my head. She wasn't just some booty call.

Dad folded his newspaper and sighed. "Cheer up, son. She hasn't disowned you yet."

My fingers found the stitching in my hat. *Have to be owned to be disowned.* "I can't believe she agreed with that pompous know-it-all out there!"

"You know, it's healthy to get a little outside criticism."

"That wasn't a little criticism. That was a ranting one-star review!"

"Don't take it too personally."

Too late. This was our business, and he treated it like some kind of hobby. "And then he asked if we had a business license."

"I assume you told him we did."

"How would I know that?" That itch crawled up my leg. The music at full blast, windows down, endless road kind of itch. I popped up and stared out the window. Ava's mattress sat in my truck bed, baking. "Wanna help me haul in the bed?"

"Nina's napping downstairs."

"Fine. I'll go work on the paddock." But that's not where I ended up. I ducked through the bars into the arena, where Denver looked bored as all get-out.

"Hey, buddy."

He stomped.

"I hear ya. I don't like being cooped up either." I slid a hand down his nose, then noticed the water bucket was bone dry, so I dragged out the hose to refill it. It made a mess because I didn't feel like going back and forth to open the valve.

Denver nosed at the puddle, then pawed it.

"You like that?"

I lifted the spray to make it bigger, and he full-on dropped and rolled in it.

Shoot. Maybe I *should* throw up a UV sail or two.

I topped off all the water buckets, made puddles for the other horses, then walked back to the house. Ava's truck was gone, and Dad was sitting in the living room flipping through a magazine.

"Where are the girls?"

He turned a page. "They went out for ice cream."

"Great. Wanna help me with the mattress?"

I'd just tipped Ava's mattress on its frame when Nina ran into the room with chocolate smeared around her mouth. Ava's bed sat in one corner, and I'd put Nina's on the opposite wall with the window between them. Seemed like a good layout.

"Yay! My bed!" she cheered. She launched herself onto it, shoes and all, making the toddler-sized springs groan with each bounce.

I snagged her under the armpits, aching ribs be damned, and swung her back to the white carpet. "All flights have been canceled until further notice." This kid needed to keep her feet on the ground while I was on probation.

Ava came via the den, pausing at the doorway. She had her hair up in a messy ponytail, shiny and just begging to be touched. But I knew that wasn't gonna happen when her eyes landed on her corner.

"Eli, please say you did *not* buy me a mattress."

"I would, but then you'd yell at me for lying."

She tipped her head back, closed her eyes, and I could just picture fire coming outta them. But instead of burning me alive, she stormed out of the room.

"Where else are you gonna sleep?" I called after her. There had to be some way to win her back over. "Did you see the walk-in closet?" No response. Glancing down at Nina, I said, "Come here, kid, let's clean you up." I took her to the sink in the connected bathroom to wipe her face. At least one of the Garcia girls wanted my help.

A minute later, Ava stormed back in, and I knew it wasn't

gonna be good. Like the time the principal caught me graffi-
tiing the bleachers after school.

"What are you doing?" she asked.

"I'm making sure chocolate doesn't get on everything."

"No, I mean, this." She drew a big circle with her arm. "The
room. The help. The bed. Are you trying to apologize? Are you
trying to seduce me?"

"Why? Is it working?"

She scoffed. But it wasn't a "no."

"Mama, what's *seducey*?"

If I weren't in the middle of getting reprimanded, I would've
laughed. Instead, I squatted down to Nina's level. "Hey, Monkey.
I bought you something."

Her eyes lit up.

"Wanna go see what it is?"

"Yes!"

"It's in the kitchen. The gray bag on the table." Her little feet
were already scrambling out of the bathroom. "But wait for me
to help you open it!"

Ava crossed her arms and glared as we listened to the baby
elephant thumps travel up the stairs.

I stood. "Relax. It's a puzzle." More glaring. "You're right, I
don't know anything about parenting. If you want me to return
it, I'll return it."

"No." She rubbed her hands over her face. The angry vibes
faded, and suddenly she looked exhausted again. "It's fine." A
long exhale blew from her lips. "Thank you. For getting us
set up."

"You're welcome." I studied the shadows that lived under
her eyes, and I thought back to those dishes that had been
waiting in the sink at her apartment. To the boxes out in the
den. She'd kill herself trying to do it all. "You should take a nap,
or something. I can watch Nina."

"No, I–"

"We'll do the floor puzzle in the den. All feet firmly on the ground."

"I can't."

"Ava, please give me another chance. I'm not gonna screw it up, I promise."

"No. I know you won't."

She did?

"I can't nap because I have no bedding."

"Oh." I glanced into the bedroom at her naked mattress. "I'm sure Dad has some."

But he didn't. Not full-sized, anyway. By the time I made it back downstairs, she was shifting boxes into her room. *Always moving.*

"What color do you want?" I asked her. "I'm gonna head out right now."

"It's fine, I'll go. I have other things to pick up, anyway."

"So do I. Guess we'll go together." I barreled on before she could argue. "Are we taking Nina?"

"Yes."

"Great. I'll drive."

I turned off the gravel driveway and onto the main road as Ava dug through her purse. "Shoot," she muttered. "I forgot my sunglasses."

"I've got an extra pair." I popped open the center console, but instead of sunglasses, I found an envelope full of cash. *Ha!* "Sneaky."

"I don't know what you're talking about." She directed her gaze to the side window.

I loved playful Ava. The air conditioning pumped, the radio played a hit, and I didn't have any plans other than her and Nina. What else did I need?

After digging around, I found my spare shades. "So, you like your room?"

"Yeah ..."

That sounded loaded. "But?"

"I guess I was wondering why Marley didn't get it?"

I veered my truck onto the freeway. "Because Marley's a brat."

A laugh popped out of Ava's mouth. "Okay. Where are her parents?"

"In Prescott. Her mom wanted to send her to boot camp. That door on the back wall of your room? It's a second entrance from the mudroom. That would've given her way too much freedom."

"So she *is* part of your kid's program?"

"I told you, it's not a program."

Ava hummed at the passenger window. "So, what about Marley? Why did your aunt want to send her to boot camp?"

"DUI."

"Yikes."

I ran a hand over my hat. "I thought a little grunt work would scare her straight, but she doesn't listen. It's like she doesn't care."

"Maybe she has low self-confidence."

I scoffed. "That girl throws more attitude than a mare in heat."

"Attitude and confidence aren't the same thing." Ava crossed her legs, and my eyes wandered. "You're the cool, older cousin. She's probably hoping to impress you."

I've had dreams about those legs. "You think I'm cool?"

"I *think* you missed the take-home."

Eyes to the road. "I doubt Marley cares what I think."

"Eli, she's a teenage girl. Of course she cares what you think."

Ava loaded Nina in a red shopping cart and led us straight to the aisle with the baby crack. She grabbed a tube for the kid and opened it right there. Nina stuck her scrawny little hand in and pulled out handfuls at a time while Ava browsed the shelves.

I trailed a few steps behind. Did grown women care what I thought, too? Is that why she kept insisting on doing everything on her own? Was she trying to impress me?

Ava tossed a sheet set into the cart.

"I'm buying that," I told her.

"No, you're not. I have to contribute *something*."

"You contribute a lot."

She ignored me and kept walking, past the plastic storage bins, past the coffeemakers. I had to take the value pack of toilet paper outta the cart and put it back on the shelf.

"Ava, you don't have to buy this stuff. There's plenty at the house."

"And we'll be using it up–Hey!"

I'd also snagged the paper towels she'd just tossed in and shoved them in an empty spot on the display as we passed.

"That's not even where it goes!" she argued.

"Then stop grabbing stuff you don't need."

She slowed by the Band-Aids and sliced a glare my way.

"What's with the look?" I asked.

"If you try to stop me from purchasing bandages, I will stick an entire package on you while you sleep. I'm taking hair, eyebrows, everything!"

I held my hands up in surrender. "Hey, you can come up to my room anytime."

"That's not what I meant!" She threw the box at my chest, and it fell to the floor.

I bent to get it. "I'm just saying ..."

"Maybe your mouth, too."

I crowded in next to her, putting my *mouth* an inch from her ear so Nina wouldn't hear. "You can have me any way you want me. Anywhere, anytime."

Her cheeks flushed brighter than the employees' shirts. "I think we're done." She grabbed the Band-Aids from my hand, then sped off with the cart faster than a horse jockey.

The hamper, her Band-Aids, meat, vegetables, random stuff from those bins at the front, and the blue floral bedspread all got loaded on the conveyor before she turned to me. "Didn't you say you needed something?"

"Huh? Oh, yeah." I scanned the rack by the register and grabbed a two-pack of Sharpies.

Her crossed arms matched the vibe of her stare. "Eli, I am two breaths away from wringing your neck."

Didn't sound like the worst thing. At least her hands would be on me. "What? I wanna sign Nina's cast."

Miracle of miracles, I caught a smile before she turned to pay.

Bags in the back, Nina still working on her snack, I pulled us outta the parking spot.

Ava blew out a breath. "This may sound nutty, but I'm relieved I didn't run into Steven."

"You said you turned off the stalking app. How would he know where you are?"

"I don't know. He's just always there. It puts me on edge."

I didn't like that. "Listen, if you run into him again–"

"I'm going to jeopardize the legacy of his family line."

"That. Was not what I was going to say. I was going to suggest a taser." I never understood how someone like her ended up with a guy like that. In fact, there was a lot I didn't know about Ava. "Been meaning to ask, how long have you known August?"

"Around four years? I met him when I started working at Hidden Meadows."

"And you're going to hire him as soon as you get your ranch?" The freeway looked like a parking lot, so I used city streets.

"That's my plan. But I may not be able to pay him. Not at first. And I don't feel right asking him to work for free."

I'd work for you for free. "Who else was on the ranch with you?"

She pivoted in her seat to face me. "You're asking a lot of questions." The move hiked up her shorts, showing off way too much bronzy thigh for my health.

I turned up the AC. "Just curious. You don't want to talk about them? Fine, what's your favorite color?"

She stared at me like she was working out a math problem. Not much to figure out. I liked her. I wanted to know more.

"Orange," she said finally.

"Like the flowers on the Oc-octo–"

"Ocotillo? Yes."

I nodded. "Mine's green. Like the thorny part."

We passed the next four stoplights in silence, Ava chewing on her lip, me trying not to imagine snagging it with my own teeth.

"It was August, Terry, Kipper, Matthew, Jason, and me," she said. "My Hidden Meadows family. Then Nina joined us." Her eyes focused on the road ahead. "Kipper ran the office with me. She kept the books. August and Mathew worked at the barn and on the grounds. Terry's the owner–you met him–and Jason. Jason trained the horses and ran the lessons."

The hum of the engine filled the cab. I stared out the windshield, not really seeing the city as it passed. She didn't have a family, so she made one. And she was working her butt off to keep it.

"Sounds like quite the team," I said.

"Yeah. It was."

It kinda made me feel like I should put a little more grease into the one I'd always had.

25

Ava

I couldn't sleep.

My imagination ran wild knowing we shared the same roof. It built whimsy, little sand castles. Played tricks on me, read into every smile, dissected every action. But then a pessimistic inner voice would wash in like a tide. *If he wanted to, he would.*

How many times had we ended up a breath apart? And he hadn't kissed me! Maybe this really was just an apology? And I was getting worked up over nothing? But then why say things like *"anywhere, anytime?"* He'd always been flirty. Was that just his nature? Did he like the attention? Well, shame on him! He shouldn't play with people's emotions like that!

Thanks to the blinds, the room remained dark, so Nina slept through my tossing and turning. I dug fingers into my hair, stretched my legs across the bed. Felt Eli's promise whisper in my ear again.

A tentative knock brought me back to reality. I sat up, discombobulated, wondering if I'd imagined it.

Another knock.

In a T-shirt barely long enough to cover my underwear, I

padded across the carpet, opened the door a crack, and squinted as light streamed in from the den.

There stood the culprit. The reason for my sleeplessness. Beaming at me with beautiful teeth and a defined jaw that I could easily imagine working kisses down my neck. My molars gnashed. In his dusty camel Carhartts and a faded blue tee, he could've just walked off the set of a small-town romance!

Staying here was a mistake.

Eli rocked on his heels. "Morning, sleepyhead. I–"

Nina's sharp cry cut him off as she thumped out of her bed and ran to the door, clawing at my leg. She probably needed another dose of painkillers. "Uppy!"

"Not right now, Crackerjack." Not unless I wanted to flash our visitor a sample of my cotton briefs. Eli slid his gaze away, and that's when I knew he'd gotten a peek, anyway. *Ugh.* I needed coffee. "What do you want, Eli?"

"I came to check on you."

"Why?"

"Because it's a little after eight."

"What! Are you serious?"

He nodded.

"I have to get ready for work!" I rushed through the bathroom to the indulgent walk-in closet, muttering, "Stupid sand-castles!"

"Want me to make you some breakfast?" Eli's voice remained den-side.

Clean underwear, pants, shirt, bra. I yanked them all in a rush, then growled when my foot got caught in the fabric of my darn capris.

"Or not," he said. "Whatever you want. You're strong and capable either way."

"I want beckfast!" Nina whined.

"Nina!" I called, "Come take your medicine." My pulse raced to a sickening degree. I hated being late. I dug through my plastic drawers for no-show socks, and the stupid thing gave me a paper cut ... a plastic cut? "Son of a Seabiscuit!" Squeezing my finger, I rushed to the bathroom sink, ran cold water over it, and dug out a Band-Aid.

Eli poked his head into the bathroom doorway. "Are you okay?"

"Get out! I'm changing!" I kicked the door shut in his face.

When I re-emerged, Eli was waiting in the den, leaning his butt against the back of the couch, his hands in his pockets.

"Where's Nina?"

"Upstairs."

"Nina!" I called. "Come put on your clothes." But I didn't have time to wrangle her out of her pajamas.

Eli followed me to the upper level. "We've got pancakes in the kitchen."

"I'm good." I couldn't eat. My heart racketed in its cage. This wasn't me. I didn't call out of work on new jobs, then roll in late like a druncle at a baptism.

"Ava, seriously. You should eat something before you go."

I had seven minutes to get into my truck if I wanted to clock in on time.

Bill fried bacon on the stove. Nina kicked her legs under the bench at the table as she bit into a silver dollar pancake.

I put the bottle of kids' grape Tylenol on the kitchen counter, and glanced around the room. "Where's Marley?"

"Helping Luke with the horses," Eli said, pulling a mug from the cabinet.

I crossed the kitchen and took it from his fingers. "I can do that." No more gallant acts for me to overthink later. A prickling feeling skittered across the back of my neck as I put a pod in the coffeemaker. "Yes, Eli?"

"What?"

I looked over my shoulder, and sure enough, he was leaning against an adjacent counter, holding his own coffee, and studying me. "Why are you looking at me like the cheat sheet to today's test?"

"I'm not doing that."

His dad laughed from the stove.

Eli straightened. "I'm not."

"Right," I drew out the vowels. "Well, can you stop?"

"It's just ..."

I sighed. *Is this worth the cup of coffee?*

His brow furrowed. "You have, I dunno, a ... a storm cloud over your head, or something."

Blame it on the pressure difference between reluctant affection and inevitable disappointment. Or my hot imagination and cold reality. Or his *"anywhere, anytime."* "May I suggest an umbrella?" If it didn't involve touching him, I really would cover his mouth with Band-Aids.

Bill laughed again, and Eli suddenly grew very interested in the marbled pattern on the counter.

"I have to go. I'll bring this back," I said as I lifted my mug. Then I bent to press a quick kiss to Nina's head. "Bill, can you give Nina her medicine?"

"Okie Doke."

As I was stepping out the door, Eli ran after me and shoved a paper towel full of pancakes at me. "Here." His hand wrapped around mine, forcing me to take it. A large, strong hand that made mine tingle with anticipation. Two strips of bacon lay across the cakey stack. Little train tracks I apparently couldn't stop myself from running down.

I only took it because to argue would've made me late.

"Bye, Nancy," I called as I walked out the door of Rock 'N Roll. "Have a good weekend!" I held my carefree smile until I pulled my Chevy onto the street. When it dropped, it was a face-gasm of epic proportions.

So far, I still had a job.

The past few days spun around me like a funhouse tunnel. Nina's broken arm, Steven's slimy power play, Eli's ... I still wasn't sure what it was.

I yanked out my ponytail and ran my fingers through my hair. Terry still waited for his visit. I'd postponed when Nina fell. Should I stop at Hidden Meadows before heading home? My brain tripped over tasks, reconciling, prioritizing. But Nina kept popping to the top. Did her arm hurt? Did she get a nap? Lunch? In the end, I headed straight for Bill's ranch.

I took my shoes off just inside the door and enjoyed the cold tile under my feet. But the stillness put my hair on end. "Hello?"

Muted voices lifted from downstairs. I found Bill sitting with Nina on the floor in our new room. No sign of Eli.

"And dis one. And dis ..." Nina's little finger pointed at all the treasures we'd proudly displayed on a cardboard box turned nightstand the previous evening.

"Those are very nice," Bill told her. "And who's this?" He pointed at a framed photo. "Is that your daddy?"

"Yeah."

"What's his name?"

"I don't know." Her voice held no sadness or longing, which should've been good, but instead it broke my heart. This little girl never knew her father. She didn't even know his name! I couldn't remember the last time I'd talked about him.

"Jason," I blurted, joining them. "She was very little when he died."

"Mama!" Nina jumped up and rushed at me, clubbing my leg with her plaster arm. Words bubbled out of her mouth like a forgotten water hose. Something about Play-Doh, and bones in the backyard.

I wrapped her in a hug, and my anxiety faded. "Wow! That sounds like an eventful day!"

Bill pushed himself off the floor. "I didn't mean to intrude on your space. Nina wanted to show me her treasures."

"I don't mind." I dumped my purse and shoes on the floor, then sank into my fluffy blue bedspread.

Bill was a godsend. What a culture shock it would be when Nina switched back to a place that smelled like disinfectant and had a ten-to-one child-to-caregiver ratio. But Bill had his own priorities—a son to convince to stay.

He picked up the framed photo. "I remember hearing something about him on the news."

"Take some salt with that. The media had their own version."

He returned the picture to the make-shift nightstand. "What's the real version? If you don't mind me asking?"

I took a minute, collecting my thoughts, waiting for that rush of sadness.

Bill's eyes dropped to Nina, misreading my hesitance. "It's okay if you don't want to talk about it around her."

"No. She's heard the story." I combed my fingers through my hair.

Where to start?

"The boys caught a wild mustang," I began. "Usually, they purchased colts or younger mares and trained them, but this stud was causing problems nearby. Maybe it caught the scent of a mare in heat. Who knows?" I lay back onto the bed, suddenly too tired to sit upright. "The boys went out and caught him. Once separated from the other horses, he calmed down. We thought he broke free from another ranch, but no one claimed him. After a month of working with him, they saddled him. He hardly flinched." My fingers traced over quilted stitching. Guilt churned my stomach, and regret burned my chest. "The mustang had a jittery personality. And there were so many people around."

Ghostly images flickered in front of me. Lazy arms draped over fences, kids running circles while they waited for pony rides, their boots kicking up plumes of dirt. Casual conversations under the canopy of mesquite trees.

"I trusted Jason's judgment. He knew horses better than anyone." My glossy eyes picked a point on the ceiling. How quickly everyone had hunted for blame. "We never would have allowed anyone else to approach or ride an unsafe horse, no matter what the news articles claimed." *All because of a stupid white trash bag.* "Anyway, the horse spooked. Jason fell the wrong way. It was quick. All of it." A single tear, like his white hat, descended.

Bill held a reverent silence for me before saying, "I'm so sorry you had to go through that."

"It's crazy because I had this horrible feeling that day. Like I knew." I inhaled a shaky breath. "I should've said something."

"Did you have family nearby when it happened?"

"Yeah." *Terry, Kip.* "But they had to deal with the fallout *and* their grief."

"But Ava, that's what family is for. All the love, the shared memories, that's what helps you through it."

I wiped my face and sat up. It wasn't my first time hearing that. Nina stared at me, probably wondering why I was crying. She didn't understand the permanence of death. She wouldn't think of all the missed opportunities and plans we'd never make. Birthdays, holidays, family trips ... I wasn't just grieving for him. I mourned the loss of all the things we had planned. That was why I had to buy Hidden Meadows. Our future was on its deathbed.

Bill gave me a sad sort of smile. He understood. This house and my ranch were the same.

I stood, shaking off a chill. "Hey, Bill? Mind if I make dinner tonight?"

Teaching Marley to fold corn husks pulled me out of my darkness. "Cooking is like meditation with a side of unfortunate cleanup," I told her as she spread masa beside me.

"You should make Eli clean up," she said. "That's what my mom does. *If you don't cook, then you clean.*" I sensed tension in her impression.

"Do you have siblings?"

"A younger sister." She thumped a fist into the cornmeal, and all the guts oozed out.

"How much younger?"

"She's twelve."

"And you're?"

"Always in the way."

I frowned. "I meant, how old are you?"

"Seventeen." She shoved the remains at me, then she grabbed another ball of masa.

"You know, I bet yours will taste the best," I added pork and folded the soaked husk until it made a perfect package.

"You don't have to do that."

"Do what?" I asked.

"Pretend I'm doing a good job. I'm only helping so Eli doesn't make me muck."

I laid the wrapped tamale in the steamer basket. "Do you cook with your mom?"

"No."

"Your Dad?"

She scoffed. "No."

"Your grandma, or an uncle, or anyone?"

"No. Why?"

"How can you expect to know what you've never been taught?"

"It's not like it's hard. You just follow a stupid recipe. Claire makes stuff all the time."

I assumed Claire was her younger sister. "Would you say you and your sister share everything in common?"

"Hell, no!"

"And there's probably something you do well that Claire doesn't?"

Marley sulked at the counter without an answer.

I moved her finished masa husk in front of me and added the pork. "When I worked at my old ranch, we had a team. I didn't do the banking because I'm horrible at accounting. But I'm good with people, so I managed clients, tours, and events." Maybe my example was too obscure? "What I'm saying is, you don't have to compare your value to other people's skills. You have your own."

"I'm not good with people. Or numbers. Or anything."

"I'm sure that's not true."

"Well, obviously, you don't know me." She threw a masa ball onto the counter with enough force that it flattened itself, and probably stuck.

Before I could backtrack, she stormed off. I spent the next several tamales reworking my words, wondering how I could've handled that differently. *Maybe I should just stick to my own business.*

Nina thumped her cast into the corner of the cabinet as she rounded the island and sagged into me.

"What's wrong, Crackerjack? You hungry?"

She responded with a long, drawn-out moan.

"Does your arm hurt?" I squatted, getting eye level with her. "Oh, what's this?" On her cast was a very odd line drawing of … "Is that a bear?"

"No! It's a monkey!" She jerked her arm away.

"Oh." I cocked my head, trying to imagine it from another angle. "Did Eli draw that?"

Another grunt.

"Can I draw something on your cast?"

"No!" She flattened herself onto the floor, right where I needed to stand, and whined into the tile.

Definitely taking a bath tonight.

Steam rose from the platter of tamales at the center of Bill's long kitchen table, alongside rice, salad, and five place settings. I waited for everyone to pick a spot before positioning Nina and me at the end of the bench by Bill. One plate remained unclaimed. "Where's Eli?"

Bill rescued Nina's water cup as she rearranged herself. "He's changing the oil in my truck. He said not to wait."

Refusing to ponder on that, I turned to Marley. "Can I get you something to drink?"

"I'll have a beer."

"Nice try, kid," Bill countered. "Get her a soda."

I set a can at her spot with a smile, then wiggled in next to Nina. As soon as my butt hit the bench, exhaustion caught up with me.

Bill used the tongs to serve himself. "Thanks for cooking, Ava. This smells great."

"It was a joint effort, so thank Marley, too."

His tamale hovered in the tongs over his plate. Second thoughts, perhaps? Was it poor form to kick your host under the table? "I assure you, they are as good as they smell. I had one while they were cooling."

The moment passed, Bill plated his tamale, and Marley didn't storm off. I served us last, enjoying the sound of clinking forks on plates as everyone tried my mom's old recipe.

Still no Eli.

I cut Nina's tamale into little pieces so it would cool. She grunted at her plate.

"Nina, I don't know what that means. Use your words."

Instead of words, she threw her fork, sending Masa chunks everywhere. Then, before I could clean the mess, she pushed at her plate, which knocked over her cup and flooded the table with ice water. Tears followed–hers, not mine, though the urge bubbled.

"I'm sorry," I told the collective stares as I mopped up the lake with my napkin. The pitch of Nina's whining made my skin crawl. "I'm going to take her downstairs."

She screamed and beat my shoulder with her cast the whole trek to the den. "No! I want dinner!" I winced with every swing. Snot bubbled from her nose. "I want dinner!"

Frustration rose like the tide. Her arm probably hurt. No doubt she was overtired. We hit the bottom step, crossed the creamy carpet, and I bumped our door open with my hip. "Nina, please stop hitting me."

"Nooo!"

When her rough cast smacked into my ear, I dumped her on her bed. "Ow! Stop it! You're making me crazy!"

She cried harder, and I bolted back to the den, slamming the bedroom door behind me. *I can't do this*. It was the first time the thought reared its ugly head in months. I rubbed at my ear. Exhaustion consumed me. But I didn't get to go to bed. I had to be Mom. Make it better. Bath her. Do her bedtime.

I sagged into the couch, burying my face in the upholstery. The weight of the past few weeks pressed down on me–a year's worth of discarded horseshoes and splintering fence posts.

I'd done it all wrong.

If I'd only stayed at Hidden Meadows, none of this would

have happened. All the moving around. Nina's broken arm. Steven.

"Everything alright?"

I whipped around to find Eli at the foot of the stairs. In his *coveralls*. "Seriously?"

"What?"

Like he didn't know he was a walking sex ad. "What are you doing under a truck? You have two broken ribs!"

In two long strides, he was in front of me, covering my mouth with his warm palm. "Can you not yell that, please?"

I pried his hand away. "The doctor said six weeks!" Anger should have occupied all my neuron receptors, but his solid presence made my knees weak, and those firm forearms burned themselves into my retinas for later.

His eyes veered to the moaning wall behind me. "Is she okay?"

I threw up my hands. "I don't know."

"Are you okay? Do you need anything? A beer? A shot?"

The intensity of his concern gutted me. I was the villain here. We didn't deserve shots.

"You want me to go sit with her?" he asked.

"No."

"Did you eat? Want me to bring your plate down?"

"No! Can you just go away?"

His scrutiny wouldn't find a needle in my hot mess because I'm pretty sure I'd lost it. "Fine," he said. "But if you need me ..." The rest hung between us. No additional words needed because I could still hear them, loud and clear.

"*... Anywhere, anytime.*"

26

———

Eli

AVA'S DOOR stayed closed all morning. I spent extra time at the stable with Luke, so I wouldn't be tempted to touch her again. Something told me she wanted space.

Luke and I were discussing going for a ride when I heard the high-pitched whine of one red Tacoma roll in. The thing literally sang for a tune-up. I followed Luke's glare to August's truck. "Hey, don't worry. He's just here to finish the fencing."

The kid yanked the watering hose so hard that it broke the wall mount right off the post, and water started spewing from the spigot. He threw the hose to the ground with a curse.

I shut off the valve. "Don't worry, I can fix it."

"Can I just go?"

"No, we're going for a ride later. Walk it off. Do your thing. I'll keep August out of your hair, okay?" I frowned at Luke's back as he stormed to the tack stall. I didn't realize he had such a problem with the guy.

True to my word, I jogged over to August as he slid out of his truck. "Are we finishing the paddock today?"

"Yes, I hope." He reached across his ripped bench seat to grab a dark brown cowboy hat.

"Great. I have better tools in the garage. You wanna come up and grab them?"

He nodded, getting back in his truck and motioning for me to join him. "You're feeling better? Your ribs?"

"Yeah."

The passenger door creaked closed when I yanked it. It took a lot of effort not to comment on the sad state of his engine as it cried up to the garage.

August parked next to Ava's truck. "She is living here now." It wasn't a question.

"Yeah. Her ex was harassing her. I suggested she stay with us." Ava could fill in the rest if she wanted to. I hopped out and led the way to the third bay.

August followed. "She will do anything for Nina."

"It was a smart move. For both of them." When August didn't readily agree, I dumped an impact drill in his hands.

That popstar smile returned. "And you'd do anything for her, *qué no*?"

Of course I would, but I sure as shit wasn't admitting it to the guy. He wasn't her dad. I dug around in a rolling chest for dill bits, shoving a bunch in my pocket. "Hey, you want me to take a look at your truck?"

August made a sucking sound with his teeth. "Jason, he fixed trucks, also."

"Ava's husband?"

"And my best friend."

I scoffed as I picked up an extra battery. "This where you tell me I don't deserve her?"

"No."

"But you're gonna watch my every move?"

"Maybe."

I grabbed a circular saw in case we needed to trim something down. "Did you love her when your best friend was married to her?"

He laughed and scratched his chin, sizing me up. I had nothing to hide. I wanted Ava for all the right, wholesome reasons. Even if some things I wanted to do with her were … less wholesome.

"I made him a promise," August said. I assumed "he" was Ava's husband.

"Lemme guess. I'm getting in the way?"

He squinted at the sky. "We better start working, no?"

He may not have said it, but I got the feeling I'd put a wrench in his plans.

"So, tell me about the band on your shirt," I said about twenty minutes in on the ride with Luke. He rode Chuck, and I rode Royal. With permission, of course.

Once he started talking, he didn't stop. From the band, to concerts, to where he got his orange Chucks. More words than I'd ever managed out of him before. It made my chest tight. Not in a bad way, but like when someone loved the gift you bought them. The sun beat on us mercilessly, and by the time we got back to the ranch, I needed a shower in the worst way.

"You hungry?" I asked as we walked back up to the house.

"Yeah."

"Great. Let's grab some lunch."

We had leftover tamales. Dad and Marley came in to join us. Still no Ava or Nina. Marley didn't surprise me, but my old man? I waited for B&B remarks, but they never came.

Marley leaned her elbows on the table, eying Luke's second helping. "That looks like one of mine."

For such a skinny kid, he could sure pack 'em away. "You made these?"

"Yup." She cut me a nervous glance, maybe thinking I'd rag on her for taking all the credit. I didn't.

"They're really good," Luke said. "Like, better than the Mexican place where my parents get takeout."

I'd never seen her smile so big. *Thank you, Luke.*

While I microwaved my second plate, I tested my ribs with my fingertips. *Still sore.* At least it didn't hurt to breathe anymore. But Ava was right. Probably shouldn't have been under a truck yet.

Dad came up next to me to stick his dishes in the sink. "Something bothering you?"

"No. Why?"

He eyed where my fingers still prodded, but instead of calling me out, he walked off.

Marley stuck around until Luke's mom came to pick him up. Then she started pulling stuff out of the pantry.

I grabbed an iced tea from the fridge. "Whatcha making?"

She *thumped* a bag of flour on the counter. "Cookies. Why? Afraid I'm going to burn the house down?"

Was Ava right? Did Marley just want my approval? "I'm sure you won't. Tell me when they're done. I'll be your taste tester."

I snuck in a shower before going down to check on Ava. *She's doing too much. She never just relaxes.* But what I found in the den were two girls curled up on the big blue couch. Nina was snoring like a piglet. Shoot! *Naptime.*

Ava's eyes sliced to me.

"Sorry." I gave her a lame wave. "I'll come back later."

Her gaze traveled over my t-shirt and gym shorts. "Were you going to lift weights?"

I shrugged.

"Should you be doing that with ..." she glanced around, "... with your injury?"

"The doctor said I could use other muscles."

The raking stare she dragged down my body made me

wonder what muscles she thought I meant. No way in hell was I leaving now. I snagged my gloves from a box near the free weights. Biceps and triceps curls were probably all I could do. Maybe some incline presses.

Sweat matted the hair to Nina's face. Ava picked up the kid's hand and pinched the tips of her fingers.

"Is she sick?" I asked.

Ava nodded. "I should've realized last night."

I ignored the dull ache as I grabbed some thirty-five-pounders and pushed out my first set of twelve. It could've been more. Ava's hungry attention made me lose count. She blinked away when I caught her, but I could feel it, like one of those infrared heaters. *Look all you want.* Hell, she could touch. I'd be lying if I said I hadn't thought about kissing her on the workout bench with her legs locked around my lap, and all that hair falling in our faces.

She switched to pinching the fingertips on Nina's other hand, and the piggy noises stopped.

I pushed through the burn of my last rep. "How'd you do that?"

"Do what?"

"She was snorting, and now she's not."

"Oh." Ava tucked her hair behind her ear. Long, wavy strands I was dying to tangle into. "The fingertips have pressure points," she said. "For the sinuses. At least, that's what my mother taught me. It works, so I keep doing it."

I watched again. Not pinching. More like a micro wax job on each tiny fingertip. "That's cool."

"It is, I guess. It works with the feet, too. The tips of the toes."

When I lay back on the bench to try pecs, my ribs barked, but only while I got settled. I extended my arms overhead, tapping the sides of the weights together, then pulled back until my elbows were ninety degrees. Pushed overhead again. I felt it in my shoulders and my chest, but no sharp stabs. I did another rep, trying to stay focused, but if stares had flavors, Ava's tasted like habanero.

Sweat pricked my forehead. "You okay over there?"

"What? No-yes! I mean ... I was just–How long did it take to build that much muscle?"

I started another rep, since she was enjoying the show. "A year? Do you lift?"

"No. But I stretch."

"Stretching is good." That strip of tanned skin on her stomach came to mind. The one that showed up when she lifted her arms. I itched to trace my fingers along it. Press in behind her as I showed her the posture for a biceps curl. Run my hands over her hips so they didn't shift. "Tell you what? I'll show you mine if you show me yours?"

Eyes dark as soda fountains drank me in. "I-I can't. Nina."

"Rain check, then." I stood, grabbing the bottom of my shirt to wipe my sweat, knowing full well my gym shorts weren't loose enough to hide what that carnal stare did to me. "You wanna watch TV?"

I snagged the remote from the coffee table, even as she shook her head. "You sure?" My fists sank into the couch cushions, brushing the outsides of her legs, caging her and a still sleeping Nina under me.

Ava's breath hitched.

I left the remote next to her. "Just in case." Then it was back to my room for a cold shower.

Monday morning, I beat everyone to the kitchen. Ava dragged herself in just after seven, slugging to the counter like a cat with a bum leg. The dark clothes seemed outta character for her.

I held out her coffee. "Are you okay?"

"It's fine. I'll get my own."

"Take it. I made it for you."

Her fingers wrapped around the cup, and she stared into it. After a whiff, she took the smallest sip known to humankind, then set it on the counter.

I frowned. "Don't take this the wrong way, but you don't look good."

"That's the stupidest saying. How else am I supposed to *take* it?"

I moved around the island and put the back of my hand on her forehead like Mom used to do. "Jesus, Ava, you're really hot."

Her pathetic swat wouldn't have bothered a fly. "It's seven in the morning, and you're flirting?"

"Ava."

"What?"

"Maybe you should go back to bed."

"I can't," she groaned, hunching over and pressing her forehead into the black countertop. "I have to go to work."

I'd seen her do this before. "Where's Nina?"

"Probably crying downstairs because I snapped at her," she said into the dark stone.

I hesitated. This situation was outside my wheelhouse. "Tell you what? I'll get Nina, and we'll make you something to eat."

"Ugh. I don't want food."

"If you feel that bad, call out."

She straightened. "I just started working there, and I've already taken two days off."

This was new. I'd never heard her whine before. "Honestly? I don't think they're gonna want you there."

She didn't move.

"Ava."

"What!"

"Call your office. Tell your boss you're staying home. Then go back to bed."

"Moms don't get to be sick. Nina needs breakfast, and I have to–"

"Dad and I will take care of it." When she glared at me, I moved in closer. If she tried to gun it for her Chevy, I could grab her. I doubted she'd put up much of a fight. "You'll probably piss off customers if you go in like this. Do you think that's what your boss wants?"

A weak protest growled out of her.

"Do I need to call Rock 'N Roll for you?" I asked.

"No. I can do it."

I followed her to the den and waited while she left a message for her boss. After which, she shot me the stink eye. "Happy?"

"Very." I popped my head into their room. Sure enough, Nina was whimpering in her bed. "Hey, Monkey, let's make pancakes."

She ignored me.

"Come on. Your mama doesn't feel good, so we're gonna let her sleep." I scooped her up, blanket and all, and ticked my head toward the larger bed. "All yours, crabby patty."

Ava brushed past and fell on top of her mattress, probably asleep before I shut the door behind us. That's how I knew it had been the right thing to do.

"Question for you, Monkey," I asked the squirming lump in the blanket. "Do. You. Like. Whipped cream on your pancakes?"

"No!" she snapped. Mama's little parrot.

"Have you ever tried it?"

"No!"

"Then I'm making you a Cubbie-Bear special." She fixed wide, dark eyes on me as I navigated up the stairs. "Oh, shoot, but it has chocolate chips and banana on it."

A toothy grin split her face, tears forgotten.

Ava appeared in the kitchen around lunchtime, wearing a pair of shorts and a baggy sweatshirt that hung off one shoulder. She filled a glass of water at the sink.

I put my sandwich down and finished chewing. "Feeling any better?"

She shook her head and downed the whole glass in a single go.

I swallowed a rising impulse. "You hungry? Want me to make you something?"

"No." She put her cup in the sink. "Have you seen my phone?"

I grimaced, sliding it out of my pocket. She wasn't going to like this. "It kept ringing. I only went in to make sure you weren't dead."

"You came into my room?"

When she reached for it, I held it away to explain. "Yeah, but when I saw you were still breathing, I left. And I took your phone so it wouldn't wake you up."

Ava dragged her fingers through the loose hair that fell out of her messy bun. "Fine. Whatever."

"You're not mad?"

"No."

I handed her the phone. *Should I push my luck?* "By the way, Nancy hopes you feel better."

She groaned. "You answered it?" After a pause, "Did she sound upset?"

"I don't know. How does she usually sound?"

"Never mind. Where's Nina?"

Her skin looked flushed now, her eyes a little red. Probably from the fever. "Nina and Dad are tinkering in the garage."

"Okay. I'm going back to bed. Get me when it's naptime?" Without another word, she thumped down the stairs.

That went better than expected.

An hour later, I snuck into the den with Ava's cash-filled envelope in my back pocket. I'd figured out a way to win our little game. When I hit the bottom step, her big blue comforter greeted me from the couch, complete with snoring.

Perfect.

I snuck into her room to find her purse, and tucked half the bills into her wallet. A couple of twenties were already clipped to the visor of her Chevy. The rest I stuck in shorts and jacket pockets so she'd have cash wherever she went.

On my way out, I peeled the edge of the comforter back so she had air. Sweat made her face shiny, but her teeth chattered. I checked her forehead again, then ran upstairs for water and Tylenol.

"Ava." I shook what was probably her arm.

She curled farther into the crease of the couch, tugging her blanket tighter.

"Ava," I tried again.

"Is it naptime?" she croaked.

"Don't worry about it. Nina's sleeping upstairs." I held out two pills. "Take these."

"What's that?"

"Tylenol. You're burning up."

"I'm freezing."

"Would you like me to take your temperature?"

"No. Go away." She burrowed her head under the blanket.

"It's a good thing you're cute, because you're grouchy when

you're sick." I sat on the couch next to her. "Take these pills, then I'll leave you to your little cocoon."

Ava shoved herself upright. The bra strap on her exposed shoulder and the drag of her fingers against my palm as she took the pills sent heat places it shouldn't. She handed back the empty glass, then sank into her nest, tugging at her comforter.

She looked miserable. She sounded worse. I couldn't leave her. "Want to watch a movie?"

"No."

The instant my butt left the couch to grab the remote, she shot her legs across all the cushions.

"Ava." I laughed. "You can't get rid of me that easily."

"You said you'd leave."

"I wanna make sure your fever goes down." I lifted her legs and slipped under them, letting her calves land on my lap.

She jerked her knees back and pushed her bare feet against my thigh. "Move! Don't you have a TV in your room?"

"This one's bigger."

"Eli ..."

"Guess you caught what Nina had." I scanned the guide for something light. Tremors still shook her body. I scooted closer. "Come here. I'll share my heat."

"No! I'm gross."

"I promise you're not."

"I don't want to get you sick."

"You won't," I told her as I scrolled page after page of channels. "Damn, you'd think with all these choices, there would be something worth watching."

"I'm not sitting by your bedside when you get sick," she huffed.

"Even if I let you read my Hustler? It has great pictures."

She groaned into her blanket.

I grinned, settling on Deadpool, because you couldn't go

wrong with Ryan Reynolds. Once the movie started, I fished under her blanket for her foot and tugged it onto my lap.

She yanked back. "Eli, what are you doing?"

"Just relax."

"I can't relax when you're touching me."

I tried not to think too hard on that. Catching her ankle again, I pressed a thumb into the arch of her foot, going up and down. I worked my way up to her toes. Did little circles. "Am I doing this right?"

"Doing what right?"

"The breathing thing. You said it worked with feet?"

She peeked at me from under the edge of her blanket, then tucked into the corner of the couch again. "Mhmm."

I pretended to watch the movie, but every little scuff against my lap–her heel, my wrist–stole blood from my brain. Hopefully, Ava didn't notice. With each pass of her toes, her breathing got quieter until I couldn't hear her at all. When I leaned over and flipped back the blanket, she was sleeping.

That tight feeling in my chest came back. I couldn't remember the last time I felt like I'd done something so worthwhile.

27

Ava

TUESDAY, I returned to work. The phones rang nonstop, several outstanding orders waited on my desk, and I spent forty-five minutes on the phone, arguing with a supplier who wouldn't deliver in our agreed-upon window. My body trudged against gravity. Congestion buried my brain in thick clouds. I would have shaved my head to be back under my blanket, even with Eli's hands all over me. In fact, that's where my brain kept going. Eli's hands on my legs. Eli's heat seeping across the cave of my blanket.

At noon, I pulled out my sandwich and turned on a fan, hoping to blow away my errant thoughts while I played around with my marketing plan for Hidden Meadows. Something that would bring income, even if the place wasn't fully running yet. Maybe a rustic wedding venue? *Very rustic.*

When five o'clock rolled around, I just wanted my pillow. The heat of my Chevy zapped what little energy remained, so to stay alert, I called Terry.

He answered on the third ring. "Hey, hon. You checkin' to see if I'm taking my pills?"

I frowned. "What pills?"

"Kip threatened to tell you if I didn't take my darn blood pressure medication."

What? "Are you okay? Did something happen?"

"It's nothing. All us old folks take 'em."

I let out a relieved breath. "Well?"

"Well, what?"

Was he being obtuse on purpose? "Are you taking them?"

His rumbling laugh vibrated through the phone. "Guess I am now."

I clenched the steering wheel as I waited for him to call me out. I still owed him a visit. But he didn't.

"So, if you weren't calling to harp on me, what's on yer mind?"

"Well, I've made some modifications to my marketing plan. And I'm exploring alternative services for income. Maybe weddings and event rentals?"

"All work ... You should take a ride. Relax a little."

"I did, actually."

"Yeah?"

"Eli kind of forced me, but it was good." I pulled up to a red light. "You know, it's not work when you're doing something you love."

Terry hummed an objection. "There's always something that's gotta be done. Especially here. And not all of it's fun. You don't want to burn out before you even start."

The seconds stretched as my fatigue tried to coax me into agreement. *No.* Tiredness was temporary. "Terry, Hidden Meadows is our dream."

"Doesn't stop me from worrying about you."

"I know."

I considered the cost of a new fifth wheel. With all the changes over the past few weeks, I knew my loan amount would be less than what Terry deserved. He should get to play in style after decades of hard work. Maybe I could wrangle Eli and August into fixing up a used trailer for him.

"Hey, Terry?"

"Yeah?"

"Take your pills."

I was so close, yet I could feel my spirit breaking.

Everything felt contradictory. Proving to Terry that I could tackle this enormous task on my own, yet relying on the help of strangers. Saving every penny toward a business while struggling to cover my day-to-day expenses. Indulging in Eli's attention, but enjoying the nostalgia of August's company and the life it represented.

I rolled down my window to let the wind drown out my thoughts. But the evening heat only melted my confidence into a self-pity puddle. What if I couldn't get Hidden Meadows running again? What if I invested all my time, my money, and failed?

I pulled up to Bill's house and climbed the porch steps while uncertainty spun donuts in my head. Eli's eyes found me the second I entered the kitchen, and without missing a beat, he opened the fridge and handed me a beer.

"I could kiss you!" I upended the bottle and chugged half its contents, fully aware his wide eyes watched me. Perhaps I should've been more careful with my words. "Where is everyone?"

He adjusted his hat. "Around."

"I'm going to change." I took my beer downstairs with me.

Business casual became a worn, wide-necked sweatshirt and a pair of loose shorts. I didn't care that my outfit screamed "laundry day." I just needed something comfortable to counter the pressure building inside. I unwound my braid and threw my hair on the top of my head with a clip. In the bathroom mirror, a stranger stared back at me until her edges blurred. She looked nothing like the woman from a year ago. Her cheeks were gaunt, and a raccoon mask shaded her eyes purple. She looked older, tired.

"I'm not burned out," I told her.

I finished my beer and headed upstairs, contemplating a second. The whole gang now congregated in the kitchen: Bill, Eli, August, Nina, and Marley. I instantly longed to retreat downstairs, where the quiet could cradle me into a false sense of security. Or dig up my worst fears. It was a crapshoot.

Instead, I went for it–the second beer. Because dinner needed making.

"Mama! Mama! Guess what?" Nina stood on the dining bench, her cast sticking up like a cactus.

I met her at the table with a hug. "Did you have a good day?"

"Yeah! August tolded me a story about my daddy!" She pronounced it "oddest," and that chipped away at some of my doubts.

"Oh yeah? Which story?"

"You putted socks on his hands! And he did a puppet show when he was sleeping!" She collapsed onto the table in a fit of giggles.

The memory unleashed a smile. He'd been on heavy painkillers for surgery on a broken collarbone. The socks prevented him from scratching his stitches. "He did. And the puppets were named Freda and Frijole."

"Doesn't frijole mean bean?" Marley asked.

"It does."

Nina shook with another round of giggles, and pleasant soda bubbles fizzed in my sternum, lifting my spirits. It *was* pretty funny, a drugged-up Jason singing love ballads to a sock. "Guess I'd better start dinner. August, are you staying? Oh, actually ..." I glanced at Bill, remembering too late that this was his house.

"You're welcome to join us," Bill said.

August flashed a paparazzi smile. "Okay. Yes, I stay."

"Great!" *Wait.* That meant I had to figure out what to cook for six people. Exhaustion crept back in as I shuffled to the refrigerator.

Eli slid up beside me and wrapped a possessive arm over my shoulders. My breath stuck as he tipped his head close to mine. "I'll cover for you if you wanna sneak off."

It could've been the beer flowing through my veins, but now I didn't want to leave. "It's fine."

"Take a load off. I'll do dinner." When I didn't move, he gave me a gentle shove toward the table. "Hey cowgirl, go sit."

Cowgirl?

As if I could. My thoughts swam through a ball pit of all the ways Eli had touched me in the past few weeks. I put my second beer on the counter, lingering. Meanwhile, he stepped around me, obviously trying not to touch me, pulling a sleeve of hamburger patties from the freezer, dumping them on the counter.

"Dad, you wanna light up the barbecue?"

Solid shoulders shifted with easy confidence as Eli pried apart the patties. My eyes dropped to the flex of his forearms. The subtle veins in his very dexterous hands. I needed something to do. Beelining to the fridge, I dug through the drawers and shelves, collecting condiments. *Ketchup, mayo, mustard, onion, lettuce ... what else?* I turned, arms full, only to collide with Eli's chest.

He started confiscating vegetables and bottles, his skin brushing mine, bodies close. "So stubborn. Just tell me what you want. I'll do it."

"Anywhere, anytime."

I knew that wasn't what he meant, but when his eyes met mine, I had no doubt he understood.

His Adam's apple bobbed. "Go. Sit. Or I will ban you from this kitchen."

"You can try." I liked Two-Beer-Ava. She didn't give one salt lick about filters.

Eli's eyes dropped to my mouth, and the muscle in his jaw jumped. In a voice so low, I could hardly make out the words, he said, "You want me to throw you over my shoulder?"

Unfortunately, his barbaric suggestion only made my core burn hotter. I gulped.

His normally amber eyes smoldered closer to burnt caramel. "You're killing me, cowgirl."

My feet wouldn't move. The new nickname didn't help.

Eli glanced around at the halted side conversations. All eyes were on us. "Be right back," he told them.

He dropped the condiments on the counter and dragged me out of the kitchen. We turned the corner into the entryway, then the entryway bathroom. Before I could blink, his body was herding me to the wall, his palms flat against the wainscoting on either side of my head. The door *snicked* shut, and suddenly, I wasn't tired.

When his mouth formed my name, I felt the atoms shift between us. Dizzying fantasies circled like drunk Tweety Birds. I yearned to run my hands up his arms, or maybe just hang on for dear life, but I was paralyzed by the firm line of his shoulders crowding me.

His eyes closed as his head dropped. "I can't–I'm trying. I don't think you realize what you do to me."

"You're the one who keeps touching me."

"You want me to stop?"

I shook my head.

His nose flared when I wet my lips. "I'm trying to be a gentleman."

The rise and fall of his chest mesmerized me. I pinched his shirt with my fingers. Issued a gentle tug. He yielded to the whispered gesture, his elbows bending in slow motion, closing the gap between us.

Impulses ran haywire. I couldn't think. Didn't want to. We could do anything in that little half bath, away from prying observations. And even if they knew? Was it so bad, Eli and I? My appetite grew for something I wouldn't find on the dinner table.

His heart pounded a new rhythm into me, his hips muting my second thoughts. I slid my hand up his body, navel to collarbone, supple cotton dragging. What would it be like to do it directly on his skin?

His breath stuttered.

"Sorry, did that hurt?" I retracted my touch.

He shook his head. "No. Definitely doesn't hurt."

Warm lips brushed my cheek, and a cool palm slid along my jaw. Fingers dug into my hair. My heart hammered so hard I passively wondered if it could punch through my ribcage. Who needed a heart, anyway? Messy things that insisted on carrying more than their weight.

"I've been thinking about kissing you for so long," he said, "I can't decide where to start."

"Are there really that many choices?"

He remained motionless for a full breath, his body pressing against mine, reverent eyes drinking me in. I snaked my arms over his shoulders to lock behind his neck. What was he waiting for? How could his mouth be so close and yet not touching? Electricity danced across my skin.

"Just kiss me, already."

With such tension singing through our bodies, his hesitant press against my lips took me by surprise. He held there, like a gradual submersion into an icy lake. Acclimating. Testing the water. Except my blood pulsed like molten lava, and if he didn't get a little more serious, I was going to erupt. I captured his mouth with mine, dragging him deeper. He inhaled sharply, then plunged.

Soft skin met scratchy stubble. Pleasure with a hint of pain. What a great motto for life. He tasted like sunshine and iced tea. Like family horseback rides and s'mores on the back deck. Slow and sweet but a shade past innocent.

His teeth scraped across my bottom lip, and a satisfied hum vibrated through him as his fingertips dusted the skin below my shirt. *Oh. My. God.*

Get an extinguisher. I was about to combust.

Then, to my dismay, he pulled his mouth away, his breathing labored. "I don't want to do this here. Come to my room later?"

The "yes!" trapezed on the tip of my tongue. This inferno needed an outlet. But sounds drifted through the wall. Kitchen sounds. Nina sounds. Sounds of responsibilities so emulsified in my makeup, I couldn't separate them.

At my hesitation, Eli inched back, then pushed off the wall. I lost all of him at once. The enthusiasm, the heat, the hand in my hair. My heart sank as his smile faded. "Sorry. Was it too much? That was too much."

"No! No ... It's just–" What was holding me back?

We stood there in silence, catching our breaths.

Eli removed his cap, ran a hand over his hair, and adjusted his jeans. "Ava, I really like kissing you."

"Me too."

He slapped his hat against his thigh. "But?"

"No 'but.' I wanted you to kiss me." We hovered on a tightrope, and I was so afraid of pushing him off. "It's okay. I'm not expecting anything long-term."

When he stilled, the small room shrank to microscopic. A strange expression flitted across his face. He shoved his hat back on. "Maybe it's better if we don't."

What? No!

"I'm sorry, Ava." He was already reaching for the door.

"Better for whom? Eli, I–"

Instead of answering, he fled the too-small half-bath. The door clicked closed, and the frigid cleanse of disappointment splashed over me. My brain spun, trying to piece together what had just happened. But the only thing I could settle on? I should've skipped that second beer.

28

Ava

ELI KEPT his distance the rest of the evening. I'm sure everyone picked up on our mutual silence, but I kept my head down to avoid any questioning glances.

As soon as we'd cleaned up dinner, I ushered Nina downstairs for bedtime. The tingling from Eli's hand on my waist persisted through teeth brushing. His voice echoed in my ear as I sang Nina's songs. By the time she'd finally fallen asleep, I must've replayed that kiss fifty times. It was an ad at every commercial break, louder than the scheduled programming, until you started thinking, *yeah, maybe I need this.*

I grabbed the TV remote and plopped onto the couch in the den. The screen illuminated the room in a bluish glow. Hundreds of choices flooded the TV guide channel, but as the minutes passed, the titles blurred into nothing but a shelf of flippers and bumpers that kept my pinball thoughts in motion.

Why had I hesitated? Did I feel guilty for wanting someone? It's not as if I could have Jason back. He wouldn't want me to fade away from life or love, or whatever fell in between. And spending time with Eli didn't take away from moments with

Nina. Often, we were all together. In fact, he engaged with her more than most people did.

I tipped my head back and stared at the ceiling; the texture resembled the contour of Eli's biceps. His jawline. The tight pack of muscles above his waistband. I should just go to bed. Sleep it off. Wake up with fortified resolve in the morning. But hyperactive energy sizzled under my skin. I didn't need my pillow. I needed a grounding wire.

Another metal ball entered the game. *"Relax a little,"* Terry had said. When? I had deadlines and promises to keep. When did it end? The constant climb? I could feel myself nearing a threshold. Waning motivation. I'd been letting things slip: Nina's extra screen time, putting off tasks I needed to finish.

I rubbed my hands down my face.

"You don't want to burn out before you even start."

Eli's kiss came in for another commercial break, and all my shiny pinballs fell through the drain.

I was tired. Tired of being responsible. Tired of always having to do the right thing. Of endlessly busy days proving my worth, wondering if I was enough, hiding my loneliness.

I wanted him. More than I'd wanted anything for myself in a year. A few hours of me time. That was healthy, right? Surely, better than burnout? A night off from being a single mom or a grieving widow. I'd been living in a state of constant exhaustion. What would one more wakeful night hurt?

If he'd have me. Not such a forgone conclusion anymore.

I crept into our room. Nina slept soundly. She'd been sleeping through the night for almost a week now. Ever since we set up house in Bill's lower level.

Could I?

Should I?

"I've been thinking about kissing you for so long ..."

I would gladly assure him that keeping his hands to himself would not be for my benefit.

The back door of our room didn't make a sound as I opened it and climbed the dark stairwell, silent as a predator to the mudroom. Maybe I *was* a predator. Or maybe I'd get to his door and chicken out.

I passed through the quiet house, into the garage, inhaling the heady blend of astringent lubricants, the bouquet of his trade. His eager and competent hands had been all over my Chevy, under my hood. Would he give me that same kind of attention? That level of care?

Wait. What if it was the kiss? Maybe, after building it up in his head, I'd left him disappointed? My feet paused on smooth concrete. What if I got to his door and he had to spell it out for me? Would I survive the embarrassment? I brushed fingers over my lips. *It couldn't have been that bad.* Not when my end exploded like fireworks. I pushed through the doubt, navigating the first tread of the stairs that would bring me to his door.

He's probably asleep. I'd probably climb up only to blunder back down in pitch dark, hoping I didn't tumble head over tail. My hand skated the half-wall as my toes searched for the edge of each rise.

What would I even say to him?

The closer I got, the worse this idea seemed, until my hand met a corner. The end of the stairwell. The raised edge of the door frame.

"Relax a little."

There were three possible outcomes: he'd be asleep, he'd tell me to go away, or maybe, just maybe, he'd pull me in and kiss me until I saw stars. One light knock. That's all I'd do. Not enough to wake him.

I tapped my fingers against the wood and held my breath.

This is stupid. If he wanted me, he wouldn't have left. This time, I couldn't blame the beer. My buzz had worn off hours ago. The seconds passed, and I considered a fourth outcome. Maybe he'd ignore me as he had during dinner. Why did that feel like the worst option? Blood swished and pounded through my head.

He wasn't coming.

I turned in silent retreat. *No chickens or predators here.* Just a lonely stray with her tail between her legs. As my bare foot met the first descending step, the door swung open, unleashing a blue glow into the stairwell that cast jagged shadows on the walls. Eli's bare-chested silhouette filled the frame.

Thrill, terror, relief, and a million other impulses overwhelmed my cognitive function. "S-sorry, I didn't mean to wake you."

"What's wrong?"

Everything. "Nothing." Suddenly, I understood my hesitation. Eli had awakened something in me that I thought I'd cremated with my husband. I may not have expected longterm, but I'd hoped for it. And that scared the S-H-I-T out of me.

My foot staggered down another step, but Eli's hand shot out to grab my wrist. His fingers flexed against my thrumming pulse, and the world hovered in a single, weightless moment. I could feel myself rising from the ashes. But what would I become?

With a swift yank, he hauled me to the landing, the azure glow painting the scene surreal. My pulse spiked. This could've been a dream. Maybe I'd fallen asleep on the couch hours ago.

But his rough voice sounded real when he said, "Don't go." And heat radiated off his skin. "Please?"

He pulled me past the threshold, into his room. Stole my breath. Filled me with hope. I'd stopped retreating, but he tipped his forehead to mine and begged again, "Don't go."

With the next inhale, his hands slid to my waist, fingers digging into the fabric of my shirt. All those looks, those touches, made me greedy for a conclusion. I wanted to feel all that glorious skin, discover what he liked. To close the space between us. To lose myself. Future-me could deal with the consequences. The percussion in his chest called to mine, lending me courage. I captured his face in my hands and brought my lips to his.

I should've been kissing him all along, because now the pressure had built, and I couldn't stop. He took my mouth like a starving man. Patient turned urgent, tentative to fevered. We toppled further into his room, sparse and cool in contrast to my heated skin.

"Ava, you have no idea ..." he breathed.

He tore my hands from his face and dragged them down his bare chest in a slow, sensuous trek over taut muscle, then back up, looping them behind his neck while his mouth moved over mine, dancing in chaotic choreography. I followed, finding his rhythm, reveling in the contrasts: demanding kiss, yielding lips. Sharp inhales, fuzzy thoughts. Awake. Dreaming. It carried me in its melody. I held on, no longer caring about tomorrow. Or the day after that. Only this moment, and what we were doing in it.

His hands skated up my sides, to my neck, my jaw, into my hair. When he tugged, urgency morphed into ravenous, demanding, all-consuming hunger.

"Dammit, Ava, why do you have to taste so good?"

His praise moved down my neck. Teasing, fluttering kisses mixed with feral bites. Moments blurred together. *Erratic breath, synching hearts. Hot skin, wet hair.* The door slammed. Our feet scuffed against the wood until my back hit the wall. I gasped and pressed my pelvis into him, thrilled at the hard edge that met me. *Mouths locked. Nails scratching.* My blood burned outward, igniting every long-ignored corner and crevice, and I ached to be closer.

Eli hooked my thigh around his hip and pressed into my soft curves. Every contact point pinged–a light-up map of travel destinations. Places I yearned for him to meet me. My humanity ebbed, and a primal Ava awoke. She made non-human noises and caught his bottom lip between her teeth. Swept her tongue inside his mouth and pulled an answering growl from his chest. At any moment, my clothes would combust.

I grabbed a fistful of my shirt, yanked it over my head, and Eli's appreciative exhale brought my nipples to hard points. Our bodies met again, skin to skin, intoxicating every nerve ending I didn't know I had.

His lips traveled across my collarbone, found the spot on my neck where my pulse pounded out of control. Warm palms slid up my rib cage, slow, reverent, stopping at the swell of my breasts.

"Ava, I can't stop thinking about you."

"Same," I uttered.

"You can't stop thinking about you?"

"About you," I laughed. This was really happening.

Teeth scraping. Hands teasing. My skin pricked with heat. He feathered a hand up my outer thigh, gripped my butt, and lifted me. I locked my legs around his waist, my elbows behind his neck, barely holding onto my feeble grasp of reality.

Was this flying? Or falling?

Eli reclaimed my mouth as he carried me deeper into the room, the strength in those brawny arms swinging me halfway to delirium. *Soft breasts, firm chest.* My fingers sank into his cool, damp hair. My lips tingled from the scratch of his stubble.

One minute, we were upright, bumping from wall to counter, to wall. The next, falling into the contours of his comforter. It hugged me like a cloud and filled my nose with the refreshing spice of his soap. We were always meant to end up here. Of this I knew. If I had just admitted it from the start, I could've paced myself.

His body hovered over mine, a Greek statue honed and

formed with attentiveness to detail. I needed to run my fingertips over every peak, smooth and hard as sculpted stone.

I pried at the waistband of his shorts, shoving them past his hips with frenzied intensity. In contrast, he pressed sweet, measured kisses down my neck. A slow, deliberate seduction. Honey dripping down the sides of the jar. How could he practice such control while I ran off the rails?

With devastating leisure, his fingers hooked my shorts and slid them down my legs, scorching trails along my skin. I moaned his name as he ran a palm up my inner leg.

"Say it again," he said to the bend in my knee.

"Say what?"

"My name." The inside of my thigh.

"Eli."

I fisted the sheets as his hand settled over the valley of my pelvis. Too close to imploding. Not close enough.

He leaned in, pressed a teasing kiss to the right, then the left, his warm breath stirring every sensitive nerve ending. Pleasure built like a riptide. If he stopped, I might die. If he kept going, I definitely would. Twelve months of pent-up everything, bubbling to the surface.

My body reached for him, and finally, *finally*, his mouth landed home. *Gentle tongue, firm fingers. Blue glow. Red hot.* A tsunami rushed in and swept me under.

I crashed out of my skin, and each wave sent me further from shore.

I gasped. Sputtered. Groaned. I may have even cried. Life was bliss in that string of moments, my problems reduced to shadows. Nothing existed aside from the two of us.

Eli moved up my body, coming into focus over my head. I pulled him to me, pressed kisses into his neck, breathed him in. A sensual mix of heated skin, fresh soap, and zesty allspice. Now, any one of those scents would transport me back here.

My fingers dug into his shoulders, finding hard, flexed muscle and unyielding endurance. "Your turn."

I shifted forward, hips searching for hips. Wanting to feel everything everywhere. To *know* the mashup of my soft against his hard. Eli's kiss turned primal as his weight settled over me. Every cell buzzed to life, my blood coursing, my heart racing.

Beneath this heady thirst shook the cowering prospect that tragedy lay on the horizon. Maybe this wasn't a good time to get involved with someone. But this man knew exactly what to do with me, and I had no intention of stopping him.

29

Eli

I must be dreaming.

Ava was there, in *my* bed. Nothing but smooth, tan skin, wild hair, and perfect curves. I was as hard as rebar when she'd knocked on my door. Even after the cold shower.

Life didn't usually give me the things I wanted. Like her mouth kissing mine, her fingers in my hair, and her naked body pressed against me. She wanted me too. She said so. And that felt best of all.

Her legs wrapped around my waist, and we almost got to the point of no return.

"Wait." It took everything not to detonate. "Let me get a condom."

I hated prying myself away and leaving her alone on my bed. This felt too good to be true. What if she changed her mind? Why the hell did I keep the condoms in the bathroom? I snagged a row of foil packets from under the sink and rushed back to Ava's welcoming thighs. She smiled, stealing them outta my hand. And just when I thought I couldn't get harder, she ripped one open with her teeth and used her long, lean fingers to smooth it over me.

Jesus Christ.

The woman undid me. She was smart as hell, with big dreams that made me wanna think bigger. Screw what Ryan said. That housebroken crap wasn't real. Just some bullshit we cooked up when we were kids. I wasn't a dog. Besides, some things were worth staying for. And I was looking right at her.

Ava fell into my sheets, and I followed, lining kisses up her neck to her jaw. Making her giggle. We coulda been on a tropical island the way her hair smelled. Long, warm days in the sun and sand. Longer nights, burning off the margaritas. Did she like to travel? I could show her so many places. White beaches in Southern California. Red sunsets in Sonora. Golden forests in Massachusetts. I'd give her all the colors.

The tip of my erection grazed between her legs.

She mewed. Like a cat.

My blood hammered through my arms and legs. It buzzed. It burned. I couldn't remember wanting anything so badly as wanting her.

"Eli," she moaned, squirming under me. "Stop teasing." Her hips flexed, pulling me in.

"I like seeing you go crazy."

"Yeah?" She snaked a hand between us, grabbing me before I could pull out of her reach. *God damn*, she was pushing all the buttons in the elevator, but we weren't getting there the scenic way. "Don't make me beg," she begged.

Ava in my bed? I should've been the one begging.

I met my forehead to hers, every muscle tight, holding back. Holding on. To give her something memorable, so she'd stay with me. "Ava. I don't know what to do with you."

"I think you know exactly what to do with me." Her purr slid with her legs around my waist and locked me in.

I didn't want it to be over. But the finish line was getting closer. I was only human. With one ripe nipple between my teeth, I eased in, enjoying how she ran her greedy hands over my body. If only I could record every gasp and groan. She closed her eyes, arched her back, fisted the blanket–

Fuck me.

One sharp thrust, and I buried home. She consumed me. Cried out my three little letters. But one single word abducted my brain.

Yours.

I'd been test-driving the label since our horse ride. Having her there, in my bed, proved that no other title would do. I never thought of myself as belonging to anyone, but if she asked, I'd belong to her. Be her home. Wall off storms, keep her warm, give her memories. A family. All of it. If she asked me to. As long as I could be hers. Was it more than I deserved? Maybe. But only an idiot would forfeit a chance this good.

Maybe it was my cock talking. Maybe Ryan's incessant texting had a point. Maybe in the morning I'd come to my senses.

Delicate fingertips traced my traps, my biceps. Heavy eyes trained on where our bodies joined. This was what she looked like when all her walls were down.

Who was I kidding? I needed all of it. This, and more. Homemade dinners at the big-ass, chewed-up table Dad insisted on buying. Horseback rides at sunset. Lazy afternoons on the porch with a beer. Ava in my truck. Ava in my bed.

I moved inside her, hypnotized by the way she drew me out. Long dark lashes against rosy cheeks. The way light skimmed over her chest, how her collarbone looked so fragile. So kiss-able. I sank my teeth into it, listening to the sounds she made. Like an archeologist, I'd figure out her mysteries. Find the Ava not hiding behind all the work she had to do.

Her body kept rising, and so did our speed.

I dragged a palm down her stomach. *Smooth and warm.* Lower, where her hips dipped. Lower.

She moaned, and I put it on my "Ava-likes-this-list."

As my fingers played, her breathing got short and pitchy. She coiled so tight all I could do was hold on. Power through. Watch her lose control and roll like waves on the beach over my bed, into me. She turned me inside out.

And I saw stars. Actual, fucking stars.

Something was wrong with my eyes. They wouldn't open. The lids were glued shut. If someone had told me I'd fall asleep with Ava curled into my chest, I woulda bet against them. I had no idea how long we'd been out, but our feet were stuck together in the sheets at the bottom of my bed. *Damn.* She fit perfectly into me.

I pried my eyes open to watch her sleep. Took a deep breath to memorize the way she smelled so I could bury it like a bone. When I slid my fingers through her hair, her shoulders tensed. But a kiss to her forehead had her settling again, humming, skating her hand up my arm to my neck.

Something almost painful panged in my ribcage. Painful and addictive.

"It's not even fair," she whispered. "I've always been an arm girl."

My laugh came out low and creaky. "I thought I was a leg guy. But honestly, I love every part of you."

I drew a slow trail with my finger down her sloping side, across her stomach, up to one dark, round nipple. She gasped and leaned into the touch.

Don't have to ask me twice. I retraced that same path with kisses and teeth until she crushed her body into mine.

"I guess you kinda like me," I said.

She hummed a "yes." Good thing we had condoms left. I moved my palms over her curves in worship. Followed her gasps and groans, giving her what she asked for. An easy task, 'cause I wanted it, too.

The clock next to my bed said 3:21.

Ava yawned and stretched, grinding all those addictive body parts into me. "I should go," she said.

I locked an arm around her and stuck my nose in her hair. Pretended we were still on that tropical island. "Why?"

"In case Nina wakes up."

"I can go check on her, if you want?"

"It's okay." She tried to pull away, but she wasn't stronger than all those arm exercises I'd been doing.

My ribs weren't even that sore.

When she laughed, the vibration traveled all the way down to my cock. Holy crap, the woman was a witch. She made me insatiable.

"I have to get ready for work in a few hours," she said.

I frowned. *Work.* She shouldn't be in a stuffy, dark trailer. She should be on the ranch with me. With the wind making her hair fly around her face, and her smile tipped to the sun. A far-fetched dream, seeing as she had her own ranch, her own people. She'd been working so hard for it.

Her eyebrows dipped as she studied me. "What?"

"Nothing. I just don't wanna let you go." I tightened my arms, pulled her closer.

She chuckled. "You'll have to, eventually. I can't survive on orgasms alone. Although after tonight, I wish I could."

My smile returned. "Fine. What if I bring your breakfast here? And make sure Nina gets hers? What time does she wake up?"

Ava's giggles were injection fluid, cleaning out all that gunk I'd been living with. I felt fresh. Hopeful. My semi pressed against her stomach as I kissed the side of her face. Her neck. Her collarbone.

"I appreciate your effort," she said into my mouth. "Really, I should go. But I promise to come back."

I sighed, pushed up on an elbow, and stared down at her. All I ever wanted blinked up at me. "Okay, fine. You want me to walk you home?"

She grinned, tossing that sexy, shiny hair over her shoulder. "I think I'll be okay. This is a pretty safe neighborhood."

That smile.

I watched her sit up, admired her in the dim blue light coming off my TV. I didn't realize it was still on. "I'm really glad you came."

"Me too."

"I'd like to make you come some more." That made her laugh. "Maybe Friday? So, you can sleep in?"

She scoffed as she shimmied her shorts up over her hips. "Nina doesn't care what day it is." All too soon, her shirt covered those lovely breasts.

Ryan accused me of being totally whipped. Joke's on him. I didn't care. I walked her to my door. "See you in the morning?"

Ava flashed me a tease of a smile and tapped my nose with her finger. "It's already morning." She padded down the steps into the dark garage.

I fought the urge to follow her. *She's not gone*, I told myself. We were still under the same roof. And Friday was only two days away.

30

Ava

My snooze rang a third time. Now I really had to get up. Extending my arms and legs, I arched my back in a luxurious stretch. Flavors from last night lingered on my tongue like a mint. Tingly. Refreshing. *Two more workdays*, I told myself.

My flouncy yellow top called to me, paired best with Bermuda shorts. Nina ran upstairs while I smoothed my hair into a high ponytail, holding back a massive yawn. I just had to survive until six. Then I could pick up takeout and collapse on the couch. Maybe Eli would join me?

We had experienced everything all at once, skipped so many intimate steps. Yet my pulse still raced at the thought of the coffee he'd present me when I entered the kitchen, and the chance hand on my thigh as we watched a show.

I wrapped the ponytail holder four times around my fisted hair. I wouldn't say the L-word, but maybe I could think it? Everything about him made me smile. His compassion, his patience, his sense of responsibility. *Those arms!* Two days or twenty-four, I recognized the blooming fullness in my chest. It was foolish to pretend I didn't.

And if last night was any indication, he felt the same. I

never thought I would care this way for anyone again. But suddenly I felt alive. Eager to push forward. I forgot how much I liked having a teammate.

I grabbed my purse and hustled to the den stairs, checking my phone to see if I even had time for coffee. When I looked up, Eli was padding down. He stopped on the tread above me, the subtle zest of his soap hitting me full force.

A tendril of that blooming fullness split my face into a smile. "Good morning."

Without a word, he slid his hands under my jaw and brought our mouths together in a prolonged, chaste-ish kiss. But then a little noise squeaked out of me, and the mood shifted. Intention followed in a slow, aching urge as strong, capable hands traveled south, past my waist, curving around my butt. Eli crowded me to the wall, the handrail pressing into my back. Teeth and tongue intruded on any reasonable arguments. This was my new favorite wake-up.

For a few fleeting moments, I considered skipping work and dragging him to my bedroom. Except Nina needed breakfast. As if sensing my resolve, he broke off the knee-buckling kiss with a low and seductive, "Good morning."

"Mmm." Agreed. *Zero regrets.*

"I got Nina some cereal."

"Thank you."

"And coffee is ready."

I frowned.

He *tsked* and pressed his fingertips into the sides of my mouth to lift them. "Nope. None of that."

My puddle of a heart couldn't deny it. The man was hardworking, humble, and sexy as hell. And I wanted all of him. "I just realized I don't know how you drink your coffee."

A sly smile spread across his features like a leisurely sunrise. "Any way I can get it."

"I meant, do you prefer it with milk? Or sugar?"

"I know what you meant. I'm not gonna tell you. Making your coffee is *my* thing."

"*Humph.*"

He kissed my cheek. "You're cute when you pout."

My bottom lip jutted out. "I'm not pouting. I'm just ... You promised coffee, yet you're holding me captive in a stairwell."

Eli grinned, sneaking in one more quick press to my lips, then he released me.

Me and my big mouth.

Nina sat at the table in the kitchen, glaring at her Rice Krispies as if Eli had given her roadkill.

I ruffled her hair. "What's wrong?"

She shushed me, then stuck her ear closer to the bowl. In a sly attempt, I wandered to the island where Eli had left his mug. He caught on and swiped it, but not before I glimpsed the deep, rich brown liquid. *No milk, then.*

"I know what you're doing," he said.

"Sugar?"

He shrugged, turning to face me with his cup at his mouth. "Doesn't matter 'cause I'm always gonna have it ready for you first."

A girl could get used to that. But because I didn't want it going to his head, "You'll slip, eventually."

"You think so?"

I turned my back on his cocky expression, addressing Nina. "Eat, baby."

In response, she pounded her spoon into the wood next to her bowl, chanting something that sounded Viking.

"Nina."

"Chun-chun-chun-chun."

"Go," Eli said, suddenly right behind me. His words tickled the base of my neck. "We're good here." When a kiss brushed on my vertebrae, it turned me spineless.

The forecasted high of 114 had nothing on me.

He wrapped his arm around my waist and pressed a cup of coffee into one hand, a food container in the other. "Don't be late for work."

Then stop touching me!

Nina glanced up with a strange expression. I slid out of Eli's hold and gave her a big, handless hug. She'd never seen me act like that, not with Steven. But I wanted her to know what love looked like. "See you when I get home, Crackerjack," I told her. And to Eli, "You too. Thanks for breakfast."

Around lunchtime, I smiled into my store-bought sub as I read my texts.

Eli: Make sure you eat.

Ava: Or what? You'll throw me over your shoulder?

Eli: No. I think you'd like that too much ;)

He wasn't wrong. I returned to browsing Rock 'N Roll's stock for ideas. What to use for the wandering footpaths through Hidden Meadows? *Wandering like Eli's tongue down my stomach.* I shook my head, blinked back to my screen. And the parking lot? Something to reduce dust? My employee discount would help, but when did everything get so expensive?

Cathy's head popped in the doorway of the office trailer. "Ava, can we chat?" Outside, the backhoes groaned and shoveled mulch and rock by the tons into pickups and delivery trucks.

I minimized my browser window and set my sandwich on

its plastic wrap. I'd expected this. Especially after the drama of a large custom delivery. "Sure."

The door slapped shut behind her. She sat in the clear plastic Ikea chair on the other side of my desk. "I know you have a young child," she started. "And things come up. Illness, car problems ..." She exhaled, her forehead a wrinkled mountainscape. "But I'm concerned about how many days you've been out in the short time you've worked here."

It looked as hard for her to say as it was for me to hear. I shoved down the panic and tried not to spiral into all that losing this job might mean.

"This position is the hub of the entire business," she went on. "It's near impossible to keep things flowing when I don't have someone here."

"I know," I told her. "And this may mean nothing to you, but these past few weeks have been the first of my life where I've been so unreliable. I wasn't lying in my interview. I *am* dependable and hard-working."

Cathy crossed a leg over her knee and leaned forward, resting her elbows on the edge of the desk. "I have to ask. Is this going to keep happening?"

I knew the answer she wanted. I knew my job depended on it. In fairness to her and her business, I gave her the same integrity I'd want from my own employees one day.

"My life is in flux right now," I admitted. "I wish I could promise things would stop coming up. But I don't know."

She nodded. "Well, I appreciate your honesty."

"I have a more stable ... situation now. If that helps." A house Steven can't get himself involved with. Someone who makes my coffee in the morning. *And makes me come at night.*

Ah! These thoughts had to stop!

If my face turned red, Cathy didn't comment. "Good." She leaned back. "I like you, Ava. You're great with my guys. Great with the customers."

Her praise felt undeserved. "I'm so sorry about the custom order. Is there any way we can return it to the manufacturer?"

She waved a dismissive hand. "We'll put it on the floor. It's more costly than our standard stock, but someone will buy it." She studied me. "Let's give it one more chance?"

"Thank you, Cathy."

"You're welcome." Her eyes fell on my turkey and cheddar hoagie. "And now, I think I'll get me one of those."

As she stood, I forced my penitent smile into a grateful one. I needed this job. For stability in my transition, for my property loan. Speaking of … When she left, I picked up my phone, called the bank, and scheduled a loan appointment for the following day. Terry kept finding holes and concerns in my business plan. I worried the more I put it off, the less sure he'd feel about our deal. And could I blame him? He had plans, too. What if, in guilting him to sell to me, I was wrecking his retirement?

Don't go there. Terry was a grown man. If this didn't work for him, he'd say so.

Fine. Settled. I would go to the bank and explain my situation. And hopefully, they'd looked at my long-term income history, not just the past thirty days. *Ugh.* How much easier would this have been if Jason were still alive?

I picked up my sandwich, but found I'd lost my appetite. This distracted, half-finished, mistake-ridden version of me soured my stomach. I could do better. By the end of my shift, my eyes may have burned with desert intensity dryness, but my heart fluttered at the thought of seeing Eli. Until I discovered a black Mercedes parked next to my truck.

"Now what?"

As I approached Roxy, Steven popped up next to the rear driver's side tire. I studied his overlong, unruly hair, the shadow of neglected scruff on his face that shouted neither mysterious nor sexy, and his wrinkled T-shirt. *T-shirt? What the heck?*

My hackles rose. "What are you doing?"

He seemed at a loss for words.

"Steven. What are you doing?"

"I–you ..." He tucked something into his rear pocket.

My eyes jumped to my tire, then back to him. "Are you slashing my tires?"

"No!"

"What's in your pocket?" It felt like I was talking to a kid.

I dumped my purse on the hood of my Chevy and marched up to him, but he skittered around the trunk of his luxury sedan. I didn't have the energy to chase him. It was too hot, and I was too tired.

He pried his door open and stuck a foot in, like it was home base. "Terry deserves better."

"Excuse me?"

"He's like family to you, right? He could be set for life. It's selfish how stubborn you're being."

I gaped at him.

His bony fingers curled around the doorframe of his getaway car. "You can't fight a corporation, Ava. They don't care about you, me, or Terry. It's all about capital." With that warning, he ducked into his leather interior and sped off.

What. The. Funnel cake? Did he start using drugs? I examined my tire, running a palm over the scorching rubber, but I found no punctures. *Would I see it, though?* Tilting my ear to the wheel well, I listened for a hiss or a sputter. *Nothing.*

I stood, staring at the tire, unease rising. AAA could check the pressure and see if it was dropping. But how long would I wait for them to show up? I could call Eli. *Nope.* How dumb would it look if it ended up being nothing? And did I need an angry bodyguard out for Steven's blood?

If it had a hole, and if I took it slow, avoided the freeway, I'd probably be able to make it to the ranch. I climbed into my truck and drove it carefully out of the parking lot, listening to the road sounds, trying to remember the usual cadence of the tread. Was it bumpier? Louder? Several stoplights later, I relaxed, concluding that if something was amiss, I would've noticed.

Adrenaline yielded to lethargy. A massive yawn made my eyes water, and as I stared at the long stretch of intersections, Steven's comment surfaced, unbidden. I wasn't being selfish, was I? Except the words weren't novel. I'd been thinking them already.

Terry had always talked about his big cross-country trip. How comfortable would he be living out of that old trailer? Climbing up to the narrow bed loft with his achy joints?

My phone pinged with a message from Eli.

Eli: Thinking about you

He attached a selfie of him and Nina doing a bicep curl with small hand weights.

A genuine smile lifted my spirits. He had appeared in my life so unexpectedly. It fueled me with hope. It reminded me why places like Bill's ranch and Hidden Meadows existed. Not because of money. I'd figure out some way to get Terry his new trailer. But in that moment, the four-lane road stretched peacefully, sparse of cars. An easy straightaway. No thought or planning needed. I just had to follow the road home.

Home.

The no-name ranch was just supposed to be a stopover. But somewhere along the way, it turned familiar, comfortable. A place I could slump into the kitchen, still wearing my PJs. A place full of people I could rely on. And Nina was so happy, with the non-stop giggles, and the excited, long-winded summaries of her days. Was it ambitious to want both? Hidden Meadows and whatever came with loving Eli? Surely, the universe wouldn't have sent me what I couldn't keep?

As I approached an intersection, another huge yawn broke free. The kind that demanded the entire face. The kind you can't cut short. I squinted through blurry eyes at the stoplight. And I thought it was green.

I swore I saw green.

The following seconds ran together. *Honking. Bang!* The world flipped. I couldn't tell up from down. Couldn't put the wind back in my lungs.

Crunching. Spinning.

My windshield became a mosaic. In a bizarre, withdrawn moment, it reminded me of a house Steven had listed on the top of the hill with the designer bathroom. So many windows. So much light diffused by crackled glass panes. I would've bought the house for the bathroom alone, but the asking price was more than I could afford.

I could afford. Afford ...

I gasped. My seatbelt was choking me, and my pulse swished so loud in my ears it was all I could hear. Shadows crept into the edges of my vision, punctuated by sharp points of pain. Little stars. *But it's daytime?* I blinked, trying to clear them away.

I needed to call someone. To tell them I'd be home late. To tell Nina not to worry. But the little stars swelled until the pain grew unbearable.

So, I closed my eyes.

31

Eli

Nina was so silly. I loved it.

She arranged my free weights in a rainbow obstacle course on the carpet. The rules were a little sketchy, but on a good day, I could bench over four times her weight, so I figured I could handle it.

Dad answered his phone somewhere upstairs, and there was something weird about his tone. I tried to catch what he said, but Nina sang at full volume as she hopped over each weight.

"*I know da colors painting fun! Grween like grwass, yellow like sun–*" Her foot snagged on a heavier dumbbell, but I caught her.

"Careful!"

She carried on, without missing a beat, "*Orange puh-kin, white snow!*"

The stairs creaked.

"*Red rose and a black crow!*" Nina froze. "Oh. Dare's no black."

"Do we need black?" I asked, shifting my attention between her face and the staircase.

In seconds, her big brown eyes put me in my place. Bottomless, like her mom's. "Okay." I scanned the room, then pulled a ten-pound plate off my barbell and added it to her hopscotch course. "How's that?"

She raised her eyebrows at me like I'd just told her Chuck was a dinosaur. "Dats not black."

"Light black?" I tried.

Dad stopped at the bottom step with a strange expression.

"Can we just pretend?" I asked her.

She sighed very dramatically. "Okay." Then she circled to the beginning to start it all again.

I left her to it, stepping over the green weights, straight to my old man. "What's wrong?"

"I, uh, need to run an errand. You good here?"

"Yeah. Ava should be back soon." I checked my phone. She was usually home already. "You need me to start something for dinner?"

"Nah. Unless you get hungry. Or I can pick something up."

My shoulders stiffened. *Something's off.* Dad offering to bring home takeout? "When will you be back?"

"Not sure. An hour. Maybe two?"

"What's with all the mystery? You're not gonna say where you're going?"

"I'll fill you in later."

When he left, I pulled up my text thread with Ava, stared at the last response from her–a heart on the photo I'd sent. I tapped out a message.

Eli: Hey, you almost here?

Ten minutes later, still no Ava, and still no response.

Nina grabbed my leg. "I'm hungwry."

Maybe Ava stopped at her other ranch? She'd talked about it. I tucked my phone away. "Okay, Monkey. Let's find you something to eat."

But Nina shook her head at everything in the pantry. I ran a hand over my hat. How did Ava feed this kid? "Okay, what *do* you want?"

"Chock-kit chip pancakes!"

I couldn't come up with anything else. My brain was spinning. "Fine. Pancakes it is."

Where's Ava? And what secret errand did Dad not wanna tell me about? I pulled out the mix and grabbed a bowl, Nina under my elbow the whole time. She grinned up at me with all those tiny little teeth and big cheeks.

"You gonna help me make it?"

"Yes, peas!"

I dragged a chair from the kitchen table to the island for her to stand on. "Oh. Hold on. We gotta wash our hands first." I wanted to enjoy the moment, but a knot tightened around my chest. I pressed a hand to my ribs, but they seemed fine.

Pancake powder ended up everywhere. On the counter, on the floor. In our hair. But somehow, six pancakes came out, fluffy and golden.

Nina ate three bites, then said, "All done."

"Really? You can't finish that one?"

"No. Can we see da horsies?"

I was beginning to understand why Ava looked so tired all the time. "Let's wait until your mom gets home."

Nina threw on her pouty face. I checked the time, then called Ava. When she didn't answer her phone, I tried Dad. "What's going on? Where is everyone?"

He met my question with a long pause. That's when I knew. Something bad had happened.

"Ava was in an accident."

"W-what?" My heart jumped out of my throat. Flat out left the building.

"She's okay," he rushed to add. "A little banged up. I'm here at the hospital. She might need surgery. That's what we're waiting to hear."

Accident? Surgery? His words swam around in my head. The hell she was okay! I needed to see her. "What hospital?"

I could hear Dad smother the speaker with his hand. I glanced down at Nina. She looked like a ghost under all the pancake powder.

"Tell ya what?" Dad said, loud and clear in my ear. "How about you come first shift tomorrow? She's feeling a little worn out right now."

Seriously? "Can I talk to her?"

After a long silence, her scratchy voice hit my ear. "Hi, Eli." For the first time, it stung to hear her say my name. Something about her tone. Like she'd rather do anything over talking to me.

"Hey." If she was okay, why didn't she answer my texts? Suddenly, I had no idea what to say. "Nina and I made pancakes." A painful pause filled the line. So long, I worried she'd hung up on me. "Ava?"

"Sorry. I'm just really tired," she said. "Can you do me a favor?"

"Anything."

"Please don't tell Nina? Can you just say I'm, um ..." her voice wobbled, then I had to listen to her take a bunch of shaky breaths.

I gripped the back of my neck, ran a palm over my hat. The need to see her made me sick to my stomach. But I couldn't go with Nina in tow. Seeing your parent all wound up in hospital tubes, that left a mark. I knew firsthand.

Ava tried again. "Can you tell her I'm staying the night over somewhere because I–" her voice cracked. "Because I was too tired to drive?"

"Yeah. I can do that. But I'm coming tomorrow, first thing."

"Fine," she sighed, and it hit like a bullet, point-blank.

After some rustling, Dad spoke into the phone. "You want me to pick up dinner?"

"No, we made pancakes." I didn't bother hiding my defeat.

"Okay. See you in a bit."

I shoved my phone in my pocket and stared down at Nina. "Close your eyes." With a dishtowel, I wiped her face, but she probably needed a bath. An uncontrollable itch made standing there in that kitchen near on impossible. But Ava needed me to take care of Nina. So that's what I'd do.

"Looks like it's you and me tonight, Monkey."

"Yay!" At least she was excited.

"If you're not gonna eat anymore, let's do bathtime."

After Nina fell asleep, I dragged myself to the kitchen to clean up. I couldn't tell if the pain in my stomach was hunger or misery. On the counter sat a pack of Reese's cups and an open case of beer. A pathetic trade-off for rejection. Still, consolation prize in hand, I found Dad on the back deck, staring at his mountain.

I slumped into the chair next to him. "Thanks."

"You bet." He tipped his own can to his mouth.

The orange bag crinkled when I ripped it open. We sat like that for a while, watching the sunset, until Dad spoke up.

"She's scheduled for leg surgery tomorrow morning."

I lifted my can, forced the warm beer down my throat.

"They're hoping to discharge her tomorrow afternoon," he added.

It all sounded wrong. *Surgery. Discharge.* Ava was young and healthy. I couldn't talk about this. Couldn't think about her lying there in a hospital bed. What the heck was I gonna do when I rolled in to see her the next morning? "Where's her truck?"

"I imagine at a tow yard."

I frowned. They should've brought it back here. I could've started working on it.

Dad took a long pull from his beer and stared at the fading purple sky. "I'm sorry, son."

"You didn't make her crash."

"Not that. I'm sorry I failed you."

I scoffed. "What are you talking about?"

"When your mom died."

Damnit. We were doing this ... I tipped my can back, knowing no amount of alcohol would make this better. "Can't blame you for getting tired of calls from the cops."

Dad shook his head. "No. You were a kid. As the adult, I should've handled it better."

It. How were you supposed to handle death? I took another swig of beer. "It's all good. I'm over it."

"I didn't know how to live without her," he said, apparently not hearing me. "It felt like I was doing it all wrong. The lunches, the school stuff. But the worst of it? The sadness blinded me to what you were going through right next to me."

"It's fine. We got the school lunch."

Dad turned and watched me unwrap a candy. "You were never a burden, you know."

"Not even when I stole the car and crashed it into the neighbors' RV?" That stunt landed me in the hospital for a week. Homebound for a month. Hannah had ripped me a new one over that. Once the stitches came out.

"You were never a burden," he repeated. "You were my reason to keep going."

I stared at him, tempted to laugh off the sappy line. But a mosh pit of feelings shoved around in my gut, and I didn't know what to do with them. I held out the Reese's bag. After a glance, he reached in and took one. There wasn't much left to say after that.

Hours later, when I finally fell asleep, I dreamed of Mom. She was smiling. I think we were at a horse ranch. Ava and Nina were there, too.

I left early for the hospital, hoping to catch Ava before her surgery. But as I neared her room, I heard, "I told you, I don't want you here!"

The nurse's station dinged. I paused at her door while blue scrubs rushed past. After a peek inside, I snuck in, hanging towards the back. Ava sat upright in her bed with her hair falling over her shoulders. A full breakfast tray waited on the table next to her. The standard tubes and wires webbed out of her arms to machines that beeped and flashed, trying to prove she was stable. But I couldn't reconcile the green numbers with the cuts on her face, or the bruises coming out from under her hospital gown. They sliced into me as if they were my own.

"Good morning, Mrs. Garcia." The nurse turned off the call button and checked her leads. "How's your pain?"

"It's fine. I'm fine. But can you please make him leave?" The IV swung when Ava lifted an arm to point at the other occupant in the room. Steven.

"I'm her emergency contact," he argued.

"Only because I forgot to change it."

The nurse's eyes toggled between the two of them.

But Steven's focus fell on me. "Oh, great. The bodyguard."

His little nickname used to bother me, but now I crossed my arms menacingly in a stare-down. He looked like he'd just rolled out of a dumpster.

"Actually," the nurse said, "All visitors need to leave. We're about to start pre-op." Ava wouldn't look at me, and when nobody moved, the nurse hung up her manners. "Come on, guys. Let's go. Right now."

I took the high road, leaving first, hoping Steven did something stupid to get himself kicked off the premises.

The stiff blue vinyl chairs in the waiting room welcomed me like a row of wasp nests. But seeing Ava alive and breathing eased some of the pressure that had been building since Dad's call. *What's a few more hours of misery?* I just had to lie low.

Steven sat in a matching chair across the room from me, under a wall of smiling portraits probably meant to inspire hope. But their white teeth and glowing faces only pissed me off. Hospitals weren't happy places.

He pulled out his phone and started tapping.

Lie low. I rubbed my hands down my face, but I couldn't let it go. "Why are you here?"

He didn't take his eyes off his screen when he answered, "She lived with me a year before she went home with you."

"Says the man who got her evicted."

"Why are *you* here?" he shot back.

"Why do you think?"

He dropped his phone in his lap and ran his hands through his greasy hair. "The ranch is a mess. It's too much for her. I'm doing her a favor."

"Keep telling yourself that."

He scoffed. "Sleeping with her makes you an expert?"

I leaned forward, elbows on my knees. "How does she take her coffee, Mr. Mercedes?" The scowl he shot back was nothing like the ones Luke could throw. "Guess living with her doesn't make you one, either."

Except, he'd made it as her emergency contact. I didn't even get a text. I wondered if she had planned to tell me at all? Or wait until she was hobbling into the house with a frigging cast and crutches.

I leaned back into my chair. The hallway smelled like lemon cleaning products. The same lemony smell from years ago, forcing up memories like yesterday's bad beef jerky. I took off my hat. Slapped it on my thigh. How long did leg surgery take?

Steven's heel started tapping the floor, and the nonstop noise grated on my last nerve. When he glanced over, I glared back.

"I know what you're thinking," he said. "But it's not true."

"What am I thinking?"

That heel ... *tap, tap, tap*. His hands through his hair again. "She showed up before I could–I didn't–Tires are durable."

"Not sure what you're getting at."

"It wasn't my fault. I didn't slash her tires."

What?

My butt popped outta the seat faster than an automated eject. Steven's phone slid across the floor, and my knuckles burned where they met his bony face. I had him up against the wall next to all those idiotic portraits before he even had time to blink.

"N-no. I didn't!" He threw his shaking hands in front of his face. Blood colored his teeth. "I swear. She showed up before–but I wasn't–I couldn't–"

"Hey!" A nurse with a head full of black braids shouted as she picked up a phone at her desk. "You two! Break it up." She was calling security.

Shit! My fist tightened on Steven's shirt as a red welt appeared on his cheek. I was not getting kicked out because of this pissant.

"You don't get it," Steven whined. "My client won't step down."

Steven wanted a bodyguard? Fine. I'd give him a bodyguard. "But you will." Because I suddenly knew without a doubt that I would kill for Ava. "I have a truck, a shovel, and if you even look at her again, I will dump you so far in the middle of nowhere, only the vultures will find you."

A pair of uniforms showed up. Protective vests and walkies. One had his taser out. I forced my fist open. Then the other, and stepped back, hands up.

Steven shot a finger at me. "He attacked me!"

Officer One put away his taser. "Take a breath, gentlemen. You," he pointed at Steven, "walk with me."

"Better check your tires, Mr. Mercedes," I said as he turned away, just to mess with him.

He looked a little green as they headed down the hall and out of sight.

Officer Two eyed me. "What's going on here?"

"This guy's been harassing my–" *My what?* I couldn't call her my girlfriend. "My friend. For weeks."

"How so?"

I ran a hand through my hair, then realized my hat was on the ground. I picked it up and put it back on my head. My heart was hammering. "You gotta kick me out?" *Damnit!* I didn't even get to talk to her!

To his credit, the officer seemed genuinely concerned. "Why don't you tell me about this harassment first?"

I called Dad from a coffee shop across the street. "Hey, so, here's the thing," I tugged my hat lower. "I kinda got kicked out of the hospital for hitting Ava's ex."

"Whoops."

"Yeah, well, he had it coming. If Ava calls you for a ride, tell her I'm hanging out to take her home?"

"Okie doke."

I drank an overpriced cup of coffee and watched Chevy

restoration videos on my phone, trying to focus on the fixing instead of how it broke. But unwanted thoughts kept popping up. Did she blame me?

Four hours later, Dad texted an update about Ava's discharge. Security watched me while I stood by the entrance. A whole dumb process considering I hardly even drew blood.

I saw the bright orange cast first. Knee to foot. Blue scrubs pushed a miserable-looking Ava in a wheelchair through the automated sliding door.

"This is our stop," the nurse said.

Ava used a set of crutches to stand. Loose fabric shifted down her thighs and hung around her legs. I'd never seen her in a dress before. It was the perfect kind for spinning her under the stars, to watch it fan out. Though if her expression was any hint, we wouldn't be dancing anytime soon.

My brain must've been fried, because the first thing outta my mouth was, "Now you and Nina match."

Ava didn't laugh. Or smile. She eyed the uniform behind me. "What's with the security?"

"Oh. There was an incident in the waiting room." I folded a hand over the bill of my hat. "With Steven."

She adjusted the crutches under her arms. "I hope you broke his nose."

That pulled a small smile out of me. If he were smart, she'd never see him again to find out. "I like your, uh, where'd you get the dress?"

"Bill picked it up for me yesterday."

I coulda done that. Woulda gladly gone shopping for her. "Do you want me to bring the truck around?"

"No, I'm tired of sitting."

I grabbed her bag from the wheelchair, and we walked at quarter speed to my truck. "I'm glad you're okay. Aside from your leg. I was–"

"How's Nina?"

A laugh covered my frustration. "She's good. She misses you." I scanned Ava's face as she hobbled, her collarbone all covered in dark bruises. "You're gonna have to tell her. There's no way the kid's not gonna see it."

"I know."

"Does it hurt?"

"Not really. But I'm on lots of painkillers." Her throat bobbed. "Does it look bad?"

"No, you're still beautiful."

She got really still. And not just because we were waiting for the elevator at the parking structure. "I meant, will it scare her?"

I blew out a breath. "She's gonna know something happened. You should probably tell her the truth."

Ava nodded. "I plan to."

"You gonna tell me the truth?"

"About?"

"Why you're acting weird with me all of a sudden?"

"Look, I really–"

In perfectly crummy timing, the elevator dinged, and the doors slid open. After people filed out, I held the side so Ava didn't feel rushed. Same when we got off. Then I held the passenger door to my truck open, but she didn't accept my help getting in.

I grabbed her crutches. "I'll throw these in the back." How did we go from touching each other everywhere to this? It felt like I was losing her.

"I need to go to the salvage yard to get my things," she said as I pulled out of the lot.

I nodded, already brainstorming how to haul her Chevy back to the ranch. I'd thrown all the equipment in the back last night, because August was right, I'd do anything for her.

When I saw Roxy in the salvage yard, it hurt almost as much as seeing those cuts on Ava's face. She hobbled to the dented passenger door on her crutches and tried to pull it open.

"I got it." I ran to assist.

Crunched roof, shattered glass. The story it told syphoned acid straight into my chest. She must've flipped the truck, and the bruise on her collarbone was from hanging by a seatbelt.

She picked around the beads of glass, collecting her things from the footwell.

I wrenched open the reluctant driver's side door to help and pulled the hood release while I was there.

"Do you see my phone anywhere?" she asked.

After some searching, I dug it out from under her seat. At least now I knew why she didn't respond to my texts. "Before we go, I wanna look at the engine."

"Don't bother."

"Why?"

"It's totaled." She could've been commenting on the weather. *Another scorcher today, folks.*

"That doesn't mean much. Insurance companies total everything." But when I popped the hood, I discovered a distinct crack along the frame near the steering box.

"See?" she said. *High of 115.*

"No, I–"

"Your face says it all." She swung the passenger door shut and hobbled back to my truck with her purse.

"I know some guys who weld." I grabbed a few photos, then closed the hood and ran to help Ava back into my truck. This time, maybe because her hands were full, she let me. "I bet we could fix it for under five grand." Free labor, of course. "Maybe not all the bodywork, but ..."

"It's fine, Eli." She handed me her crutches, then she yanked her seatbelt across her chest and hugged her bag to her stomach.

I didn't get it. Ava loved her truck. I just needed a clue. Something to explain what was going on in her head. "These trucks are solid. They–"

"I said it's fine!"

Finally, an emotion, but not the one I expected. Her words echoed across the rusted metal graveyard, over hundreds of vehicles, all decrepit and forgotten. But her truck carried stories and memories. It didn't belong with bottomed-out Buicks and boxy, doorless Corollas.

"I'm gonna get a guy to come look at the frame. If he can weld it, I think we should buy it back for scrap."

She dropped her face into her hands, her fingers digging into her scalp.

"Hey." I lowered my voice. "If it's fixable, I *want* to fix it."

"Well, I don't!" she cried. "Can you please just take me home?"

A second passed. Then another. "Yeah, sure."

I checked her leg before closing the door.

The silent ride to the house nearly suffocated me. Ava waited in the passenger seat while I grabbed her crutches. She grimaced when she shimmied to the ground.

"You in pain?" I asked.

"Not really."

I reached past her, dug the prescription oxycodone out of her plastic hospital bag to read the label. "Every six to eight hours." I looked up at her. "How long ago did you take some?"

"Right before discharge."

"Okay." I counted the hours in my head. "Give me your phone."

"Why?"

I bit back an annoyed sigh. "So, I can set an alarm for your next dose."

"I can do it."

"Then do it now. Seven o'clock, before you forget." Why did she have to be so stubborn?

When she unlocked her screen, our text thread popped up, including an unsent message on her end that she quickly swiped away. I shoved that to the overworked muscles at the back of my jaw, and waited for her to set a timer.

"Happy?" she asked.

Not really. "Thank you."

Was that why she got into an accident? Because she was on her phone? With me? I grabbed her stuff and followed her to the house, ready to catch her at every wobble. But she didn't need me.

"We're back," I called to the quiet house, closing the door behind me.

Little thumps rounded the stairs. "Mama!" Nina appeared at the top, with a huge smile that dropped as soon as her eyes hit Ava's orange cast.

"Hi, baby. I missed you!" Ava dumped her crutches and bent with arms open for a hug, which Nina fell into carefully. "I broke a bone, just like you, so I had to go to the doctor."

Guess the truth was gonna come in small doses. If I got mine at all.

The hug lasted so long, I had to wonder if, somewhere in the whole ordeal, Ava thought she wasn't coming home. A stab of guilt had me crossing to the kitchen. "Anyone hungry? I can make something."

"It's a broken leg," Ava huffed. "I'm not an invalid." She reclaimed her crutches and shuffled into the kitchen, dragging the extra weight of one little girl with her.

But I saw the strain on her face. "Let me help. Until you get used to your new legs."

She ignored me, pulling things from the fridge, one ingredient at a time. I caught the mayonnaise jar when it almost fell from her grip. Picked up her crutch when it slid to the floor. Handed her a paper towel when the French's bottle exploded.

She took it all reluctantly. "I'll have to figure out how to do this on my own, you know."

"But not today." She wouldn't shut me out. There was something there, between us, worth fighting for. I leaned against the counter next to her as she cut a sandwich into quarters.

She dropped the butter knife with a clatter. "Do you have to be right *there*?"

"This is my kitchen. Where should I be instead?"

"Literally anywhere else."

I moved closer. "Better?"

With a sharp inhale, she said, "Nina, take this to the table, please," handing the kid a plate with four little sandwich squares.

I waited a beat. "Are you mad at me?"

"Look, I appreciate your help. But I'm not a stray that needs saving anymore."

I frowned. "Who said you were a stray?"

"No one. But that's how you're making me feel."

I studied the side of her face. Tried to read what she wasn't saying. "I found a stray once, behind the grade school. Lured him home with a ham sandwich. Best dog I ever had."

"You're not helping."

I crossed my arms. "What's going on? Why are you angry with me?"

"I'm not angry."

"I don't believe you."

"Fine. I'm not angry with *you*," she said.

"Then who are you angry at?"

She didn't respond.

"Okay. Answer me this, then. It kinda feels like if it weren't for the bright orange cast, you never would've told me what happened."

"What am I answering?"

"Why didn't you call me from the hospital?"

She glanced at Nina, then to the second plate on the counter, sporting a half-made sandwich. "Terry didn't have your number. So, he called Bill."

"You called Terry?" Why did it feel like a half-truth?

"It's the only phone number I know by heart."

"And he called Dad? That sounds like a stretch. How would Terry have his number?"

"They never delete anything in their system."

Something wasn't lining up. "So why didn't Terry come?"

Her top teeth bit into her bottom lip as she decorated half a piece of bread with cheese and lettuce. "I didn't tell him."

I opened my mouth to ask why, then shut it. *Nope, stay on track.* "Okay, so when I had you on the phone, why wouldn't you talk to me?"

"For the same reason I didn't want Terry coming to the hospital."

"Which was?" Pulling teeth had to be easier than this.

She shoved the top bread onto the bottom half of her sandwich. Mayo and mustard oozed out the sides. "Will the right answer make you stay?"

"Maybe." A wrong answer, judging by her frown.

She pressed her palms into the counter, glanced at Nina again. Then dropped her voice. "Eli, I was so tired, and overwhelmed, and ... distracted that I *drove* into a commercial truck! I'm lucky I walked out alive. Lucky nobody else got hurt!" Her eyes found mine, and they were full of pain. "I don't need more. I need less."

Guilt rose like battery acid up my throat. I held her stare even though it ripped me apart. "I'm guessing I'm the more?"

"I think you should stay. Here, on the ranch with your dad. But don't stay for me."

I nodded once. Then again, wanting not to believe her. But

she'd confirmed what I already knew. I would've given my best socket set, hell, my whole damn truck, to go back to being ignorant. "I'll be around. Call if you need anything."

The spray of toothpaste mucked up my bathroom mirror, just like all my stupid fantasies. Horseback rides and dinners together. Dancing under the stars in that dress. I wasn't helping her. I was making things worse. Keeping her up late when she was already exhausted. Sending her texts when she needed to focus on driving. I'd never told her why I chose the road. Now she knew.

The only thing I had done since being on Dad's stupid ranch was help build a paddock and get my hopes up. For what? This place had three horses, two boarders, and one sad excuse for a son. The best I could do was get out of everyone's way.

I threw my hat on the floor as I snagged my duffel. If I couldn't keep my promise to Mom, I didn't deserve it anymore.

32

Ava

I KEPT SEEING the fire die in his eyes. Over and over. I'd wake up, shift positions, drift off, and there they'd be, dull and dark as charred debris. *"Call if you need anything."* Still giving, still helping, while simultaneously plundering my chest, stealing my last shred of sanity. Because want and need weren't the same, and Nina came first.

As sleep dragged me under again, I prayed I'd done the right thing.

A song repeated, and something poked at my arm, though I hardly felt it over the pain that clawed up my leg. I pried open one eye to find Nina standing at my bedside, holding my phone. With a few blinks, the numbers focused, and I recognized the song for my alarm. But the clock didn't match the time I'd set it for.

"Mama, who's calling?"

Fuuunnel cake.

It had been singing for hours, and I'd slept through it!

"No, baby. It's an alarm to take my medicine." Which I'd left in the bathroom. Along with my water.

I forced myself up and threw my legs over the side of the bed, an action I immediately regretted. Splintering pain and heavy pressure pulsed under my cast. For a few uneasy seconds, I worried I might hurl right onto the carpet. I should've staged everything on the box next to my bed before falling asleep. That's what Eli would've done. Heck, he would've snuck downstairs to make sure I took it.

"I'll be around."

My heart gaped like gills out of water, and I deserved every sharp spasm. "Nina, can you get my crutches?"

I downed my pills at the bathroom sink, meeting my hollow gaze in the mirror. For the first time in years, I missed my mom. I hated her for giving up when my dad died, but suddenly I understood. You could be as hard as a river rock, but life's non-stop current still wore you down. My husband was dead. My truck was dead. And if I didn't act soon, my ranch would be dead. Did she know something I didn't? What would she tell me now?

I dropped my head and stared at the sink. Promises, responsibilities–I had to offload *something*. To get out of the current, before it left Nina without a mother.

When I'd woken in the ambulance, it wasn't Jason's face I searched for, or his voice I longed to hear. It was Eli's. But I couldn't sacrifice everything for a man I'd just met. I still loved Jason. My feelings for Eli could never replace him. The reasons that had sent me running from Hidden Meadows a year ago were now my reasons to keep it. To show Nina her father in the shift of horses. To hear him with every hoof-clomp. To feel him on the breeze as it passed through the sweeping mesquite trees. We were happy once. I had to get back there.

For Nina.

Instead of tossing in my bed for hours, I tucked her into her blankets and migrated to the den, only to scroll blindly through the TV guide. The pain medication wasn't working, hunger gnawed at my insides, and when sunrise hit, I would have to get dressed and get myself to work. Assuming I still had a job. Then I realized something. I had no car! My head fell against the back of the couch. I could *not* call in sick. And I loathed the thought of asking Eli for help. Somehow, I knew if he overheard me ask Bill, he'd sweep in and insist on doing it himself.

I swiped away frustrated tears, idly remembering to elevate my leg. Not that lifting it hurt any less. How did I make it stop? The pain, the guilt, the rising panic in my chest. I had all the same tasks, but now I had to do them truck-less, with a broken leg! And shy an ally. I'd pulled the Cinderella card–been sent back to the beginning. Again.

And my hope was somewhere in the discard pile.

The sun squinted through the French doors when August found me and Nina firmly planted under a blanket, watching Paw Patrol. "I was looking for Eli," he said. "But I find you like this?" He gestured to my cast. "*Mijo*, what happened?"

I tried to make light of it. "Oh, this ol' thing? Nina and I decided to be twins." The stolen joke made me frown. I rubbed at the pinch in my chest.

August hissed his disapproval. "Where is Roxy?"

Unwanted emotion expanded in my throat. I blinked back to our show. "The scrapyard."

"*¿Qué?*"

"And I'm not going to fix her, so don't ask." I didn't deserve her anymore. I didn't deserve a lot of things. And still, I had the audacity to ask August a favor. "Can you–" I shifted Nina, deciding. "Can you give me a ride to work?"

His furrow almost surpassed his chin. "You should rest, no?"

"If I don't go, I will lose my job."

His hand cupped the back of his neck as he watched me get to my foot. Perhaps contemplating how I planned to make myself presentable in thirty minutes. "If I take you, you will tell me what happened?"

I glanced at Nina. She was completely engrossed with the dogs on the screen. Still, "I'll tell you on the way."

Twenty minutes later, I hobbled up the stairs, creaking and thumping in yesterday's dress over a pair of shorts and a messy top knot. With each step, my pulse increased. Would I run into Eli? What if he handed me a cup of coffee? Or lifted Nina in a football hold just to make her giggle?

But the kitchen was empty. No coffee waiting. No plated pancakes. Just a sinking anchor where joy used to be. *This is what you wanted, Ava. Less. Remember?* When I turned to the window, only Bill's truck sat out front, and that sinking anchor smashed into the ocean floor.

It sure as heck didn't feel like less.

I hobbled to the coffee maker to fill the water tank. *It was the right thing to do.* The timing sucked. My life consisted of too many variables. I was stretched too thin, and everything was suffering. My job, my business deal, my health. I couldn't take care of Nina if I didn't earn money, if I didn't have a home for us.

Water flooded over the side of the tank and onto the counter. "I can't even pour water right!" I yanked a paper towel off the roll to clean up the spill.

I hated this version of myself, doing everything just well enough to stay afloat, but nothing well. We'd basically been couch-surfing! That wasn't stability. Had I been impulsive? Did I let my attraction for Eli color my choices? *What a mess!* I'd become a woman I hardly recognized. So far from the girl who booked horse lessons in the margins of a calendar and bought white cowboy hats. Or painted her nails in bright, bold colors only to chip them off a day later. I didn't even have time to paint my nails!

"Where's E-why?"

I turned to see Nina enter the kitchen with Bill.

Silence descended.

Where was Eli? He could've been running an early errand. Pulled his truck into the third bay? But I knew better.

"He had to go, Kiddo," Bill said.

"Why?" she asked.

Because I ripped his heart out. And apparently mine along with it.

"He doesn't live here. Guess he had something to get to."

"But I want choc-kit chip pancakes."

My insides shattered. How did I think I could do this?

"Well, you're in luck." Bill crossed to where I stood to collect a plate from the overhead cabinet. "There's some in the fridge."

"I'm sorry," I mouthed to him. Two silent words that would fix nothing.

He put the plate on the counter and studied me with a wrinkled brow. "You know, staying doesn't mean much if you're not true to your boots."

A desperate laugh popped out of me. "You sound like Terry."

"We have a few things in common."

"You both own ranches?" I asked.

"We both want what's best for you and Nina."

I stared down at my cast. "Well, this isn't the boot I normally wear."

Eli never stayed in one place. He said as much from the very beginning. But Nina and I? Where did we belong?

Cathy said nothing initially, probably because she was

processing my termination paperwork. It put me on edge all morning.

The pain medication plagued me with mental fog while also not numbing the discomfort. At best, it shaved off the piercing edge. And because of that, my tasks took twice the effort. I started questioning everything I'd ever said and done. Especially when I hobbled down the block to the local taco truck for lunch, realizing too late I had forgotten my purse. When I dug in my pocket for my phone to pay digitally, I found a twenty-dollar bill folded inside a sticky note with the message, "xoxo."

What have I done?

I could live with the pieces of my shattered heart–I'd survived before. But to run off Bill's son? To sentence the older man to lonely dinners at an empty table? He'd sell the ranch, and Eli's mom's house would be lost to them, decorated by someone who never knew her.

Because of me.

Six o'clock finally rolled around, and I wanted to rip out of my skin just to escape myself. Or run to someone strong enough to absorb all my frustrations. To tell me it was okay, that they'd fight for me. Even if I didn't deserve it.

At least Cathy hadn't fired me yet. Maybe she'd keep me out of pity. Why did that feel worse?

August's red truck waited in the lot. As I eased down the steps, he swung the passenger door wide. "You sure you wanna go? You look a little, eh, like you–"

"Tired?" I supplied.

"*Sí.*"

I'd texted him earlier with a request to take me to Hidden Meadows. I'd put it off too long, too busy playing house. "I have to speak with Terry. Face to face," I said. If he regretted our deal, I'd see it. If I were being selfish, I'd know once and for all.

It had to be 110 degrees outside. August's AC tried, but with my leg accessory, I graduated to a new level of misery.

"There is a water," he said, pointing to my door pocket.

"Thanks."

He didn't pressure me for conversation as we drove the windy path to where we'd first met, a concrete ribbon to the past. If I closed my eyes, I could pretend we were returning from a used trailer show, Jason complaining about the prices of fifth wheels, but I had my sights set on a 30-foot Coleman. Willowy mesquite branches would wave us in the long driveway. We'd pass families unloading their vehicles for a day at the ranch, wagons with coolers, kids in cheap cowboy hats, their faces white with sunscreen. Friendly horse-hands standing by in their worn and dusty denim and boots. A rainbow of horse breeds saddled and waiting in the arena.

But when I opened my eyes, I saw only the skeletal remains of a past I desperately sought to reclaim. As soon as he'd parked, I teetered out of August's truck with my crutches. He ran to meet me, offering a hand.

"I'm good," I said. "Can I just have a minute?"

"Of course."

My extra legs *clacked* and *clicked* as I worked my way down the ghost of a path alone, towards Jason's favorite trailhead. The ranch hadn't changed since last I'd come, but everything about it felt wrong. Broken fences shouted like live-auction bids—money spent for wood and screws instead of new toys for Nina. The nearly empty barn wept lonely tears, a time-abyss to recruit new boarders. I'd miss out on floor puzzles before lunch, and ice cream dates when the days hit triple digits. I no longer saw potential; I saw a thief. What else would it rob me of as I fought to bring it back to life? We had so little time already.

The sun beat mercilessly on my skin. The dust made my eyes dry. Terry and Kip were probably in the air-conditioned office, taking a break, or wrapping up for the day, but that wouldn't be my reality. I'd be out there every day, all day, making up for the lack of staffing. Building equity with my own sweat. Terry's words echoed in my mind. *"Just because you can, doesn't mean you should."* He was right. He'd been warning me from the start, but I'd been too naïve to realize that cost meant more than money.

When my truck flipped, I'd been sure I'd never see this place again. And I didn't care, because nothing overshadowed the fear of leaving Nina behind.

Hidden Meadows had changed, but so had I.

My crutches swung me past the leaning arena with its uneven gate, past withered sheds with their peeling paint, splintered picnic tables. Decorative stones used to line the path to the trailheads at the east end of the ranch, but now stringy weeds and burrs danced around my ankles.

My trek ended at the mouth of Jason's trail, where we'd scattered his ashes. I wasn't wearing boots or denim. I didn't have my cowgirl hat. And the tangerine sleeve on my leg ensured I wouldn't ride for weeks, maybe more.

We'd built our life's routine around a single goal: Hidden Meadows. Every choice, every sacrifice pivoted on how to make it ours. I knew nothing else. But did I really *want* Hidden Meadows? Or was I seeking the connection to Jason that it gave me? "You're probably wondering what I'm doing here like this."

The mountain felt massive to a little seed like me, seeking somewhere to land.

"What am I saying? I bet you already know." A tear slid down my face before I could sniff it away. My voice shook. "I screwed up, Jason. I lost sight of what mattered. I don't even know how it happened. I did everything I was supposed to. Stayed strong for Nina. Focused on the goal, kept busy. But ... I'm not happy."

No sudden gust of wind stirred at my words. No burst of rain erupted from the cloudless sky. Jason wasn't here. No one was. Maybe that's why the truth I'd been holding back finally burst free.

"I know we promised each other a home here, but I can't keep doing this. I'm tired of fighting. A day in a stuffy office is better than one that doesn't end with Nina."

Next to Jason, I knew where I belonged, what came next, and how to get there. But without him, I was shifty. Uncertain. A horse without a herd.

My vision blurred. He was supposed to be there. To reassure me.

Sweat ran down the opening of my cast, and my flamingo leg shook from heat and strain. "I'm really sorry about Roxy." Somehow, I'd known that I couldn't raise the dead with her. Why did I think I could do it with a ranch?

"I wish you'd say something."

But he wasn't there.

Of course he wasn't. He hadn't been for a year. I was just too grief-stricken to see it. Jason had so much passion for the ranch. To fall in love with him meant falling in love with Hidden Meadows. And I had hoped that reviving it would keep him alive. But it felt impossible to do it without him. Because it was him, and he wasn't coming back.

I pivoted on a single crutch, leaving a circular gouge in the dirt that mirrored the one in my chest where all my whimsical plans gushed out. Then I scraped and sweated across the ghostly ranch to the single-wide until the office door loomed in front of me. I knew the hinge would squeak when I opened it, and the interior would smell of paper, Sharpies, coffee, and horsehair. Kip would probably be leaning over the books, pencil in hand, readers fixed at the end of her nose. Terry might watch her with a half-smile as he jumped between slurping his third or fourth cup of coffee and catching up with August. A little pocket of familiar bliss.

And never had I been so terrified to enter.

I stood on the bottom step, my heart galloping up my throat. No plans, no direction, no idea what came next–a foreign predicament that chafed against my very nature.

What do I do?

Then, like a sigh, an invisible weight settled over my shoulders. It closed around me, holding me together. Fed me strength. A sun-soaked cocoon. And within that breath, I believed everything would be okay.

Tears rolled down my cheeks. I didn't know who I was supposed to be anymore. Without him. Without Hidden Meadows. But I needed to find out. Because I couldn't live in the past and be present for Nina. I pressed the heels of my hands into my eyes and wiped away my doubts.

It was never about a place.

It was about a family.

33

Ava

Kɪᴘ sᴛᴏᴏᴅ at a file cabinet near the kitchenette. Terry sat on the corner of Kip's desk, coffee in hand, chatting with August. The ceiling fan whirled, spinning the cobwebs into dizzy dance partners. The exact picture I'd imagined.

Until all motion stopped and three sets of eyes fell to my mandarin boot. Maybe I should've picked something more discreet?

Terry spoke first, popping off the desk. "What the heck happened to you?"

A dozen delicate responses mingled, but the straightforward one shot through the fray. "I totaled my truck."

"Well, shit." In the seven years I'd known him, I'd never heard him cuss. He put his cup down. "Glad to see you're in one piece."

"Yup, thanks to a metal plate and eight screws."

"Ouch," Kip chimed in with a grimace.

"That's more hardware than I have on the main gate," Terry joked half-heartedly, moving in to give me a side-hug.

"You can have them when I'm done."

"They rated for all weather?"

"I have no idea."

"Terry, stop it," Kip scolded, swatting his arm as she passed.

But his teasing lifted my confidence. Actually, more like hauled it up by its suspenders and told it to stop letting fear make my choices for me. "As much as I enjoy showing off my new boot," I didn't, not even a little, "I'm here for something else."

I leaned into my less sore armpit and tucked a loose hair behind my ear. August offered a nod of support. But he thought I planned to deliver a closing argument, not a white flag.

In the spirit of straight deliveries, I said, "You were right, Terry."

He beamed, glancing at Kip. "You heard that, right? You wanna jot that down?"

Kip rolled her eyes. "You might want to check where this is going before you start bragging."

Terry smoothed out his mustache with weathered fingers and turned back to me. "What was I right about, hon?"

"This place. It-it isn't meant for me."

"Ah." His slow nod told me he was neither surprised nor disappointed.

Still, I felt I owed him an explanation. "I hate that I'm breaking my promise, but it's too much. Nina's still so little. And I'll always be comparing it to how it used to be before ... You know. And I think I was just trying really hard to keep Jason alive." Out came the tears.

"We just want you to be happy," he said, wrapping an arm around my shoulders again. A year's worth of unrequited hope spilled out in salty waterfalls. A final farewell to the life I'd never end up living. But it made room for relief.

I curled into Terry's shoulder and cried for Jason, for Hidden Meadows, for Nina, and then finally, for myself. I cried until my throat ran dry and my nose plugged up. Past polite tears and into ugly, body-raking sobs. I'd been trying so hard to hold everything together, to appear confident and in control when in reality, I'd been ignoring the tear as it ripped wider.

Kip appeared behind Terry, holding a box of tissues.

"Th-thank you." I took one, then another, blowing until my head floated with the clouds.

Terry stepped back to stand with August. Kip remained, handing me another tissue.

"I really wish–" I paused to wipe my eyes. "I wish this didn't mean Steven won."

Terry laughed. "He sounds like a bit of a twerp."

"I had a more colorful term in mind, but yes."

I tossed my wad of snotty tissues in the trash. I felt better. Exhausted, but for the first time since I can't remember when, I didn't have that constant urgency straining against the inside of my skin. With a sniff, I told Terry, "You deserve every bit of that offer. Buy yourself something ridiculous."

He shrugged. "You gonna be okay? You need help gettin' around? Or figuring stuff out?"

My nose twitched with the threat of another outpouring. "No, I'm good. I just … it still feels like I'm deserting him."

Terry clicked his tongue, lifting his eyes to the fan overhead, and watched it spin. Then he gestured to the room. "Jason isn't here." He pressed his palm to his chest. "He's here."

"I know."

Kip handed me the tissue box and crossed to the kitchenette. "How about a cup of crappy coffee, fancy pants?"

Caffeine? This late?

I glanced at the can of cheap bulk grounds on the folding table. "Actually, yes. That sounds good."

Terry knocked back the rest of his cup and moved towards the door. "While you do that, August, I need your help with something." His eyes flashed with mischief.

"*Sí.* Of course."

The door thwacked shut, leaving just me and Kip.

"I'm proud of you," she said, handing me a chipped mug with black coffee, then turned to dump three packs of sugar in hers. I was the only one who took cream, so they wouldn't have any.

"Thanks." I braved a tentative sip. The bitterness honed my focus down to a single pushpin on a map. If I were emotion, Kip was logic, so I asked, "What do I do now?"

"What do you mean?" She turned to me with her own cup.

"I've been working towards Hidden Meadows for years. I don't know what to do."

"That's easy. Do whatever you want."

My laugh was more of a desperate exhale. "What if I don't know what I want?"

There were things I wished I had, but they lacked the bigger picture. They were effects of a lifestyle. Time. Love. Togetherness. Not items on a checklist.

"What makes you happy?" Kip asked me.

"Nina."

"And?"

"Horses?"

"And? What else?" Her question forced me to dig deeper.

I thought about how the past few weeks had infused color back into our lives. Joyful meals at the dinner table with people I cared about. Teaching Marley to cook. Saturday morning pancakes. Terry's hugs. Kip's rare smiles. Eli's unwavering support.

She gave me one of those hard-earned expressions then. A smile. "I see you've discovered something."

My isolation had always been self-inflicted. "I have a family."

"Well, of course you do!"

Without business plans, loan paperwork, and confrontations with Steven, I'd have the time and luxury to reconnect with people. *They* were my roots. All I needed was a home base and a table big enough to feed everyone. I could do that. Though my heart clenched thinking there'd be one face missing.

Kip sipped her coffee. "What made you change your mind?"

I stared down at the toes that stuck out of my cast, now dusty from all my trekking. "I drove into a commercial truck a few days ago. It was my fault. My mind was in a million places, and I was tired," I shook my head. "I could've hurt someone. Or worse." What was I trying to say? "I just ... I realized I've been so busy I'm missing everything. What if something happens to me? What memory would Nina carry? That her mom was so obsessed with a dead man's promise that she was never around? I'd hated my mom for leaving me. How is what I'm doing any different?"

Kip's face softened. "A lot to think about. You didn't ask, but my two cents?"

"Hit me."

"You made the right choice."

I nodded, expecting immense sadness, but saying goodbye to Hidden Meadows felt more like releasing a wild bird I'd been caging inside of me. I loved it, but it clawed at me because it was never meant to be mine alone. And with its release came freedom. Time to meander, to appreciate what I had, and maybe spend an entire weekend in my pajamas–wherever we ended up.

I sipped my black coffee, letting myself explore where our new home might be. Oddly, every version had rusty mountains framed in a forget-me-not sky, and a kitchen with black coun-tertops.

"What will you do when he sells?" I asked Kip.

She inhaled deeply and let it out slowly through her nose. "I think I'll join the bocce league."

My brow shot up. "You play bocce ball?"

"No, but I've always wanted to try." She shrugged in an unusual show of uncertainty. "Maybe I'll travel. Who knows?"

"Where would you go?"

Her eyes drifted to the window, and I got the distinct impression she wasn't seeking something, but someone. "Don't know."

Let her have her secret. "I should probably get going. I'm sure Nina's getting hungry. Once I'm more settled, would you like to come over for dinner?"

"Depends, whatcha making?" She gave me a wink.

"Thank you, Kip."

"For what?"

"For being patient with me."

Her eyes rolled in exasperation. "Stop it. I've been saying it all along. That's what family does." At my wobbling smile, she added, "Go on! Get. Feed Nina. We're not going to sell this place overnight."

We? "Yeah, okay." Instead of goodbye, I said, "See you soon." I had feared a farewell, but this turned out to be a reunion.

The boys were waiting by August's truck for me. A potted tree sat strapped in the bed.

"What's this?" I asked.

Terry landed his hands on his hips like a proud dad. "It's a mesquite sapling. Grew it from a cutting before they all got sick."

"Oh, my gosh!" I rushed up to inspect it. A baby legacy! "Where's it going?"

"Home with you."

"What?"

"Plant it somewhere special."

"Oh." A jagged fissure raced through me. I really wanted it, but, "I-I don't have a–"

"You will." When my waterworks sprang again, Terry came

in for another hug. "Make sure she hydrates when she gets home," he told August.

I was sobbing over a tree. *A tree.* Water was good, but a beer would be better.

August drove us under the iron arch that marked the entrance to Hidden Meadows. "It changed," he said.

I twisted to watch it shrink in the rear window. "Yeah. Losing someone does that to you."

He glanced across the cab at me. "Yes."

"I'm sorry I didn't warn you. I got out of this truck intending to buy a ranch."

"*Mijo*, you don't need to explain to me."

On a heavy exhale, I slouched in the passenger seat. "I miss him."

"I miss him, also."

"He'd probably be furious with my choices lately."

"Some, yes," August agreed.

I stared out the window at the winding road that cut through the rocky landscape. It must've added thirty minutes to the drive, cupping each bluff, following the natural grooves in the mountain. But a straight shot would've been too steep, impossible to traverse. I, too, had taken the long way around.

We had no time machine to bring us back, and I was not the same person I'd been. It could never be the same. I understood that now. I let Kip's words ruminate. "*What makes you happy?*"

As if on cue, my phone pinged with a text from Bill.

Bill: Nina and I are going to the library. We will pick up dinner on the way home. See you soon. :)

I smiled at his full sentences and use of punctuation.

What makes me happy? A simple answer to a simple question. And horrible timing. Without Eli, Luke probably wouldn't stay. Marley had to go home–she'd be starting school soon.

When Terry closed escrow, he'd drive off to live his best retired life, maybe with Kip. Bill would also sell.

Everyone was leaving.

I leaned my head against the seat and closed my eyes. The sun baked my skin, and the wind whipped my hair in every direction. My path had a few more curves to go.

"Drink water," August said as soon as we entered the house. He left my sapling in the truck and trailed me into the kitchen. No doubt to ensure I followed directions.

While I hydrated, my eyes skated over the doorway that led to the garage via the mudroom. I'd once speculated on Eli's science of leaving. Owning only enough to fit inside a single duffel. But I'd never expected him to disappear so quickly. It led me to a single conclusion: his only reason to stay was for me. *If he'd planned to stay at all.* And that wasn't good enough. I didn't want to be the source of resentment five years down the road if things fell apart. To owe him for giving up his life for me. Bill was right. He had to do it because he wanted it for himself.

How could he just up and leave, though? He told me he'd be around! What if I needed him to ... to teach me how to lift weights? Not even a goodbye!

I left my glass on the counter and collected my crutches. "I'll be right back." Maybe Bill misunderstood. Maybe it was just an overnight errand. Maybe Eli left a note. That was his thing, sweet nothings signed xoxo.

My underarms burned, and my back spasmed as I climbed the studio stairs, but his door stood ajar, like a welcoming wave inside. I had to see for myself. To understand what he was thinking. Because a part of me wanted to call him and tell him to turn around.

I stormed into the room, my eyes scanning inch by inch for a Post-it or an envelope. An easy task, because every surface–the counter, the nightstand, the desk–was bare and bland, as if he'd never been there at all. No wrinkles in the made bed. No papers on the desk. No coin piles on the counter. The emptiness seeped into my skin, changing the laws of gravity. I suddenly struggled to hold myself upright.

He'd done what he'd always intended to do. To veer back to his old life. Could I blame him? I'd given him all the green lights, then suddenly barricaded the road. Seeing it made it real. He left. And it wasn't *less*, not by a long shot. I moved deeper into the room, desperate for something. A small piece of him. If it hadn't been for Eli, who knows where we would've ended up?

My crutch sent something skidding across the smooth wooden floor.

A frayed baseball cap.

Eli's baseball cap.

I thought I had nothing left to break. But as my crutches fell to the ground, my heart cracked in two. *I did this.*

Footsteps thundered up the stairs, and a moment later, August appeared in the doorway. "You are okay? I heard a loud noise."

I bent to pick up Eli's trademark cap and ran my fingers along the worn brim. I wanted to take it all back. To suck the words straight from the source into the vacuum of space so he'd never hear them, not even by accident. "I lied, August. I told him I didn't want him."

August sighed, taking Eli's hat from my fingers. "He's not so stupid. He knows better."

"Then why would he leave?" It was easy to say he needed to stay for himself, but to honor that proved a much harder challenge.

August's mouth twisted to the side in uncertainty.

How could I fix this? Whether by happenstance or divine intervention, I'd found exactly what I'd been looking for. Eli wasn't *more*. He was the balance I couldn't seem to give myself. The rest in between hectic ambitions. A teammate, not an extra inning.

My kindhearted boy who rescued strays with peanut butter cups and ham sandwiches. Such a simple act. A breath amidst chaos and desperation. Was it any wonder I fell so hard?

Maybe that was it? He thought we didn't need him because we weren't stranded anymore? I had a down payment in my savings account. We could buy a house. Something outside the city with a yard big enough for a horse, maybe two. *Or a boarding ranch with a mountain view.* Was it wrong to entertain that fantasy when this place was meant for Eli?

"Hey, *Amor*." August smacked my head with the soft side of the baseball cap. "Stop what you're doing. It's no good."

I grabbed Eli's prized possession from his loose grip and curled my fingers over the faded bill. "What am I doing?"

"You think it's because of you. He's a man. He makes his own choices." August picked up my crutches and held them out. "Come. Have a beer with me. And more water. You cry a lot today."

As I sat at the kitchen table with my untouched beer and Eli's cap in front of me, a new emotion surfaced. Why was this here? Was he okay? When I pulled out my phone, I stared at the screen for a good ten seconds. If the roles were reversed, would I answer? I honestly couldn't say.

My finger tapped the call button, and I held the phone to my ear.

It went to voicemail.

34

Eli

I WAS BLASTING a local country station while driving through Albuquerque when I got the call. My halfway point to frigging nowhere, Texas. But I didn't wanna be in New Mexico. Or Texas. Or anywhere Ava wasn't.

Nothing but a sad sap, stuck in a country song. I unpeeled another Reese's and tossed the wrapper into the footwell with the others. I hated how the wind blew my hair everywhere. Hated all the hats for sale at the truck stops.

I hate this damn music!

I punched off the radio, but the silence was worse.

My fingers choked the steering wheel. I'd left a mess, and something didn't sit right about Luke's mom's call. His mom never called. Not once in the whole time Luke worked the ranch.

Frigging-A.

I veered off the exit and flipped around, catching I40 west.

Six hours later, I was driving past remodeled houses with big trees, fancy paver driveways, and three-car garages. My butt ached from sitting, the road vibrations scrambled my brain, and I had no idea what to do when I got to Luke's place.

I stopped in front of a gray house with a yellow door that screamed 2.5 kids and a dog. In the cupholder, my phone rattled.

Ava.

All I wanted was to hear her voice, even to chew me out for leaving without a goodbye. Anything she could dish I'd already thought, or worse. But the best I could do was to stay out of her way and stop giving her more to think about. I let her call go to voicemail as I threw my truck into park, and stared out the passenger window.

Luke's house wasn't what I expected. But I knew a perfect exterior meant squat. Mom's cancer didn't care that we had clean shutters. Just like depression couldn't be redirected with a fancy leaf-shaped downspout. I hopped out of my truck and walked up a slate stone path.

The front door opened before I could knock, and Luke's mom rushed out, shutting it behind her. "Eli, thank you so much for coming. I didn't know who else to call." Her voice leaked hope like a broken pipe.

"No problem. What's going on?"

She shook a prescription bottle of Percocet. It rattled like it had maybe three pills left. "I take these for my back, and last week this was full."

I frowned. "You think it was Luke?"

She nodded.

A shadow in the front window caught my eye, but I pretended not to see it. "Did you ask him about it?"

"Yes. He started shouting all kinds of horrible things, then locked himself in his room."

"What kind of things?"

"That he hated it here, and he wished he were dead." Her lip quivered, and words started rushing out of her. "I just ... I don't know what to do. My husband doesn't have the patience for this kind of behavior. Luke's been in there all day. He hasn't eaten, I don't think he's even come out to go to the bathroom, and now he's not even responding when I go to check on him. I don't know if he's okay. Or what he's got in there. His music is too loud to hear anything–"

"Okay. Okay, slow down. We'll figure this out." I scratched at my stubble while she caught her breath.

It was pretty clear the ranch plan had failed, and chances were, nothing I could say would make a difference. She'd be better off sending him to an actual program. But he'd think he was being offloaded onto someone else. "Let me see if he'll speak to me."

She did one of those baseball bobble-head nods. "Thank you."

I followed her into a tidy house. Past a spotless living room, and around a giant rug scored with vacuum lines. I could just imagine the woman trailing behind her son to catch the dirt when he came home from the ranch.

We stopped at a white door that matched all the others; no band posters or handwritten "stay out" signs.

I didn't expect much, but I knocked, anyway. "Luke?"

The reply through the door was a definite, "Fuck off."

I ticked my head toward the front of the house, suggesting Luke's mom step away. After eying me, then the door, she zipped off, and seconds later, the hum of her vacuum bounced down the hallway.

I knocked again. "Luke, I can't hear anything. Your mom's vacuuming. Can I come in?"

No response.

"Eventually, you're gonna have to come out." I couldn't break down a stranger's door. And barging in would only road-kill the kid's trust. "Come on, man, talk to me."

But did he trust me? Maybe I was being delusional. My hand reached for the hat I'd left behind. Where did I go wrong? I'd failed everyone. Luke, Dad, Ava. Mom.

Popping pills? Right under my nose? I leaned into the door. "Hey, Luke?"

"What do you want?" It swung open to the scowling teen. He wore his usual black, plus all the piercings, but something about him looked different.

"I want you to talk to me."

"No."

"Fine. You wanna talk *at* me?"

He scoffed. "How's that different?"

"I just shut up and listen."

His eyes narrowed. "Why? So, you can tell my mom? Fuck you."

Come on, Eli. Fix this. What set him off? "What's with all the cussing?"

He crossed his arms. "What's with all the shit in your truck?"

He saw that? Of course, he did. I'd parked right in front of the house. My whole life sat in the bed of my truck. I linked my fingers behind my neck. "I need to go to Texas. For a job."

"Bullshit. You said you'd be here all summer."

"It was a last-minute thing."

His face fell flat. "You're so fucking full of it."

My arms folded over my chest. "Excuse me?"

"You always tell me to go home and sleep on shit."

"I *did* sleep on it." Or at least, I tried to. "This isn't the same thing. I'm an adult. I don't live with my dad anymore."

"Yeah. You don't live anywhere."

Ouch.

"I fucking hate it here," he said, "but *I* stayed."

I was losing an argument to someone half my age. Worse, he had a point. "Look, you gotta finish school. Plus, you can't get an apartment as a minor."

"Why did I fucking listen to you? You're such a hypocrite. You have one fight with your girlfriend, and you run away."

"That's not–Ava's not my girlfriend." And it wasn't even a fight, because I couldn't argue against the truth. "Wait, how did you know about that?"

"The little kid told me."

"When?"

"This morning, when I showed up, and you didn't." I could hear the hurt.

Shit. My fingers raked through my hair, then I remembered how Steven did that at the hospital, and I shoved my hands into my pockets. Luke found out from Nina?

"So, it *is* 'cause she dumped you?" he said.

"No." *Not technically.*

"Is it because you hate your dad?"

"No."

"So, what? You got tired of checking on me?"

"No! Of course not." Then I did the thing Dad used to do– the chin dip and the stare down. "Do I need to check on you?"

That made him pause. "Whatever. Just fucking go. I don't care."

I don't care. The biggest load of crap ever spoken. When people said that you doubled down. "What's going on? You promised you'd stay out of trouble if I gave you a job."

"Yeah, well, you're leaving, so ..."

Damnit. I'd been so fired up about Ava, I wasn't even thinking.

"It's fine," he said. "I'll go be someone else's problem."

"Luke." *No.* "That's not–you're not a problem."

That's when I realized why he looked different. Not once in the conversation did he flip his hair out of his face. Shoulders hunched, arms crossed–he was shrinking. Last time he'd been that small, I'd caught him sneaking out of a Circle K with booze under his sweatshirt. That was the day I met him. All those hours on the ranch, and we ended right where we'd started. He thought everyone was better off without him. Suddenly, I saw my younger self staring back at me, and I laughed. This kid had my number in more ways than I wanted to admit.

He tried to slam the door in my face, but I sliced a hand into the jamb. The temporary pain mattered so much less than proving to this kid that he mattered. The effort spent helping him didn't take away from my life or anyone else's. I thought back to what Dad said. It was true, having a worthwhile purpose pushed me through the daily grind when everything else hit the fan.

Ava called it a youth program. Maybe I missed how great the ranch was before she showed up, but Luke didn't. He found a place he wanted to be. How could I take that from him?

The vacuuming stopped. *Great.* Just in time to overhear my confession. But I'd do it anyway. Luke needed an outlet. A place where he could get messy. Somewhere without grades and judgment.

I shook out my throbbing hand. "You're right. I'm a hypocrite. This is about Ava. She has me in so many knots I can't think straight." Luke rolled his eyes, but he wasn't shutting the door on me anymore. "It's messing with me. But I'm doing my best."

After a long pause, he said. "I'm sorta into Marley."

I held back a laugh. *Duh.* "Did something happen?"

"We, uh ..." His face turned candy apple red.

"You made out with her in the tack room?"

"What? How'd you know?"

"Lucky guess." Why else would Marly go down to the stables in the mornings? I didn't say anything because I'd figured they'd do it anyway.

"I thought she liked me," he said. "But she got all weird."

"Is that why you started stealing your mom's pills?"

He shrugged. At least he admitted it.

"Girls are brutal," I told him. *"I don't need more. I need less."* The truth of it split my chest in half. "Ava yeeted me, too."

"No." Luke shook his head. "Nobody says that. Never say that again."

"What? Why? Isn't that the slang?"

"You didn't even use it right!"

"My bad."

Luke shook his hair out of his face. Finally, we were getting somewhere. "Girls suck."

I blew out a breath. "Yeah." I would've stayed for her. Woulda done a whole lot more–fences, welcome mats, and good school districts. I scrubbed my hands down my face. "Luke, you're not some problem I have to deal with. I like having you at the ranch."

In fact, I'd been happier doing that than bouncing around Podunk cities for a decade. All those miles I'd traveled, and I never got anywhere. I was the same sad kid who lost his mom. Maybe not with drugs or alcohol, but I was still throwing my life away, avoiding everything that felt hard and calling it happiness. "You were right," I told him. "I was gonna run. But maybe I should sleep on it, first?"

"Yeah. I guess."

"And maybe I'll see you at the ranch tomorrow morning?"

Luke lifted a skinny shoulder.

"Well, I hope I do. You're the best ranch hand I've got."

"I'm your *only* ranch hand." But there was a smile under the attitude.

"Same rules though. No drugs. No alcohol. You're feeling low, we'll go for a ride. Or I'll hang a punching bag in the garage, and we'll beat the crap out of it. Deal?"

"Yeah. Cool."

It felt like a miracle, and I wondered if a man was entitled to more than one? "See you tomorrow."

Luke's mom walked me to my truck with tears in her eyes. "That was-you're just-If you ever need anything, ever, please ask."

"Luke's a great kid." With thoughts and feelings that had nowhere to go. I pulled open the driver's door. I had no business telling his mom how to parent, but I could give him space every morning to do his thing. "Bring him by at seven?"

"Absolutely!"

It seemed all my dumb choices finally turned into something useful. Funny how that made me regret them a little less.

There were no trucks out front when I pulled up to Dad's ranch. *Weird. Where is everyone?* A lucky break, though. That gave me time to work out what to say. A pitch for the plan that started brewing when I pulled away from Luke's house.

How do you start a youth program? *Ava would know.* She was smart, resourceful, and organized. She could write business plans in her sleep.

But first ... I shoved my keys into my pocket and circled the hood of my truck to the mudroom entrance. Up the studio stairs, into the room that started off as a prison. I'd pegged "home" as fences and HOA rules decorated to disguise your cage. But maybe I had it wrong. Maybe home wasn't a cage. Maybe it was a safety net while you figured everything else out? A place where you could sleep on it.

I stopped in the middle of the studio and did a full 360.

Where is it?

I checked all the drawers, under the bed, and in the bathroom, but my hat wasn't anywhere. *What the heck?* Down to the garage, I dug through toolboxes and all the crap on the workbench. That's when panic started rising. How frigging stupid was I? *Why did I leave it?* I didn't remember going there, but I stomped through the mudroom into the kitchen, flipping on the light.

My feet froze.

"Were you looking for this?" Ava asked. Her back was to me. She was sitting at the table, facing the window, and there, in her hands, was the thing I'd been looking for.

My heart thudded. "Yeah. Where did you find it?"

"In your room."

Ava was in my room? Hope turned me drunk and reckless. I crossed the kitchen and took a seat opposite her. She was tracing the stitching on the bill of my hat and avoided my eyes when she handed it to me.

"Thanks." I didn't expect to see her yet. I had no idea what to say.

She twisted a can of beer that sat in front of her. "I didn't mean you had to leave, you know."

"Yeah, I know."

The focus she gave her drink would've made any man jealous. She'd told me she wanted less, so how did I tell her that just being in the room with her felt right? Making her smile was like smiling myself. Holding her grounded me in a way I never knew existed. That I didn't just *like* her. The words were begging to come out. But if I blew it?

I turned my hat over in my hands. "Where is everyone?"

Her eyes finally found mine, so dull and tired. "At the library."

"This late?"

She shrugged.

My foot tapped under the table. I glanced behind me at the bed of my truck, full of stuff. I couldn't do it. Couldn't let her sit there like that and keep my feelings to myself. For once, I wasn't itching to escape. I itched for a plan. "Good."

"Good?" Confusion looked beautiful on her. Everything did.

Why couldn't this work? We liked each other, and we made a killer team. How could that be *more*? There had to be an overlap between the two ranches. Heck, I could complete the stuff at Dad's in a few hours with Luke and give her the rest of my day. I'd do it for free. And if it was too much, I'd wait. She wouldn't be overwhelmed forever.

"Good," I repeated. "'Cause I wanted to talk to you."

"Eli, I–"

"Are you gonna drink that?" I nodded to her beer.

"Probably not." Her eyes grew wide as she watched me chug half the can.

At least now I had her attention. "I need your help with something. Advice. On how to start a youth program."

"I–A–" she stammered, blinking hypnotic lashes at me. "You want to start a youth program? Where?"

"Here."

"Here?"

I nodded, tracking every little change on her face. How her eyes cut again to the window, and all the evidence of my failed escape. To think I was gonna drive off and never see her again.

"Yeah. Luke called me out today. It was brutal, but true."

Teeth dug into her bottom lip. Her chest inflated. "What did he say?"

"Told me to sleep on it." I met her eyes dead-on. "Thing is, everything I want is here." She opened her mouth, probably to shut me down. "Let me finish? You can try to change my mind when I'm done."

She pressed her lips together.

I slid my hat home, no idea what came next, only that it had to sweep her off her feet. "Have you ever had powdered eggs?"

Her forehead wrinkled.

"Hotel breakfasts. The eggs are always powdered," I explained. "Well, sometimes they have hard-boiled. But the powdered ones, they taste like crap." I scanned the black counters that Ava called sexy. "I never appreciated a good breakfast. Or good coffee. Or good company." Color started coming back into her cheeks.

Keep going.

"But it's more than the eggs. It's a house full of people. And working with Luke. And horseback rides. Not so much the heat, but I can live with it."

The day granted me a second miracle: Ava snickered, and that familiar light flashed in her eyes.

"And it turns out," I went on, "my dad doesn't hate me."

"Of course he doesn't!" When I gave her a look, she playfully zipped her lips.

I readjusted my hat, pretty sure it was going well. "I think we need a plan, like you made for Hidden Meadows, so I know how to help you without making it more. I'll do whatever. At home or at your new ranch. Fix dinner, fix fences. Watch Nina. And I promise I won't keep you up late. Not if you don't want me to." A beat passed. Maybe I had more to say, but I couldn't think of anything. "Okay, I'm done."

Seconds ticked by, and she didn't respond. I considered polishing off the rest of her beer. Instead, I held my breath. My heart revved a million revolutions a minute until finally, she spoke.

"Somewhere in there, you'll have time to run a youth program?"

"I was thinking before and after school. The middle of the day would be for you."

"Even in triple digits?"

"I'll throw up some misters. Shades. Whatever it takes. I wanna be on your team, Ava. Part of your Hidden Meadows family."

Her smile faded. "Eli, I don't need your help with Hidden Meadows."

"I know you don't *need* it, but I want to–"

She stood abruptly from the table, making the bench drag across the floor. I stood too, fear taking over. *No, I blew it!* I should've waited. Thought it through. "Ava, I didn't mean you weren't capable enough."

Her voice cracked when she asked, "Are you hungry?"

"What?"

She hopped across the kitchen, using the counter for support. I followed her to the fridge, where she started pulling food out. This all felt so familiar.

"Ava, what are you–give me those." I took the loaf of bread and the condiments. "Look, I know you want less, but what I'm trying to say is, I can make it less. Let me take stuff off your plate."

She added sliced cheese and ham cold cuts to my load, then hopped to the cabinet and pulled down an actual plate.

I dumped the food on the counter. "Please don't shut me out. Let me try." Then I watched helplessly as she started making a frigging sandwich. "Will you talk to me? Did I get it wrong? Am I just being an idiot here?"

She topped the thing with bread and slid the plate across the counter to me.

My gut bottomed out. "Thanks, but I'm not hungry."

"Seriously?" Annoyed–that's how she sounded.

Well, join the club! I was giving the woman my heart, and she responded with a damn ham sandwich? Maybe I said too much? Not enough? What more could I do?

She inhaled sharply and spread her fingers wide on the countertop. "You told me once about a stray you lured home with a ham sandwich."

I blinked.

"Best dog you ever–Forget it." She reached for the plate. "Never mind."

I shot out a hand to stop her. Something big was filling me from the inside. So full I would probably rip right down the center, but it just might've been the best feeling I'd ever felt in my whole damn life. "You're trying to lure me home?"

"Never mind. It was stupid. I don't even have a home right now. I–" The words got stuck, and she cleared her throat. "I gave up Hidden Meadows."

"What? Why?"

"Because I can't build a future if I'm living in the past."

My head exploded with possibilities, like watching a science video of the Big Bang. She and I, working side-by-side. Family horseback rides. Dancing under the stars with her in that dress.

Maybe even a dog.

"Okay," I said, "this is gonna sound dumb, but am I in that future?"

"I hope so."

I grabbed the butter knife she'd used for the mayo and cut the sandwich in two, taking one piece for myself and pushing the plate back her way. I held my sandwich in the air. "To finding homes?"

She picked up the other half and tapped the corner of her bread to mine.

Hands down, it was the best sandwich I'd ever had.

35

Ava

BILL'S EXPRESSION was impossible to interpret when he stepped into the kitchen. He nodded a greeting to his son. To me, he said, "Sorry we're so late. They had a puppet show going on at the library tonight." He set two takeout bags on the counter.

"Well, that's cool." Did I sound too chipper?

"Yeah. So cool," Marley deadpanned, appearing behind them.

Nina wrapped her arms around my leg. "Mama, Mama! They have a big poo!"

I stared at her, trying to dissect that. "A what?"

"There was a life-sized stuffed Pooh Bear in the kids' section at the library," Bill explained.

Nina added, "And the boy had a magic cock!"

Marley snickered.

"Rooster," Bill said. "In the puppet show. The farm boy had a magic cock, or *rooster*, that gave him gold feathers and crowed when danger was near. Right, Nina?"

"Uh huh. And look!" She held up a gold-colored feather pendant attached to a black cord. "I got a cock fedder!"

Marley lost it. She threw herself against the wall and folded in half, laughing. I choked, trying to keep a straight face.

Eli patted my back. "Breathe, Ava."

Bill adjusted his glasses. "The script was a little dated. But the antique marionettes they used were in great condition."

"Yeah," Marley screeched between hysterics. "We learned old cocks can still crow."

Bill cut her a warning glance. "Are you done?"

"You're the one who made me go. I wanted to stay home." She wiped a tear, her chest still shaking. "But seriously, I've never heard that word so many times in one hour."

Eli's hand lingered on my back, and an addictive awareness trickled down my spine.

"Sounds like quite a show," I said. "I'm sorry I missed it." But not enough to trade the past hour Eli and I had spent in the empty house making up.

"Mama?"

I smiled at Nina. "Yes, Crackerjack?"

"Why your shirt is outside-in?"

"What?" I glanced down and saw that in my rush, I'd slipped my top back on inside-out. "Um ..."

Eli's self-deprecating laugh only made it worse. "Can't get away with anything."

I jabbed him with my elbow.

"Oh, my God!" Marley gagged. "Ew. Just, ew."

He flung a dismissive hand at her. "Don't you have angry girl music to listen to, or something?"

"Why's dat ew, Mama?"

"Heeey, Dad," Eli cut in. "Can I talk to you real quick?"

"Sure. Let me grab a beer. Meet you on the deck?"

I hopped to the counter where Bill had left the takeout. "I can plate the food. Is there enough? Should I prep something to go with it?"

Bill turned to his son. "You staying for dinner?"

It amazed me that his voice held no hope or disappointment, judgments or guilt trips. It was just a question. He truly wanted this to be Eli's choice. I pressed my lips together, trying not to give away the plan Eli and I had concocted between greedy kisses.

"Was kinda thinking I'd stay for more than that," he told his dad.

That's when Bill's face morphed into the joy of a man who got all he'd ever wished for. "Sure, Ava, if you wouldn't mind."

The house was quiet except for Eli's soft thuds up the garage stairs as he returned to the studio. Nina had finally settled into bed, and I should've followed suit, but uncertainty swirled around me like fog. This all happened so quickly. It felt too easy. After years of fighting for everything, I didn't expect to have it handed to me on a hay bale. Bill seemed pleased during dinner, but did he consider all the details?

If he agreed to hire me, the posted salary for Bill's ranch manager position left little room for both rent and preschool tuition. And Eli would be busy building his youth program. Maybe even taking some psychology classes and earning a credential. That meant childcare fell to him alone, for however long this worked. Forever flashed through my brain, but I had to be practical. We weren't in a fairytale. Things happened. People changed their minds.

I snuck out of our bedroom, a three-legged circus act, cringing at every click from my crutches, psyching myself up. *Stairs, Ava. You got this.* I hadn't checked, but I was fairly certain my underarms were purple.

However, by some miracle, I found Bill on the couch in the den, staring at the French doors and the darkness beyond.

Relief rushed out in a loud exhale. "Oh, good! You saved me a trip up the stairs." I eased onto the cushion next to him and propped my leg on the coffee table.

He waited for me to get settled. "Eli told me about your ranch. I'm sorry, kiddo."

I smiled at the term of endearment. "Thank you."

He turned to me then, his brow sinking. "I'm worried–I hope you didn't give it up because I told you I wanted Eli to stay."

"No! No, you were right. He needed to decide for himself, and not for nostalgia or some romantic whim." Although I didn't hate that his feelings for me turned him tongue-tied. "It was because of my accident. It put things in perspective. I realized I can't do it all. And I certainly can't revive the past." I shook my head, accepting the weird sinking feeling that rose up my throat instead of down. The sting as my words fought past it. "Even if I could, I'm a different person now. It wouldn't be the same." I pulled my good knee to my chest. "I feel like I failed my husband. But I think it was the right decision."

"That's something I admire about you, Ava. You're not afraid to make hard choices."

"Just because they're hard doesn't mean they're the right choices."

"Right choices, wrong choices," Bill shrugged. "I think if you commit to it, and you work at it, it all comes out the same in the end."

"That being said," I twisted to face him, "I want to make sure you're okay with me working here."

"Of course! I would've hired you on day one."

"Really? Because if I remember correctly, you scolded Eli for feeding me breakfast."

"And then you insisted on mucking in those silly heels."

"Touché." I paused. "I know you said you would watch

Nina, but if I work here, and if Eli starts his program, I'd need help with her *every day*, and–"

"Ava."

"Yes?"

"You are a gift sent from God. You returned my son to me. I will do whatever it takes to keep you here. Plus, I'm pretty fond of peanut in there."

My chest swelled, forcing up mushy tears. How much did Eli tell him? The whole grand plan, or just the highlights? We still had kinks to work out. A credential to earn. Some financial issues to address. But I had a down payment with nowhere to go. I wondered whether Bill would consider a partnership? A conversation for the morning, maybe.

"Thank you, Bill." I bit my lip, shifting to ease the soreness in my hip. "I have one more favor to ask."

"Shoot."

"Can I stay here until I have a few pay stubs? For an apartment application? That kind of bit me in the butt at my last place."

He frowned. "Why would you move?"

"I don't want to take advantage of your generosity."

His laugh lit his face and made his glasses shake. "You cook, you clean up after yourself, and I wake up hearing voices and laughter. Feels like I'm getting the better end of the bargain here."

No arguing with that. I stared down at my cast. "In that case, can I start my official manager position in six to eight weeks?"

I could not wait! Seven days until my cast came off! Honestly, that was eight days too many. Showering had become such a hassle. I probably had a trough worth of sweat down there. And *actual* trough water.

I reached over the seat to hand Nina a tube of Gerber baby puffs. They cost as much as a retail chain coffee, but they lasted longer than a bag of Cheerios. Call it a world wonder. Her recently liberated arm seemed to have no problem with dexterity, despite the fading rash and skinnier appearance.

Eli cranked up the AC, then leaned over the center console of my new truck to steal a kiss. "Be right back."

Maybe not steal. That implied an unwilling partner in crime. "Make sure they include the radish and the pickled vegetables."

"I'll ask for extra." He pressed another quick kiss to my lips and left me grinning like a Cheshire cat.

I admired the way his butt filled his jeans as he walked up the sidewalk. He fit the stereotype now, his gait a lazy ramble in his new cowboy boots. I liked the work boots, but he insisted new beginnings needed new footwear. A sentiment I understood. That's why we opted for takeout.

We had spent the entire day hunting for a truck, with a stop at the ice cream shop thrown in to appease Nina. My legs ached from all the standing around, which was why I let Eli drive my certified pre-owned electric-blue Ram 1500 off the lot. He'd gone in for the kill, popping the hood and drilling the salesman, Clint. Poor Clint. But how refreshing to have someone fighting in my corner! Another apparent weakness of mine, which meant Eli and I would need some alone time later. After elevating my leg.

I stared at the front of the Mexican takeout place at the end of the strip mall. The same shopping center where we'd met. It turned out this little hole in the wall had the best handmade tortillas in South Phoenix.

The *For Lease* sign still hung in the bare storefront two doors down. I guess Chinese food did not woo Mister Robert

McClintock into a contract. *Serves him right.* I wanted to be the forgive-and-forget kind of person, but with Steven, my feelings swayed toward vengeance. The passive sort, since he deserved none of my time. Thankfully, he'd stopped harassing me after his altercation with Eli. My only regret was that I didn't get to punch him, too.

The rattle and cascade of baby puffs leaving their container and hitting the floor had me twisting to Nina.

She stared down past her legs. "Oopsies."

"Nina, baby ..." Did they sell these things in bulk?

"It's okay, Mama. I will still eat them."

"Off the floor?"

"Eli said they're still good."

I blinked at the full sentence with correct verb conjugation. "Did he?" When did that happen? When did my little girl start acting like a big girl? Before the thought could rip a new hole in my recently patched heart, my phone rang.

"Where are you?" I murmured, digging through my purse. I answered an unfamiliar number on the last ring. "Hello?"

"Hi, is this Ava Garcia?"

I hesitated at her agitated tone. "This is. Who's calling?"

"My name is Lindy Watkins."

Lindy. Where did I know that name?

"I've been trying to reach Steven Craig for weeks now. He's not returning any of my emails."

"I'm sorry to hear that. Unfortunately, I no longer work in his office."

She went on as if I hadn't spoken. "You tell that man he had better call me! I've invested too much to lose my hotel to a greedy land shark!" Fury shook her words.

Now I remembered. Lindy Watkins, independent hospitality chain. She sought a plot near the airport. "I think he's understaffed." Wait. Why was I making excuses for him? And why was she calling me? "Can I ask how you got my number?"

"Someone in your office gave it to me."

"I don't work there anymo–"

"This is discrimination!" she went on. "I'm not afraid to walk in with a lawsuit!"

Discrimination? That could cost Steven his license. "Lindy, I am truly sorry about your hotel." The driver's door opened, and the aroma of Mexican delicacies wafted toward me, making my stomach grumble. Time to wrap up the call. "I think you're right, go for the lawsuit. And best of luck." I hung up and tossed my phone into my purse.

Eli gave me a look as he handed me the white takeout bags. "Lawsuit?"

I placed them on the floor between my feet. "*That* is Steven's problem, not mine." I lifted a Styrofoam lid, a habit I'd developed after many nights without the proper condiments.

"*Extra* radish," Eli said.

"Look at you! I might just keep you."

He grinned. "I hope you do."

I would never tire of that expression. How one side of his mouth reached higher than the other, how his eyes winked at me from under his baseball cap. "Hey, before you get in, can you help Nina with her puffs?"

He glanced at Nina, then at her dangling feet. "You dropped your baby crack?"

"Baby crack?" I asked, but he was already opening her door and scooping up the pieces.

He dumped them in her lap.

"Tank you!"

"You're welcome," he said, ruffling her hair. "But don't drop them again."

She would. And we both knew it.

Eli climbed into the driver's seat of my new Ram and fastened his seatbelt. "Home?"

"Yes," I beamed. "Let's go home."

Epilogue

"Could you have made this any bigger?" Eli grunted as he and August shifted the large steel archway upright in the bed of his truck.

"I didn't make it," I countered.

"Yeah, well, you ordered it."

I was prying off the smaller wooden sign we'd mounted to the fence a year ago. "Remember when I offered to pitch in for a crane?"

He laughed through another grunt. "Next time, remind me to shut up and listen to you."

I walked to his truck and shimmied the old ranch marker into the back seat. "Hey, Eli?"

"Hm?"

"Don't break my sign."

"Yes, dear."

The new hires, Jamie and Brick, snickered as they waited beside Eli's Ford, ropes at the ready. I stepped back to watch Eli's plan play out. He'd assured me that leverage and manpower could lift the massive metal ranch sign eighteen feet in the air. Up to the horizontal beam of the wooden frame he'd built the week before.

"Stop worrying," he said. "We've got this."

I must've been biting my lip.

If the past year had taught me anything, Eli's forte was team-building. After looping the ropes through the sweeping letters, then up and over the beam, he and August hopped to the ground, and the four of them lifted the 300-pound beast out of the truck bed, one swaying foot at a time.

"How's that?" he called when it hovered just below the frame.

"Higher on the right," I said. "No, back down. Okay, stop!" When it appeared level, I gave a thumbs up.

Eli and August abandoned their ropes to grab the four-by-fours out of my truck. Meanwhile, Jamie and Brick dug their heels into gravel, struggling to keep the sign aloft. Brick's arms started shaking, and his face transitioned from red to purple.

"Eli!" I tilted my head to the young new-hire. Contrary to his nickname, he stood almost six feet tall and weighed a hundred and forty pounds wet.

Eli about-faced to trade places with Brick. "I gotcha, man. Go get a post." He looped the extra rope around his bent elbow, and when he caught me ogling his bulging biceps, he shot me a dirty look. So, I flashed him my bedroom eyes, to which he cursed under his breath.

August and Brick wedged the four-by-fours under the sign to offload the weight. Then, with a ladder, an impact drill, and a pocket full of bolts, August began mounting my metal baby to the beam. When he finished, Brick kicked out the four-by-fours.

I pressed my palms together, stomach tight.

Don't fall. Don't fall.

Eli and Jamie eased the ropes until they hung slack. A

moment passed. Then another, and nothing came crashing down. I finally allowed myself to breathe.

"See?" Eli said, a little winded. "No problem." He directed the kids to help August pull the ropes free as he meandered my way. "You like it?"

Sweeping black letters stood prominently against a forget-me-not sky. 'Rusty Mountain Ranch,' it said with rearing horses on either end, manes wild and free.

Perfect. "I love it."

"You'd better," he teased. "Damn hunk of metal cost a fortune." Sweat highlighted his arms and neck.

I tapped the brim of his hat up and nodded to his handi-work. "Do you think it should hang more to the left?"

He shot me a scalding look.

I laughed. "I'm kidding!" Sometimes I worried he took my every desire too seriously.

"Well, if we're giving feedback," he hooked his finger in my belt loop and pulled me close. "You cannot look at me like that with the guys around."

"Like what?"

"I think you know."

Some of the boys assumed Eli and I were married. They teased me for never wearing my ring. Eli and I stopped fighting it. He'd stayed. What did I need a ring for?

"I can't help it. I'm an arm girl."

"If you're not careful, you're gonna be a pregnant girl."

Oh? We hadn't talked about that yet. We hadn't talked about any next steps that didn't pertain to the ranch. I assumed he wasn't ready. Between Nina, college courses, and the youth leadership program, we had our hands full.

Eli slid his finger free of my belt loop and stepped away with a sly smile. "I'd better help the boys pack up."

He's joking, right?

Still, the idea of a baby sent a pleasant rush through my chest. "Oh, I forgot to tell you! Terry's back in town today. Do you mind if he and Kip come for dinner?"

I hadn't seen Terry for six months. He'd been across the country, visiting old friends in his decked-out RV, thanks to some European heiress, or actress, or something, who came in with a bid that put Steven's client to shame. Her only stipulations: a short escrow, no questions asked.

"Sure. Might have to hit the store, though. At this rate, I shoulda bought the whole pig."

"I'll go right now," I offered. "Luke gave me a check this morning. I can deposit it and pick up more snacks while I'm out." Eli's five teens/preteens could clear out the pantry in two days flat, but with the annual funding generously donated by Luke's dad's business, we kept it well stocked.

I gave Eli a quick kiss. "See you back at the ranch."

Nina stood on the kitchen bench, towering over Bill, when I hauled the first load of groceries from my truck. "Mama, look! I did Abi's hair!"

Bill pivoted his head for my inspection, looking content as a lion with its pride. "What do you think?" Sparkly clips and bows glinted in his short, white mane. Every hair accessory we owned found a spot in there.

I dumped my armload of bags on the counter. "Very nice! Hey, have you seen Eli? I have a truck full of groceries I could use some help with."

"He's uh ... he's working on something." Bill's tone gave me an odd aftertaste. "But I can help you."

"Me too!" Nina insisted, full of enthusiasm.

"Great. It's all in the truck bed," I told them.

While they brought in the remaining groceries, I played Tetris in the pantry. I had just forced the last box of protein bars onto an already overflowing shelf when Eli wandered into the kitchen.

I felt oddly relieved. "There you are!"

He tackled the haul of produce, arranging and rearranging fruit in the wire basket on the center island without reply.

I gave one more solid shove to a few boxes and pointed a finger at the precarious stack of snacks. "Stay." When I exited the pantry, he'd taken everything out and started again. "Should I make the boys a snack before they head home?"

"No. I took them to Taco Bell while you were out."

Did he change his shirt? An apple fell and rolled onto the floor. Eli picked it up and put it beside the basket. Tension clung to him like a staticky sock from the dryer.

I frowned. "Are you okay?"

"Yeah. Can I borrow you for a sec?" he asked without looking at me.

I didn't realize we had other projects lined up for the day. "Okay. When?"

"When you're done. Grab some water and meet me by the stable?"

"Sure."

Then he left. *Weird.*

Eli had Denver and Jessie saddled at the stables when I got there. Jessie was our newest rescue from a breeding operation. A painted-quarter mix with an unusual spot pattern and a thick white stripe down her muzzle. While reserved in the ring, she packed quite a punch on the open trail.

And she was my preferred mount. "We're going for a ride?"

He looked up from the strap he was tightening. "Yeah. You up for it?"

A little late to be checking with me now. I glanced at the house. "Sure. Let me tell Bill–"

"I already did."

"Oh?" In the past, these impromptu rides revolved around sorting out feelings. Usually, frustration and overwhelmingness. "Is everything alright? Are your classes okay?"

He adjusted his hat. "Just itching to spend time with you."

I stopped badgering him. If he had something on his mind, it would come out, eventually. Eli led us up to the ridge. We stopped with our backs to Phoenix, appreciating the spread of high desert to the south in comfortable silence. The Gila River wove like a green snake through the abundance of tans and browns. Steadfast and evolving. It had to be, to survive.

"Have you been up to Hidden Meadows recently?" he asked oddly.

I gave him a questioning look. "No. That's called trespassing."

"Oh, right."

"But August told me that the new owner isn't tearing it down," I said. "In fact, she's hired him to fix a few things."

Eli laughed. "I've heard *all* about that. Apparently, she's a piece of work. And here, I thought August got along with everyone."

This was news to me. Then again, I'd been busy helping in Nina's kindergarten classroom.

"Do you regret it?" he asked suddenly. "Giving it up?"

This question had chewed me up for months. But I finally had an answer that satisfied me. "No, because letting it go gave me more than what I sought to keep."

I wondered what spurred this line of questions. Did he have regrets?

Eli took off his hat, scratched his forehead with the bill, then slid it back over brown locks that curled around the edges. "Remember the first time we rode up here?" He turned to catch my gaze. "You were really grouchy. And you assumed I couldn't ride?"

"I never said that!"

"But you were thinking it."

"No. I *thought* you were being overconfident."

"You said," he made air quotes with his free hand, "'For a mechanic, you ride well.'"

I pressed my lips together. "Fine. Yes. I remember that day." My first ride after Jason's death. How could I forget?

He smiled finally, and the tightness in my chest eased. "Do you remember what else you said?"

I shook my head.

"You told me you felt lost." He turned and stared at the view. "That's when I knew."

I waited, but he didn't continue. "Knew what?"

"That I wouldn't love anyone else."

I stared at his profile, realizing why he'd been acting so weird, and my heart kicked up to a canter.

"You put words to what I'd felt for years," he said. Eli removed his hat, turning it over in his hands, staring at it as he went on. "I always figured hanging around meant responsibility. And responsibility meant giving everything up. That's why I became a mechanic. So, no one got stuck where they didn't want to be."

Surely, he knew he didn't achieve that by only fixing cars. "I thought you told me you weren't a mechanic? It was just something you happened to be good at?"

He pointed a bashful smile at his lap. "Yeah, well, I was trying to show off. Anyway, then you had your accident, and I realized what the word "home" meant. It's not a building. Or a ranch. It's a feeling you get when you're with the right person."

These were not impromptu words. He'd been practicing.

As if I needed more encouragement.

"Ava, I know I dragged my feet," he continued. "But I didn't want to rob you of your dream. I had to make sure I didn't hold you back."

"I have no complaints."

"Good." He eased Denver in beside Jessie so our legs brushed. "Listen, I know you've done the marriage thing already ..."

Suddenly, I couldn't breathe.

"... and I get it if you don't wanna do it again. But I have to at least ask." He shifted in his saddle, folding his hands over the bill of his hat so tightly that I worried it might snap.

I reached out to save it. "Hey–"

He grabbed my hand. "Ava, I want to put a ring on your finger. So, the boys will stop teasing you about losing it. So that everybody knows I belong to you. So you know, wherever you are, and whatever kind of day you're having, that someone out there loves you and Nina more than anything else. That to someone, you are home."

Wow. Whoever helped Eli with his speech needed to join our marketing team.

His fingers wove into mine. "I wanna be your family. Nina's dad. Make roots with you."

A joyful tear slid down my cheek.

He pulled his hand out of mine to wipe it away. "Is this because you're happy, or because you're about to bite my head off?"

I choked out a watery laugh. "You were on a roll, don't stop now!"

"Okay, good." He shifted to dig into his pocket.

A smile split my face. We were back to the unscripted Eli. He pulled out the ring. It wasn't in a little velvet box. Horse people didn't need boxes. Dirt and sweat measured the quality of our days. He turned it in his fingers so I could admire the design: two diamond-studded white gold bands intertwined. Subtle and graceful. My breath hitched.

"Is it okay?" A hint of uncertainty lingered in his voice.

"It's perfect." I did the girly thing and held out my hand between us, letting Eli slide the ring on my finger, and together, we stared at the glimmering stones against my tanned skin.

Eli closed his eyes and let his head fall back. "God, I'm glad that's done."

"Did you think I'd say no?"

"No. Well, maybe. I was worried I'd mess up the moment. Or if you weren't ready to, you know, go all in."

I picked up his hat from the saddle horn and shoved it on his head. The poor keepsake was nearly threadbare. I'd patched the frayed bill several times over. In turn, Eli salvaged my Chevy's license plate and turned it into art that he hung in our bedroom.

Now, he leaned in, priming to press his lips to mine, but Jessie was apparently done with all the mushy stuff. She sidestepped, and Eli wobbled back into his own saddle, laughing in that shy, self-deprecating way that made my knees weak.

"I swear these horses have it out for me."

"How about," I said, collecting Jessie's reins, "we head back so you can kiss me in the stable?"

I didn't have to ask him twice.

Later that night, I walked around the kitchen table to each place setting, brandishing a pair of tongs and the tamale tray. The long wooden surface mirrored a rural harvest painting with its massive platter of corn, a giant bowl of salad, and a collection of mismatched plates and cups. The murmur of side conversations and clinking forks rose in symphony. Loud like a restaurant, cozy like home.

"Marley, you made these?" August asked as I stopped at his spot. He eyed my ring.

"I did," she answered. "And if you say they suck, I will throw this corn at you!"

"No need to waste good corn, hon," Terry interjected, smiling under his bushy white mustache. The thing had to be twice the size since he'd gone on his trip. "Just cut off the hot water. That boy hates cold showers."

"Hey!" August protested. "I work hard! It helps my muscles."

Marley pulled a face. "Ew. Why would I be at his house?" We had seen her every week since she started on-site classes at the University of Phoenix. Apparently, the dorm food sucked, and the laundry room smelled like gym socks.

August requested three tamales. Before I could move to the next plate, he grabbed my arm. "You," he said softly, "are not smiling big enough."

I gave him a comically large grin. "Better?"

He *tsked*. "You have been wanting for this guy so long, I almost beat him up. You should be happy, no?"

I peered at Eli, who leaned back in his chair, arms crossed, smirking. "I'm thrilled," I said. "But I'm also trying to feed everyone a hot meal." I moved on to Eli.

"*So long*, huh?" he teased.

I dumped two tamales on his plate and continued on, ignoring him. "How many, Brick?" The kid came from a large foster family, so he stayed for dinner a lot.

"Four," he said. As I served him, he blurted, "Hey! You found your ring!" Turned out, everyone knew Eli's plan, except for Brick.

"Mama's getting married!" Nina sang. "And I get a baby sister!"

Kip honked out a laugh.

"That's a separate thing," I said as Eli announced,

"Or a brother."

"Eli!" I scolded.

"You don't want more kids?" Disappointment coated his tone.

"Can we talk about it, *not* in front of everyone?"

His chair scuffed as he stood. "Brick, finish passing out tamales, will ya?"

Kip wiped amused tears from her eyes at my expense. Marley pushed her plate away, muttering how gross we were.

"I-I didn't mean right this second." All eyes bounced between us. With a sigh, I handed my tray to Brick. "Fine."

Eli snagged my arm and dragged me out of the kitchen, around the corner, and out of sight. "Tell me quick," he said. "It's not a deal breaker, but I don't wanna get my hopes up." When I lacked a ready response, and why should I? We'd only just gotten engaged, he added, "Honestly, Ava, I really wanna make babies with you."

Who knew that hearing a man say that would be so ... arousing. And he said babies. *Plural.* "H-how many?"

"I dunno. What do you want?"

"Two? Is two good?"

He shrugged.

"Three?"

"Depends, I guess."

"On what? Four?" I asked in disbelief.

He crowded me against the wall, his hips finding mine. "Ava," he rumbled, sending warm licks down my spine, "if you don't stop upping the ante, I'm gonna have to haul you to the bedroom right now."

I bit my lip, and Eli's eyes smoldered.

"You two okay out there?" Bill called.

"Yeah!" Eli hollered back. "She said four!"

"I did not!" I slapped his chest as it shook with laughter.

"Better eat a good dinner," Bill muttered loud enough for us to hear.

"Thanks a lot," I growled, ready to fall into a cactus just to avoid the embarrassment of returning to the table after *that*. But as I took my spot between Nina and August, I noticed pink on the tips of Eli's ears. At least we were in this together.

Our boots brought us home.

Author's Note

Art mimics life. Ask any graduate with a Fine Arts degree, and I'm sure they've heard the phrase. The most moving pieces connect us to unspoken truths. Make us feel seen. Unite us with someone we've never met. But what we see, hear, or read comes as a result of experiences and emotions. That's the order. Life first. Art second.

So, imagine my surprise when I wrote this book, and my life deigned to copy it. Not an identical twin, but I experienced my first soul-shattering grief when I lost my father. Instead of using my own experiences to paint Ava's loss, I found myself nodding in agreement with her as I worked on my drafts, understanding her motives better than when I'd first written them. Learning that grief is not linear. It doesn't care about time. And something as trivial as the wrinkles in someone's jeans can lead to a metaphorical leaky pipe.

My father used to print business cards with my book information and hand them out to strangers. He'd bragged about "this fresh new author" to any listening ear. And he didn't know it, but this was his book. I had always intended to dedicate it to him–the one we discussed together at the local café over coffee and a breakfast sandwich every Friday.

For a tech guy, he had impressive intuition about storytelling. He helped me find my plot arc. He fueled scene ideas from his youthful years on a ranch. He taught me the intricacies of silent support-the kind that doesn't tell you what to do, but leads you there gently. There was no way I could have predicted that even in death, he would help me still, providing raw insight to what had previously just been research, speculation, and a strong empathy for others.

I don't believe it's a coincidence that every book I've picked up in these past two years has told a story of loss. Because it's a universal experience, no matter our gender, sexuality, origins, or even political beliefs. And how we cope is as varied as the embroidery patterns on a pair of cowboy boots.

But the most amazing thing about romance novels? They are our safe catharsis. They crack open our chests and force us to rain when we want to hold it in, all with the promise that in the end, we will be okay. My favorite authors gifted me advice right when I needed it: shower every day (Everyone is Beautiful by Katherine Center), do what brings you joy (The Seven Year Slip by Ashley Poston), and honor your love for someone by turning it into something beautiful (Sounds Like Love by Ashley Poston).

Dad, you are in these pages. You are in the heart of everything I write. Never underappreciated, never forgotten.

Acknowledgments

To quote a famous Disney medic bot, "I am not fast," but I finished! And I have an overflowing well of gratitude to those who helped me get here. Firstly, I would not be the writer I am today without my amazing writer critique groups. Benicia Outlaws–Tim, Wayne, Keith, Anne, Karen, and Jim–you were my first, and I hear your voices in my head whenever I'm redrafting. You turned a novice storyteller into a confident writer. And Epic$hit!, what would I do without you guys? Lee-Eric, Carlye, Lloyd, Maureen, Jill, Ellen, Suzanne, and Myles, you are all such amazing, inspired authors. Thank you for elevating the quality of my work with your observations and great writing. We really do produce some Epic$hit!

Many thanks to my beta readers–Christine, Myles, and Keith. Several major changes were made per your reactions and suggestions. And your notes made me laugh when drafting turned tedious.

A huge thank you to my copyeditor, Roberta Maguire, for both your corrections and your motivational words. And to Martha Barragan for helping me present English as a second language with cultural sensitivity.

Thank you, Dawn. You are my soundboard when I get stuck, and my ever-present cheerleader. And Yuko, for being there when my dad died, and for always listening with an eager ear as I went on and on about plots and characters, and cover designs. To Dwanna, for the time and space to crunch out half a book while the kids were busy playing. And Monica–your ranch was an inspiration (and your horses will undoubtedly appear in my marketing campaigns). Thank you, Diane–staying in your trailer inspired the first wisps of this story, though the black tank event didn't make it into the final version. And, Jay, for letting me grill you on horse terms and behaviors.

To the amazing community of romance writers (from my unicorn authors to my fellow indie authors on Instagram) who find and focus on beauty in a word with so much ugliness. You create much-needed respite. You bestow empathy and hope to your readers when we need it most.

Thank you to my dad, who was thrilled when I opted to do something in a saturated field that makes no money and takes forever to complete. And Mom, for your unwavering support, thoughtful advice, and for always keeping my freezer well-stocked with my favorite coffee beans.

A huge shout-out to my daughters, who give me daily inspiration for my work, and finally stopped playing musical instruments during my critique meetings.

And finally, to my amazing husband. You know how much emotional and mental fatigue comes from writing a book, and you still support my dream and joy of writing. Not just in words, but in actions. You are, and forever will be, my muse. I am truly blessed.

About the Author

Lexie Sloane writes emotionally rich, character-driven contemporary romance with a side of humor. She lives in the Bay Area with her husband, two kids, and two rabbits. She loves cooking, singing, kickboxing, and overcommitting. Occasionally, you'll also find her finishing a baby quilt just in time for the recipient to head to college. Other works include Broken Summit (2022).

Find out more at: Lexiesloane.com

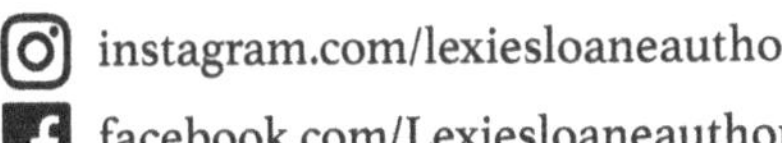

instagram.com/lexiesloaneauthor

facebook.com/Lexiesloaneauthor